DEATH & DRAGONS

Witch of Ware Woods

BOOK TWO

Death & Dragons

SONJA F. BLANCO

*For Mia and Jason ~
My beloved house squirrels, anything is possible*

An apple's perfection is in baring its bruise.

CHARACTER LIST

Sullivan Family
White Ash
Kinetic Witches

Kane
Abigail/Abby
Thomas
Violet
Connor

Lochton Family
White Pine
Psychokinetic+ Witches

Sara
Ann* *(Sara's
great-grandmother)*
Gran/Rosetta
(Sara's grandmother)
Alice *(Sara's great-aunt)*
Charlie *(Sara's father)*
Ted *(Sara's uncle)*
Ian *(Sara's half-brother)*

Cahill Family
American Chestnut
Earth Witches

Eliza* *(Sara's mother)*
Uncle Larry
(Sara's grandfather)
Helen
Eddie
Rebecca/Becca
Caleb
(Sara's second cousin)

Atwell Family
Black Gum
Air & Water Witches

Kingsley	Lily
Orsen	James
Elizabeth	Johnny
Claire	Ophelia
Ben	

Walker Family
Sugar Maple
Shifters

Albert
Bill
Shannon
Moira
Matthew

Blue Ridge Pack
Red Spruce
Shifters

Dean	Tobio
Moesha/Mo	Luke
Alesha	Wes
Iesha	

Additional Characters

Mary* *(Sara's
great-great-grandmother)*
Winona* *(Ian's mother)*
Naomi *(Ian's aunt)*

Lethal
Ryujin/Jin
Samson
Kira

Makwa/Tituba*
Dorcas
Brad
Shadow Mother

*Deceased at the start of Book 2
+Lochtons have a variety of magics
(named characters only)

OUTER FOREST
Atwell
CEMETERY
COUNCIL
STAGE
BIRCH
GROVE
Walker
Cahill
MAIN HOUSE
Lochton
Sullivan
OUTER FOREST
Ware Woods

CHAPTER 1

INDIGO CLOUDS PRESSED upon the forest, threatening to smother Sara. She pushed back her shoulders and lifted her chin, scanning the predawn sky, its bruised darkness at odds with the humid warmth radiating from the forest and kissing her skin. With a deep inhalation of berry-ripe summer air, Sara leapt from the second-story deck.

Silent as a shadow, she flew her routine vigilance through Ware Woods. First was a zigzag maneuver over four soul trees and the central Main House, followed by a sweep of the lake and recessed island to check on the fifth tree, then a flying run atop the forest's entire stone-wall boundary. The pattern had been practiced so many times, she wasn't even winded.

After completing a full round without spotting any sign of dark magic, she hovered above the wall, one hand testing the elastic resistance of the invisible barrier. A breeze grazed her legs, and Sara glanced down at the gray T-shirt barely skimming the tops of her thighs.

Crap. She had forgotten to grab shorts. Again. Definitely unbecoming of a High Witch.

She dropped her hand, shoulders sagging, before retreating into the forest's upper canopy and perching atop the favored outstretched limb of an old-growth pine. The bark beneath her feet was smooth with her frequent visits. She tilted her head and listened, hyperaware of every waking beetle, bird, and furred animal.

This forest with all the wondrous magic inside it was hers to protect—an honor and a responsibility that weighed on Sara like a heavy cloak and made it nearly impossible for her to sleep.

She placed a hand to her chest, atop the bloodstone amulet that amplified her powers, feeling her heart beat in time with her ancestor's magic.

Mary had spoken to Sara only once—right after she'd been awakened by Sara's blood coating the stone. At the time, Sara had believed Mary's prophetic words stating Sara was meant to be High Witch. But now, having realized the safety of the forest and its five magical families rested in her novice hands, Sara doubted she was the leader they needed. After all, leaders were confident and powerful, not worried and unsure of themselves. Since her pleas for further assistance had gone unanswered by Mary, perhaps she could magically unearth a book titled *How to be a High Witch and Everything Else You Need to Know to Protect a Sacred Site and Everyone You Love.*

Sara's stomach twinged with unease and hunger. "Gaa." She shook her head as if she could shake off her tension. Despite the ground resting somewhere far below, buried beneath a thick under-story, she padded along the limb and pressed her back against the broad trunk. The energy of the tree vibrated through her. She relaxed, imagining herself becoming one with the pine, reaching through its roots below and branches above to connect with the forest's power.

It had been two weeks since she'd awakened from her magical stasis and recovered from overexerting herself—from killing Makwa, the bear witch who had cursed her and tried to destroy Ware Woods. Two weeks of meeting with the Ware Woods Council, of questioning her father, and of drilling her brother, Ian, for information on other sacred sites and the Global Council that supposedly oversaw the three magical factions of witches, shapeshifters, and vampires. Two weeks of attempting to contact them, only to be met with silence. Two weeks of self-doubt creeping back into her life, of her hatred for Samson growing like poison ivy.

She dug her fingers—all nine of them—into the grooved bark and inhaled to the slow count of three. The dark witch, Samson, had taken more than her pinkie finger. He had taken her sense of security. And she'd be damned to let him live much longer before hunting him down and eliminating the threat he posed. As High Witch of Ware Woods, Sara would do anything to protect her sacred site and forest family, including embracing her own darkness to destroy Samson and any other menace salivating at their wall.

The understory trembled, stirring the heavy air with a whisper of magic. Sara's skin prickled. She knew this deadly kinetic power, its familiar source traveling along the forest floor. Preferring to remain hidden, Sara flattened against the pine. Below, a young witch with long black hair and multiple deadly edged weapons raced along the spine of the stone wall, disappearing to the north. Not until every pine needle and blade of grass stilled did Sara exhale.

Despite the stoic tree at her back and the deep breathing her mother once taught her, Sara's anxiety held a firm grip. Today, she and her new friends were departing for a three-day vacation, yet instead of excitement, Sara felt dread. The idea of leaving Ware Woods, even for a quick trip to the beach, seemed ludicrous, especially with Samson still out there.

When she told her grandmother the dark witch couldn't possibly be dead and would come back soon to attack their forest, Gran shrugged and said, "You're going to the beach and that's final. With our powers back, Alice and I can hold down the fort for a while." And to further thwart Sara's protests, Gran had confirmed Dorcas, the witch who was once Makwa's companion, was cheerfully assisting the Cahills in removing noxious parsnip from the marsh.

Apparently, being High Witch did not make one immune to

Gran's orders. And apparently, Gran had known all along that Samson still lived. Devious, psychic grandmother.

From her perch, Sara rested a few more moments, surveying the outer forest. The silence did not reassure her. Rather, it suffocated like the eerie calm before a storm, and all Sara could do was wait, fearing she was not ready to protect the forest from whatever horrors were brewing.

A wood thrush broke the stillness, its song drifting through the tree canopy as Sara considered the brightening sky. If she hurried, she could sweep the entire boundary once more before—

Energy crackled in the air, and her heart skipped a beat. A fluttering to her right, accompanied by an intoxicating musky scent, brought her solo rounds to an end. So distracted by her worries, Sara hadn't sensed Thomas wake, much less follow her, their bond naturally drawing them together as if they were magnets. She smiled, shifting her shoulders to face him. Clad only in jeans, his hair mussed from sleep, Thomas landed with a slight bounce, clearly checking the strength of the wide branch.

Though his expression was casual, brow slightly raised with concern, his blue eyes bore into her, assessing. "You know, she'll think you don't trust her to run patrol if she catches you out here." He flicked his gaze to the dense forest floor, where his dark-haired sister had passed by. Violet had recently turned seventeen, one year younger than Sara, and had earned permission to guard the boundary by herself at night.

"Of course I trust Vi. It's the rest of the world I don't trust."

Thomas approached her, his steps sure and confident despite their precarious position, and cupped her face. Light-blue energy snapped between them as his thumb brushed her cheek. "Where is this coming from? Talk to me."

Sara turned into his touch and placed a hand over his. Judging by the set of his jaw, she would have to tell him about Samson now instead of after the beach trip like she had planned. But doing so would certainly put a damper on their getaway.

When she bit her lip, Thomas pulled her to him, enveloping her in his warmth. He held her to his bare chest with a tenderness few people ever witnessed from him.

"We're not moving from this tree until you tell me what's eating you." His husky voice tickled her neck, and she shivered, only to feel him smile against her skin. "Yeah, I noticed, and I gave you time to come to me." His tone slightly rose, revealing a bit of hurt before dropping low again as he continued, "But I can't stand to see you brood anymore. You can trust me with everything."

She knew that fixed tone. It was no surprise he noticed something was bothering her. The deep bond they shared went beyond being able to locate one another. It physically sizzled between them—their souls and magic craved one another as if they were meant to meld together. Indeed, sometimes Sara swore he was an extension of herself.

Before her mother had been killed, her parents had a bond, though according to her father it had been nowhere near as strong as the pull between her and Thomas. He cautioned her that such a connection came with fierce emotions and the urge to protect a bonded mate could often cloud judgment. She hadn't had the heart to tell him that as High Witch, she was duty bound and determined to protect them all. Regardless of her bond with Thomas, her judgment was already clouded.

Thomas gently squeezed her, bringing her back to the present. *Alrighty, then.*

Sliding her hand between them to rest on his firm chest, she uttered the sinister mantra playing on repeat in her head: "Samson is alive." Her confession hung in the air like nails about to be driven into a coffin. She felt their hearts skip a beat.

To his credit, Thomas didn't deny her statement or ask questions. Instead, he tightened his grip, arms banding around her. "Then we will deal with him." His voice held the promise of death. "*Together.*"

Nope. Not gonna happen. As High Witch, this is my problem alone to be faced outside *the wall.* She wiggled, attempting to loosen his embrace. "I don't want anyone getting injured. Or killed. In fact, I wanted to cancel our beach plans. Except Gran insisted we still go. She and Alice said—"

"You told them but not me?" Thomas stiffened and pulled back, the hurt in his eyes visible in the early dawn light.

Sara froze. *Oh shit.*

The muscle along his jaw twitched. "Please don't keep secrets from me." His voice rumbled from deep in his chest, as if coming directly from his heart.

"I—I didn't want you to worry," she said, her last word falling flat, her own heart aching with her epic failure. If he hadn't been holding her, she would have tumbled from the branch, taking her shame with her, and crawled into the nearest snake hole.

He arched a brow at her, piercing her with his gaze.

"You're right. I should have told you sooner."

His brow climbed higher. "I know you. There's more you aren't telling me. What else is stressing you?"

Damn him and his smoldering blue eyes. Sara cracked. "Okay, fine—*everything* is stressing me. I have no idea how to be High Witch, and I'm constantly worried about dark magic attacking us, about the ice splinter in Ian's heart killing him, and about you . . . dying." She whooshed a breath, relieved to have spilled her guts yet frustrated to have no recourse to do anything about it.

Surprise flashed in Thomas's face before his expression softened. He grinned. "There now. Was that so hard?" he teased, ignoring her scowl. "The threat of dark magic will always exist. And it's not your responsibility to handle it *alone.* You offend everyone in Ware Woods if you think otherwise. We're not fragile, and we don't need protecting. On the contrary, it is Samson who needs to be afraid of us." His grin turned positively wicked, blue flames of energy flickering around them. "Ian is not going to die, and neither am I."

He had told her exactly what she wanted to hear. And despite knowing she could not hold him to such an assurance, she said, "Promise?"

His eyes blazed. "Promise. As I recall, I also pledged to never let go of you." He kissed her forehead and hugged her until she relaxed her shoulders, tension melting. "Now," he said, leaning back again to study her face, "we're going to the beach today. You need a break, and the whole gang needs to let loose and just be normal for a moment. Besides, Samson is too smart to approach us in public. Even if he did, I'd gladly face him."

Sara straightened, eyes widening. "You'd stand against him—outside the forest and without your magic." As High Witch, Sara was the only one who had the ability to use magic beyond the wall. Either Thomas truly had a death wish or the bond was clouding his judgment. Perhaps both.

He pressed his brow to hers. "For you, I will stand against anyone." He ran his hands up her sides and cradled the back of her head, fingers winding into her hair. "I'm not going to die for a ridiculously long time, and I *swear* to the Mother and the Father I will do everything I can to keep you safe and be worthy of you—as my High Witch and as my love." His chest shuddered, the thud of his heart racing in time with hers.

My love. Such an oath was both insanely loving and dangerous. Due to her role as the forest's leader, she was a target for dark magic, and as her bonded mate and best friend, so was he. Her heart tightened at the gravity of their situation. He would willingly sacrifice himself yet still felt inadequate.

"Thomas." She placed her hands on the sides of his face. "You are worthy."

At this, he closed his eyes, jaw clenched. She knew it frustrated him to have his magic bound to the forest, feeling lesser than her because of this restriction. However, something else was troubling him. Something she sensed he was ashamed of. Secrets, indeed. Yet it didn't bother her. The love she had for him would never falter; besides, she hadn't shared everything with him either.

While her personal secret wasn't something to casually mention at the start of a relationship, they were bonded mates—she presumed for their magically long lives—and she would have to disclose what made her feel unworthy of him. Soon. Not quite yet though. Stars above, she loved him with the very seed of her being, and she selfishly hoped he would still love her despite her unique aberrancy.

The stubble on his cheeks grazed her palms as her fingers ran through the downy hair at his temples. Blue flames flickered around them again, and a lazy smile spread across his face, heating her core.

"We have a few hours before we leave," she whispered.

His lashes lifted, revealing a devilish gleam in his eyes. "True. Do you want to go back to my studio and get some sleep? Or . . ." His gaze fell, taking in her bare legs.

"Well," she drawled, failing miserably at hiding her smirk and delighting in his aura's fiery shift. The ability to see auras had manifested after her magical stasis and, she had discovered, was a fascinating indicator of raw emotion. "I'm not tired."

In one swift motion, he scooped her into his arms and pushed away from the pine tree, launching them into the sky. "I was hoping you'd say that," he said into her windswept locks.

Her surprised yelp turned into a bright laugh as she snuggled against him. Kissing the tender spot between his shoulder and neck, she allowed his diversion to momentarily ease her worries. Perhaps the beach trip would be more exciting than terrifying. Nonetheless, a crew of eight magicals in a normal world would be anything but dull.

She hoped they would all survive.

CHAPTER 2

BLACK DUFFEL BAG slung over her shoulder, Sara descended the curved treehouse stairs, hand trailing the buckled oak bark. The tree shivered and sighed under her touch. "I'll only be gone a few days." She paused at the base of the stairway, where she took in the surrounding cemetery. A soft breeze ruffled her hair as a low-hanging branch swept forward and nudged her away like a mother shooing a child outside on a sunny day. "Okay, okay. I'm going. Behave yourself and keep the squirrels out of my bedroom. They race around and knock books off the shelves." The tree shook again, creaking and snapping while proudly straightening its thick branches toward the sky. A sky now bright with the start of a new day.

Wonderful. I'm late.

She adjusted her bag, hastily filled with a few days' worth of clothes after leaving Thomas's studio. It was all too easy to linger in his embrace and forget time. If only she could forget the responsibility of being High Witch for just a moment to calm her mind from the shit storm of worries plaguing her.

She blew back a strand of hair and gazed at her mother's grave, at the latest garland of sunflowers her father had placed atop the headstone. With a swirl of her index finger, Sara whished the drooping flowers back into position and lifted the blossoms of the wildflowers surrounding the stone.

"Morning, Sara," Naomi's husky voice called out before she popped through the bushes at the rear of the cemetery. The apples of her cheeks shone as she approached the oak tree, swinging a basket at her side.

Sara studied the jovial sepia-skinned witch who had once helped her break out of a mental ward and who also happened to be Ian's aunt—the last known survivor of the Hills sacred site. "You're suspiciously chipper for this early in the day. What are you up to?" Sara peeked at the gleaming pruning shears in the otherwise empty basket.

"Such a busybody." Naomi chuckled and switched the basket to her other arm. "Ever since you revealed yourself as High Witch, you've seemed overly concerned about everyone else."

Sara folded her arms. "You say that like it's a bad thing." This was her role—her responsibility—to protect the forest and everyone she loved within it. In accepting her role, she had vowed to keep them all safe from dark magic. A vow that made her overprotective and a wee bit sleep deprived.

Naomi pointed her chin toward the adjacent grassy clearing and lake beyond it, her line of sight on the little boat waiting patiently at the shoreline. "I'm off to search the outer forest for ingredients to finish my protective charms. *Don't* even think about stopping me. I'm on a mission to make a charm for every child in our forest before school starts."

Sara furrowed her brow at the challenge. While the younger children were homeschooled, older kids attended the nearby town's public high school. It was a way to socialize with normal people and the outside world, but it also put them at risk. Without their powers beyond the boundary of Ware Woods, they were vulnerable to the dark magic that hunted them.

Naomi put a hand on her hip, a spark of a dare glimmering in her playful expression.

A cottontail rabbit darted across the field as Sara stared past the island toward the far shore, weighing her options. Few people knew Samson was still alive and likely biding his time before attacking them again. Sara was intentionally waiting until their next Council meeting to tell the entire forest. She was not looking forward to bursting their bubble of contentment with the threat of dark magic so soon after their battle with Makwa.

Closing her eyes, she focused her power on a sweep of the outside forest, searching for any outsiders. All remained quiet. When she opened her eyes, Naomi was already halfway to the shoreline.

Seriously? "Be careful and return well before dark," Sara called after her.

Naomi waved off her monition. "Have fun at the beach," she replied, the familiar laughter in her voice conjuring images of roses and cherries in Sara's mind.

With a lighthearted grumble, Sara pivoted and sprinted through the path opening at the rear of the cemetery. Though it would be quicker to fly to the meeting point at the Walkers, she needed a jog with a specific stop along the way to stretch her legs and settle her nerves before leaving.

Sensing her intent, the forest path yawned into a straight course, allowing her to run until her legs ached before ending at a freshly mowed backyard.

Sara veered around Bailey's more-decorative-than-used doghouse, then rushed across the yard and bounded up the back steps of the Lochtons' brown house, her uncle Ted's handmade whirligigs clicking furiously behind her. She dropped her duffel bag onto the screened-in porch floor, entered the kitchen, and halted.

Gran, Ted, and her dad, Charlie, sat at the blue diner-style table with chrome edging, coffee cups in hand and mild amusement on their faces. At the far side of the table, Ted set down his cup, whished a pair of heavily tinted sunglasses into his palm and offered them to Sara.

The glasses were visibly finer than the lopsided drugstore pairs she used to burn through as a means to hide her eyes—eyes which startled people not because of their cauldron-black coloring, as she'd once thought, but because they shimmered with magic.

Sara gulped a lungful of air. Instead of taking the sunglasses, she aimed for the plate of pastries on the table. With a grunt of appreciation, she snagged a mini muffin and shoved it into her mouth, the sweet flavor replacing the awful taste of the protein shake she had shared with Thomas earlier. An image of his pristine yet meagerly stocked kitchen flashed in her mind. Next time she visited his studio, she'd bring him some real food.

Gran dumped a spoonful of sugar into her coffee and then shifted, her chair scraping the floor as she eyed Sara. "You should have left by now."

Sara fought to swallow the muffin along with her worry. Thomas was right; she didn't want to offend them by implying they couldn't protect Ware Woods without her. After all, they had done so for centuries before she showed up a few months ago.

"I—I wanted to say goodbye." She forced a smile and turned to Charlie. "'Bye, Dad," she whispered in his ear before kissing his cheek. Leaving the forest was hard enough, never mind leaving him, even for just a few days. The death of her mother and nearly losing her father, all caused by Samson, were still fresh wounds in Sara's heart.

She cursed herself as grief flickered in her father's pale blue eyes, his empathic powers likely sensing her emotion. In a blink, he smiled warmly, gave her shoulder a reassuring squeeze, and said, "Love you, firecracker. Now go before your brother's impatience gives us all a headache." He inclined his head toward the seldom-used front door.

As if on cue, Ian's voice rang in her mind, *Why are you at our house instead of the Walkers?"* He mentally huffed his exasperation. *"Never mind. The guys and I are leaving now. Moira will pick you up. She wanted you to ride with her, which made Thomas grumpy. And now Bailey and I have to spend a few hours with a sullen Sullivan."* He huffed again. *"Keep your phone on 'cause none of us will be able to talk telepathically with you once we cross the wall. And take the sunglasses!"* His assertive older-brother tone bit her before his last word faded away.

Sara straightened. *"What the Hells? I thought I was the one who gave orders around here. Speaking of, make sure you bring* all *the medicine I packed for you last night. And since you forgot, I don't have a phone anymore. Cranky pants,"* she added with a mental image of herself sticking out her tongue. She timed her send-off just as she sensed his annoyed presence leave the forest.

Her subsequent chuckle was drowned out by the aggressive hum of chunky tires racing down the old road in front of the house. Sara's gaze shot through the kitchen and out the open windows of the adjacent living room before settling on the stone wall at the far end of the front yard. A blur of rusty orange flew into view as Moira Walker floored her shifter family's Suburban in reverse and screeched to a stop just outside the forest boundary. All the car windows were down. Violet Sullivan, Thomas's raven-haired younger sister and a kinetic witch who loved razor-edged weapons, adjusted her headrest in the front seat. In the back seat, Lily Atwell, a serene water and air witch with strength that defied her delicate appearance, turned her porcelain-pale face toward the house.

Ted wagged the glasses at Sara while Charlie and Gran snickered into their coffee cups.

"Gaa!" Sara snagged the glasses, whished her bag alongside her, and hustled out the front door. "I'll be back soon," she called over her shoulder, leaving the door open in her haste.

"Hurry," barked Moira. "We need to catch up to Thomas and Caleb."

Thomas had mentioned they would be taking three vehicles. Since Ian and Bailey were riding with him, she assumed Moira's nearly identical twin, Matthew, was riding with Caleb, a gifted earth witch and Sara's cousin.

Sara piled into the back seat beside Lily and, eyeing the rear crammed with coolers and camping equipment, stuffed her duffel under her feet. "We're only going for a few days, right?" There may have been a touch of panic in her question.

Moira stomped on the gas, throwing Sara against the seat, and the Suburban roared down the road. Exchanging a wide-eyed glance with Lily, Sara scrabbled for her seat belt. Wind smelling of pine and sunbaked grass swirled around them, whipping their hair until Moira pressed a button on the console and closed the windows.

Violet swung her head around and lowered her sunglasses, indigo eyes flashing. "Yep. Three days of beachy bliss." She jerked her chin at the cargo. "That's mostly food. The guys eat a ton and Caleb loves to cook, so they packed enough for an army. Here, this is from Ian." Violet tossed Sara a shiny new phone. "Our numbers and a digital credit card have already been entered, along with a shared location app. The rule is to always keep your phone with you and never go anywhere alone. Oh, and no looking anyone in the eye."

Sara sucked in a breath. Her old phone had been unsalvageable, smashed into a million pieces during the car accident. The new device in her lap was larger and felt odd when she gingerly picked it up. She had once been nearly addicted to her phone, back before everything changed—before her mother died and before she found Ware Woods and her true magic. A phone hardly seemed necessary now. She touched the cool black surface, and a locked-screen image popped up of Bailey's furry face, wet nose front and center. Sara blew a short laugh at the yellow Lab's photo and tossed the phone into her bag.

Violet glared at the discarded phone, then dragged her disapproving gaze to Sara. "This applies to you, especially. Don't even think about using the slightest bit of magic, or a dragon will take you."

Sara dropped her grin. Right. Ian had once told her if normals witnessed magic, a dragon would correct the situation by wiping the normals' memory and taking the magical responsible for the infraction. For this reason, good magic was bound to the safety of sacred sites, with the exception of a site's leader—their Magus, either an Elder Vampire, an Alpha Shifter, or a High Witch. The problem with this supposed regulation was that dark magicals were not bound to a sacred site. Instead, they roamed freely, hunting good magicals and taking their power.

Sara swallowed. The reminder of her role as High Witch and the steady drone of the engine made her weary. She threw a hollow smile at Violet. "A dragon will never take me. I'd be too much trouble for them." When Violet's glare did not budge, Sara rolled her eyes. "I'll put the phone in my back pocket after I take a nap." She faked a big yawn. "Your brother kept me up all night."

Violet scrunched her face in disgust and turned back to the front seat.

A pillow smacked Sara in the face. Hard. "Lily! All Hells, you almost broke my nose." Gently flaring her nostrils at her, Sara grabbed the pillow and propped it against the door. She eyed Lily's petite figure and arched brow of bemusement. With syrupy-sweet innocence, Sara leaned into the pillow and said, "Thomas and I were playing *cards*."

Moira snorted as Sara closed her eyes. Content in this moment, despite the threat of dragons and dark magic, she let the drive lull her to sleep.

CHAPTER 3

S ARA JOLTED AWAKE, her head smacking against the window, as the Suburban roughly halted. Drool chafed the corner of her mouth, which meant she had been asleep for far longer than the minute it seemed. And it also meant Moira would probably tease her. Sara wiped her lips across her shoulder and looked up at Moira, who had twisted around in the driver's seat to stare at her. Panic fluttered in Sara's stomach.

Why did we stop?

She shifted her gaze out the windshield, scanning for dangers both normal and magical. The Suburban idled near a guard shack. Parked in front of them were Thomas's lifted black truck and Caleb's SUV. Her nerves settled at the absence of Samson's telltale black, smoky clouds.

"Guess that's yours now," said Moira, nodding at the damp pillow in Sara's lap.

Sara stifled a groan, expecting Moira to laugh at her, but she merely turned to face the guard shack. "Put on your glasses and watch this." Though her tone was playful, tension filled the Suburban.

Sara squinted at the bright sky and donned the sunglasses Ted had given her. The black frames fit perfectly, slightly wrapping at the sides. Although heavily tinted, they provided crystal-clear vision. "What are we watching?" asked Sara, her voice thick with sleep. She took in the small building and drifts of sand smearing the single-lane road. A giant red barrier arm, reading ALL CAMP-SITES FULL, blocked their path.

Sara swung her gaze back to Thomas's truck and placed a hand to her chest. The bond still pulled at her heart, invisible threads connecting her soul with Thomas's, yet she couldn't sense his phys-ical presence and emotions *or* his fervent magic. She pressed her hand harder, the bloodstone steadily pulsing against her palm. Being outside of Ware Woods, where he didn't have his powers, tempered the bond like fog dampening an otherwise sunny day.

Thomas exited his vehicle, strolled up to the guard shack, and paused before the open door. When a young woman stepped out, he flashed a smile and began talking. Sara unbuckled her seat belt and leaned into the front of the Suburban, straining to hear their conversation over the air conditioner and through the closed win-dows. The woman blushed, flicking her ponytail and laughing at whatever Thomas had said to her. Sara's cheeks burned as her finger-nails dug into the console. Thomas raised a hand, bicep stretching the tight sleeve of his black T-shirt as he briefly lifted his sunglasses and flashed another smile.

"Did he just intentionally flex for her?" grumbled Sara, white flames of energy shimmering on her skin.

Moira's feline smile grew ear to ear. "Thomas can charm the skin off a snake," she purred.

Energy crackled.

"Calm down," hissed Violet, motioning to the magic quivering along Sara's arms. "He knows what he's doing."

"That's *exactly* the problem," growled Sara. Clearly, he had plenty of practice with charming others. The idea of him with someone else heated Sara's blood, wavering her vision.

She shook her head and willed her magic to still. *No. This is completely absurd. He's just asking the attendant to double-check for vacancies. Right?* Mother below. Even dampened, the bond made her insanely jealous. She pursed her lips, attention focused on the guard, who was nodding with such enthusiasm her ponytail swing could have cut down a soul tree.

After pointing down the road behind her, the guard disappeared into the shack. Within a heartbeat, the barrier rose.

Thomas pivoted and strode for his truck. His rigid posture, and the fact that he didn't look at Sara, suggested he knew exactly what he had done and how it had affected her. Which meant he had the same intense feelings.

Her heart fluttered, and not in a good way.

Great. As if Samson and dragons weren't enough to worry about, now she had to consider the distinct possibility of Thomas turning murderously territorial if anyone looked in her direction. This was going to be a very dicey few days.

After they had settled into a remote campsite at the far end of the beach, Ian assured Sara it was the same spot they had visited over the past few years, and they never had any run-ins with other magicals—good or bad. To set her mind further at ease, he explained they would do the same activities they always did: wait until dusk to hit the boardwalk for food and fun, sleep in and play all day on the beach before having an epic BBQ and bonfire, then pack up and leave on the third day.

One tent was designated for the guys, one for the girls. Facilities, including hot showers, were a short trek down the beach at the end of the boardwalk.

Sara blinked, stunned by his rapid-fire instructions and grateful for the hot showers. The *"never running into other magicals"* was not very comforting—there was always a first time for anything.

As Sara helped unpack the vehicles, she studied the surrounding beach—the grassy dunes behind them, the kites and seagulls in the clear sky above, and the stretch of sand before them with people idly combing the ocean's edge. The steady breeze smelled of seaweed, brine, and sunscreen. Gentle, crashing waves, squealing laughter, and the sharp call of sandpipers filled the air. Yet despite the cheerful location and lack of anything out of the ordinary, Sara remained on high alert, absently assisting Caleb in handing out a prepared lunch that instantly disappeared among the crew. She hadn't noticed the headache at the base of her skull until a sniggering Violet told her to give up the hypervigilance and insisted she play cards with her while everyone else set up the tents or tossed a Frisbee.

Though Sara feigned offense and secretly welcomed the distraction, she strategically sat at the worn picnic table with her back to the vehicles and her gaze toward the public beach. She tried not to watch the sun hang lower and lower on the horizon while Violet shuffled and dealt hand after hand of frayed Uno cards. In true Sullivan fashion, Violet showed no mercy, burying her with wild draw fours and sweeping every game. Sara might have won a round or two had she not also been distracted by a shirtless Thomas nailing in tent spikes and playing Frisbee with the others.

By the time the sun set and the beach scene darkened to a rich periwinkle, everyone was ready to hit the boardwalk—everyone except Sara. She hated crowds, and the idea of eight magicals blending in without an unfortunate altercation was ridiculous.

Laughing between themselves, Violet and Lily strolled away from the campsite. Ian and Thomas followed, herding Sara along with them.

She dragged her feet in the uneven sand. "You're sure Bailey is okay staying behind by herself?" Sara stole a glance over her shoulder at the yellow Lab sprawled between the tents. Playing Frisbee and tearing up and down the beach all afternoon had completely worn her out.

Ian checked his phone and slipped it into his pocket. "She's not the one you should be worried about." He whirled around, turning Sara with him, and motioned at the remainder of their group as they zipped up the tents and hurried to join them.

Sara stumbled. She would have eaten sand if Thomas hadn't steadied her.

There strutted trouble in triplicate: from Moira's skimpy tank top to the bounce in Matthew's step to Caleb's mischievous gap-toothed grin.

Sara muttered, "I'm convinced everyone has their own reckless agenda, and I'm the unwitting chaperone."

Matthew responded with a coy wink, which sent her spluttering. She lunged to punch him in the shoulder, but Ian grabbed her and redirected her into Thomas's open arms. He lifted her off her feet, chuckling at her yelp, before gently setting her down and clasping hands. A zing of energy tickled her palm.

Although his expression didn't change, Thomas tightened his hold, his thumb stroking the top of her hand.

Sara debated if she should tell him his caress was the opposite of calming.

Ian slowed his pace, letting the eager trio pass them before turning conspiratorially to Thomas and Sara. "I'll keep an eye on Matt and Caleb, and Lily and Violet will wrangle Moira. Absolutely no fighting"—he pointed at Thomas—"and no magic"—he pointed at Sara.

They both avoided his stern gaze. If Samson dared to show, Sara wouldn't hesitate to use magic, and she knew Thomas wouldn't hold back from attacking him or anyone bold enough to get close to her.

Ian sighed. "Just behave and take this opportunity to enjoy a proper date." He pushed back his thick, curly hair and raised a brow at them.

Sara grinned and projected into his mind, *"Will you and Lily be going on a date as well?"*

His eyes widened, a silent gasp on his lips. He leaned toward her and whispered quiet enough for Thomas not to hear: "We're close, but not in that way. And no more magic." Ian pulled away and frowned at her.

Sara replied with a playful scowl.

"Midnight curfew for *everyone*," he added in a louder voice as they approached the expansive boardwalk stairs, the first few wooden treads dusted in sand. The twins immediately groaned.

Sara's scowl slipped. She may be High Witch, but Ian was definitely the chaperone.

A breeze floated from the colorfully lit shops and restaurants, welcoming them with raucous music and the scent of fried foods and sugary sweets. Sara's mouth watered. Perhaps a date would be nice—one free of magic and death.

"Let's go," sang Moira, linking arms with Lily and Violet. Giggling, they ran up the stairs, cell phones perilously tucked into back pockets, and disappeared into a throng of people.

The moment she lost sight of them, a chill washed over Sara. She contemplated using her power to track them when Thomas jerked her hand and broke her concentration. He stopped on the beach, holding them back while Ian, Matthew, and Caleb sprang up the steps and trailed a group of college girls in sundresses.

Once the guys vanished into the crowd, Thomas faced Sara, standing between her and the wooden stairway. He pressed against her, his lips to her ear, sending an electric current down her spine. "I don't know what you were about to do, but you *can't* use magic here. Even if a dozen Takers show up, you cannot summon one bit of your powers. Because if a dragon takes you, I will ravage the entire world to get you back."

His tone of voice and steady grip on her hand struck her soul as their bond flared, unseen energy crackling between them. *Oh! This is his greatest fear.* Her entire body tingled at both his fierce love and his solemn disclosure.

He sealed his statement with a prolonged kiss to the back-arching sensitive spot behind her ear. Sara would have melted to the ground and taken him with her had they not been in public.

"Now," he said, his breath warming her skin. She may have moaned. "Let's have a sweet, memorable, and dragon-free date." And before she could plant a firecracker of a kiss on his wicked mouth, he whisked them up the steps and into the heart of the boardwalk.

CHAPTER 4

Sara and Thomas strolled the carnivalesque thoroughfare, keeping to the shadows wherever possible and avoiding direct eye contact with others. The latter proved difficult for Sara, considering the frequent stares in their direction, which she attributed to Thomas's muscled physique. Though her headache persisted, she refrained from using her healing magic and genuinely enjoyed the festive moment. A few months earlier, she had been a social outcast whom people hated and feared; now she had family and friends and Thomas by her side. With a smile, she swung their clasped hands.

Behind them, a group of young men whistled, and someone taunted, "I'll take your mother when you're done with her."

A growl promising pain erupted from Thomas.

Sara glanced at her long, unbound hair, its silvery-gray color a result of breaking her curse and embracing her magic. *Shit. I should've dyed it.* Ducking her head, she pulled Thomas into the nearest shop.

The brightly lit interior sparkled with hundreds of gemstones, from small, polished crystals to glowing salt lamps to boulder-sized geodes—each and every one calling to her magic. Sara ran her hand over a display table of pocket-sized gems, their energy swirling and tickling her skin.

Thomas drew her away from the display. "How about you look but don't touch," he whispered, a hint of laughter replacing his deadly growl.

Pleased to have diverted his attention, Sara leaned into him and whispered back, "I want one of everything."

"Of course you do. You're a witch."

"So are you," she murmured.

"True, and we're drawing attention." He let go of her and stepped back. "I'll wait for you by the door while you take your time *looking*." Thomas strode off, hunching his wide shoulders and scrolling through his phone. He appeared every bit a bored boyfriend, yet she knew his downcast eyes surveyed every patron in the shop.

Contrary to the soothing flute music drifting lazily through the store, a distinct feeling of excitement tugged at Sara. She whirled around, following the sensation to a shelf of crystals along the back wall. Among a rainbow of stones glinted one golden piece with a shimmering aura. *No touching* be damned. Sara picked it up, its fractured cubist shape fitting perfectly in the palm of her hand, and had a distinct vision of Naomi, head thrown back in laughter. A stiff white card with black text read:

PYRITE

A powerful protection stone that detects
and shields against dark energy.

Sara chortled, causing Thomas to look up. When she held out the pyrite, his alarmed demeanor faded into relief, his gaze sliding back to his phone with a shake of his head. She bit back another laugh.

This stone was perfect for Naomi, a witch with spell-breaking and shielding abilities. Sara squeezed it in her palm and meandered her way toward the register. As she passed a cluster of pre-teen girls exploring a display of turquoise jewelry, a table of silver rings caught her eye. She paused.

Each exquisitely crafted piece bore a gleaming gemstone. Forgetting herself, she selected a deep amethyst ring with an intricate band of twining branches and slipped it onto her middle finger. When she stretched out her hand to admire it, the pre-teen girls gasped and broke into nervous giggles, their eyes glued on Sara's four-fingered hand.

Double shit.

Sara hastily pulled off the ring, plunked it back on the table, and made a beeline for the register where Thomas stood, ready to pay.

As they exited, the door tinkling shut behind them, Sara shoved her hand and the pyrite stone into her front pocket and walked at a brisk clip away from both the shop and the stares at her back. *Still an outcast among normals, but at least I have friends.* Sara's headache pounded, anxiety gripping her. After turning a corner, she slowed her pace and scanned the many vendors and groups of people milling about the center of the boardwalk. Where was everyone else?

Thomas gently grasped her other hand and, in a low voice, asked, "You okay?"

Sara cringed. She was not okay. Pretending to be normal would never work for her—for any of them. Yet neither would hiding in a sacred forest for the rest of their unnaturally long lives.

She sighed, her frustration turning into guilt. They were on a *date*, and this beach trip wasn't about her—it was about the whole gang having a reprieve between battles, a chance to feel normal before facing darkness again. The clackety-clack of a skateboard brought her flustered mind back to Thomas standing before her, looking for all the world like he wanted to ignite the crystal shop and everyone in it. What a dangerous pair they made. Her lips curved upward, and Thomas returned her grin as if reading her thought.

"I'm starving," she said, which was true. It had been hours since they'd eaten the late lunch Caleb and his mother, Rebecca, had prepared for them.

"Me too. I know the perfect place with the best Mexican food. And everyone else will be there, so you can stop searching the crowd." His grin deepened, and she gave him a mock glare.

Of course he had noticed her constant surveillance. She bumped him with her shoulder, only succeeding in bruising herself against his rock-hard chest.

The Mexican restaurant, named MANINA'S in a sign with green glowing letters, did indeed have excellent food. It also had a lively bar with throbbing music and extremely lax security when it came to checking IDs. Although Sara and Thomas drank ice water, most of the young crowd clutched a beer or margarita—or both.

While sitting at a coin-sized patio table and scarfing down tacos with the best flour tortillas she had ever tasted, Sara keenly studied the entire riotous restaurant. People enjoying heaping plates of food and pitchers of alcohol occupied every table on the patio overlooking the beach. Open rolling doors gave way to an interior dance floor, writhing with sweaty dancers, and behind it stretched a long bar packed with customers jockeying to get drinks.

A server who could have passed as a high-schooler, wearing a whistle and a name tag reading PACO, approached their table and offered them shots of tequila. Directly from the bottle. Having once gotten sick from tequila at a college house party she had snuck into, Sara grimaced and gave him a hard no. He merely shrugged, bused their table, and disappeared into the dance floor melee.

Thomas chuckled. "So, you've drunk before." Not a question.

She grimaced again. "It seemed like a good idea at the time, except I honestly thought I was going to die the next morning."

"That's because of our magic. Alcohol is poison to us. Well, I suppose it's poison to everyone, but more so to us." Thomas clearly didn't care if anyone overheard them. Probably figured they were too buzzed and the music too loud for anyone to grasp their conversation. He glanced around and, in a commanding voice similar to his father's, stated, "Exit doors are off both sides of the bar, and you can easily jump the patio's low wall and be on the beach. Matt is at the pool tables"—he jerked his chin toward the darts and billiards in an adjoining outdoor space—"and Caleb is holding court with that fine group"—he turned his amused gaze to a throng of young women howling with laughter beside the bar.

Sara craned her neck to see over the dancers. Her jaw slacked at the sight of her cousin in the center of the clique. His rugged good looks clearly had them mesmerized, along with whatever tale he was telling. She dragged her eyes away from him and spotted Matthew playing billiards—men and women watching him intently. He gave his audience, including his rakish opponent, a smooth smile as he chalked his cue stick. With a flick of his russet hair, Matthew tossed the chalk to the handsome contender, sat on the pool table rail, and expertly sank a behind-the-back shot.

Hells. They were having a good time. They were also attracting many adoring fans. Perhaps too many. Sara chewed her lip, unsure if the unease she felt was simply nerves or some kind of magical warning of Samson about to make a smoky appearance.

Thomas rose from their table and extended his hand to her, a devilish look on his face. "The rest of us are on the dance floor."

Sara pushed back in her seat, shaking her head. "Oh no," she protested, but he firmly took her hand and led her onto the dance floor, bumping past dancers until they reached Moira, Violet, Lily, and Ian near the center of the swarming mass.

"Sara!" screamed Moira, barely audible over the pumping

music, as she pulled her into their circle. Her face was flushed, her red hair wild. She looked full-on blissful, her curvy body grinding to the beat. Even the normally reserved Violet was letting loose and undulating, arms waving overhead. Beside her danced Lily, face shining with a bright smile, body moving with fluid grace. The pale blonde witch laughed at Ian and grabbed his arms, stopping him from flailing about like a dying fish.

A familiar, brazen hand gripped Sara's waist and spun her around. She raised a fist, considering how hard to punch Thomas for dragging her onto the dance floor only to trip into him. He caught her fist in one hand, wrapped his other arm around her, and drew her against him while moving to the music. "I'm thinking lack of rhythm is a Lochton family affliction," he teased, his stubble grazing her cheek as she stepped on his foot.

Sara groaned. "Please tell me I'm not as uncoordinated as Ian."

"Relax," he coaxed in a low voice, running a hand possessively down her back and swinging her away from a shirtless, brawny guy who had gotten too close.

The bond sparked inside her, and her legs molded to his, letting him move her.

He murmured into her ear, "That's better. More like we're in bed instead of sparring."

Sara's core ignited from the rumble in his voice and their tightly aligned bodies. When she lifted her chin and met Thomas's burning gaze, she came undone and smashed her lips to his. Her hands splayed across his broad back, needing to draw him closer.

Multicolored lights flashed in time with the pulsating music. Sara closed her eyes, moving with Thomas on the dance floor, their kiss deepening. Heat built inside her—not from the summer night or sweaty bodies pressing in around them, but from her magic searching for his power and wanting release. With each seductive sway, it built and built. Her entire body vibrated with the effort to hold in her magic until a tiny fraction slipped past her. She snapped open her eyes, abruptly stopping their kiss. Too late. A jolt of energy surged between their hearts and visibly sparked around them.

Thomas froze, eyes wide and protectively holding her to him. Around them, people laughed and rocked, completely oblivious, while music continued blasting and overhead lights flickered. "Don't move," he rasped, his gaze searching the beachfront and night sky outside the rolled-up doors.

Sara held still, anticipating a dark, shadowy dragon ripping off the roof of the club and spewing fire at her. Sweat trickled down her chest and pooled around the bloodstone hidden beneath her shirt.

After a few heart-pounding moments, Thomas loosened his hold and steered them away from the dance floor and toward the end of the bar. Finding a pocket of space at the edge of the surging dancers, he rubbed the back of his head, his blue eyes fixed on her. In a voice barely loud enough to be heard over the rousing club, he said, "I'm sorry. I didn't think our bond would do that outside of the forest. Without my powers, the fire between us feels like a faint ember." Despite their steamy dance, his face had paled.

Her insides flipped. The spark of magic had been her fault, not his, and she refused to let it ruin their night. Intent on wiping away his serious expression, Sara placed a hand on his chest, leaned into him, and teased, "Bond or not, you completely seduced me— drove me wild—and now you're acting like our date is over. I don't think so."

He reared back and blinked once, twice, then gave her a heart-stopping, wolfish grin. "*Completely* seduced you?"

"Yes, so now you need to be a perfect gentleman and bring this date to a happy ending." She folded her arms and fought the urge to look to her left—one of her tells he was acutely aware of.

Delight flashing in his eyes, he placed his hands on her hips and brushed against her. "I'm always a gentleman. What exactly do you have in mind?" She could have sworn he angled his head toward the quiet beach.

"Ice cream," she beamed, smugly pulling the rug out from under him.

He choked a laugh, then nipped the tip of her ear, sending a zap of electricity along her skin. "Ice cream it is. My wicked little monster." With a kiss to her nose, he stepped back. "May as well bring everyone with us." He gave a resigned sigh and shifted aside as Ian and Lily joined them, their faces glowing.

Sara glanced at the dance floor behind them, her anxiety returning in full force. "Where are Violet and Moira?"

Ian swiped his sweat-slicked brow and pulled out his phone. "They danced off with a few dudes."

Sara stiffened. Even without the threat of fire-breathing reptiles and dark magic, "*dancing off with a few dudes*" was never a good idea. What were they thinking?

"They're at the opposite end of the bar. Must be in the restroom," said Ian, studying the locator app. His calm voice was betrayed by a nervous flick of his wrist, shifting the corded charm bracelet that had once saved his life.

Sara whipped her attention toward the far end of the room just as an invisible icy talon jabbed between her shoulder blades and dragged down her spine. Her back arched, goose bumps spreading across her skin. The bloodstone pulsed, a faint red light shining through her cotton T-shirt. Three sets of wide eyes met hers before they all turned toward the crowd between them and the opposite side of the bar.

Sara shouted over the music, voice fraught with fear, "We need to get to them."

CHAPTER 5

W HEN THE BLOODSTONE beat again, Sara shoved aside a dancer, then another and another, fighting for every inch forward. Someone pushed back at her, and Thomas's fist shot out, sending the offender into the patrons lining the bar. The sharp sound of breaking glass rang out, followed by a chorus of angry hollers. A pack of frat guys slid from their stools and faced them, shirts drenched with beer, fists at their sides.

Thomas rolled his shoulders, an eager gleam in his eyes. "Seems we'll have to fight our way through." He shifted his stance, blatantly adjusting his weight and sizing up his targets, a predator preparing to pounce.

"No fighting!" Sara yelled over the pounding music. Another frozen talon raked her back, and she gasped. Violet and Moira needed her. *Now.*

Sara frantically shook out her hands, magic tingling in her palms. *Think.* Pushing through the solid crowd would take too long. There had to be another way.

She raised her gaze over the sea of dancers to the colorful banners and lighting overhead. The urge to fly above the crowd had her trembling, and she stumbled, stepping between Thomas and the oncoming frat pack.

Thomas roared, "No magic!" But Sara was already in motion.

She ducked under the frat boys' raised fists and surged toward the bar. With one quick swipe, she cleared half a dozen beer bottles and scrambled to stand atop its slippery lacquered surface. To her left, Thomas swung away, his trained focus crushing his opponents, while Ian and Lily stared up at her, mouths agape. To her right, Paco and another bartender took a step back and gave her wide grins.

The bar erupted into chaos—customers and staff cheering. Whistles blew, hands grabbed at her legs, and more than one person yelled, "Take it off!"

Sara shoved down the urge to flatten them all with a violent microburst. Magic howled in her ears and threatened to engulf her in flames, but she ground her teeth, willing it to remain hidden, and set her focus on the far end of the bar. Among a stream of people entering and exiting the restrooms, Moira's flaming-red hair stood out—as did the hulking man pinning her to the wall.

Sara kicked back the meaty hands on her calves and sprinted down the bar, leaping over pitchers and crashing through stacks of shot glasses. Partiers shrieked, grabbing at their drinks, as she barreled past, launched herself off the end of the bar, and nearly took out an unfortunate server before slamming into the floor with the force of a raging bull. Customers scattered, creating a momentary opening toward the restrooms. Sara lunged for the gap and half ran, half skidded to where Moira lay slumped on the floor with her back against the wall—Violet beside her.

"What happened?" Sara cried, her heart racing while she scanned the immediate area. No sign of the hulking man.

Violet swung a plastic cup at Sara. "Some cute guy bought us punch," she slurred. Moira lifted her head, her eyes glassy.

Shit.

Sara grabbed the half-empty cup, sniffed the red drink inside, then poured its remaining contents onto the grimy floor. When she peered into the cup again, a pasty white substance clung to the bottom.

That was punch alright—as in, punch you out. "You've been drugged! You're never supposed to take a drink from someone you don't know."

They stared at Sara, tears welling in their eyes.

Ah, Hells. Of course they wouldn't know this. They hardly ever left the forest and certainly didn't grow up in a debauched college town like she had.

A hiccup-burp escaped Moira. "I'm gonna puke." She pressed a hand over her red-lipped mouth. Before Sara could drag them into the restroom, Thomas, Lily, and Ian grabbed the three of them, threw open an adjacent service door, and pushed them all out onto the beach.

Cool, quiet air smelling of salt and stale beer kissed Sara's face. Relief flooded her. No dragons, no dark magic—just a normal scumbag she wanted to slowly choke for preying on her friends.

Moira leaned against the side of the building and vomited. Violet immediately followed, emptying her stomach while Lily held back her hair. When Moira heaved again, Sara cautiously gathered her ginger locks, unsure if the fierce shifter would bat her hands away. While she wanted to soothe Moira and Violet with her healing power, she held back from pressing her luck and inadvertently summoning trouble.

Over the muffled thumping of music, a thunderous crash rattled the service door as if a full-on brawl had exploded inside the bar. Sara shot her gaze at Thomas, whose grin radiated pure joy despite the bruise blooming on his cheek.

Perhaps they had *started a brawl.*

She swept her gaze to Ian, who backed away from the shaking door.

He turned to her with a pinched expression. "What got into

you—with the whole gasp and glowing bloodstone?" He scrunched his nose at Moira and Violet. "And what happened to them?"

"I thought I sensed"—Sara stopped herself from saying Samson's name—"dark magic. Except it seems some normal asshole drugged both of them. They've vomited most of it and will be alright, but they need to get cleaned up and sleep it off."

The gleam faded from Thomas's face, replaced with anger and concern. He gently put an arm around his sister and steered her toward their campsite. Lily gathered Moira to her side and did the same.

Sara hesitated, glancing back at the club. "What about Matt and Caleb?" She sounded too much like an overprotective parent.

Ian tugged out his phone and quirked an eyebrow at the screen before shoving it back into his pocket. "They're fine and promise to be home before curfew. And don't ask any questions unless you're prepared for the answers," he warned, dashing after the others.

"Pfft!" Sara hustled to catch up with them. This trip was going to be the death of her. If not by dark magic and dragons, then surely by cavalier attitudes.

It had been hours since they'd showered, rehydrated, and settled into their respective tents. Hours since Matthew and Caleb had slipped back into camp at precisely 12:03 a.m., and Sara still could not sleep. Had dark magic truly attacked them at the club, she would have instinctively used her powers to protect them. But doing so would have called a dragon and made Thomas's greatest fear a reality.

She loosed a quiet sigh. Being High Witch was testing every fiber of her complicated soul. In her heart, she desperately wanted to pack up and return to Ware Woods. However, the leader she was trying to be knew they needed this rare moment to be free of magic—both light and dark.

Moira rolled into her for the third time, her soft sighs akin to a kitten's purr. Shifters. Even in their sleep, they sought the presence of their pack. Sara wondered how Thomas was faring crammed in a tent with the other guys. All night she had listened for the faintest sound of him having one of his nightmares—terrors that left him ashen and trembling even after she woke him and clutched him to her. But she had only heard Caleb's lion roar of a snore.

She inched away from Moira and silently extracted herself from her sleeping bag. Having forgotten pajamas, she had changed into fresh clothes before bed. Her hand settled atop her shorts pocket, where the lump of pyrite bit into her upper thigh. The gemstone had kept her company during the night, her fingers rubbing it and memorizing every smooth angle. Perhaps a walk to pass the last hour before dawn would settle her nerves and occupy her time before the rest of the group woke for breakfast.

With the stealth of a leopard, she unzipped the tent, crawled onto the sand, and came nose to nose with Bailey. The yellow Lab wagged her tail and licked Sara's face.

Okay. Not so stealthy. Sara rose and put a finger to her lips, and the Lab quieted. *Good dog.* Jerking her head for Bailey to follow her, Sara strode off down the beach, toes digging into cool sand.

After a quick stop at the facilities building for both of them to do their morning business, Sara ran for the shoreline, Bailey sprinting alongside her. With the ocean breeze lifting her hair and spirits, Sara threw back her head and took in the lightening sky— not a white or smoky cloud in sight. Bailey brushed against her legs, and Sara gazed down at her furry companion with a wry smile. Technically, she was not alone; plus, plenty of pre-dawn joggers were around, ensuring dark magic wouldn't dare appear.

Keeping a polite distance from others, Sara slowed her pace and walked on the wet sand beside the water's gently lapping edge. When an icy wave washed across her feet and ankles, she yelped and jumped to higher ground. The cold reminded her of the icy touch at the club—a touch that must have been her High Witch senses detecting a threat to her forest family rather than the presence of dark magic. She chewed on this thought while she wandered farther down the beach, Bailey racing around her as they passed the sleepy boardwalk.

Another wave lapped at her feet, and Sara stopped her ruminating to glance at the ocean. A portion of its previously calm surface now churned as if a deadly rip current lay beneath. The back of her neck prickled. A warning. Sand vibrated under her feet while overhead a flock of gulls screamed in a rush back to the mainland. Bailey ran to her side with a whine, and magic crackled in the air. When Sara whirled to find the source, a rogue wave slammed into her.

She fell back just as a sizzling sphere of black energy skimmed her shoulder.

Shit!

Sara grabbed Bailey and jumped up to face three monstrous Takers running straight at her with dark energy swirling in their palms. The shirtless Takers were reminiscent of Samson's men, except these sycophants had bruises around their eyes, the marks appearing like the empty sockets of a skull.

Sara stepped in front of Bailey and surveyed the beach. To her distant left, near the grassy dunes, were a pair of female joggers and a man on a fat-tire bike. They stopped and gaped as the beastly men hurled sizzling, dark voids of power at Sara. Judging the normals were far enough back to be out of harm's way, she hugged Bailey and summoned a protective shield around herself and the dog. Her shield had barely formed when the Takers' black energy struck it with a deafening crack.

The women screamed. Their shrill cries echoed through the coral-hued morning and were immediately answered by an explosion of water as a dragon erupted from the sea.

CHAPTER 6

THE DRAGON'S MASSIVE head shimmered with seawater and fiery scales. Spikes edged the sides of its face, and atop its skull, multiple gilded horns splayed in the manner of an imperial crown. A long tentacle-like mustache fluttered from an open mouth lined with gleaming white teeth the size of daggers. Salt water sprayed forth and rained upon Sara's shield in fat drops as the dragon's long, sinuous body rose from the ocean. Every inch of the magical creature was power and magnificence, from the curved spikes running along its spine to each ruby-red and golden scale glinting like fire in the rising sun. Though it lacked wings, the dragon looped and swam through the sky with serpentine ease, speeding toward Sara and the Takers.

All three Takers cursed and seized the stone pendants around their necks like lifelines. Their black encircled eyes remained fastened on the charging dragon as sooty wisps slithered from the pendants and curled around them.

Sara's shield sputtered, her focus shattered at the sight of the Takers using the same dark smoke Samson used to transport himself. But before the wisps could swell into inky clouds and magically dispatch the lackeys, the dragon spewed a jet of fire. Flames engulfed them; their yells cut short as the surrounding sand liquefied into molten glass.

Fire billowed and raced down the shoreline. Sara screamed, pouring energy into fortifying her shield while the flames licked around her and Bailey.

The dragon jerked back, the fiery onslaught stopping. It swung its head toward her, jaw snapping shut, gaze locking on to her, as though surprised at her presence.

Bailey whimpered. Sara dug her feet into the sand, strengthening her stance. She refused to look away, choosing to meet death with a mix of awe and contempt for the splendid dragon. When it drifted close enough for her to see its silvery eyes and vertically slitted pupils, her heart skipped a beat. "Don't touch this dog," she growled, her hands burrowed into Bailey's fur.

The dragon snorted a puff of smoke at her shield, which promptly winked out like a birthday candle.

Great. I'll go out as beach BBQ.

Maintaining eye contact with the dragon's surreal gaze, Sara slowly pulled one hand from Bailey. While part of her yearned to touch the dragon, the distinct possibility of losing her arm stayed her curiosity. Instead, she clutched the bloodstone through her shirt and silently begged for her ancestor's help. Her great-great-grandmother Mary had spoken to her once in her time of need. Perhaps she might aid her now.

The dragon tilted its head. Sara's heart skipped again. Flames of white energy gathered on her skin and stretched toward the dragon. It snorted another puff of smoke, blanketing her with velvety warmth and smelling not of death but, surprisingly, of rain. When Sara flared her nostrils, wanting another whiff to confirm the fresh scent so at odds with its ferocious appearance, the creature swiveled its grandiose head toward the growing crowd of people on the beach and the many phones recording its every move.

With a roar that tremored the entire beach, sending people screaming in all directions, the dragon swept a figure eight pattern in the air, forcing Sara to shut her eyes against a whirlwind of sand. Though she couldn't see it, she *felt* it flying low overhead and heard the thunderous rasp of its scaled body. After a heart-pounding moment, the sandstorm died. Sara cracked her eyes open just in time to see the dragon dive back into the sea. Water punched skyward in a giant plume, the ocean's surface churning with white-capped waves until the dragon's entire blood-red and golden body disappeared. A flame-like spear on the tip of its tail was the last Sara saw of it before a glassy dark circle marked its descent and the sea returned to normal.

Expecting the dragon to return and swallow her whole, Sara remained frozen, scanning the gentle ocean waves until a jogger passed and broke her stupor. She tore her eyes from the water and took in the unmarred sand, the people casually enjoying early morning workouts on the beach, and the flock of gulls softly crying overhead.

Normal. Everything was positively normal, as if nothing magical had ever happened.

Bailey shook herself, dislodging Sara's protective hold, and trotted back toward their campsite.

Brilliant idea.

Sara sped after the yellow Lab, eager to put distance between herself and wherever the dragon had disappeared to. Brushing off sand as she hurried along, she swiped her hand across her shorts and felt the lump of pyrite in her front pocket. Either the stone was indeed a powerful protection charm or her ancestor had somehow intervened. Regardless, Sara was grateful to be alive.

Apparently, Bailey was too. The dog barked and circled her, tail wagging.

"I won't tell anyone if you won't," said Sara. Sharing what had happened would *completely* freak out Thomas and Ian—they would never let her out of their sight again—and their little "normal" vacation of reckless abandon would come to a screeching halt. Besides, one of those hulking Takers must have been the man hounding Moira and Violet at the club. And since they were undeniably gone, Sara could lighten up and enjoy their day at the beach.

The scent of bacon and eggs greeted her as she and Bailey jogged up to their campsite. Everyone except for Matthew was up and ready for the day.

"Hey," she panted, stopping before Thomas and narrowing her eyes at his grumpy vibe and disheveled hair. Clearly, she wasn't the only one who'd had a rough night.

"See," chirped Moira, all too cheerful for her usual self. "I told you she was walking Bailey."

Thomas shoved Sara's phone at her. "You forgot this," he grumbled.

Electricity sparked between them when Sara took the phone. She met his eyes, his unspoken fear squeezing her heart. She shoved the phone into her back pocket and deflected his concern with her own. "You're still hurt from last night," she said, reaching for his bruised cheek.

Thomas jerked back. "No magic," he whispered harshly.

If only he knew a small spark of healing energy was *nothing* compared to the magic she recently witnessed. Determined to lighten his mood, Sara smiled and flicked his nose. "Suit yourself."

He grabbed her hand, interlacing his fingers with hers, and eased his expression. "You're pale. Are you okay?"

The guys' tent rustled. With a yawn worthy of raising the dead, Matthew stumbled out and joined the others, who were all sitting at the picnic table, watching her and Thomas.

Thomas's gaze never left her face.

Carefully maintaining her smile, Sara offered a slight shrug. "I'm fine." *Nope, not really. Just survived three Takers and a freaking dragon.* "Couldn't sleep is all." Hoping Thomas wouldn't see the lie in her eyes, she dropped her gaze and tugged him to the table.

After a banquet-worthy breakfast, Sara pulled out the thick fantasy novel she had brought and settled into a folding chair under the shade of a rainbow-striped umbrella. Lily, Violet, and Ian slathered on sunscreen while Matthew and Thomas dumped a bag of sports equipment onto the sand. Donning their sunglasses and grabbing a volleyball, they all took off for an open section of the beach.

The sight of Thomas in black-and-gray plaid swim trunks launched her heart rate until she noticed Matthew's low-slung Hawaiian print shorts and debated yelling at him like a twitchy mother to yank them up.

A tent zipper ripped behind her, followed by a hoarse choking sound from Caleb. Sara twisted to see Moira in her flaming red-hair glory and a barely there bikini.

"Well, it's an improvement from the spider-thread suit you last wore," drawled Caleb after clearing his throat. He wore hunter green shorts and a light-gray swim shirt stretched taut over his broad chest.

Moira twirled, dangerously pleased with herself. "You approve? Gran made this one too."

"It's *crochet*!" cried Sara. "Father of Night, at least put some shorts on."

Among the clusters of people wandering the shore, a squad of high school boys stopped to gawk, throats bobbing.

"Keep walking," ordered Caleb with a firm jerk of his thumb down the beach. Moira shoved him, succeeding only in bouncing off his stocky build. Chuckling at her, he turned and sprinted for the ocean.

"Caleb Alexander Cahill! I told you not to get in my way," she growled, and gave chase. The rest of their group dropped the volleyball and followed them into the water.

How they could jump into that icy ocean was beyond Sara. Not to mention all the things lurking beneath the waves. Perhaps the dragon would keep the sharks away . . .

With a pat to Bailey lying protectively at her feet, she inhaled the salty air and dozed off to the serenity of waves and seagulls.

Sara sprang awake at the sensation of someone being too close and taking something from her. White energy buzzed at her fingertips as she snapped open her eyes to find Moira and Violet staring at her. They stepped back, Violet holding Sara's book before her as if it were an offering.

Sara willed her magic back inside herself and straightened in the chair. "Burning Hells. Was I drooling again?" She wiped her mouth and stilled the tremble in her hand, cursing herself for being so jumpy.

"Didn't mean to startle you. We were just curious to know what book you *weren't* reading." Violet sniggered, inspecting the back of Sara's book. Her eyes flared a shimmering indigo. "This sounds *spicy*. Can I borrow it?"

Moira glanced over Violet's shoulder and raised a manicured brow. "Ooh, can I borrow it too?"

Sara blew a soft laugh through her nose. "Sure, just don't fold the corners or salivate on the pages." Eyeing the beach, she stood and stretched. "Where is everyone?" She hoped her tone was casual despite the panic squeezing her chest.

"Probably the volleyball courts by now." Moira gave a shrug. "I'm surprised Thomas left. 'Course, he made us *swear* to keep our eyes on you."

Resisting the urge to whip out her phone and check the locator app, Sara ruffled Bailey's fur and turned her attention toward the boardwalk. The corners of her mouth curled up at the opportunity to stealthily watch over the others while finally enjoying the treat she had been craving. "Let's get some ice cream and catch up with them. But first," she said, considering the girls' bikinis, "put some shorts on."

Moira groaned as she and Violet ducked into the tent, tossing the book into Sara's duffel bag. "You're worse than my mother."

"I pity your mother," said Sara, grabbing her sunglasses. "I swear, if my hair wasn't already gray, it would be by the end of this trip."

CHAPTER 7

AS THE THREE of them strolled along the wooden board-walk, Moira bumped shoulders with Sara. "Look at us, besties," she crooned, dipping her sunglasses. Glee flashed in her honey-colored eyes, along with a tender authenticity Sara had not expected.

Moira had once threatened to kill her if she touched Thomas, who was as much a brother to her as her twin, Matthew. The red-headed shifter exuded confidence and a tough exterior, yet her recent change in demeanor suggested a softer side Sara never thought existed. Sara regarded her. A shifter who wanted friends. Perhaps she and Moira were more similar than she'd ever thought possible.

A group of skaters clacked beside them, catcalling and openly wagging their tongues. "What's up, Grandma?" jeered a reedy boy as he swerved in front of Sara before gliding off with his snickering companions.

Sara rolled her eyes so hard that she turned her shoulders to the nearest shop and braked, Moira and Violet slamming into her. Taped to its display window and open door were dozens of tribal tattoo sketches and flash art in a riot of colors and intricate designs. While they were all stunning, one drawing in particular snagged her attention. It was a combination of the infinity and yin-yang symbols and was nearly identical to the still circle tattoo her father had on his upper back and the brand Thomas wore on his forearm—the mark chosen to remember someone they loved. An image of her mother smiling over a bouquet of lilac hydrangeas flashed in her mind.

Sara strode into the shop.

After a few minutes of Moira and Violet repeatedly asking her if she was sure, Sara exiled them to a bench outside the tattoo parlor, where they were all too happy to "see and be seen." Within moments, Sara met with an artist, sketched the still circle design, and lay face down on a padded bench—shirt off.

The artist gently adjusted the straps of Sara's camisole, transferred the purple stencil to the center of her upper back, and handed her a mirror to confirm the placement. "This looks nice with the faint line you have on your spine," said the woman, her gloved hand swiping Sara's backbone. "That must've hurt."

Sara frowned, having forgotten the unusual birthmark running down her back. It was so pale and out of sight, she never gave it much thought. A memory of Thomas brushing his finger up and down her spine while murmuring, "*Beautiful*," had her cheeks flushing.

An hour later, Sara exited the parlor, taped bandage concealed beneath her shirt and loose hair. With an ear-to-ear grin, she hauled Moira and Violet from the bench and dragged them to the ice cream shop. A couple of teen boys trailed behind but, much to Sara's relief, moved on before the trio received their frozen treats and hit the boardwalk again.

Violet licked her rocky road and, with a hint of warning in her tone, said, "I'm sure Charlie will be cool with it, but my father would kill me if I got a tattoo."

Sara snorted and lapped the ice cream melting down the side of her cone. Since her father had the same still circle tattoo, she doubted he would disapprove—especially because it was to remember her mother. However, Violet's father, Kane, may very well wring her neck. Ever since he'd found out Sara was High Witch of Ware Woods, he acted like a father to her. His constant training sessions and overprotectiveness had become more intense once they all realized how strong the bond was between her and Thomas—his oldest living son.

By the time they approached the sand volleyball courts near the end of the boardwalk, Sara had devoured her double scoop, mint chip ice cream and had a skip in her step. The sunny yet breezy weather made for a perfect day, not to mention surviving a dragon, getting a tattoo, and enjoying her favorite dessert. Now all she had to do was ensure the safety of her crew by simply watching beach volleyball.

On the court closest to them, Thomas, Matthew, Ian, and Lily were holding their own against another four-person team. Despite a lack of magical power, Lily crushed her serves, and the boys set, dug, and spiked like professional athletes. Sara gawped at their flawless teamwork, as though they practiced often and instinctively knew how to maneuver every play. When they won their last set, they took a water break and joined Sara, Moira, and Violet on the side of the court—the other team waving as they took off.

Sara's attention darted among the other courts, searching for Caleb until Ian said, "He's at camp prepping for our big BBQ dinner."

"Alone?" she countered.

Thomas flashed a bright smile. "We thought you three were still there, playing cards and sleeping all day."

"It was just a short nap." Sara eyed the sand sticking to his abs. Thank the Mother she hadn't slept the entire afternoon.

Sara pulled her focus away from Thomas. "I'll go hang out with Caleb. I'm terrible at volleyball anyway and would probably lose my head to one of those serves." She sized up Lily, completely mystified as to how someone so petite could be so strong without her witchy powers. Sara turned to leave but stopped dead when two people, magical auras flickering around them, approached the opposite side of the court.

Black shadows clung to a tall, muscled male wearing sunglasses, his creamy skin flushed with the start of a sunburn. Beside him, a liquid silver aura, similar to Lily's, fluttered around an umber-skinned female wearing long braids and a face mask over her mouth. No glasses covered her onyx eyes. With a curious cock of her head, the masked female waved her hand down low—the expected greeting between magicals.

Sara returned the acknowledging hand wave and whispered to Lily beside her, "I can't tell if they're good or bad. Is this typical?"

"No," said Lily. She locked her attention on the female and bared her teeth, a response so different from her usual pleasant self that Sara's jaw dropped.

Ian stepped forward, the confidence in his stance further lowering Sara's jaw. In a tone of authority he stated, "You need to leave."

"Aw now," drawled the male, striding across the court. "I don't think so." He struck Ian square in the chest, sending him flying back with a crackle of dark power.

Shit.

Sara's skin prickled with magic, but before she could strike the male—physically or magically—Ian looked up at her and shook his head, silently pleading her not to engage.

"Asshole. That wasn't part of the plan," hissed the masked female, rushing to Ian. When she grabbed his arm as if to pull him up, magic sparked between them, and she jumped back with a yelp. Eyes wide, she looked from Ian to Lily, who was now helping him to his feet.

Lily snarled, her lips pulled back in a murderous grimace. The female gasped, her surprise evident through her black mask, and murmured, "Your teeth are . . . straight."

The hostile male turned to Sara. Arrogance seeped from him as he slowly lifted his sunglasses, revealing brown eyes glinting red in the summer sun. With a twist of his lips, he leered at her.

Recognition punched her in the gut, and she cursed. Loudly. The last time she had seen Brad, the sadistic orderly from the questionable mental facility where she'd been held, he had been vomiting with a concussion she had gifted him. Now he radiated dark magic and had openly struck Ian. And, judging from Moira's narrowed stare at Brad's hulking figure, Sara was sure he was the scumbag—and not a Taker—who had drugged her and Violet.

Sara should have strangled him in the facility when she had the chance.

He loosed a throaty laugh and winked at her before lowering his glasses back into place. Thomas growled, his hands curling into fists. Brad ignored him and raised his pale, muscled arm to Sara. "Remember this? I see it every day and think of you." Two arched scars marked his forearm, a precise match to Sara's bite pattern. When he dropped his arm, she glimpsed a touch of black stain smearing his palm.

Well, shit. Was this why he poisoned himself with dark magic and somehow found her? For revenge?

Sara grinned and snapped her teeth. "Are you wanting a matching set on your other arm? 'Cause I can do better than that now." She slipped her hands, palms burning with energy, into her pockets and clasped the pyrite.

Burning Hells! This was going to get ugly. Before she could bark an order for her crew to run, Thomas launched himself at Brad.

Thomas's rapid assault nailed three blows, each punch a sickening crack, before Brad could counter with a wild jab. Thomas dodged the strike and feinted, leading Brad right into a hook and sending him to his knees. Brad roared as Thomas landed a kick, and then another.

Shadows much too dark for a summer's day exploded from Brad, throwing Thomas back. Quicker than Sara had ever seen

Thomas fight during their sparring, he sprang up and hurled himself into Brad. They fell to the sand with Thomas on top, relentlessly whaling on him. Even without his magic, Thomas was beating him—brutally. He'd kill him, Sara realized at the same moment black flames flickered in Brad's hands. Unless Brad killed him first.

Sara lunged forward, and it was as if time slowed. Distantly, Ian and Lily shouted, and then came a bone-snapping crack as a wild fist connected with Sara's jaw. She flew back, instinctively healing herself before she hit the sand.

"STOP!" screamed Violet. "You'll summon a dragon, and we'll all die."

Everyone froze, even the cluster of normals who had stopped to watch the fight.

With a grunt, Brad shoved Thomas aside and jumped to his feet, wiping sand off himself with a whisper of black smoke. "Dragons. Soon they won't be a problem," he muttered and spat blood so dark it appeared black. He aggressively beckoned to the masked female and in a louder voice said, "Come on, Kira. It's done. Time to go."

"You're disgusting," she lashed at him, onyx eyes full of fury. With a final piercing glance at Ian, she marched off the beach and into the crowded boardwalk. Brad gave Sara a parting middle finger and strode after Kira, quickly disappearing with her into the mass of people.

Someone yelled, "Dungeons and Dragons forever," followed by laughter as the surrounding normals returned to their activities.

Though Sara longed to pursue Brad, she tore her gaze from the crowd and swung around to face Thomas. The savageness in his eyes stole her breath. If she had been able to feel the full brunt of his emotions through the bond, she had no doubt she would have collapsed. His entire body trembled as if consumed with rage and adrenaline, his shredded knuckles bleeding rusty blots onto the sand.

Moira leapt between them. Hands on her hips, she stared down Thomas. "Go run it off, you idiot."

He cracked his neck, cursed, and sprinted down the beach—away from their campsite.

Matthew pivoted to follow, but Sara grabbed his shoulder and held him back. She swept her gaze among the group, assessing their morale. Violet nervously watched the surf, Ian seemed in utter shock as he gaped at the boardwalk, and the rest of them stared at Sara with wide eyes, awaiting her direction.

Brad's last words repeated in Sara's mind. While she had no idea what he meant by "*It's done,*" it was certainly time for all of them to go. First, she needed to wrangle Thomas. She chased after him, calling over her shoulder, "I'll handle him. The rest of you go back to camp and pack up. We're leaving today."

By the time Sara caught up to Thomas, they were at a secluded stretch of beach miles from camp. His stride never tired until she pleaded with him to stop and even then, he only slowed to a jog.

"You shouldn't be around me," he snarled.

Hells! He wasn't even winded.

Sara gulped down salty air and perhaps used a teensy bit of magic to keep up with him. "Don't be ridiculous," she panted.

"I never wanted you to see me like this. When my fighting instinct takes over, I have *very* little control. I'm dangerous. You should leave me. I don't want to hurt you—again." He stopped jogging and walked, sides heaving with frustration. "I didn't even see you until it was too late. I *hit* you. And made you use magic. And if . . ." His hands fisted, reopening cuts and leaking scarlet blood.

Sara rushed in front of him, grabbing his upper arms and pressing herself against him until he fully stopped. "Shh." She tried and failed to catch his averted gaze, and because she didn't know how else to calm him, she kissed him.

He stiffened, and still she kissed him until his shoulders relaxed and his thumbs swiped her cheeks. When at last she pulled back, he groaned and rested his brow against hers.

"Sara," he whispered, love, regret, and vulnerability swirling in his crushing blue eyes. "I know we're bonded, but . . . you deserve better than me."

Her heart fractured.

To hear him say such a thing was shocking, but either his acute emotion penetrated the hazy layer on their bond outside of the forest or her soul naturally responded to his, for she *felt* his anguish. It was wholly devastating, partly because he truly believed it and partly because she knew *she* did not deserve *him*.

Tears pricking the backs of her eyes, she held his intense gaze. "There is no one better than you. You are the only one I want to be with. The only one I will *ever* love so fiercely. The only one who has my heart. Now and forever."

His hands shook as he held the sides of her face, his aura blazing in response to her words.

She tilted her chin, bringing her mouth to his. With a soft groan, he shuddered against her and parted his lips, accepting her kiss and returning it with a hungry sweep of his tongue. Her insides melted, a flush of heat rushing through her and into him. Energy popped and cracked around them.

Thomas released her, pulling back and staring at his hands. They had completely healed. He stole a nervous glance at the sky, then returned his smoldering gaze to hers. "We are resuming this kiss as soon as we return home. And I will show you *exactly* all the ways I love you now and forever." Another spark of energy snapped, and Sara's legs threatened to give out from their run and his heated words.

He rested his brow to hers again, and in a low voice said, "I don't know who that asshole was, but please tell me he never laid a finger on you." His bare chest vibrated with a deadly growl.

Sara swallowed. Thomas would certainly kill Brad the next time they met, especially when he learned Brad was the one who drugged his sister and Moira. "Asshole, indeed," she said, deciding to keep certain cataclysmic information to herself. "I bit him and knocked him out before he had the chance."

A wicked grin spread across his face. "That's my monster."

Though Thomas didn't need to know all the nasty details about Brad just yet, Sara needed to tell him something else. If he could open up and admit he didn't feel worthy of her, then she could do the same for him. But while his violent instinct to protect was a concern and something they could work on together, her personal complication was irrevocable.

Both of their phones pinged with messages, which they ignored. Sara wrapped her arms around his neck. "Thomas," she said, her tone serious.

He immediately sobered.

Sara pursed her lips, buying another moment for courage, then said, "*You* deserve better than me—I need to share something with you." Before she could reveal the troubled piece of herself, a piece that could be crucial to their future together, their phones pinged again and again.

And then rang.

CHAPTER 8

Sara Pulled Out her phone, which had abruptly gone silent after two rings, and held it between her and Thomas. The screen lit up with message after message after message, all reading the same thing:

COME HOME NOW

They sprinted back toward camp, adrenaline and fear fueling Sara's tired body as she matched Thomas's punishing pace. Their bare feet pounded the wet sand along the shoreline, each wave biting Sara's raw heels with a salty sting. Beachgoers scrambled out of their way with a mix of shrieks and grumbles.

When her phone rang again, Charlie's name popped up. She punched the speaker and shouted, "Dad! What's going on?"

"Thank the Mother you're okay." Charlie blew out a rush of air. "Is Thomas with you?"

"I'm here. What happened?" Thomas said to the outstretched phone, his voice strained.

A moment of silence followed, leaving Sara fearful of a lost connection.

At last, Charlie said, "Samson took Connor." His words were a death knell.

Sara faltered, almost dropping the phone as Thomas surged toward the barely visible boardwalk and campsite beyond, sand kicking up in his wake. Dizziness descended upon Sara, her legs turning leaden. Thomas had already lost two brothers to Takers. Violet and Connor were his only remaining siblings, and now Samson had his little brother.

Father above.

Sara tripped again. This was all her fault. She should *never* have left Ware Woods, should never have left her forest family unprotected. She was a failure and a fool to think they could ever be normal and have a moment of peace from dark magic. If anything happened to Connor, Thomas and his family would be devastated—all the families would be. And she was to blame.

White-hot flames flickered along her arms. The power inside her flared with her emotions and her urgency to return to Ware Woods—to hunt down Samson and, Mother willing, rescue Connor.

Instead of following Thomas, she scanned the bright-blue sky stippled with cottony clouds. Maybe she could summon a rain cloud for coverage and fly—

Her insane idea halted as a thunderous wave crashed and shook the beach. She glanced at the ocean and her flames guttered out at the sight of a fiery scaled serpent twisting and churning in the foamy surf.

Seriously? Is this dragon following me?

"Sara," crackled her father's voice, reminding her he was still on the line. "Samson said he won't harm Connor as long as you meet him in the outer fields tonight."

She tore her eyes from the leviathan and resumed her sprint, legs on fire.

This was so like Samson. Sick bastard. Using a child as a bargaining chip to get her to face him. Little did he know she needed no coaxing. She looked forward to seeing him again and, whether or not she could guess his true name, she would end him. Even if it cost her life, she wouldn't hesitate to eliminate him and keep Ware Woods safe. Thomas would eventually get over her and meet someone else who wasn't so troubled—someone who could give him everything he could possibly want.

"If you leave now, you'll make it home before dark. Drive safe and don't use any magic." His last words landed with a fatherly severity, as if he knew a dragon lurked beside her.

She shot a glance at the nearby surf, both relieved and a tinge disappointed to find a wave of pure blue gray and not magnificent, fiery red.

"And Sara," he continued, "I'm sensing Samson doesn't want to harm you either. He's impossible to get an accurate read from, but . . . I think he needs something from you—from all of us."

A bitter taste coated her mouth. *Yeah, more fingers or maybe even my heart.* She would slowly carve his out first. Though she painfully lacked experience as a High Witch, Sara figured unleashing the full extent of her monstrous powers would surely end Samson—just hopefully not herself and everything around her in the bloody process.

Her father might fall for Samson's tricks, yet Sara refused to believe this forced meeting was anything beyond a ploy to hurt her.

She said, "We need to be prepared for whatever he throws at us. Have everyone inside the wall and ready with all the arrows we have."

"We're gathering everyone now." He hesitated. "Be careful and stay calm. High Witch or not, your words and actions are as powerful as your magic. You don't always need to fight for what you want."

True. Except words would never bring back her mother or the Hills witches or her finger. And fighting Samson—killing him— would ensure he hurt no one else she loved. She chose not to acknowledge her father's advice. "No matter what happens, keep everyone inside the wall." And before he could further lecture her, the phone lost reception.

Sara passed the boardwalk, dodged joyful beachgoers, and

rushed into their campsite—already packed up and picked clean as if they had never been there. Caleb and Moira edged their vehicles onto the service road while Thomas's truck idled, front passenger door open and waiting for her.

To say the mood in the truck was tense would have been an understatement. For hours, Thomas hardly spoke a word—his furious gaze set on the road. When they briefly stopped for gas, he pulled on a shirt, laced up his shoes, and tucked an arsenal of knives into his waistband and cargo pockets.

Sara eyed him warily as they peeled away from the gas station and sped toward Ware Woods. Weapons were useless against a dark witch like Samson; besides, she had no intention of letting Thomas get close enough to use knives. With a muttered, "Thanks," to Ian for grabbing her duffel bag, Sara tugged on her worn canvas shoes and braided back her hair.

In the rear seat, Bailey sprawled across Ian's lap as he continually checked his phone and provided updates from their father. Kane and Abby—Thomas's mother—were enraged over Connor's abduction and distraught that Thomas and Violet were outside the protection of Ware Woods. To keep the Sullivans within the forest, Charlie had used his magic to mentally ease their emotions. He reported that everyone was concerned and tense, assembling into position along the wall before the Sullivans' house and watching the ominous clouds gathering above the forest and outer fields.

Samson's clouds.

Sara chewed her lip. Though the entire situation screamed *TRAP*, it was also unusual for the wily dark witch to blatantly announce himself. She focused on gathering her magical power, grounding herself, and redirecting her frantic anxiety into the confidence she needed to exude as High Witch. Her repeated attempts did little to calm her rapid heartbeat. Too much was at stake, and her guilt for leaving the forest and shirking her duty clawed at her like a rabid beast.

As they drew closer to Ware Woods, Thomas roared his truck ahead of Caleb and Moira. His aggressive driving and clenched jaw had Sara clearing her throat to remind him for the tenth time that he and the others were to run to the safety of the forest wall while she dealt with Samson. But she checked herself when Ian suddenly ceased his manic texting with their father and looked at her with watery eyes.

His golden complexion faded to ghostly white. "Naomi's dead." He slumped back in his seat. "They found her in the outer forest, on the far side of the lake."

Sara froze. Impossible, yet the tremor in his voice said otherwise. "Oh, Ian," she breathed. Naomi had been her friend, but she had been so much more to Ian. His aunt had been his last blood relative on his mother's side—the last of the Hills witches—all others murdered by Samson. And now, it seemed, Samson had killed her too.

Sara ached to deny this horror, to pretend hard enough that it hadn't happened until Naomi magically manifested back to life. If only such magic existed.

Thomas cursed and floored the gas, racing the truck down the private road and toward the outer fields.

Heedless of the jostling truck and thick clouds overhead, Sara stared unblinkingly at Ian. Her brother had already endured more trauma than anyone should ever face. It wasn't fair. He was the bravest and most compassionate person she knew, and despite the crap that fate kept throwing at him, he never judged others or wallowed in self-pity.

Sara placed a hand over the pyrite in her shorts pocket.

She should never have left. The apology she owed Ian—owed Naomi and everyone in Ware Woods—stuck tight in her throat.

Thomas threw the truck into park beside the fallow fields and jumped out. To Sara's terror, he ran, not toward the forest wall and their families lined up and waiting with an armament of bows and arrows, but toward the center of the cropped grassy plain, yelling at the dark sky for Connor.

In response, the riled thunderclouds flashed with lightning. They swirled and stretched, forming a tornado that struck the ground with a deafening howl. In a burst of light, the dark clouds collapsed and skittered across the field, dissipating into ribbons of ash.

There stood Samson, clad in his black military-style jacket and top hat. Flanking him were half a dozen Takers, as well as Brad and Connor.

CHAPTER 9

Thomas's younger brother was upright and bound by smoky coils but appeared unhurt, his face rosy and with no sign of poison. In fact—Sara squinted—his lips were tainted a sticky blue, not inky black. He had snuck off—again—to the neighboring town to buy candy, and Samson had taken the opportunity to snatch him while Sara had been occupied at the beach. "*It's done*," echoed in her mind. Samson had clearly sent Brad to ensure her distraction.

Sara flew from the truck and landed between Samson and Thomas, pushing Thomas back with a gust of wind and placing an invisible protective dome around him and the rest of the gang, who had sprinted over to join him.

Of course they hadn't run for the wall. She'd lay into them later for not heeding her orders. With an admonishing frown, she twisted back to Samson and drove a white-hot spear of energy directly at his head.

He jerked to the side, eyes wide as the lethal pike skimmed his top hat and exploded behind him in a plume of dirt and rock. The hat disintegrated at his feet, and he swore. "I liked that hat." Without even looking in Sara's direction, Samson casually held up an ink-stained hand, creating a magical shield against her ensuing barrage of magic.

Bastard. No matter what she hurled at him, it fizzled out when it hit his shield. Panting from her efforts, she stopped and glared at him.

He arched a brow. "Are you done yet? Because I'm not here to fight."

"Then let him go," she snarled, stealing a glance at Connor, who looked slightly amused.

"I'd love to. He's already gutted me like a fish." Samson drew his gaze across the families lining the stone wall, arrows pointed at him. He didn't bat an eye. In a voice loud enough to carry across the field, he addressed them: "Even your spawn is insufferable. Who sends their kid to the store with multiple weapons? You're the animals here, not me." He placed a hand dramatically on his skinny chest.

With his attention shifted to the wall, Sara threw another blast at him, only for it to splinter like broken glass against his invisible aegis. "That's rich. You just killed Naomi," said Sara, and although knowing it was futile, she launched a few more spheres of energy at him.

Keeping his hand on his chest, Samson whirled to her with genuine surprise and, had she not known better, a bit of worry on his face. "I didn't kill her," he said, his tone sincere and not mocking for once. "Pity. We all could have used those special charms it seems only the Hills witches know how to make."

Sara wavered, her internal bullshit detector recognizing this as a true statement. But if he hadn't killed Naomi, who had? Her gaze flicked to the wall and stopped on Dorcas. At hundreds of years old, she was the eldest witch in Ware Woods and the only one with dark magic in her past. Yet Dorcas's recent actions had been helpful and her demeanor pleasant, as if she had indeed turned over a new leaf since Makwa's death. Even from afar, Sara could see shock on the witch's youthful, pretty face.

Sara's stomach clenched. This confrontation was not going as planned. Though she knew she wasn't worthy of being High Witch and was definitely in over her head, she couldn't let Samson know this. Couldn't let all of Ware Woods lose faith in getting Connor back. And she couldn't let Thomas and his family down.

Think.

Resisting the urge to look to her father or anyone else for help, Sara inhaled for the count of three. She couldn't beat Samson magically, at least not yet without further honing her powers, and she was at an utter loss for words, which left her with her oldest and most faithful weapon—swagger.

She dragged her gaze back to Samson and grinned, his resulting stiffened surprise further fueling her fake confidence. Casually slipping her four-fingered hand—the hand *he* mutilated—into her pocket and clutching the pyrite, she drawled, "Soo, why *did* you take Connor? Afraid to pay a visit without a bargaining chip?" She popped the 'p' on her last word and tilted her head.

For a moment, she swore he raised his brow in respect before his face darkened with a fiendish scowl. "Apologies, but I needed something to get you to *listen* to me." He straightened, pinning her with his pitch-black gaze. "A threat far more dreadful than me is coming. And it will take our combined powers to stop it. If either of us wants a chance at survival, we must work together. Consider this my favor to you, seeing as how all of this is *your* fault." He gave her a dismissive wave, smoke tendrils extending from his stained fingers.

Sara recoiled, her swagger threatening to crumble as his ridiculous statement struck her like an icy blade. Her fault. Thomas growled behind her, the sound shaking off her daze, but not before Samson's leer deepened, showing he knew he'd hit his mark.

Damn it. I'm going to tear off your fingers, one by one, and shove them up—

"Tut, tut," he warned. "You," he spat, pointing his pinkie finger at her, "unleashed a Pandora's box of magic when your blood mixed with your ancestor's stone."

Sara's vision clouded with rage. How dare he—

A series of knives screamed past her so quickly she didn't realize what they were until they thudded to the ground before a very sour-faced Samson.

He pinned his gaze on Thomas, who was now standing, coiled with tension, beside Sara. Samson snarled, his eyes flashing red. Ice crystals spread up his sleeves as dark smoke grew behind him, creating a set of dusky wings. "Do that again, and I'll throw them all back."

Cursing herself for dropping her containment shield around Thomas and the others, Sara stepped protectively in front of him. Thomas growled again. His rage and pride were about to get him and everyone else filleted. If they survived this, she would throttle him. She shot him a stern glance over her shoulder and noted the flames in his eyes and determination in the set of his jaw. Mother below, this bond may very well get them all killed. But Samson hadn't attacked yet, and Sara needed to know why.

She projected into Thomas's mind, *I know you said you would stand against him, but please don't.* Though the muscles in his arms rippled as he fisted his hands, to her relief, he yielded the slightest of bows to her. Sara sighed through her nose and turned her attention back to Samson.

The dark witch had the audacity to roll his eyes before charging ahead with his rebuke. "Once you activated your extraordinary powers, you threw an epic tantrum and *then* you killed Makwa. Did you not think there would be a price to pay? You've upset the balance, and now the Shadow Mother is coming for all of us."

"Shadow Mother?" Sara blurted, forgetting her tenuous swagger and confident High Witch façade.

Samson turned his incredulous glare back at the wall—at Gran and Alice. "Honestly. Do you teach her *anything* in that bubble of yours?" Smoke billowed, snaking around him while the bald Taker standing closest to Connor folded his massive arms and gave a throaty laugh. Brad merely stood with a smirk on his face, as if watching his favorite team destroy a bitter rival.

Samson pivoted, looking every bit the general his military jacket suggested, and faced Sara. "The Shadow Mother is evil incarnate and will turn our entire magical *and* normal world upside down. So we"—he gestured between himself and Sara, smoke extending to the Takers and the families at the forest wall—"will have a truce, and you will accept my generous offer to join forces."

Sara bristled. No one told her what to do. "You do not order me around. I choose my path." Seething, she gathered her energy, white flames snapping in her palms.

Samson grinned. "Not yet, little lamb. Right now, you need my help far more than I need yours. We have until Winter Solstice—the darkest day of the year—when she will attack. In the meantime, I suggest you perfect your magic. You'll need it," he warned. "And to ensure our alliance, I'll keep the boy."

"No!" screamed Abby from the forest wall. Bill Walker and Uncle Larry—two of the largest and strongest in Ware Woods—strained to hold her and Kane back from storming the field. Charlie pressed his fingers to his temples, eyes fixed on the Sullivans. Her father could easily mentally incapacitate them and was no doubt struggling with the fine line between respecting their free will and keeping them safe.

Beside Sara, Thomas unsheathed more knives, the blades singing with anticipation. Violet came from behind and did the same.

Sara whipped her focus back to Samson. Maybe she could pledge herself to him or offer a magical bargain in exchange for Connor. But before she could form a coherent scheme, Ian stepped forward.

"Take me instead," said Ian. "It's me you want, anyway." His golden-brown eyes held not the slightest trace of fear as he stared at Samson—the dark witch who had killed his maternal mother and nearly killed him with a splinter of ice to his heart. The daily medicine Ian depended on to keep his pulse normal was a constant reminder of his frailty.

Words completely escaped Sara as she gaped at him.

"No!" yelled Charlie, his voice frantic. "I'll go." He joined the Sullivans in struggling to cross the forest wall as Sara threw her power into holding them back and keeping them safely within the protective barrier.

Samson's abrupt laugh became a violent cough. He spat black phlegm and swiped his mouth with a wisp of smoke. "Everyone is lining up to help—it's disgustingly sweet. Tempting as it is to get my hands around your throat, Charlie, I'll take Ian in exchange for the spitfire boy." A serpentine swirl of smoke shot out, curling its ends around Connor and Ian. In less than a heartbeat, Connor was tucked into Thomas's side and Ian tottered beside Samson.

Bailey's distressed whine echoed across the field.

With a roar, Sara surged toward Ian and Samson. "Are you kidding me? I don't trust you with Ian. You attacked him as an *infant* and wanted to kill him—all of us—just a few weeks ago." The bastard kept Ian too close for her to launch her magic without risking her brother's life. She skidded to a halt before Samson and cringed at the power and acrid malodor radiating from him.

He looked down at her. Mother below, he was much taller and sicklier looking than she remembered. In a quiet, raspy voice, he said, "I thought I had no choice then. But when I got a taste of your power, everything changed." His black eyes flicked from her four-fingered hand to the forest wall and narrowed. "Speaking of change, I'll be taking Dorcas too."

"Wha—No!" Even though Dorcas appeared untouched by dark magic, Sara did not know the extent of the witch's powers or if she had Makwa's bloodstone. Besides, Mary had bound Dorcas to Ware Woods.

"Hush," whispered Samson. Sara gagged at his stench. "I'm doing you a favor. While I'd prefer the small blonde"—he stabbed his sharp chin at Lily behind her, and this time it was Ian who growled—"I'll settle for Dorcas." Samson chuckled wetly and dabbed his mouth with a satin scarf he pulled from his ice-encrusted sleeve. "I promise I'll keep her on a short leash, and I won't harm Ian so long as you join me against the Shadow Mother." His bright white grin was positively deadly as he held out his hand to Sara. "Do we have a deal?"

Shit.

Striking a deal with this devil was the last thing Sara ever wanted to do. She had no idea who or what the Shadow Mother truly was. Not that she had to. Samson's genuine concern had her downright terrified. And he needed her help, desperately enough that he was taking Ian *and* Dorcas as collateral to ensure her willingness. Perhaps he needed her more, and this was all a ruse and part of some sick plan of his. Tricky bastard was probably bluffing about everything. Regardless, until she could learn more about the Shadow Mother—if indeed there even *was* a Shadow Mother— Samson held all the cards.

Or did he?

She took a step back to escape his poisonous odor and get a better look at him without craning her neck. A touch of anxiety hunched his shoulders and slightly lifted his brow. When she swept her awareness over him, he grimaced but allowed her to read his intentions. He seemed to be telling the truth. And she was right— Samson needed her. Which meant she had some bargaining power.

Sara folded her arms, pretending to be a calm and clever High Witch. "Ian needs his medicine," she stated, and with a flick of her wrist whished a small red cooler from the back of Thomas's truck. Precisely eleven bottles of pine green medicine rested on ice inside the hard plastic cooler. She had packed a dozen—sisterly overkill for a weekend trip—and personally handed him the one he already drank. "Here's what *you* will do for me. You have one week to reverse the damage you inflicted on his heart and fully cure him." Her own heart pounded while she waited for his reaction. Because if the Shadow Mother did exist, she would need Samson just as much as he apparently needed her. And if everything went according to the crazy plan she'd just hatched, she could cure Ian and stop the Shadow Mother—whatever she was—and *then*, when their momentary truce was over and her magic was honed to perfection, she would go after Samson. For causing her mother's death, killing the Hills witches, and *eating* her finger, she would end his dark days.

Samson shrugged. "Fine." He whished the cooler into the arms of the bald Taker and pointedly looked at his still-outstretched hand.

Mother below, he didn't even fight her and now she had to go through with this pact. With what she hoped was a cocky grin and not a wince, she extended her four-fingered hand. "Fine," she agreed.

As their hands clasped, a slip of smoke cut between their palms. Sara bit back a gasp as their blood mingled and a spray of white and red sparks sealed their bargain.

"Excellent," jeered Samson, obviously pleased at getting his way. Little did he know. "Now, for the first test of our agreement, you need to invite Dorcas to exit Ware Woods. While she is bound by your ancestor's magic, your command will allow her to leave."

Sara felt the blood drain from her face as Dorcas practically danced at the wall, giddy with excitement. "Multiple short leashes," she muttered at Samson.

He eagerly licked at a touch of black stain on his lips. "Indeed."

Sara fought the urge to dry heave. After mentally apologizing to Mary and to all of Ware Woods and the world, she invited Dorcas to leave. A shot of electricity raced down the wall, simultaneously ripping through Sara and ending with a large crack as Dorcas and her cat appeared before them.

Like a teenager at an all-you-can-eat buffet, Dorcas painted her hungry gaze up and down Samson. With a toss of her long flaxen hair, she purred, "The cat comes too."

Samson glared at the enormous lynx-like animal. It sat back, extended a leg and began grooming itself, flexing the many needle-sharp claws in its double paw. A cruel smile spread across Samson's face as he shifted his glinting eyes to Dorcas. "Fine, but it does not sleep in our bedroom, and if I find one cat hair in the meals you prepare for me, I'll reach into its throat and turn it inside out."

Without another word, he turned on his heel and strode toward a black cloud gathering in the field, his dark magic pulling the Takers and Ian with him.

Dorcas tittered a schoolgirl laugh and skipped after them, the cat slinking beside her. "I'll keep a close watch on Ian," she sang, her charming voice drifting to Sara.

It should have been reassuring, yet Sara's panic flared. She locked eyes with Ian, silently promising she would find him and bring him back, when Samson called over his shoulder, "Don't bother looking for me. I'll return in one week to check in on your magical *refinements*. And we'll finally have a nice dinner together—finger foods optional." His raspy laugh echoed as the cloud swallowed them all, contracted upon itself, and disappeared with a frigid puff of air.

CHAPTER 10

A s soon as Sara lost sight of Ian, she spun around and rushed to Thomas and Connor. Crouching at the boy's eye level, she asked Connor to recall exactly what had happened to him.

He shifted nervously. "I was riding my bike home and—poof. All I saw was black smoke, and then I was in a big tent filled with toys and candy. I swear I didn't go quietly." He looked up at Thomas, who gave Connor an encouraging smile and waited for him to return his attention to Sara and continue. "I stuck a lot of them before they took my knives. But they didn't hurt me, and Mr. Motley—the bald one—kept me company the entire time. It was . . . kinda nice."

Nice? Sara frowned. Samson was definitely up to something.

She asked, "Did you see anything else? Anything to give us a clue as to where Samson is hiding?"

"No, there were no windows or doors . . . I'm sorry, High Witch," he added, shame in his big blue eyes.

Sara stood and ruffled his hair, coaxing a smile from him. "I'm just Sara. And you have nothing to be sorry for, except maybe ruining your dinner from all the candy."

With a glance toward the forest, she released her power holding back the families at the stone wall.

Thomas reached out and clasped the side of her face, turning her gaze to his. "Thank you," he said, voice hoarse. His other arm held Connor close to his side.

She nodded and turned away, swallowing against the lump in her throat. The magnitude of bargaining her own brother and a potentially psychotic witch into the hands of her greatest enemy threatened to debilitate her if she didn't keep moving. She flew to her father, Ted, and Gran—her remaining immediate family. Rather than landing in their arms, she hovered out of their reach, ashamed of having bartered Ian, and in a quiet voice asked, "Naomi?"

Gran's lip quivered, distress pinching her face. "In the cemetery," she said.

Instead of a chorus of peeper frogs and crickets, the late-summer evening was unnaturally quiet, as though the forest shared Sara's suffocating anguish. Even the mighty oak tree slumped in grief. One of its lower branches stretched to the ground, reaching for a small flowering tree. Not just any tree but a cherry tree, blooming out of season and surrounded by roses of all different colors.

Roses and cherries. The sound of Naomi's laughter echoed in Sara's heart. She knelt before the fresh grave and choked on a sob. An immediate burial suggested Naomi's body had been horribly desecrated. The thought sluiced down Sara's back like glacial ice.

This was her fault. She wanted to go back in time and never leave the forest—never leave any of them unprotected.

She dug her hands into the soft soil, aching to cry and ignite the world with her power, just as she had done for her mother. But it couldn't bring them back, and Ware Woods needed a High Witch right now—not another mourner.

Instead of shedding tears, Sara needed to know what dark magic had killed Naomi—and to hunt it down. If it hadn't been Samson, and she wasn't ruling that out yet, perhaps it had been another dark witch clawing at their forest or . . . the Shadow Mother. Neither possibility boded well for Ware Woods. She truly hoped it was Samson.

Sara pushed herself up and, as she brushed off her hands, felt the lump of pyrite in her pocket. A lot of good this did Naomi now. Sara clenched it in her four-fingered hand, letting it cut into her palm. While it may have protected her from the dragon, she had no use for it now. She would never leave the forest again, and neither would Naomi. Her pathetic gemstone gift—similar to her attempt at being High Witch—fell short. She would have to do better. So much better. To cure Ian and protect them all, she would have to become a High Witch of legend. Somehow, she would find a way to do this. Even if she had to befriend monsters or become one herself.

With a flick of her finger, she magically buried the pyrite beside the cherry tree and turned to face the path at the rear of the cemetery. Gran, Charlie, Ted, and the heads of the Atwell, Cahill, and Walker families approached her, nodding and talking in quiet conversation. The Sullivans were undoubtedly comforting Connor and patrolling the wall.

Sara took in her Council's grim expressions and stuttered, "I—I'm sorry. For leaving and causing—"

Her father pulled her into a crushing hug, silencing her apology. "This is not your fault." When she wiggled, he eased his grip, allowing her to pull back.

Uncle Larry Cahill, who was technically Sara's grandfather on her mother's side but preferred to be called Uncle, agreed with Charlie. His booming voice joined the agreement of Bill Walker, the twins' father and the forest's resident alpha shifter.

Sara shook her head. *Not true.* "What happened to Naomi?"

Lily's fair-haired father, Orsen Atwell, glanced at Naomi's grave and said, "We found her on the far shore. It appeared as if she had cut out her own heart with . . ."

"Pruning shears." Sara finished his reluctant account. Naomi grieved her slain people and had once confided in Sara that she felt guilt for being the last of the Hills sacred site witches—for fleeing and not turning back. Yet Naomi would never have willingly ended her own life.

Orsen nodded. "We found no trace of Samson's poison. No trace of anything."

"Maybe it was the Shadow Mother," said Sara, fear prickling her scalp. She shifted her gaze to Gran. "What do you know of her?"

In the dying light of the day, Gran's steel blue eyes glimmered, not with her usual sharpness but with silent remorse, as if sharing Sara's regret for not being prepared for this potential new threat. "Nothing yet. Alice and I know where to seek the information, though."

As Sara shot her an inquisitive look, Ted spoke up. "Charlie and I will continue our efforts to find the Global Council. Once we are able to contact them, they should assist us as well."

Sara bit her lip. The Global Council's elusiveness was troubling. What if they never responded?

"Until we know more about the Shadow Mother," said Charlie, "we have decided to continue our daily operations—including duties outside the forest. Ware Woods has faced threats before, and we know the risk. Dark magic does not control us." He gently squeezed Sara's arm in emphasis. "While I'm not at *all* pleased that Samson took Ian and Dorcas, I think he is telling the truth, which means we have until Winter Solstice to prepare for whatever may be coming. I doubt there will be any more attacks. Naomi's death wasn't random—it was intentional. She was the last of the Hills witches. It seems a force darker than Samson was hunting her."

He failed to mention that Ian was half Hills. His mother, Winona, had been Charlie's first love and had also been Naomi's sister. Sara swallowed. This connection could put Ian at great risk. Her father's knitted brow and glossy eyes confirmed he feared the same.

Ted cleared his throat and said, "Ian is brave, and the rest of us need to be brave as well. I agree with Charlie. Samson is difficult to read, but I don't think he will harm Ian. Besides," he added with a faint grin, "Dorcas will likely run him ragged."

Sara paled at the implied innuendo and the distinct possibility that Dorcas may very well put Samson in his place and assume his role as the greatest threat to Ware Woods.

Ted continued, "Ever since Makwa's death, Dorcas has been kind and helpful. I'm sure she will keep watch over Ian."

Sara frowned.

Seriously? Are you all delusional, or am I the only one completely freaked out by the impossible situation I have just created?

Charlie squeezed her arm again. "You're doing your best and—"

"And a lot of good that did us. Naomi is dead!" Sara shrugged off his touch and paced among the gravestones. "I saved Connor only to lose Ian and Dorcas in a *bloody* bargain with a devil—the very same devil responsible for my mother's death!" Sara panted with rage, white flames sparking around her.

Everyone took a step back except her father.

He grounded her with a parental look—love, reprimand, amusement, and concern all rolled into one. "Your best will always be good enough. *You* are good enough."

"Pfft!" Sara threw both hands into the air. Having a father who was a metaphysics professor was downright infuriating at times. She quieted her power before facing the heads of the families. They needed their High Witch.

Bill folded his arms, his amber gaze studying her. "Kane and I will obtain more weapons, and we'll double up on wall patrol. You're not alone in this, Sara." His voice was firm, yet not unkind.

Sara nodded. The gesture was appreciated even though they all knew physical weapons were useless against dark witches and she was the only one able to magically defend the forest from outside the wall.

She pulled back her shoulders and addressed her present Council, ticking off items with her five-fingered hand. "Tomorrow, we will have a glorious celebration for Naomi—filled with colorful flowers, food, and laughter. Exactly as she would want it. After her party, duties both inside and outside the forest will continue as normal. Gran and Alice will assist me in learning about the Shadow Mother. Bill and Kane will increase our physical defenses. And Charlie and Ted will continue to search for the Global Council."

Energy sizzled around her as she held their gaze and silently made her final pledge. *And I swear I'll never leave this forest again.*

The heads of the families nodded their acknowledgement and murmured tender goodbyes before disappearing into the woods. Only Gran and Charlie remained, worry etched in their faces.

Psychic families. Of course they would be concerned about the shit storm of emotions churning inside her. Before she could politely wave them off, her stomach turned—the heart-wrenching choice to bargain her brother coupled with the imagined horror of Naomi's last moments had taken a physical toll. She rushed past them and retched at the edge of the cemetery.

Within a dry heave, her father and grandmother appeared at her side. Gran handed her a thermos, and Sara gratefully sipped the cool water it contained. It was as if Gran had expected this. And in true Gran fashion, she bluntly asked, "Are you pregnant?"

"No," cried Sara and Charlie at the same time.

Gran quirked a brow.

When Sara remained quiet for fear of opening her mouth and vomiting again, her father gave her an apologetic look and explained, "Sara has a condition which makes pregnancy nearly impossible."

Sara took a long pull of water, wishing she could swallow her embarrassment with each gulp. Long before she'd arrived at Ware Woods, sharp internal pains had prompted an emergency doctor's visit and a deluge of tests. The doctor had scratched her head at the results and admitted she had never seen such an unusually shaped uterus. When she had told Sara the likelihood of her becoming pregnant and carrying a child was extremely slim, Sara had seen it as a blessing. At the time, she had misunderstood her magic and considered herself a monster, unworthy of love and certainly not interested in reproducing. But now . . .

She dismissed her father's worry with a wave of her hand, carefully keeping her face hidden behind a veil of hair that had escaped her braid.

Here was the troublesome piece of herself that even her healing magic couldn't fix. The monthly pains she endured for years had never subsided—altered slightly once she wore the bloodstone, but never gone.

This was the reason she felt unworthy of Thomas—her bonded mate who was endearingly protective of his siblings and likely wanted his own biological family someday. A future she recently began to yearn for but couldn't give them.

Father above, this was the worst day ever.

Gran shook her head, utterly puzzled and speechless—which was a first for Sara.

Charlie put his arm around Sara and guided her toward the stone cottage on the other side of the cemetery. "You should get some rest. Do you want us to stay with you tonight?"

"Thanks, Dad. I'll be fine by myself." Not really, not in the least bit, but she craved some quiet to process her situation.

As he pulled her in for another hug, his hand snagged on the bandage at her upper back. With a crinkly prod and a twinkle in his eye, he asked, "What's this?"

Sara stiffened. She had forgotten about the tattoo—the still circle to remember her mother and now to remember Naomi too.

Instead of lecturing her, Charlie asked, "May I see?"

With a nod, she swept her hair to the side and gingerly removed the dressing.

His soft smile of approval glowed in the early moonlight. "Nice line work. Mom would love it." He kissed her cheek before striding off after Gran. "Good night, firecracker."

CHAPTER 11

AFTER NIBBLING A few crackers and taking a long, hot shower, Sara flew from the cottage to her treehouse bedroom. The oak rustled its leaves in greeting and gently rocked her bed back and forth as she slipped under her favorite blue blanket. Though she was physically exhausted, her mind spun with thoughts of Naomi, Ian, dragons, Takers, and . . . Thomas. His musk-and-ash scent floated from the extra pillow beside her—and then filled the room.

In a burst that quaked the oak tree, Thomas rushed through the window opening, whished off his shirt and shoes, and slid into bed beside her. He pulled her to him, their arms wrapping around each other with a fierce hold as if they could crawl into each other's skin and become one. With her cheek on his warm chest and his lips on her brow, they simply held each other, eventually drifting to sleep.

The soft mossy slumber enveloping Sara ripped away with a violent shake. Her eyes flew open. Hazy moonlight filled her room as the entire bed convulsed again.

Thomas!

She turned to him. His body was rigid, his face wrenched with pain. Energy lashed tightly around him, pulsating a grievous blackened blue.

Sara grabbed his shoulders. The nightmare gripping him hissed against the touch of her white flames. *"Wake up,"* she mentally projected, but he remained stiff, eyes rapidly moving beneath closed lids.

A tear squeezed free and ran down the side of his face, wetting his already damp hair.

Her heart raced. When shouting his name and shaking his body still did not wake him, Sara braced herself and slipped into his mind.

Pain lanced through her soul as Thomas's nightmare of memories flashed around her. From experience, she knew to expect the remembrance of his two older brothers protecting him from an attack of Takers only to then die before him, the magic leaving their eyes as Thomas collapsed in a pool of their blood. And she recognized herself lying broken and unconscious before the bear witch, Makwa. But here were two new terrors of Brad leering at her and Connor bound beside Samson. Sara gasped from the ferocity of Thomas's anguish—his guilt and fury at not being able to protect his loved ones. Though she had spoken with him multiple times, trying to help him disarm his guilt and fears, the nightmares still plagued him.

She let her love for Thomas surge like an exploding star, pushing back the pain, as she projected, *"Thomas! I'm here with you. Wake up!"*

They both jolted, suddenly back in bed and staring into each other's eyes.

Thomas, his expression tormented, heaved a sigh. "I'm sorry for—"

"Don't apologize for needing me. Just tell me how I can help you." Her voice cracked from sharing his pain.

The treehouse gently swished its leaves as his gaze softened. After a few mingled breaths, he pulled her to him, burying his face between her shoulder and neck. "Hold me."

"I am."

"Hold me closer."

Sara twined their legs together, wound a hand into his hair, and slipped back into his mind, letting her love and magic fill him, body and soul.

Thomas relaxed into her, his warmth enveloping her in response, their hearts slowing and beating together. Light-blue energy blanketed them, its quiet hum drawing them back to sleep.

Dawn had already broken by the time Sara woke, still tangled with Thomas. He lay peacefully beside her, his eyes closed, face calm. Zero indication of his nightmare. When she stirred, hoping to sneak out and fly a quick survey of the forest wall, his arms tightened around her.

"Don't even think about leaving," he said, his husky morning voice rumbling through her.

Sara melted into his embrace, tucking her head into the crook of his neck and placing an answering kiss on his collarbone—the collarbone she'd once healed.

His pulse quickened, and he shifted his hips away from her.

"Do you want to talk about it?" asked Sara, referring to the nightmare or Naomi or any of their recent trauma.

"Yes." He hesitated. "I have a few things to say to you. And I want you to listen without comment."

Sara stilled. This was his lawyer-in-training tone, as if he were about to plead his case. *Oh, this is serious.* She nodded against his chest.

Thomas inhaled, trembling slightly beneath her cheek. "There is a very dangerous side of me that I sometimes cannot control, especially when people I care about are threatened. Our bond has intensified my need to fight—to protect you. But when this *need* takes over—like at the beach—I can't control it. At least not yet. I'm trying. And it took *everything* in me to not foolishly launch myself at Samson yesterday. It drives me mad that I don't have magic outside the forest and can't properly protect my family and you. I'm sure this triggered the nightmare."

Sara raised her head and met his brilliant blue eyes. Her heart flipped. "You—"

He placed a finger to her lips. "I know. You don't need protecting, and I love this about you, but since we're bonded, I know you feel the same way about me." Sara nodded, and he continued. "I'm asking you to accept that I will *always* be driven to protect you." When she nodded again, he held her face and ran his thumbs over her cheekbones.

"Thank you for saving Connor. What you did wasn't easy, and I'm proud of you for holding your ground with Samson and for mostly remaining calm." A slight smile tugged at his mouth and then was gone. "Naomi's death is not your fault. And she wouldn't want you thinking you were responsible in any way." He held her gaze until she dipped her chin again, her eyes watering.

"And lastly, I promised you—and I never break my word—Ian and I are not going to die. I also promised to never let go of you when you graciously let me catch you weeks ago."

Thomas pulled her into a tight embrace and held her until their rapid heartbeats finally slowed.

All day, he remained by her side and was a comforting, supportive presence as they celebrated Naomi. Despite the music and flowers and pleasant reminiscing, Sara's heart remained heavy. And from the sad eyes and dark-blue aura of the families, she knew the entire forest grieved as one.

As she exchanged words of encouragement with others over finding Naomi's assailant and bringing Ian and Dorcas home, Sara leaned into Thomas. He never faltered, holding her hand throughout every conversation and meal, and holding her to him all night again too.

By the following morning, Sara was done ruing. The families didn't need her saddled with regret or crippled with grief like she had been after her mother's death. What they needed was a High Witch capable of exacting justice for Naomi, of besting Samson, the Shadow Mother, and whatever else lurked outside their wall. She threw off the covers, eager to meet with Gran and Alice and learn whatever they had up their magical sleeves.

Complementing her hopeful mood and welcoming her to a new day were clusters of cheerful sunflowers and goldenrod atop the bedroom windowsills. With a soft smile, she swept a hand over the still-warm space where Thomas had lain beside her. He had mentioned needing to meet his father early at their office and that he would be busy all week with a trial involving pollutants leaching into the Ware Woods lake.

The reality that they had to defend Ware Woods against normal threats such as pollution and development in addition to dark magic had surprised Sara. So much remained for her to learn about Ware Woods and the magical world, including how the elusive Global Council could help them.

If the Council was as important as she hoped—and deigned to respond to her father and uncle—perhaps she wouldn't need Samson to deal with the Shadow Mother. Teaming up with the Council's powerful Magi was more desirable over having any contact with Samson and his dark magic.

Sara shuddered at recalling his acrid stench and hacking cough. All she wanted from Samson was for him to heal Ian—either by reversing his own damage to Ian's heart or by dying and taking his dark magic with him. Preferably the latter.

Careful not to disturb the sunshine-yellow flowers, Sara flew between the treehouse and cottage, preparing for a long day. While braiding back her silvery-gray hair, she mentally reached out to Gran. *"Where are you?"*

Gran's chuckle echoed in her mind. *"Good morning to you, too. How are you holding up?"*

"I'm ready to find Naomi's killer and bring Ian and Dorcas home, if that's what you're fishing for."

"Atta girl. Pure Lochton fire." She paused. *"Alice and I are at the blue house. And yes, we have breakfast."*

Sara sighed. Thank the Mother they were ready to go . . . and with food. Her stomach grumbled in response as she flew directly to the old Lochton home—the one whose second-story dormers hung like sad eyes. To her knowledge, the home was vacant.

Sara landed in the backyard, the sweet scent of muffins greeting her. When she approached the open rear door, an underlying odor of dust and neglect smacked her nostrils, triggering a sneeze.

"Excuse the mess," trilled Alice, her lilted voice floating from inside the home.

Sara crossed the threshold and froze. The small living room had been turned upside down, sofa cushions strewn about, open books stacked upon themselves in piling heaps. It appeared as if someone had been searching for something.

Sara swiped a finger through the thick skin of dust coating an end table—its single drawer ripped out and discarded on the oval area rug—and frowned. Whatever had happened had occurred long ago.

She picked her way through the jumbled mess and toward the light and warmth spilling from an adjacent room. A teakettle whistled as she stepped through a wide archway and beheld a kitchen and dining space twice the size of the disheveled living room.

To her right sat a long farmhouse table; behind it stood a wall of white-framed windows with views of the front yard and old gray road. In front of Sara stretched a kitchen counter of butcher-block wood, striated and scored with years of cooking, baking, and—she figured—spell casting. Near the center of the overhanging counter,

Alice perched on a barstool, her long white hair flowing down her back, her mother's bloodstone nestled in the hollow of her throat. On the opposite side of the kitchen counter, Gran stood facing a brick stove and fireplace along the rear wall. The kettle ceased its scream and, as if invisible hands held it, poured its steaming contents into a pot, which then whished to the wood counter and plunked beside three cups.

Gran turned around from the stove with a plate of muffins and set them beside the tea, while Sara pulled out a stool alongside Alice.

"Thanks," mumbled Sara, snagging a muffin and swiveling her head to take in the floor-to-ceiling corner fireplace and overhead pot rack adorned with bundles of dried herbs and flowers so ancient she feared they would disintegrate into her breakfast. She leaned back, muffin held close to her chest, and raised both brows at her grandmother and great-aunt.

"I've let this house sit for too long," said Gran. She waved a hand, and a myriad of jars and containers on the shelves behind her straightened themselves, taking turns lifting into the air as a towel wiped the kitchen's many surfaces. "When your parents left before you were born, I had a stitch of a fit."

Alice snorted and lightheartedly shook her head at her sister.

Gran shot Sara a grin. "When Ted and I moved into the brown house to raise Ian, I turned my back on this mess. And when Ian grew older and didn't need my help, I moved into the Main House. But it's time I returned to Old Blue." The magical cleaning continued as she poured three cups of tea. "Besides, the Main House is getting crowded."

Sara paused her chewing, mouth full of muffin.

After Makwa's fires burned down the original Main House, Gran had instructed the Cahills to build a much larger version, one that currently had multiple empty rooms. Before she could prod Gran about possible premonitions, a book thumped onto the counter as if dropped from the ancient herbs hanging overhead.

CHAPTER 12

SARA YELPED, NEARLY choking on her breakfast, and whished her trembling teacup with its sloshing contents away from the unexpected book.

With a demure sip of her tea, Alice nudged Sara and said, "This is the family grimoire—a collection of spells and history and whatever else you need. Place your hand on top."

The bloodstone around Sara's neck pulsed with energy, flushing her body with tingling warmth. She swallowed the last of her muffin, staring at the slim, unassuming book for a curious moment before shifting her gaze to Gran and Alice. "Seriously? We have a *real* spell book, and you haven't thought to show it to me until now?"

Alice took another sip before turning her amber eyes to Sara. "The Book disappeared when our mother died—your great-grandmother Ann. At the same time Makwa bound our powers." When she said Ann's name, she lightly touched her bloodstone. In her other hand, Alice used her teacup to gesture at Gran and herself. "Rosetta and I hadn't seen the Book until the day you left for the beach, and it simply appeared here, in this kitchen, while we were checking on the house. When we opened it, the pages asked for you."

Sara widened her eyes at the innocuous book. "It *asked* for me?"

"The Book does as it pleases." Gran shrugged, spooning sugar into her tea. "It only opens for descendants of Mary and selectively reveals spells and information when needed. I recall it being quite helpful at times and obstinate at others."

The Book shuddered, seemingly offended and jumped closer to Sara.

"Go ahead," said Gran. "It'll unlock when you touch it."

Sara wiped her hand on her T-shirt and placed her palm atop the cover. In a flash of white light, the Book transformed into a thick, leather-bound journal with worn parchment pages sticking out from its edges. "This is unreal." Sara traced her fingertips across the scarred cover. When she attempted to open it, the Book expanded as if taking in air, then flipped itself open with an impressive rustling until finally resting at a page near its beginning.

The page was blank save for one word in curly script near its center:

Hello.

Sara's jaw fell slack. "Uh, hello." She gave a slight wave.

The Book ruffled its pages and slid closer. Power radiated from it with a soft hum, tickling Sara's cheeks.

Unable to resist, she placed both hands on the yellowed paper. Energy surged through her, crackling along her skin before dissipating into whorls of smoke. "Mother below," she whispered. When she pulled back her hands, the Book slowly turned its pages, revealing a multitude of richly illustrated spells and helpful instructions before stopping at a double-page spread illuminated with golden ink.

Sara raptly took in the ornate drawing of the Mother sitting in a resplendent garden of flowering trees and plants of all shapes and colors. Her elegant robes were a mosaic of sunny yellow, grassy green, ocean blue, and garnet red. Upon her head of cascading locks rested a crown of woven branches with gemstones so carefully tucked into the design they appeared to have grown into place.

At her feet rested a menagerie of animals from bear and deer to falcon and viper.

A sense of peace and hope washed over Sara. If the Book knew the Mother, it had to know the information she sought. Sara tore her gaze from the grimoire and looked at Gran and Alice. "Did you ask it about the Shadow Mother?"

The Book snapped shut with such force, the overhead arrangements trembled and released a puff of bygone blooms.

"Yep," said Alice with a cough, waving dust away from her tea. "And we received the same answer."

Sara squinted at the Book. Like Hells she was going to accept that response. Clearly, the grimoire knew something. Perhaps it just needed the proper persuasion.

She placed her hand on the cover again, letting her energy—the forest's energy—connect with the Book. In a silent plea, she projected, *"Please, tell me what I need to know about the Shadow Mother."*

The Book shivered and opened to a page coated in black ash. White curly script appeared and disappeared one word at a time as Sara read the message in her head:

Extreme Caution.

The Shadow Mother is wholly fear and deceit.

Her presence symbolizes a dangerous imbalance.

Do not stand before her alone.

The powerful magic inside Sara shrank upon itself. Had she upset the balance like Samson said? She chewed her lip. If she had, and this was her fault, why would Samson want to help her? Why risk his magic—his life—to ally with her in facing the Shadow Mother when he could hide in whatever dark cave he called home? Her chest constricted. A cave her brother now called home, thanks to her.

She inhaled deeply, filling her lungs while desperately trying to settle her terrified mind.

Okay, one thing at a time. The Shadow Mother seemed to be another dark witch. Perhaps the female equivalent to Samson. Regardless of exactly *what* she was, Sara intended to get rid of her—either with help from Samson or the Global Council—and then dispose of Samson. It was a somewhat duplicitous and tenuous plan, and the best she could come up with.

Though having a plan, no matter how crazy, should have calmed her, the idea of multiple dark witches coming after Ware Woods made her wish she hadn't eaten her muffin so quickly.

Her gaze flicked back at the ashy page. Knuckles white from her death grip on the counter, she asked, "Who killed Naomi?"

The Book skipped to a page undulating with smoky shadows, eerily similar to Samson's. Gran and Alice joined Sara in leaning over the grimoire, waiting for the shadows to unveil a name or likeness. But they remained in constant motion with no grand revelation.

"Could be Samson or the Shadow Mother," said Gran, casually refilling her teacup.

Hopefully, the Book was indicating one of them and not another dark witch. Sara sighed. *Did I just make the world's biggest mistake in bargaining with Samson to take on the Shadow Mother?*

The Book riffled to a page with one word:

Trust.

Myself or Samson?

No response from the Book. "Who *is* Samson?" Sara asked out loud, hoping it would tell her his true name. The page flipped and revealed the same message:

Trust.

"Pfft! He has seven days to cure Ian and even then, I won't trust him." She shook her head at the grimoire.

Gran and Alice sniggered.

"Told you the Book can be obstinate," said Gran.

Sara sat back and folded her arms. "It's a persnickety Magic 8 Ball." She swore the Book huffed indignantly.

"No," said Alice with a gentle firmness in her tone. "The Book is a resource and a tool, not a fortune-telling crutch. It provides the information you need to know, when you need to know it. Only you can make the choices that control your destiny."

"Point taken," Sara mentally projected to Alice, earning a nod and warm smile from her great-aunt. "Fine. I'll just take it back to the treehouse so I can study all the information it chooses to reveal." She shut the grimoire and tried lifting it from the table, but it refused to budge.

Gran chuckled again. "Apparently, the Book stays here. You'll just have to visit us two little old ladies for breakfast every day to glean your knowledge." A twinkle shimmered in her steel blue eyes. She pushed the plate of muffins toward Sara. "Grab another for yourself and one for the shifter waiting patiently at the back door. You both share a need to play with your power and grow stronger. Winter Solstice isn't for four months, so you have plenty of time to have fun while you work.

"Now," said Gran, straightening her back and whishing her cup to the sink, "you'll excuse us as we kindly evict the bats in the attic." And with that, Gran and Alice swooped from the room and up a narrow staircase.

Sara patted the Book, her fingertips tingling with energy from the touch, and said, "See you tomorrow." With a bounce in her step, she grabbed two sugar-crusted muffins and headed out the back door to where a red fox sat beside a gooseberry bush. "Hey, Moira," she called, tossing a muffin in the air. "Catch."

Moira instantly shifted into her human form, unbound hair

flaming around her shoulders, and snagged the pastry. "How'd you know I was here?"

"Gran told me. Plus, your whole family has a particular . . . scent," said Sara, strolling with Moira for the Lochton soul tree—a towering white pine atop the hill before them. The pine's blight damage caused by Samson and Makwa had completely healed save for one of the lower limbs, which had blackened and disappeared into ash.

Moira gave herself a curious sniff, shrugged as if in agreement, and bit into her muffin.

"I didn't mean that in a bad way. It's warm, wild, and spicy." Sara's cheeks burned. Eager to change the subject, she asked, "Why didn't you just come into the house?"

The shifter crowed a laugh, spraying her mouthful of muffin. "Too much magic in there. Makes my fur stand on end. Besides, I have nothing but time. Everyone else is busy. Caleb is making furniture, Thomas and Violet are at the office, Lily is taking care of the lake, and Matt's at the clinic." She scrunched her perfectly freckled nose. "My folks still want me to be a vet too, but I'd rather roam the regional forests as a ranger than be cooped up in a building all day."

Sara stuffed her face, hoping Moira didn't see her budding smile. Although they'd had pleasant conversations during the beach trip, Moira hadn't shared any personal information. Clearly, today she had a pent-up need to express herself. With a quick swallow, Sara imitated her father's stealthily inquisitive manner and quirked an eyebrow. "Oh?"

Moira drew in a breath and, as if releasing the lake's dam, spewed, "Yeah. But I can't be a ranger because I'd run into other shifters who would either shun me or kill me."

"Why would they do that?" Sara sucked on a tooth. Maybe this was typical predatory behavior among shifters.

"I don't know. For whatever reason, the regional packs don't care for my family. My older siblings had to travel overseas to find mates in accepting packs and pledge to different sacred sites." She hopped over a tree stump with quiet grace as Sara slowed her ascent.

Well, this was unexpected. "You have older siblings?"

"A dozen," said Moira, the mid-morning sun illuminating flecks of gold in her amber eyes. "Matt and I are the babies. So our folks don't want us going overseas too." In a subdued voice, she added, "Which will make it very difficult for us to find mates."

Sara frowned. Why would other shifters attack the Walkers? Perhaps the Book would tell her tomorrow.

Moira blew back a tuft of red hair and slid an inquisitive look at Sara. "What did you want to do? Before you knew about all of this," she said, waving her hands at the surrounding forest.

Sara's frown deepened. What *had* she wanted to do? Before Ware Woods, she had only wanted to hide from the world and the powers she didn't understand. She had eked out a quiet existence, working for her mother's floral business and occasionally aiding her father's metaphysics research. She gave a one-shoulder shrug. "I wanted to help my family."

A grin lit up Moira's face as she rubbed shoulders with Sara. "Same as you're doing now. Must feel good, knowing what you're meant to do."

Sara stifled a bitter laugh and forced a smile at Moira. *I have no idea what I'm doing.*

"Come on." Moira tugged her into the static hum of the Lochton pine. "Let's practice at my place. I know you're itching to improve your powers and find a way to beat Samson. Your eyes were practically *glowing* with hatred when you bargained with him." Her husky laugh disappeared into the whooshing beat of the pine as they looped to the maple soul tree and popped out at the base of its trunk, the Council stump stage to their left.

"Race you," said Moira, phasing back into a fox and streaking for the fields and pond behind the Walkers' sprawling, double-story, green-paneled house.

For the remainder of the day, they practiced their magic—Moira phasing into a variety of animals and Sara summoning kinetic energy. Sometimes they jeered and sparred with one another or used wooden targets, other times they worked solo in companionable silence. Though they took breaks to grab meals at the Main House, they were both sweaty, muddy, and thoroughly exhausted by dusk.

Before turning in for the evening, Sara snuck into Thomas's studio with an assortment of foods from the Cahills' farm. Thomas had been practically living at his office in the adjacent town, coming home late and going in before dawn. Bringing him food seemed the best way—the only way—to help him, since she knew nothing of legal matters and his place was already spotless. Besides, Sara missed him, and simply being in his studio eased a certain tightness in her chest.

Just a week, she reminded herself as she prepped the meats, veggies, and fruits and placed them in his fridge along with a reheatable container of Helen Cahill's freshly made pot pie.

The following morning, purple asters adorned her windowsills.

Sara smiled at Thomas's flowery thank-you and tucked a few blossoms into her braided hair, readying for her own busy day. After scooping drowsy squirrels from her shoes, she rushed to the blue house, threw down breakfast with Gran and Alice, then glued herself to a barstool.

The family grimoire landed with a thump onto the counter before her.

"We'll leave you to your research," said Gran as she and Alice traipsed down the basement stairs located on the far side of the dining room. She muttered something about inspecting every fermented jar of magical and vegetable origin before calling out, "Tell the boys they don't need an excuse to pop in."

What boys?

The back door creaked open, and soon Charlie and Ted entered the kitchen, coffee mugs in hand. Her father and uncle looked nearly identical with sandy blond hair, blue eyes, and youthful yet charismatic appearances, the exception being that Ted was slightly shorter than her father and had a goatee he tugged when deep in thought.

"Morning kiddo, or should I say High Witch?" greeted Ted, standing on the opposite side of the wooden counter and whishing a bowl of blueberries to him.

Sara cocked her head. "Are you checking up on me?"

"We ran out of coffee," said Charlie, lifting his nearly full mug. He topped it off from the pot beside the stove while adding, "And yes, we wanted to know how you're doing."

Polite of him to ask when he could easily read her mind. She sighed, knowing he wouldn't accept "fine" as an answer. "I'm furious over Naomi's death, I miss Ian—not so much Dorcas—and I'm incredibly frustrated at not knowing what to do. I'm hoping this Book has the answers."

"Well," said Charlie, completely unfazed by her admission, "we grieve and miss them too. Even Dorcas, who has been rather pleasant lately." He stole a blueberry from Ted, ignoring his brother's side-eye, and peered down at the Book. "But we've only recently become aware of the grimoire, and it wouldn't open for us. Fascinating, isn't it? And selective. Maybe with the three of us present, it will reveal what we need to know."

The Book clattered on the counter before them and threw itself open. Sara jerked back, the leather cover narrowly missing her nose. Pages fluttered before coming to a stop at a section on sacred sites and the Global Council.

Sara gasped as all three of them leaned in.

CHAPTER 13

To Sara's surprise, the grimoire displayed page after page of information about sacred sites all over the world, and the vampires, shape shifters, and witches who protected them. According to the Book's gilded script, the three magical factions seldom interacted with one another, the only exception being Global Council meetings. Each sacred site had one Magus—an Elder Vampire, Alpha Shifter, or a High Witch—who had power outside of their site and had a seat at the Global Council.

Charlie ran a finger down a page, scanning the information. The Book vibrated like a content cat. "We already know this. Outsiders who have come to Ware Woods, like Caleb's father, have told us the Global Council monitors threats to all sacred sites, with like factions occasionally assisting one another, but we don't know where or when they meet."

"Can't Caleb's father ask his original site for this information?"

"He's tried, but once an outsider comes to Ware Woods, their birth site severs communication with them."

Sara puckered her face at this.

"We know. It's odd to say the least," said Ted.

"Then how are we supposed to find them?"

The Book fluttered to a page with a single tree drawn in the

90

center. She bent forward, hand extending toward the image. "I don't understand. Do they meet in a tree?"

With an agitated huff, the Book turned the page, showed the same tree, then slammed shut, nipping Sara's fingertips. Her resounding yelp was answered by a howl outside the rear door. Sara jumped out of her seat, eyes wide, barstool screeching behind her.

"Moira's been waiting for you," said Ted, popping another blueberry into his mouth and whishing the bowl away from Charlie.

"Go on," said Charlie, waving Sara away and kinetically opening the rear door. "We'll let you know if we find anything on the internet about a special tree." He stole the last of the berries when Ted turned to refill his coffee mug.

Moira's voice drifted into the house, "Is everything okay? Please don't make me come in there."

With a goodbye kiss to her father's cheek, Sara sped from the kitchen, grabbed Moira, and took off for the Lochton pine. Before she and Moira looped to the Walkers', Ted projected to her, *"He ate all the blueberries!"*

Sara's resulting snicker vanished when they walked onto the fields and Moira, with a sly curl to one side of her painted mouth, announced she had a surprise to show her. All day, Sara warily studied her while they practiced their magic—Moira shifting into a falcon and dodging Sara's bolts of energy, and Sara summoning wind to push back Moira's grizzly bear assault.

It wasn't until late in the day when Sara lunged at Moira in fox form that she instantly phased into a porcupine. Quills plunged into Sara's chest and covered her arms like fur before she skidded to a halt, stunned by witnessing Moira's new animal form—and by the pain. Lots of pain.

Moira returned to her human self, shock on her face. "I didn't think you'd get so close, especially after I warned you. Don't just stand there. Heal yourself!"

In a flash of warm light, the quills disintegrated, and Sara stumbled back, unscathed.

Moira rushed to her side. "Are you okay?"

"Perfectly fine. But I dare say we just took the 'good friends stick together' saying to a whole new level."

A smile as bright as the sun lit up Moira's face. "Good friends, huh?"

Moira's reaction hugged Sara like a cozy sweater, staying with her throughout the evening and into the night as she lay in bed overthinking her predicament. Maybe this could work—learning from the Book, strengthening her magic, and suffering Samson all to heal Ian, avenge Naomi, and keep Ware Woods safe. Father above, she hoped so.

The treehouse swayed, the scent of wet oak and leaves filling the bedroom while a nighttime rainstorm softly pattered the forest, lulling her asleep.

Sara held the door open as an opossum with a passel of babies on her back ambled into the blue house, shook the dew from her pink feet, and promptly curled up on the couch. The day before, a skunk had been lounging on the floor of the living room until Alice had sent him off to the gooseberry bushes with a biscuit breakfast.

With a faint grin and shake of her head, Sara entered the empty kitchen, whishing herself a cup of tea, and pulled up a seat. The Book landed before her, excitedly fluttering its pages in what Sara hoped was an amiable mood.

"Well, good morning to you too. Are you going to show me where Ian is?" Though Samson had agreed he would heal and not harm Ian, torturous thoughts filled her mind. Samson had one day left to make good on his bargain. The bastard had strung her out all week, resulting in a tremor in her hands as if she had drunk too many espressos.

The grimoire shook itself, pages remaining in constant agitation.

Sara sighed. "Okay then, show me something that will help me protect the forest."

The Book fell open to an image of a stunning dragon, its horns and scales dusted with gold, its long body weaving across a two-page spread.

With a surprised squeak, she whished her teacup aside and pulled the Book closer.

Unlike the blood-red dragon she had witnessed at the beach, this depiction was such a dark green it almost appeared black. While Sara knew dragons regulated the balance between light and dark magic and corrected situations if normals observed magic, the Book explained that the Father above pulled dragons from the Aether where he resides and gifted them to the Mother below as a means to monitor the magical factions.

Sara gripped the tattered edges of the Book. More ink bled up through the paper and formed a second dragon image, this one grotesquely bloated and with cold, solid black eyes.

Flat-eyed dragons, the grimoire's curly text explained, were devoid of conscience and blindly followed the direction of the Mother or of higher-ranking elysian-eyed dragons.

Sara impatiently tapped her finger on the magnificent dark-green dragon with slit-pupiled, piercing eyes. The Book further explicated:

Elysian-eyed dragons are discerning personal servants to the Mother. They are rare and oversee all flat-eyed dragons and the entire magical balance.

Two types of dragons. Sara slumped back in her chair. Perhaps it hadn't been the pyrite in her pocket that had stayed the elysian-eyed red dragon. Perhaps it had discerned to spare her. But why?

Deep in thought, she absently flipped the page as Gran bustled into the kitchen, her hair tied in a kerchief and her hand clutching a wand that smelled of cedar.

Gran whished a container of salt overhead and, with her other hand, grabbed a dustpan of brick powder by the hearth. "Alice and I are negotiating attic space with the spiders. Tough lot they are." She whirled around with a wink at Sara. Eyeing the open grimoire, she paused. "Doing research on your bond with Thomas, I see. I'm sure it won't be easy for either of you when he leaves for fall semester."

"What?" Sara stammered, confusion threatening to topple her from the stool. Lightheaded, she clung to the countertop and glanced at the open book. What had been a blank page was now inscribed with the following large curling font:

Bonded Mates

And in slightly smaller font:

Ordained by the Mother and Father.

Fateful partners with intense magical connections.

"Oh," exclaimed Gran. The salt crashed to the counter. "I thought—"

She cut off as the back door threw open and Charlie sprinted into the kitchen, shaking a cell phone at them.

"Ian is on the phone!"

Sara didn't fully register what her father was yelling; all she heard were echoes of Thomas leaving the forest.

Sliding from the stool, she placed a hand over the bloodstone at her chest. The stone and her heart beat much too rapidly. "Thomas is *leaving* for school?"

No.

He wouldn't think of leaving, especially without telling her. Would he?

She turned from Gran to her father, hoping it was a practical joke for any of them—much less Thomas—to be away from Ware Woods for months while dark magic threatened them.

Charlie froze, hand still in the air with the cell phone. He inclined his head and said, "Yeah, we agreed to continue normal duties inside and outside the wall. He and Matthew have to attend a semester in person. But"—he shook his head, waving the cell—"Ian is on the phone! He wants to talk with you." Charlie thrust the phone at her.

Sara stared, internally skipping between shock, disbelief, and a touch of white-hot anger that Thomas hadn't told her. When Ian's voice shouted her name from the phone's speaker, her jumbled emotions skidded to tingling relief.

"Ian! Where are you? Did Samson cure you? I swear to the Mother, if he touched one hair on your head, I'm going to incinerate him."

Ian's laughter floated from the speaker. "I'm fine. More than fine, actually. Except he can't cure me, and I need more of my medicine. Ted is packing another week's worth until Helen can make more."

"That's *not* the bargain I made," Sara seethed. "If he can't cure you, I want you home. Now." The idea of Ian, Thomas, and Matthew all away from Ware Woods crashed into her. She was now clutching the bloodstone, its throbbing beat both a comfort and a reminder to calm down and behave like a High Witch. With that thought, she released the bloodstone and grabbed the phone, checking the locator app. It only showed a death spiral.

"Where are you? I'll come get you myself." She had no idea how she would do such a thing, but she would gladly turn the world inside out to bring him home.

"I can't tell you. Just trust me that I'm okay. I'm needed here and . . . I kinda like it."

Sara jerked back. Distinct joy colored his voice. What the Hells had Samson done to him?

He laughed again, as if he were reading her mind through the connection. "Samson isn't the monster you think he is."

Sara groaned in disbelief, Gran and Charlie joining her.

Wonderful. Her own brother was allying with her greatest enemy. Did he not remember all the horrible things this witch had done?

Sara drew a steadying breath and, in a funeral-quiet voice, said, "Ian, he killed our mothers." She locked eyes with their father, seeing the grief that never fully left his expression.

A heavy pause from the other side of the phone ended with Ian clearing his throat. "He didn't want to, Sara. You can trust him."

"What are you talking about? If we can trust him, why isn't he here?" Sara paced around the farmhouse table. "Why isn't he bringing you back?"

The phone crackled, struggling to maintain service. "He has good and bad days. He'll come when he can to tell you more. I want you all to know I'm choosing to stay here for now, where I can best help Samson and Ware Woods. In the meantime, you have until Solstice to hone your powers."

Sara ground her teeth, annoyed to be at Samson's beck and call and genuinely concerned that Ian had been brainwashed. "You promise us"—she swept her gaze around the group, which now included Alice and Ted, who had silently joined them—"you are okay." Her voice may have wobbled.

"Yes," Ian responded without the slightest hesitation. "Mr. Motley will come to the wall for the medicine. I'll call Dad and Ted each week to check in and arrange for a fresh batch from Helen."

"Call us *every* day!" interjected Charlie. "I just got you back in my life, and I refuse to let another dark witch come between us." His voice hitched on his last word, and Sara's heart clenched.

Ted shifted Ian's medicine to his other hand and drew an arm around Charlie's shoulders. With a reassuring look, Ted mentally projected, *I know Ian. He's speaking the truth and acting on his own free will.* " Charlie's rigid posture visibly relaxed.

"Dad? I—" Ian's voice grew faint and murmurous, a higher tone joining his in hushed conversation. The murmurs stopped, and someone sucked in a breath. "Nothing will come between us again," said Ian with a sudden fierceness. "Reception is spotty. I'll call and text as much as I can. I love—"

The connection failed. Beyond the dining room's wall of windows, a cloud of black smoke erupted outside the forest wall. In a blink, the smoke cleared, and a familiar hulking, bald Taker stood waiting.

With a clatter of barstools, Sara and her family rushed out the front door and to the wall.

Mr. Motley, his stance tense, fixed his wary gaze on Sara. One gigantic, stained hand grasped the black stone pendant hanging from his thick neck. In his other hand, he held out Ian's plastic cooler, which Ted gingerly took, careful not to touch the Taker's poisoned hands, and replaced with a new cooler. Mr. Motley never took his red-rimmed stare off Sara.

She shot him a devilish grin and delighted in his flinch. But before she could threaten him with a slow, painful death if he even looked at Ian cross-eyed, he cleared his throat and darted his gaze among them.

In a voice like crushed granite, he said, "Ian is a fine boy. He is safe with us." Then he squeezed his pendant, releasing coils of inky smoke, which swirled and swallowed him whole, doubtlessly transporting him back to whatever hell he came from.

Charlie and Ted released heavy sighs while Gran and Alice, popping star mints into their mouths, calmly turned and strolled back to the blue house.

"I have a witchy feeling that Ian is more than safe," projected Gran, an obvious chuckle in her tone.

"Pfft! He better be safe," fumed Sara at the dissipating smoke as Trouble—Moira's raven—landed on her shoulder. The bird bobbed its head while Sara poked at the phone she still clutched. The locator app refused to function, and though she wanted to call Thomas at work and rip into him, she tossed the phone to Ted and stalked off for the Walker homestead.

When Sara marched onto the fields, white flames sizzling around her, Moira took one glance at her before phasing into a hawk and wisely flying off with Trouble.

Alone, Sara let her temper and magic flare, tearing apart and restoring the Walker fields over and over again.

Trusting Samson went against her heart's desire to destroy him. And Ian choosing to stay with him was salty icing on a bloody disastrous cake. But what really irked Sara was *knowing* Thomas withheld information from her.

Before the sun went down, she flew to his studio, grabbed a shower, and waited not-so-calmly for him to arrive.

CHAPTER 14

S ARA SAT, LEGS folded under her, in an upholstered chair beside Thomas's bookshelf of perfectly aligned poetry and law texts. His studio above the Sullivans' massive four-car garage was part spotless gym with floor-to-ceiling mirrors and part private quarters with kitchen, living space, and a grand master suite.

Through a window facing the forest wall and old road, she spied his black truck pull into the drive, dusk darkening the sky. Her heartbeat quickened, as it always did when he was near. Yet she waited in silence, listening to him park and ascend the interior staircase.

His footsteps hesitated, and a tingle of electricity brushed her lower back.

"Well, this is a pleasant surprise," he said. "Although, I can feel you are pissed about something. Did practice involve another mud bath today?"

Her fingers drummed the arm of the chair. She was pissed about so many things, but especially Thomas's withholding of his imminent departure. It made her a hypocrite and that much more frustrated with herself and her predicament.

With a noticeable hop in his step, he crested the stairs. And when he turned to face her, Sara's breath hitched. Besides his dazzling gaze, he wore gray pants with a matching vest over a pale blue shirt and cobalt tie. His clothes were expertly tailored, accentuating his broad shoulders and trim waist. The finery was part of his arsenal in winning over normals and winning in legal matters. He wore it with ease.

Damn him. She nearly forgot her fury before pinning him with an icy stare.

He stopped, his countenance turning grave. Without taking his eyes off her, he whished his jacket and briefcase to the nearby couch. "Is this about me leaving for university in a week?" His tone was careful. Oh so careful, as if he were dipping a toe into a river with demons lurking beneath the surface.

One week. Her eyelids shuttered. No words could escape her constricted throat nor convey her fractured heart.

Thomas remained frozen by the stairs. "I'm sorry I didn't tell you. With everything going on, I never had a good opportunity."

Though he didn't mention Naomi's death and Ian's absence, she still winced.

"And I admit, I was scared of this exact reaction. Rolling your eyes proves my point." He gave a soft chuckle. A weak attempt at lightening the heaviness between them.

He raked a hand through his sable hair. "And because I'm torn. I need to go—to meet the in-person requirements for my law degree, just like Matt needs to fulfill his physical labs to be a vet—but the idea of you and me being apart for months makes me ill."

He flew to her, his musk-and-ash scent stirring in the air as he knelt before her and took her hands in his. "I'll be back before Solstice. And once I complete this last semester, I'll get my degree, pass the bar, and then I can protect Ware Woods in my own way—without magic."

Her anger and disappointment instantly dissolved. This was the path he'd been on long before she arrived at the forest. In addition to patrolling their wall, the Sullivan family protected Ware Woods by mastering the laws of normals—because dark magic wasn't the only threat they faced. This on-campus semester, conveniently coinciding for both Thomas and Matthew, had probably been planned for years. Sara couldn't deny him this right to protect them, even if it meant being apart.

Her heart felt ripped open, knowing she needed to let him go yet wanting him to stay. Not to mention her terror at the mere thought of him being attacked outside the wall—defenseless, without magic. If any harm ever came to him, she would destroy the world and herself in the process. Shivering, she strengthened her grip on his hands, their white and blue flames merging and flickering around their clasp.

Reading her emotions through the bond, he said, "We'll be in a secure dorm at a very busy university. And I'm not exactly defenseless outside the wall." He angled his head toward the gym and its racks of deadly edged weapons.

Physical threats weren't her only concern. "What about your nightmares?"

"Matt's used to them. He throws water on me. Effective, though not as pleasant as waking up to you."

When she remained quietly staring at their grip, he withdrew a hand and gently raised her chin with his finger. Blue flames shimmered in his eyes. "We can't stop living today for what may or may not happen tomorrow."

Her stomach clenched with guilt. He was right. Mother, he was right in so many ways. And perhaps it was presumptuous of her, but Sara had to share her condition with him.

She swallowed, hoping the confession she was about to make wouldn't completely turn her world upside down. With a stuttering heart, she said, "Thomas, remember on the beach when I said I had something to tell you?"

He gave her a soft smile and caressed the side of her face. "Yes. And I know you'll tell me when you're ready. Although I am curious," he admitted.

She tried to turn her head and avert her gaze, ashamed of her unusual circumstance, but he held her chin, refusing to let her look away. In a voice as small as she felt, she said, "I don't know what may or may not happen between us, but you should know that I cannot have children." A tear slid down her cheek.

Thomas stared at her. Though his face remained emotionless, she saw his aura flare a variety of colors. The urge to read his mind and know his thoughts was nearly overwhelming. She bit her lip, waiting for him to say something—anything.

He dragged his calloused thumb across her cheek, swiping away the tear. And with a predator's slow and smooth poise, he leaned in and softly sighed across her neck.

She stifled a gasp, her back arching with another zing of electricity.

"Sounds like a challenge to me," he declared, his husky voice turning her center into liquid fire. He leaned back with a lazy grin, energy pulsing between them.

Father above, he was downright wicked and perfect in every way.

"Does it, now?" she teased, dishing it back at him.

In a solemn voice, he added, "For when we're ready, of course."

She nodded and with fingers trembling from both relief and need, she untucked his butter-soft satin tie from his fitted vest. Thomas smirked as she fisted the tie, wrapping its length around her hand, and tugged him closer.

"So aggressive," he murmured, his stubbled cheek grazing hers, and gently nipped her jaw. "Do *you* remember at the beach when I told you we would resume our kiss and I would show you exactly all the ways I love you?" His words tickled her ear.

Oh, yes. White flames erupted along her skin in response.

His chuckle was positively sinful as he nuzzled her neck and, in one swift motion, picked her up and rushed them both to his master suite. With a chaste peck to her cheek, he placed her on the bed and stepped back out of arm's reach. "I'm wearing far too many clothes for what I have in mind." He visually feasted on her while slowly undoing the buttons on his vest. Pure devil.

Sara narrowed her eyes at him. *Alrighty, then. If you want to play games . . .* Though her nose twitched from holding back on whishing off all his clothes, she merely returned his smirk.

As he made an elaborate production of hanging up the vest and removing his shoes and socks, Sara flopped onto her belly, propped her chin in her hands, and casually kicked up her bare feet behind her. She wore one of his T-shirts—snagged from his closet after her shower—and cut-off shorts, her shoes long discarded. She pretended not to notice when he stole a glance down the front of the gapping shirt before blatantly tracking the movement of her legs.

Oh, she was going to win. She may have wiggled her hips.

Thomas advanced toward her, eyes blazing.

"What happened with the trial?" she asked, struggling to keep her voice light and innocent. Her inquiry was equal parts teasing and genuine concern.

He jerked to a halt. "You're asking me this *now*?"

She held her sweet smile.

"We won, of course."

Relief washed over her. "Your confidence is duly noted."

"I deserve a reward." Flames reignited in his eyes.

She licked her lips, noting his laser focus on her mouth, and in a much lower voice said, "Agreed."

A growl escaped him, the only warning before he pounced—shirt gone, cufflinks and buttons skittering across the floor.

Sara yelped as he lifted her on top of him and wound his hands into her hair. Blue and white sparks burst like fireworks in the dimly lit room, casting them in a soft twinkling light. Instead of fiercely claiming her mouth, Thomas gently kissed each corner, his lips impossibly soft given his chiseled exterior. And despite his rapid pulse, he hesitated a hair's breadth from her parted lips. Not teasing but waiting for her to make a move.

"Kiss me," she breathed, baring her body and soul to him. Energy surged between them, flooding Sara with tender warmth while tightening their embrace.

With a groan that tingled her core, Thomas obliged. His lips parted hers and his tongue swept in, leisurely devouring her and ratcheting her heart rate until all she saw were stars. When she whimpered and dug her fingers into his bare shoulders, Thomas broke their kiss and pinned his shimmering eyes on her. "Ready for more?"

Heavens, yes.

His silky grin ignited her, white energy glowing on her skin. But when she tried to undo him by kissing the still circle branded into his forearm, he teased her further by pulling his arm down to his side. "Don't you dare do that yet," he rumbled.

Done playing games, she whished off the rest of their clothes and pressed her body against his. From the feel of him beneath her, he was done playing too. But despite his own need, he idly swirled his calloused hands up and down her back, holding her to him. She kissed his neck, savoring his scent and the low groan he gave in response. Sara closed her eyes and sighed, committing this moment to memory—to hold on to for the coming months.

His hands paused, splayed across her back as he placed his mouth to her ear. "I need you to say it," he said, his words clipped with a barely there restraint.

"Yes, please. MORE," she projected into his mind.

"Good," he murmured, voice thick as honey. "Because I'm going to take my time and enjoy every inch of you so that neither of us will forget the feel of one another, not just for the fall semester, but for forever."

The room exploded with his blue energy as he flipped her onto her stomach and kissed her lower back with a jolt of electricity.

"Thomas," she pleaded, trembling with the need for him to fully consume her.

He chuckled and slowly dragged his finger up her spine, one vertebra at a time. "You are so special," he whispered, his words barely audible. Her hair whished aside, either by her will or his, for him to continue his playful ascent up her back. Thomas stopped and, with delighted amusement in his voice, said, "And you snuck off at the boardwalk to get a tattoo. My little monster." He purred his last few words and laid a very wet kiss on her upper back. Electricity swept through her again.

Enough.

She leapt up, pushed him onto his back, and straddled him. The sheer bliss reflecting in his face sent her heart soaring. "Are *you* ready for more?" she panted.

His chest heaved, eyes widening. "Hells, *YES.*"

Blue and white energy crackled again in the room as she accepted his answer and took in every bit of him until she thought she would explode with consummate joy.

Thomas's grip tightened, his fingers digging into her flaming skin, eagerly meeting her need to be closer. Lightning shot through her—through him—and the room blazed light blue. Here were passion, love, and acceptance, burning and fusing them together until all she felt was their hearts and souls beating as one.

Later, when they lay exhausted beside one another and her stomach growled, Thomas rolled out of bed and made them spaghetti. Though he apologized profusely for his lack of cooking skills and for already having eaten the food she brought over earlier in the week, it was the best spaghetti Sara had ever tasted.

Sitting beside him at the table, she held his hand in hers, their powers sparking at the connection. An ache unlike anything she had ever felt before filled her and threatened to shatter her being. It was a swirling potion of happiness for their love and of hope for their future—and of fear for their upcoming separation while dark magic loomed like a deadly storm.

CHAPTER 15

S ARA SCOWLED AT the Book. Again, she had asked for information about Samson. And again, all it said was "Trust."

Fine. "If Samson can't reverse the damage he did, what *can* heal Ian's heart?" Pages flipped, and Sara widened her gaze. Hopeful.

Love.

"Thanks," she mumbled. "Another cryptic answer. I assume this is a specific type of love, seeing as how everyone already adores him, including Mr. Motley." Sara grimaced at mentioning the Taker. "Care to share any *helpful* specifics?"

Hearts of all sizes bubbled up on the page.

Sara snuffled a laugh through her nose.

For the rest of the week, she continued practicing with Moira during the day and, at night, enjoying what little time she had left with Thomas. On his last evening, they met the gang for dinner at the weathered gray picnic table behind the Cahills' farm. Ian's absence weighed heavily in the cool air, and though it was a nearly full moon, no one was in a partying mood to show off magic and chase one another through the adjacent field of grass.

Lily and Caleb were particularly quiet, their thin smiles indicating unspoken worry not just for Ian, Sara guessed, but for Thomas and Matthew as well. The only crew member genuinely excited was Matthew, who bounced around like a fox during mating season—ecstatic to be going to university.

"I pity you for rooming with this wild idiot," said Moira to Thomas before throwing a frown at her twin, whose fidgeting shook the entire table.

Matthew flicked back his mop of wavy copper hair, amber eyes shining in the early moonlight, and sliced a grin at her. "Is that your way of saying you're going to miss me?"

"I won't miss sharing a bathroom with you. You've been stealing my shampoo and conditioner again. Don't think I haven't noticed," said Moira with an exaggerated glare, though sadness hid in her voice.

Sara pushed her plate aside, stomach tied in knots. The twins had probably never been apart, and the fall semester would be hard, not just for Sara but for Moira too. An odd sense of comfort passed over her at knowing she and Moira would spend the next few months practicing, commiserating, and counting down the days until Thomas and Matthew came home.

"Don't worry," said Thomas, clearly addressing Moira's concern for her twin. "I'll keep a close eye on him so he doesn't get into too much trouble." He shifted his attention to Matthew. "I doubt your labs will leave you much spare time, and I'm not letting you binge-watch anime and nature documentaries, howl at the moon, or sleep until noon."

Matthew sat back, his lightly freckled face full of incredulity. Sara stilled as he considered Thomas's challenging grin before flicking his keen gaze at her and everyone else at the table. His stunned expression melted into pure vulpine craftiness, his eyes dancing with an inner fire. "Bro, you gotta let me have *some* fun. How about sorority parties?"

Sara spluttered her birch beer.

"No," said Thomas.

"*Fraternity* parties?" Matthew's beguiling smile deepened.

"No."

"If there're no parties for me, then there're no fight clubs for you."

"Fine."

Matthew snorted, as did Violet. "Let's compromise and join the university lacrosse club. I know you've been itching to pick up your stick again." Matthew's gaze cut to Sara. "We haven't played in two years. Not since we were seniors when I scored the winning state championship goal and Thomas attacked the other team's goalie for cussing me out."

Sara's gasp was drowned out by Caleb's whoop of laughter. "It was a spectacular game," he gushed, high-fiving Matthew.

"Dad made you run the wall for two days," said Violet to Thomas. "I felt so bad for you that I snuck you water whenever he wasn't watching."

Another laugh, this time from Lily. "I did the same."

"I was very grateful," said Thomas with a deep chuckle.

"Hmph," grumped Sara. "I'm not surprised Kane punished you. And please tell me you're *not* entertaining the idea of—"

"We're not joining any clubs or teams," interrupted Thomas. "Matt is playing you. He knows we need to keep a low profile."

Sara threw a scowl at Matthew.

He winked at her and, with a definite foxiness in his smooth voice, said, "I wasn't kidding about the parties. But it seems my witchy brother has outgrown his need for a good fight club." He folded his arms, amber stare kindly assessing Thomas. "I like this calmer version of you."

"Me too," said Thomas, the corners of his mouth turning up. He grasped Sara's hand under the table and gave it a squeeze.

With a slow blink, Matthew redirected his gaze to Sara. "He rarely smiled before you came to Ware Woods."

Sara's cheeks burned. She too had rarely smiled before Ware Woods. Unsure of what to say, she returned Thomas's squeeze, releasing a snap of light-blue energy between them.

"It's true. We used to call him Sullen Sullivan," said Moira, tossing back her red mane. Sara could have kissed her for picking up the conversation. "I'll miss both of you grinning knuckleheads, but with you gone"—Moira speared her fork in Thomas's direction—"Lily, Violet, and I can spend more time with Sara. We can finally have a 'girls only' night." She beamed a smile at Thomas, who gave a polite laugh. Then she swiveled to face Caleb. "Since you'll be the last male standing, you can hang with us too."

Caleb choked on his second piece of pie. With a fist pound to his brawny chest, he said, "Hang out with four gorgeous *yet* sisterly females? Hmm." His green eyes glittered as he drew a finger in the air, pointing at the four of them. "Only if there will be pillow fights. I'll take you all out."

The following morning, after hardly getting a wink of sleep, Sara lingered beside Thomas's truck—its bed packed with belongings and dormitory supplies. Behind her, in the Sullivans' front yard, stood most of their forest family. They had already said their goodbyes and best wishes and stepped back for immediate family members to give a last round of hugs.

Bill and Shannon Walker embraced Matthew, followed by Moira, who rumpled his hair until he playfully put her in a head-lock. When she cocked back an arm to slug him, he let go and slipped into the safety of the front passenger seat with a smooth grin.

Similarly, Kane and Abby hugged Thomas, followed by Violet and Connor, who tried to jab Thomas, only to be deftly blocked and gently cuffed upside the head. "I expect your sparring to improve by the time I get back," Thomas chided his younger brother. They fist-bumped, and Thomas pretended to wince at Connor's punch before turning his smile toward Sara. Her heart stopped when he embraced her. She buried her face into the spot between his neck and shoulder, inhaling his musk-and-ash scent as if taking in his very essence. With a squeeze and quick nibble to her ear, he released her and hopped into the truck.

Everyone drifted closer to the wall, respectfully leaving Sara, who rose to her tiptoes and leaned into the driver's-side open window. In the front passenger seat, Matthew idly played with his phone, focusing anywhere but in their direction.

"I know you'll be crazy busy, so I'll only call once a week," said Sara. Since the treehouse had no reception, she would have to call from the Lochtons' brown house, where service was strongest.

"You can call or text as often as you want," said Thomas, clicking his seat belt.

And because they had already said their private goodbyes all night, she gave him a quick peck on the lips and stepped away from the truck.

"This isn't goodbye, Sara, just 'see you later,'" he said, eyes blazing. And though he gave her a broad smile, his posture remained taut with tension. He slowly pulled out onto the old road, tires bumping over the stone wall where it stitched under the driveway, and waved his hand down low out the window. Everyone in the front yard responded with a cheerful wave above their heads.

The bloodstone thumped against Sara's chest as she lost sense of Thomas's presence through the bond, a portion of her soul ripping away when he crossed the boundary. With her hand pressed over the glowing stone, Sara flew as high as she dared, Moira joining her in hawk form. Together, they watched the truck until it disappeared into the normal world.

Moira's piercing cry echoed throughout the forest and within Sara's heart.

Determined to busy herself for the rest of the day and not obsess over Thomas and Matthew, Sara trailed her father and Ted to Ian's high-tech office in the basement of the brown house. For hours, they scoured the internet for possible leads on the Global Council and how to contact them. But they still discovered nothing—not even the faintest whisper or urban legend about a secretive group with a special meeting tree—and none of the other sacred sites would respond to their inquiries. It was as if Ware Woods didn't exist.

Sara slumped back in Ian's computer chair, Bailey napping at her feet, the Lab dreamily twitching her paws and fluttering her jowls while Sara checked her phone's locator app for the umpteenth time. Her shoulders relaxed a smidge when Thomas and Matthew reached the university and texted their safe arrival.

Leaving Charlie and Ted to continue their efforts, Sara looped from the Lochton pine to the Cahill chestnut and, with a hard swallow, shoved her phone into her pocket and joined the Cahills in preparing the meal for the evening's full moon Council meeting.

After a restless afternoon of food prepping, Sara took center stage and began her first forest meeting as High Witch with the customary hand wave and pledge to Ware Woods.

Plastering on a smile, she assured the families that Ian was doing well and had chosen to remain with Samson of his own free will, and she promised she would find the darkness that had caused Naomi's death.

She left out the part about slowly killing whoever or whatever was responsible.

And when the meeting ended, Sara welcomed her father's company as he walked her to the treehouse and sat with her in the main room, softly droning about Aristotle and the history of metaphysics until, despite the hole in her heart, she nodded off, sprawled out on one of the couches.

CHAPTER 16

SARA PACED THE treehouse's turret deck, torn between wanting the coming months to speed by—until Thomas, Matthew, Ian, and Dorcas were back in Ware Woods—and wanting time to crawl and delay the Shadow Mother. The fact that Ian chose to remain with Samson ate at her, and Thomas's absence was a throbbing ache. But instead of folding to her panic, she scanned the lake and surrounding forest, taking in its inherent energy, and renewed her commitment to refining her magic. A commitment she would throw herself at. Surely, a grueling practice schedule would perfect her skills *and* keep her mind from unraveling with worry.

First, she sought out the Cahills and concentrated solely on improving her earth magic. With help from Caleb and Uncle Larry, she practiced opening deep fissures in the forest floor, stacking boulders into towering walls, growing and bending trees to her will, and commanding the serpentine choking nature of vines. From Helen and Rebecca, she learned how to entice a flower to bloom out of season, cultivate the softest moss, and finely tune the burgeoning fall leaf colors into an array of dazzling hues.

Despite dropping a boulder on Uncle Larry's foot—and promptly healing him—Sara's magic improved. By the time Mabon arrived, a crystal-clear sky pleasantly marking the autumnal equinox, her powers instinctively dug deep into the ground like roots tapping directly into the Mother's magic. To celebrate, Sara stood in the center of the Cahill common and—with a wink at Helen and Gran, sitting in rocking chairs on the Main House's expansive deck—she flourished her arms, letting magic course through her. In a surge of energy, she decorated the house with clusters of plump apples, dried corn stalks, and mixed berries. Helen dropped her quilting squares and applauded while a beaming Gran whished a collection of candles to join the offering.

Buoyed by her progress, Sara next set her focus on honing her water and air magics. With assistance from Lily, Orsen, and Kingsley Atwell, she learned how to stretch her power up to the sky, as if reaching into the arms of the Father above, and summon fierce snowstorms, tornadoes, and violent thunderclouds, their bellies swollen with torrential rain.

One afternoon, while standing with Lily in the meadow beside the lakeshore, Sara froze a blast of lake water and kinetically suspended many glistening blades of ice. It was a grand achievement, but when Caleb popped out of the forest's edge and whistled in awe, Sara's concentration splintered. The ice melted, and a deluge of water dumped upon Caleb, stopping him mid-whistle and drenching him to the bone. Sara wavered, unsure if she should hit him with a warm jet of air or run.

Caleb tossed his head, spraying water from his sandy hair, and set his green eyes on her. His mischievous twinkle launched her feet into a sprint for the shore, hoping she could successfully run on water as well as Lily. Sara didn't make it two steps before Caleb's power shot out, ensnaring her with a thick patch of clinging mint.

"How about a hug, cousin?" he sang over her playful shrieks, the mint pulling her into his arms. He wrapped her in a snug embrace until she was equally soaking and laughing along with him and Lily. Sara's hair was still damp when she conducted the Council meeting later that night—a meeting in which she discussed the upcoming harvest and not the impending Winter Solstice of doom.

With autumn in full swing, its crisp nights triggering brilliantly colored foliage, and time ticking down for dark magic to rear its ugly head, Sara joined the Sullivans in physical and kinetic sparring. Thomas's parents were delighted to have her over for family dinners and instruct her in ruthless fighting matches.

From Abby, Sara discovered how to pull kinetic energy from the air and create deadly spheres anywhere she desired, including behind an opponent, where a direct hit was least expected. And from Kane's brutal lessons, Sara learned how to hone her focus and find an opponent's weak spot. Working with Kane was always unpredictable. At times, he was downright scary when he pushed her to her limit with promises that dark magic would be merciless, and at other times, he was fatherly, sweet, and patient, like when he instructed her on compartmentalizing her emotions. She failed that lesson repeatedly. His resulting laugh reminded her so much of Thomas, her chest squeezed, and she had to look away to hide the pain.

Occasionally, she teamed up with Violet. Sara enjoyed sparring and racing with her—urging each other to fly faster and faster—but Violet was often busy with schoolwork. She was currently enrolled in an online undergraduate program, following in Thomas's footsteps to be an environmental attorney and work for their family practice. Connor would likely do the same. Attorneys by day, deadly kinetic witches by night.

When Kane began another trial, this one relating to an encroaching development, and needed Abby's assistance, Sara moved on to try her hand at shifting. Such a talent would be advantageous in fighting off dark magic, and something Samson would not see coming.

She wandered to the cemetery's oak tree, deep in contemplation. If her great-aunt Alice could shift, perhaps with some quiet concentration Sara could too.

How hard can it be?

Sara sat cross-legged in the center of one of the treehouse's vacant rooms, an extra-large window opening overlooking the pines behind the cemetery. With a stiff roll of her shoulders, she closed her eyes and focused her mind on becoming a wolf. Minutes dragged by while she imagined a furry coat, perked ears, a mouth of sharp teeth, and enormous paws. The result was nothing but a headache.

Maybe a wolf is too ambitious, and a rabbit will be easier.

She scrunched her face, grunting with effort as she concentrated on an image of a cottontail rabbit—long, soft ears, cute little tail. Her body trembled, and then stilled. Nothing. She sighed and opened her eyes to two ravens cocking their heads and blinking their black-seeded eyes at her.

"Gaa!"

Moira shifted into her human form, and Trouble flapped to the windowsill.

"What are you trying to do? Visualize world peace?" inquired Moira.

"Something like that." Sara groaned, and instead of humiliating herself further, she asked Moira to dinner at the Main House, where they discussed the finer points of having a bathroom all to oneself.

The following morning, Sara asked the grimoire for an explanation on shifters. According to the Book, shifting was a biologically based magic, not something that could be learned. Sara frowned when she read this. It struck her as odd how Alice could shift, but not her sister—Gran—nor anyone else in Sara's immediate family. Which meant Alice could have a different father than Gran. Sara kept this suspicion to herself, not daring to inquire about such a sensitive subject either during their morning tea or later when Alice calmly instructed her on how to control witch fire—a rare and dangerous magic Sara struggled to command.

Despite her inability to shift and other occasional failures, the long weeks of grueling practice were satisfying. Her routine of practicing magic and searching the Book also included calls with Thomas and texts with Ian, checking in with Charlie and Ted on any leads regarding the Global Council, and lots of waiting.

Waiting for Thomas and Matthew to come home. Waiting for Ian to be miraculously healed. Waiting for Samson to show up again. Waiting for dark magic to attack on Winter Solstice.

Sara hated waiting. It made her skin crawl and squeezed every fiber of her being.

By the time the second full moon was nearly upon them, she had exhausted all her resources within Ware Woods. Yet, for all her magical improvements, Sara knew she was still shamefully unprepared for Samson or any other darkness as strong as him—or stronger. Thank the Mother and Father for the blessed stone wall which was impervious to dark magic and kept Ware Woods safe. A wall that was also their prison if Sara couldn't keep darkness away.

Hells, not just away. Sara wanted darkness to be terrified of her. And perhaps this made her a bit dark herself. But this need to protect at any cost was a part of her. She had knowingly killed a threat to a friend a long time ago—long before she even knew she was a witch. And though it weighed on her, Sara knew she would kill again and again to ensure the safety of her forest family.

She brushed past a honeysuckle bush, absently walking a path back to the treehouse after another tiring day of practicing her magic. The rich humus and brisk scents of fall fluttered around her as she kicked up a pile of golden leaves.

Autumn had settled with a nip in the air and a warm kaleidoscope of foliage colors, from pale yellow to flaming orange to apple red. The forest was a living mosaic of brilliance. It stole Sara's breath whenever she flew above the treetops and viewed Ware Woods below her. How normals failed to see and feel the radiant thrumming energy of the forest was a mystery. Perhaps the wall also shielded Ware Woods' shimmering power from the outside world.

She paused. Maybe this was why the Global Council and other sacred sites had never reached out to them. Maybe they couldn't detect them through the protective barrier.

Ian had once explained that Ware Woods was left alone because it included a mix of magical factions: witches, shifters, and apparently two reclusive vampires whom Sara had yet to meet. But this explanation seemed wrong to her. Why would a mix of factions be ignored? If anything, working together to protect sacred sites would be an advantage against dark magic, not something to be scorned.

Sara resumed walking and pondering—the physical movement enabling her to focus.

Think.

How could a High Witch grow stronger and magically gain the centuries of knowledge and power and experience needed to defeat something as dark as the Shadow Mother?

A spark of enlightenment hit her at the same time the toe of her boot caught on an errant root. Surprised by both her revelation and clumsiness, she pancaked to the forest floor, ripping the knees of her jeans and grinding dirt into her palms. Instinctively healing herself, Sara rolled to a sitting position and grunted a laugh. Beside her, a swath of ferns tinged autumn brown nodded as if in encouragement.

Clearly, she needed help. And only the best would do. What she needed was the aid of a cunning Elder Vampire, formidable Alpha Shifter, and expert High Witch. If a spell had once worked to break the curse Makwa had put on her and release her magic, a spell would surely work to bring Sara the aid she desired to improve her powers.

She tapped her chin. Who would know of such a powerful spell?

Naomi had known the spell to break Makwa's curse, but Naomi . . . Instead of finishing her thought, Sara slipped her hand under the back collar of her sweatshirt and touched the still circle inked just below the nape of her neck. All thoughts of Naomi and spells abruptly halted as a whistle of death shot straight at her.

CHAPTER 17

Sara pivoted and froze a familiar bone-hilt dagger in midair, less than a foot away from her chest. She spat a filthy curse, then hollered, "Hells, Vi. You could have killed me."

"Thought I'd test your reflexes outside of designated practice," said Violet, emerging from the understory with a smirk and a strut in her step. She plucked the blade from the air and dropped her grin. "You should always be ready for anything."

True, especially if there is a Sullivan around.

Sara's mind instantly conjured an image of Thomas, and her toes curled in her boots. With her lips pursed, she took a deep inhalation through her nose and then released it, calmly dispersing the energy that had sprung up around her.

Great.

Now she was conflicted between spending the night racking her brain for a clever spell or running to her father's house and calling Thomas like a love-sick puppy. They'd talked for hours the night before, and she knew he was currently busy memorizing case studies for an upcoming exam. Despite the aching pull in her heart, she would have to endure another week before hearing his voice.

She loosed another sigh and lifted her chin at Violet. "What are you doing out here? I recall you saying you had '*poop loads of homework this weekend.*'" Sara eyed the backpack slung over Violet's shoulder and the dagger in her hand, which she idly spun and flicked with ease.

Violet ceased her toying, hand gripping the hilt of what Sara hoped was animal bone, and lifted a brow. "Didn't Moira tell you that we're meeting at *your* place tonight? You were too busy for a party last month, and since tomorrow is a full moon—on Samhain no less—we thought tonight would be perfect for a nearly-full-moon all-girls' night." She waved her dagger at the dimming forest and added, "Well, we invited Caleb too, but I doubt he'll sleep over. Which is a good thing, since he snores like a bear."

Crap.

Moira may have mentioned something, but Sara had been too focused on her High Witch duties—like keeping them all safe from whatever impending horror was to arrive on Winter Solstice. And this would explain why Gran had dropped off an armful of quilts the day before—partly for the coming winter but also for this sleepover.

Sara regarded Violet's hopeful expression. Spell casting would have to wait.

"A big loveable bear," Sara said with a snicker. Her cousin's sleepy rumbles had been a gentle comfort when she had lain awake all night on the beach. Sara rose from the forest path, hovering before Violet. "I'm sure the cottage kitchen has plenty of food, even for Caleb. Race you." She took off above the trees and would have won had Violet not thrown her dagger at her *again*, forcing her to barrel-roll to the side.

Violet passed her with a grin and flew straight through the open door of the brightly lit cottage. In a gust of wind, Sara landed behind her, eyes wide at the full spread of food Caleb was unpacking and laying out on the kitchen island. Behind him, Moira rolled out pastry dough while Lily peeled and cut a bowl of apples. The entire cottage buzzed with warmth and a mix of delicious smells. A memory of making applesauce with her mother on Green Brier

Lane, of cozy laughter and cinnamon, washed over Sara and she leaned against the door frame, her vision flickering with the image. Sara blinked and found Lily staring at her with a glowing smile.

"You could use a shower before we eat," Lily said, pointing with her paring knife at Sara's disheveled appearance.

Moira glanced up, and Sara gave a double take at the flour dusting her perfectly freckled cheeks. "Don't look so surprised. Gran and Alice have taught me how to make an apple pie worthy of winning over any alpha." She dropped her grin and eyed Sara up and down, wrinkling her nose. "Are ripped jeans a thing again?"

Caleb paused from his unpacking. "Since I don't have your fancy electric magic to power this kitchen, I pre-made everything: beef Wellington, roasted root veggies, and frisée salad—oh, and a cheese-and-bread board." He nodded at the nearby coffee table and a platter overflowing with delectable cheeses, red grapes, and a selection of freshly cut breads.

He had definitely gone all out for this get-together. Sara's mouth watered.

"Speaking of which," said Moira with a head tilt to the oven, "can you—"

Without even flicking her wrist, Sara willed the oven to heat for the pie. "Done." While all her practice made such a simple task effortless, she knew she still lacked the power to stop a dark witch without destroying herself in the process. She stuffed down the thought and poked at the torn edges of what had been her favorite pants.

Violet dropped her bag beside the fireplace, which was already aglow with cheerful flames, and plunked onto the small couch, snagging a piece of Cahill cheddar as she went. She gestured to the bathroom behind her and spoke around her mouthful, "We'll wait for you. But can't say the cheese will." She grabbed another slab as Sara flew to the shower.

Both Caleb's meal and Moira's pie were deliciously filling, as was everyone's playful banter. When their lighthearted conversation—pointedly avoiding talk of dark magic and the three missing members of their group—turned to their public high school experiences, Sara was astounded they'd suffered similar challenges. It seemed normals were inherently intrigued yet dangerously fearful of all magicals no matter how well they blended in or how kind they were to them.

While most of the gang had completed the four years of "being socialized," as the forest called it, Caleb had switched to homeschooling for his last two years—the same as Sara. She couldn't fathom anyone bullying her humorous and brawny cousin, yet when she gently prodded him for the reason he chose homeschooling, he busied himself with clearing the table. Sara dropped the subject, and when they all pitched in to clean up, she tried to convince him to stay the night.

For all their sweet cajolery and false promises of clay masks and pedicures, Caleb laughed them off, insisting they enjoy an all-girls' sleepover. As consolation, he strolled home with the rest of the apple pie. When his cheerful whistling faded into the forest, Sara followed a giddy Violet, Moira, and Lily toward the treehouse.

"I'm excited to spend a night in the oak," gushed Violet, running her hand along its knobby trunk as they ascended the treehouse stairs. "Thomas says it rocks you to sleep and whispers its leaves all night."

Sara snorted. Apparently, Thomas liked the magical tree despite his occasional grumblings of its *attentiveness*.

The tree swayed, stretching its massive branches and rustling its nut-brown leaves.

"Show-off," teased Sara. With half a thought, she lit the many white candles placed about the treehouse. The flames were similar to the energy that often danced along her skin—bright but not hot unless she wished for heat. She had the Book to thank for teaching her this enchantment.

Violet and Moira leapt ahead and burst into the lower deck's main room, which had recently been decorated with a pale-green area rug, two plush couches, a coffee table, and four wooden chairs grown by Caleb. The pair twirled among the furniture and richly grained open space before rushing to explore the new rooms, turrets, and decks added after Sara and Naomi broke Makwa's curse, when the oak and treehouse—entwined as one—had exploded with growth. While Sara's original bedroom remained a level above, tucked against the right side of the trunk, surrounding it was now a smooth wooden mansion of cozy bedrooms, lounge spaces, and even an expansive meeting room with round table and chairs.

From the outside, the treehouse appeared modest in construction, blending into the gnarled gray trunk and sprawling branches. From the inside, the entire house unfolded into grand spaces that often magically appeared and disappeared. The many windowless openings and expanded doorways created an airy ambiance, which sun- and moonlight took turns illuminating.

Moira squealed in delight from somewhere far above. "I claim this room," she called out.

"I get this one," hollered Violet in response, her voice carrying down a stairway to the left of the main room.

Lily started for the flowing stairway when a slender branch extended from the ceiling and pointed her up the original narrow set of stairs beside the trunk. Sara matched Lily's wide-eyed wonder and shrugged. To her knowledge, the only room off the original stairway was her bedroom. But, similar to the Book, the oak tree did as it wanted, and Sara was learning not to question the forest's magic.

As they topped the stairs, Sara gaped at a stately new chamber, nearly equaling hers in size. Its polished wood floor and walls gleamed from dozens of flickering candles. Before the center of the far wall rested an ornate bed with scrolled posts fit for royalty. A lustrous gray quilt edged in black velvet draped its fluffy, cloud-like mattress.

Lily padded into the room, placed her bag on a chair overlooking a private deck, and gently sat on the edge of the bed, sinking into the soft covers.

Sara squinted at the bedding. Gran must have made the beds today too, but why hadn't the tree brought Lily to a room with the buttercup-yellow quilt Gran had proudly shown her? Bright yellow seemed a much better fit for Lily instead of cool, stone gray.

"I love it," breathed Lily, smoothing the cover with her delicate hands.

Before Sara could comment, footsteps thundered throughout the treehouse, followed by Moira's husky voice from the main room. "Come on you two! Time to tell Sara some embarrassing stories about Thomas." Her howl of laughter drifted up the stairs and trembled the leaves in the vaulted ceiling.

By the time they crashed into their respective beds, they had laughed so hard they cried—each sharing embarrassing stories, from Violet and Thomas pretending to be wolves when they were little and wearing out the knees in their pants, to Lily accidentally spotting her great-great-uncle Kingsley skinny-dipping, and to Sara's grade-school dance instructor who was convinced Sara was having a seizure. But hands down, they decided Moira had the most hilarious story—at the age of eleven, she barged into her parents' room "to see what all the noise was about."

To everyone's glee, the treehouse did indeed sway them to sleep.

For the first time in weeks, Sara slept soundly and didn't wake until mid-morning, along with the rest of the treehouse. As a bleary-eyed team, they stumbled down the stairs and into the cottage, where they were pleasantly welcomed by Gran and a brunch of pastries, eggs Benedict, and fruit.

"It's about time you all woke up," chided Gran with the usual twinkle in her steel blue eyes. She handed Sara a mug of coffee. "I haven't seen you this content and well rested in ages."

A sleepy smile twitched on Sara's lips. Last night *had* been a wonderful sleepover filled with friends and laughter, as opposed to the last sleepover Sara had experienced, when she killed a vile man and lost all her hair. She grabbed her ponytail, confirming her silvery-gray locks were there, loosed a sigh, and pushed aside the murderous guilt still weighing on her. "Thanks," she mumbled, taking a grateful sip of coffee and gesturing to the food.

"Don't mention it. Thought I'd feed you all before we build the bonfire and decorate for Samhain tonight. I need everyone's help." She handed an herbal tea smelling of liquid sunshine to Lily, then turned back to Sara. "But first, you need to go to Old Blue. The Book is asking for you. Been rattling about for hours as if it had wood lice."

The Book.

Sara jolted awake. Perhaps the persnickety grimoire was in an agreeable mood today and would help her with the spell she needed.

She gulped down a quick breakfast with the rest of her coffee, heated the cottage's water supply for Lily, Moira, and Violet to enjoy hot showers, then gave a round of hugs before jetting directly for the blue house.

CHAPTER 18

As soon as Sara entered the kitchen, the Book halted its clattering on the farmhouse table.

"Hello." Her wary greeting sounded like a question as it echoed in the empty kitchen. "Did you summon me because you know I need a spell?"

Silence.

She eyed the closed grimoire as though it were a feral animal. When it declined to open, Sara cautiously slid into the chair before it. She sat on her hands—afraid to touch the Book. Afraid it wouldn't help her and she would remain at the mercy of Samson, waiting for his wretched appearance and whatever chaos the Shadow Mother would supposedly unleash on Winter Solstice.

Sara swallowed. The Book had told her to trust. Perhaps she could use this to her advantage in convincing it to provide a spell.

"I need help," she admitted. The Book puffed itself up with what Sara hoped was pride. Encouraged by its reaction, she explained her crazy-ass idea. "To stand against dark magic and be the High Witch that I need—*want*—to be, I seek the knowledge, power, and experience only a Magus can teach me. And not just one Magus. Three. One from *each* of the magical factions: vampires, shifters, and witches. Because if the Shadow Mother is as sinister as you have portrayed her, we may need to combine our powers to defeat her." Sara fidgeted in her seat, palms hot with nervous energy. "I *trust* you will provide a spell to summon the aid I seek."

For a heart-pounding moment, the Book remained still.

"Please," whispered Sara, placing her hand atop the Book. White energy surged from her touch, wrapping around the grimoire while the bloodstone at her chest pulsed, combining its energy with Sara's.

The Book fluttered open to a blank page. Sara stared, not daring to move, as ink bled up and formed curly scripted words:

Tonight.

When the land of the dead listens in the cold of night, cast a circle among them and recite:

The instructions faded away, yet no spell appeared in its place. Sara wrung her hands to stop herself from flipping the page and, not-so slowly, counted to ten before asking, "Recite what?"

One word appeared and vanished before the page tore free from the Book and floated toward Sara:

Trust.

Gaa!

Sara considered the empty page for a long moment before picking up the parchment and carefully folding it into a palm-sized square. Perhaps the spell would miraculously appear later tonight. Mother below, she hoped so. The fate of Ware Woods was literally in her hands.

"Thank you," she said to the Book, pushing back her chair and rising from the table. The Book closed with a soft sigh as Sara tucked the paper into her jeans pocket and flew from the house.

For the rest of the afternoon, Sara followed Gran's directions in harvesting pumpkins, picking the last of the apples, and decorating for the evening's celebration. Even with magic, it took her and the entire forest family until the setting sun to decorate the cemetery with a bright spectrum of flowers, black and white candles, and jack-o'-lanterns of all sizes; prepare and arrange an epic feast in the Council clearing; and create a sculptured peak of bonfire brush in the now-fallow fields by the Cahills' barn.

Despite the spell paper tingling in her pocket, and despite the marked absence of Ian, Matthew, Thomas, and even Dorcas, Sara smiled easily. The bliss of spending the prior night with good friends followed by a day of mirthful labor with the families warmed her soul. This was worth it. Whatever the spell may bring or whatever she would have to endure to protect Ware Woods and everyone she loved, Sara was ready. For them, she would do anything.

She shoved off the Council maple tree trunk, grabbed a heaping plate of food, and joined Ted at the Lochton table. Earlier in the day, she had set this table herself with a cheerful jack-o'-lantern surrounded by wild sunflowers and extra place settings for the deceased: Eliza, her mother; Naomi; a grandfather she never met; and Winona, Ian's biological mother. She regarded their apple- and nut-laden plates and gently touched the still circle tattoo on her upper back. Soon, she would determine Naomi's killer, destroy the Shadow Mother as well as Samson, and finally bring Ian home.

"I see you wisely insisted Alice and your grandmother conduct tonight's celebration," said her father, interrupting Sara's thoughts as he set down a plate of food and sat between her and Ted. Charlie acknowledged the extra place settings with a sad smile, his eyes glistening with affection and a tinge of grief. When a squirrel popped up and snatched a hickory nut, his face brightened, and he let out a laugh, sending the furry thief up into the maple.

Sara beamed at her father, amazed at how easily he could smile despite his losses, and then wandered her gaze across the crowded clearing. She *had* insisted Gran and Alice lead the evening activities, partly because this was her first Samhain in Ware Woods and she had no clue how they celebrated, and partly because she was preoccupied with a very important, yet invisible, spell.

She nodded toward the stump stage—at the two older witches, playfully wearing black pointed hats. "They're positively giddy, as are all the children," said Sara, waving hello to Connor as he raced past in a wolf costume holding a fistful of Rebecca's handmade skull-shaped lollipops. Truly, everyone was in high spirits.

"This has always been our favorite holiday. And with a full moon, tonight is very special," said Charlie. He took a swig of his birch beer and tucked into his food while Gran approached the center of the stage and held up her palms.

A hush fell across the Council clearing, and Gran lowered a hand, waving down low. The families, including Sara, responded by raising a hand and waving back. Greetings completed, Gran launched into the forest's familiar blessing, everyone joining in and reciting the pledge in such unison it was as if they all breathed as one.

Giving a respectful glance at the Sullivan, Walker, and Lochton tables, Gran said, "While a few of the living are not with us tonight, we are assured they are well and will be home by Solstice."

Cheerful yells and clapping rang out, along with a slightly wistful howl that Sara assumed came from Moira. She texted her twin more often than Sara checked in with Ian and Thomas.

The light waned as a hazy cloud drifted before the full moon. Gran continued, "As for the dead, they are with us tonight. Their love surrounds us today and every day, so we are never alone, and neither are they. On Samhain, the veil between living and dead is spider-thread thin, and we honor those who have fully passed onto the spirit realm. With the full moon, we must listen carefully and speak wisely, for many spirits are among us, and magic is wild tonight."

Gran paused, taking her time to scan the crowd with her sharp gaze. "Always be mindful of wishes and intentions, both spoken and unspoken, for our power is greater than we know."

Everyone fell silent, Gran's solemn reminder ringing through the gathering like a prophet's divine insight. Ever since Gran's magic had been restored, including premonitions, the families were rapt for her advice. But after talking with her over many breakfast pastries and cups of tea, Sara understood Gran's premonitions were usually so vague she couldn't tell what was foresight and what was flight of fancy until the time came to pass.

Gran pushed up the brim of her hat and stepped closer to the edge of the stage. "Lest we all forget how precious life is, I have a cautionary tale to tell." She bent down, scooped up one of the fat black candles with all the ease of a young woman, and stood before them, the flickering light casting shadows on her lightly wrinkled face.

The clearing stilled. Even the costumed children playing on the ground before the stage settled, the candies in their hands momentarily forgotten, their eyes glued on her.

"There once was a witchling with nails as black as night whose mother was such a powerful High Witch that some say she was descended from the Mother and Father themselves. In this regard, the witchling was blessed. However, the magical balance works in mysterious ways, for the witchling's father was a dragon. Not just any dragon—but one of the ancients pulled from the Aether and capable of assuming human form when desired."

A paper dragon shot up from behind the stage and hovered above Gran. The cluster of children gasped along with Sara as she beheld the resplendent effigy. From its flared nose to its pointed tail, the dragon was nearly the length of the stage. Its airy, hollow body was colorfully mottled with smoky black, seawater green, and dusty gold.

Sara craned her neck and spotted Connor, face glowing with pride, at the side of the stage. He held up a hand, using his kinetic power to gently sway the dragon and give it the appearance of flying. The paper creature's fluttering movements and many horns and spikes were remarkably similar to those of the red dragon Sara had seen on the beach.

Gran hunched over her candle and continued her story. "Of course, the dragon did not know he had a child, for if he knew, he would have killed her—such are the ways of fierce dragons. So the High Witch mother remained quiet, secretly raising the witchling in an enchanted forest where the trees and animals talked and magic sang in the air.

"But the witchling was not a dreamy, content witch. She was headstrong and fiercely protective of her forest and curious about everything—her father in particular. As she grew older and more powerful—mastering all kinds of magics—she decided she was strong enough to find her father. So she left the enchanted forest that nurtured and loved her beyond measure and sought out the ancient dragon."

Connor shook the dragon and roared dramatically while the rest of the children tittered with nervous laughter. Every adult had stopped eating, their hands in their laps, their focus on the stage.

Sara swung her gaze back to her grandmother, apprehension coiling in her belly as to where this theater production was headed.

Gran paced the front of the stage. "Now, some think the witchling found her dragon father, and they had a joyful reunion . . . until a dark witch with ice in her heart attacked them both." She pretended to stab her chest, face twisting with pain.

"Aye!" interjected a male voice from the rear of the tables. Sara twisted to see Kingsley Atwell jabbing the air with a forkful of cake. The Atwell tables laughed, and Sara caught Lily affectionately shaking her head at her great-great-uncle.

Sara turned back to the stage, catching Gran's frown at Kingsley, and thanked the Mother she hadn't been raised in Ware Woods and subjected to such dark bedtime stories.

In a louder voice, Gran said, "But most believe the deadly dragon—like all dragons—was void of love and stopped his daughter's heart with one cruel stare. Regardless of what happened, the curious witchling used the last of her power to return to the enchanted forest and take her dying breath—surrounded by those who had always truly loved her."

No one said a word. The children, including Connor along the side of the stage, stared wide-eyed at the seemingly innocent paper dragon. Charlie and Ted both chuckled beside Sara as Gran drew a finger across the crowd, her intense gaze sweeping them all before extinguishing her candle.

"How can you laugh at this morbid tale?" projected Sara with a slight scowl.

Charlie leaned toward her. "She's been telling this story every year since we were little."

"Ayuh, and she gets more dramatic every time," added Ted with a jerk of his chin. "Here's my favorite part where Alice reels her in."

From the shadows near the back of the stage, Alice stepped forward, hands on her hips, long white hair flowing like streaks of moonlight around her. "Honestly, Rosetta, you scare half the children to death with that story."

"Gaa!" exclaimed Gran, setting down her candle and relinquishing center stage to her sister. "It's good for them, like cider vinegar."

"Then I shall temper your sour story with a sweet ray of light," said Alice in her pleasantly lilted voice. With a flick of her hand, the dragon burst into amber witch fire. The entire clearing oohed and aahed as the embers turned into twinkling starry lights and floated above the crowded tables.

"Like the witchling's enchanted forest," said Alice, "Ware Woods is our special home. A place filled with joy and magical wonder. A sanctuary that connects us with the Mother below and the Father above, as well as our past, present, and future loved ones." She pointed at the earth and sky and then, with both hands, gestured to everyone in the clearing. Gran approached and clasped hands with Alice, and together they recited the last verse of the forest's blessing:

"For I am you and you are me,

We are the light, so mote it be."

By the end of the phrase, all five families had joined in and raised a glass to the full moon.

"Now on to the festivities!" proclaimed Gran.

A roar of applause filled the clearing. Children resumed racing around as a few of the Cahills and Atwells, including Kingsley on fiddle and Lily on flute, played lively Celtic music.

Sara pushed back her chair, mouth slack at the musicians. "I didn't know Lily—"

"Come on," said Moira, hooking arms with Sara and dragging her toward the rear of the clearing to the horse trough—cleaned and brought over from the Cahills' barn that afternoon and now full of water and apples. "Let's see if that big mouth of yours can beat mine at apple bobbing."

CHAPTER 19

Hoping she wouldn't make a fool of herself, Sara held back her hair, bent over the metal trough, and sought out the smallest apple. When she tried nimbly biting it, the apple rolled and dipped, evading her until she smelled Caleb's mossy green scent and her entire head was pushed into the freezing water.

Her teeth bit into the fruit, water flooding her nose and ears. With the apple stuck in her mouth, Sara reared up, spluttering and swiping her face. Caleb whooped with laughter and dashed off among the tables, dodging kids and an excited Bailey. Sara gave chase and, ignoring all pretense of being a poised High Witch, chucked the apple at his head.

Caleb caught it and took a bite, looking quite pleased with himself until Violet kinetically snatched the apple and pelted him with acorns. He held up his hands in surrender and snagged one of his younger siblings, placing the little costumed vampire on his broad shoulders and jogging back to the horse trough.

After taking turns holding the younger kids for apple bobbing and cleaning up the tables, Sara, Moira, Violet, and Caleb looped through the Council maple to the Cahill chestnut and moseyed out to the bonfire field.

Alice and Gran greeted them with a wave as they talked among the families, many of whom were cupping steaming mugs of apple cider. Within a few moments, Lily and the rest of the band arrived and resumed playing while Alice lit the bonfire. Amber flames licked up at the full moon while people danced around the towering blaze. Moira hooked arms with Sara once again, and they joined Caleb and Violet, moving to the festive beat of the music. Sara threw back her head, laughing and enjoying the merriment, even as her hand repeatedly strayed to the spell in her pocket.

By midnight, with the moon high overhead, most everyone had returned home—save for a handful of Cahills banking the last of the bonfire and Bill Walker, who was patrolling the wall. The shifter had been particularly eager to scare off any teens from the adjacent town who were either on the wrong side of a dare or foolish enough to think of approaching the Ware Woods wall on such a night.

Zipping her black jacket against the chill, Sara walked her father and Ted back to the brown house, where they exchanged fierce hugs. From their drawn expressions, Sara knew they shared her longing for absent loved ones—both living and deceased. When the screen door finally bounced shut behind them, Sara rocketed for the cemetery, eyes leaking tears from the cold sting in the air.

She landed with a reverent gentleness at her mother's etched headstone. Beside the candles and flowers she had placed that afternoon was a mug of tea and a silver framed portrait of her mother laughing in her flower studio, no doubt left by her father.

Samhain had been her mother's favorite time of year. A time, Sara now realized, her mother could be her true self—an earth witch. Every Halloween among normals, she had delighted in wearing striped leggings and a floppy witch's hat as she handed out homemade candies to the neighboring children. Ever since Sara was old enough to remember, she had helped her mother make the flower-shaped candies, carefully layering white and dark chocolate to resemble petals.

Sara fisted her hands. Samson would pay for causing her mother's death, for taking her away from her and Charlie and Ian—from everyone in Ware Woods. The air stirred with a hint of lilac. The candle flames snapped, burning brighter.

"Mom?"

A breeze kissed her cheek, then flitted away.

With a soft smile, Sara touched the side of her face and swept her gaze across the cemetery. It was a visual celebration of colorful flowers and hundreds of glowing candles and jack-o'-lanterns.

Captivated, Sara wandered through the flickering cemetery, visiting every grave and honoring the dead. At Winona's lichen-crusted headstone rested a photo of her pregnant with Ian. And at the graves of Thomas's two older brothers stood photos of them laughing and sparring—their dark hair and blue eyes so similar to Thomas's that her heart ached.

When she approached Naomi's cherry tree, Sara sank to her knees. "I'm sorry I left and didn't protect you. I promise I'll find your killer and destroy them." She blinked back tears and glimpsed a golden shimmer near the base of the tree. With a swish of her finger, Sara magically brushed off a smudge of soil and spotted the pyrite she buried two months ago.

She gnashed her teeth, feeling foolish she had thought a simple gemstone could help any of them. Ware Woods didn't need a shiny bauble; it needed a High Witch with enough magic to obliterate darkness. Magic she could only hope to master with the help of Magi from all three factions.

The cold, damp from the ground seeped through her jeans as she sat cross-legged and pulled out the spell paper. Icy wind blew through the cemetery and rustled the oak's remaining brown leaves. An owl hooted overhead, and from across the nearby clearing, lake water shone silver under the full moon. With a shaky breath, she unfolded the paper and smoothed the folds with her four-fingered hand.

The page was blank.

Come on. I'm definitely in the land of the dead, and it is freezing cold out here.

She hunched into her jacket and contemplated whishing a quilt from the treehouse. Instead, she summoned her energy to heat her frozen marrow and wrap around her—the cozy white flames identical to the hundreds of candles twinkling throughout the cemetery. Sara straightened, her gaze panning the lights.

How could I forget!? The Book said to cast a circle.

Raising her hands above her head, she whished dozens of candles into the air, arranged them into a wide circle around her and the cemetery, and gently set them down.

The lilac-scented breeze returned, softly brushing back her hair. *"Now, invoke the four Elements,"* said her mother's feathery voice.

Sara startled, unsure if her mother's spirit truly spoke to her or if she imagined it. "I don't know how," she whispered.

"Yes, you do. You've known since you were old enough to follow me into the garden. Remember twirling among the flowers, laughing and singing?"

Of course Sara remembered. She would spin and shout their simple song until she grew dizzy, tumbling to the petal-strewn path in a fit of giggles. Smiling at the memory, Sara chanted:

"Earth below me,
Water beside me,
Air above me,
Fire within me."

Scripted ink immediately materialized on the paper. Sara huffed, awed relief hanging like a specter before her. Eyes wide, she soaked up every word, memorizing the spell before the ink began to fade. And when the page was blank once again, she recited:

"Of earth and stars and true magic made,
Sisters and brothers lend me your aid.
Knowledge I seek from one old and divine,
A vampire with cunning greater than mine.

Strength I beseech from one great and their all,
A shifter with power to guard my wall.
Expertise I ask from one of my kind,
A witch with mastery for me to find.
In the name of the Mother, I call you to me.
In the name of the Father, so mote it be."

From beneath her many layers, the bloodstone at her chest pulsated. The cemetery trembled. Grave site flowers swayed, photographs rattled, candles guttered, and the oak groaned as a power from deep within the ground welled up toward the surface. Sara slapped her hands on the cool, dewy grass to steady herself, staring at the quaking cemetery and half expecting all three Magi to pop out of the earth. With a spark of magic, her hands stuck to the ground, fingers digging into the soil as if she were a lodestone drawn to a force beneath her. The trembling stopped, and Sara stiffened. Glowing orbs of different colors and sizes flowed among the graves while whispers lifted her hair and tickled her ears. The perimeter of the circle swelled, earth and candles rising a hand's length above the rest of the ground. With a sonic whoosh, the raised circle fell and rippled inward—directly toward Sara.

She squeezed her eyes shut, bracing for impact as a surge of energy slammed through her and up into the night sky. Her back arched, hair whipping about, mouth open at the sheer magnitude of power rushing through her and skittering along her bones.

Though Sara had felt the forest's energy before, this was something profoundly more. Orbs swirled around her, and she felt her mother's warm embrace—heard her murmur Sara's name. Before Sara could thank her, Naomi's sweet laughter rang out, followed by dozens of well-wishing voices and smiling gossamer spirits from old women to young boys, even a pair of fair-haired twins. They zipped around Sara, pausing once when the bloodstone shone through her layers, casting them in a reddish glow, before they disappeared with a satisfied sigh.

Magic crackled around her. In one final charge, it shot away from her, extinguishing the candle circle and vanishing into the forest. The ground released her hands, and she fell back, her head nearly smacking the ground before a gust of wind pushed her upright. The spell paper in her lap disintegrated, invisible flames eating its edges until it too disappeared into the night. Sara heaved a breath, her heart pounding from the flush of energy and blessings of the deceased.

Father above, the spell she'd cast felt far more powerful than the one Naomi performed to break Makwa's curse. Hope and fear burned inside Sara.

Either I just invoked our salvation . . . or my doom. For no matter what happened, if it came to it—she would sacrifice herself to save them all.

Still trembling from the heady rush of the spell, Sara levitated to the treehouse, barely making it to her room before collapsing face first onto her bed.

"SARA."

A sudden shout in her head ripped through a dreamy scene of a waterfall and cherry blossoms.

"Sara!" called her father's voice again. *"Wake up. It's late afternoon and there's . . . something at the wall you need to see. NOW."*

"Sara Lochton!" This time it was Gran's voice.

"Yeesh. Alright. Alright. I'm coming," Sara projected back to them, dragging herself out of bed and pulling on fresh clothes. She squinted at the sunlight filling her room, unable to recall the last time she had slept so late, and remembered the Samhain magic that had rushed through her. No way had the spell worked that fast. Besides, they all could wait an apple-peeling minute while she attended to her needs in the cottage bathroom and grabbed a thermos of sap to settle the queasiness in her stomach. Too many

of Caleb's caramel-drizzled desserts last night. Sara's sweet tooth was becoming almost as bad as Gran's. Almost.

To appease her father and grandmother, she scrapped the idea of walking over to the Lochton homes and instead rose above the trees and headed in their direction. As she passed the Lochton pine and spotted the stone-wall barrier, she hesitated.

Parked on the old road before the blue house was an SUV limousine. Inside the wall stood her father, Ted, Gran, and every Walker and Sullivan in the forest.

Her heart skipped a beat. Maybe Thomas and Matthew had come home for a visit. But this vehicle was ostentatious, definitely not the forest's unassuming style and definitely not Thomas's black truck.

Flying closer, she *saw* the unease rippling from her forest family like heat waves radiating from a pyre. Her flash of elation at possibly seeing Thomas was snuffed out by sickening dread. If anything had happened to them . . .

She dropped onto the ground between her father and grandmother.

"It's about time," hissed Gran. "And no, this doesn't concern Thomas. In fact, he and Matthew are safest being far from here."

Her father tapped his temple and said, "I told the Atwells to stay on the island."

"Good," replied Gran.

Sara looked back and forth between them. "What the Hells is going on?" She scrunched her nose at an odd, musty scent in the air.

"Something wicked," whispered Gran, taking a step back from the wall and tugging Sara with her.

The rear door of the limo opened, and Sara felt her soul try to leave her body as indeed something *very* wicked slipped from the vehicle and faced Ware Woods.

CHAPTER 20

Sara had no words of comfort to offer her family as they sucked in a collective breath, waiting for the visitor to do something—anything to relieve the pressure holding them stock-still like terrified deer. Gone was her swagger, replaced by the alarming instinct to run. This was no Taker or dark witch; here was something she had never even considered to walk the earth.

Beautiful death incarnate.

The visitor's face rivaled classical paintings of angels, neither male nor female but captivatingly transcendent. Golden hair flowed past their slender shoulders, the softness offset by the sinewy muscles evident through their worn black leather pants and on their corded arms, where the sleeves of a linen shirt had been casually pushed up.

Though they appeared human, the deadly calm and centuries-old awareness emanating from them was undeniably ancient magic. If not for the blessed wall, Sara had no doubt they could tear apart the forest without getting a speck of dirt—or blood—on their polished appearance.

The striking visitor dragged their stony gaze from one person to the next, eliciting a growl when they hesitated on Bill and a snap of kinetic energy when they paused on Kane. And when their assessment swept over Sara, the bloodstone beneath her jacket released

140

a tingling beat of power. Gran tightened her grip on Sara's arm, and the visitor stopped with their eyes set on the older woman.

"This is a cluster. Which one of you is the Magus?" Even their voice defied logic—being at once smooth and abrasive like a notched blade.

No one answered.

Sara was both dumbfounded by the visitor's presence and unaccustomed to being called a Magus. And it seemed no one else wanted to reveal her.

The angel of death didn't move—didn't alter their almost-bored demeanor. "You disturbed my peace and pulled me across the seas with your insolence. The least you could do is give me a proper greeting."

Charlie and Gran slowly turned their heads to Sara. *You summoned this creature?* Gran shouted in her mind.

Sara flinched, and the deadly angel pinned her with ice-gray eyes.

Crap.

"You?" they said, and the faintest of smiles drew up one corner of their perfect lips. "You're a mere child."

The comment sparked Sara's temper, and before she could clamp a hand over her smart mouth, she shot back, "I could say the same of you. What are you, barely eighteen?"

Charlie and Ted choked. Gran looked liable to flay her alive if the angel didn't do it first.

They grunted and held their stare. "I was, once. Over a thousand years ago."

Sara dropped the thermos of sap she had been clutching, her hands suddenly as useless as her common sense.

The angel offered a sliver of a half-smile, revealing an upper fang.

Vampire. The back of Sara's neck prickled.

They smoothly motioned to themselves and the wall. "I'm here. *Invite me in.* Then we'll talk like civilized monsters, and I'll decide if I care to assist you with whatever insane campaign of murder you're planning."

Gran yanked Sara aside. *"Why in all Hells did you summon an Elder Vampire?"*

"We need help to deal with Samson and face the Shadow Mother." Sara stole a glance at the vampire, surprised and slightly encouraged to note a touch of amusement on their perfect face. *"They can't be that bad if the Book gave me the summoning spell."*

With a shake of her head, Gran projected, *"Elder Vampires kill anything and everything, especially vampires they deem lesser. If you invite this monster in, they will likely kill the vampires who hide in our forest—our family."*

Sara's legs threatened to buckle. *"I didn't know this. I don't even know who our vampires are, and I'm High Witch. Why doesn't anyone ever tell me anything?"*

"Because I didn't think you'd do something this drastic."

Sara threw her hands into the air and kicked the thermos. It hit the stone wall with a dull clang. Somewhere behind her, Trouble squawked and flapped away.

"Firecracker," her father mentally nudged in the following silence.

Sara held her gaze on the metal container, mind pinging with an absurdly simple answer to her vampiric pickle. She shot her father and grandmother a triumphant smile.

"I know how to fix this." She grabbed the thermos, hopped over the wall, and faced the angel of death.

As one, everyone inside the wall let out a gasp and took a step back.

If the vampire was dark, they would surely attack Sara. And if so, she wanted it to happen outside the wall, where no one else would get hurt. She may have held her breath for a few heartbeats as they stared at one another. The vampire didn't move. They appeared every bit a veritable statue.

Alrighty, then. They passed the first test.

Sara cocked her head. "I summoned you for knowledge on how to handle a particular problem. Thank you for coming." *And so quickly, from overseas . . .* No matter. She'd ponder their rapid travel another time.

Now for the second part of the test.

"I'll invite you in, but first you must promise not to kill anyone inside this sacred forest, and you must drink this to ensure your intentions are pure." She spun off the cap and held out the thermos.

The vampire accepted the container, a slight clink resounding at the handoff, as if they wore a metal ring. They peered inside, sniffed, and then drank the entire thermos, sap dribbling down their chin. "I won't kill anyone inside your forest," they droned and thrust back the container.

Instead of keeling over dead, the vampire rapped twice on the vehicle's window, and a woman emerged from the driver's side. Her posture was stiff, her eyes downcast. "This is my confidant, Wren," they explained, meeting the woman at the rear of the limo and, with her help, removing two body-sized trunks. "I figured I would be staying a while and packed accordingly."

Presumptuous. Sara frowned at the trunks.

The vampire whispered to Wren, their lips grazing her neck like a lover, then watched intently as the woman got back into the vehicle and drove away. They slowly slid their gaze to Sara and waited.

"Oh, um, who are you? I mean, what's your name, so I can invite you in?" Sara cringed at her bumbling.

In a distinctly arrogant tone, the vampire replied, "I'm not a who, but a what. And the name is Lethal." They approached the stone wall and held out their alabaster hands, no doubt feeling the forest's vibrating, invisible shield.

Sara jerked back at the stone-cold promise in their voice. Perhaps she had bitten off more than she could chew with this summoning spell.

On the other side of the wall, Gran pursed her lips and gave Sara a quick nod. Sara glanced at her father, Bill, and Kane. Though they also gave their approval, all three quivered with tension, ready to release their power at the slightest provocation.

Sara shifted her weight to the balls of her feet, physically preparing while coiling her own power in case this went badly. "As High Witch of Ware Woods, I, Sara Lochton, invite you, Lethal, into our sacred forest." She hoped her words were formal enough to appease the protective barrier.

The vampire leapt over the wall, their sensuous top lip curling into a deadly four-fanged smile—two upper teeth of pinpoint murder on each side.

Shit.

CHAPTER 21

LETHAL LANDED INSIDE Ware Woods and audibly inhaled, head tilted back as if tasting the entire forest at once. Their gaze again took in every present member, and instead of bored disinterest, astonishment glowed from their angelic face. "*Strabilianti,*" they whispered.

Bill growled again, edging himself before Moira and his wife, Shannon. Similarly, Kane stepped in front of Violet and Abby, palms open and sizzling with energy.

Lethal pivoted, their movement as fluid as a silk snake, and regarded the wall with a keen eye. "If this barrier ever breaks, it will be like a bomb detonating."

"Oh?" asked Charlie in his inquisitive professor tone. "And why is that?"

"Even for a sacred site, this forest has incredible energy. You all do," they added with a lazy gesture before stopping to point at Sara. "Let's talk someplace more hospitable than a sodden lawn, shall we?" Their voice held a pinch of disdain.

Sara bit back her scowl. Either Lethal was implying the families were backward for not recognizing the forest's power or they were insulting the Lochton homestead. Perhaps both. Arrogant vampire. The fact that they casually left their trunks in the old road, expecting someone else to fetch them, didn't escape her either.

She squinted at Lethal. The meeting space in the basement of the nearby brown house was indeed damp, and no way would she invite them into the blue house, where they might sense the grimoire. The Main House would be full of Cahills, making too many casualties should something go bloody wrong. Sara needed to keep this vampire very close to her. Which left one location.

"We'll meet at my place," said Sara, hoping she sounded like a Magus, and turned to the present families. "I want heads of households present as well. Bill, Kane, Charlie." She nodded at them as she said their names and then glanced at her grandmother. "You too. 'Cause I know you won't stay away *and* because I need your blunt input. And bring Uncle Larry with you." Sara did not mention Orsen Atwell. Though Lethal downed the sap and never flinched, she still didn't trust them and had no idea who was or wasn't a vampire among the Atwells.

"Give me an hour to escort Lethal and get them settled. Then, meet us in the conference room on the second level. The tree will show you the way," said Sara, whishing Lethal's trunks into the air. With a wince at the trunks' unexpected heaviness, she marched for a path yawning open at the rear of the yard.

Kane huffed. "You have a full-sized conference room in your treehouse?" he called after her.

"Yes, and apparently a vampire roommate."

Thomas will not be pleased.

Lethal easily fell into step beside her, their footsteps silent on the leaf-speckled forest path. Their gray gaze widened as trees bowed out of their way and pulled back their branches to accommodate the enormous trunks trailing in the air.

"Please tell me there are no bodies in there." Sara jerked her chin toward the baggage.

Lethal slipped their hands into their pockets. "Not exactly."

Mother below, what kind of answer is—

The nape of Sara's neck prickled again. *How could I be so stupid?*

She pressed a finger to the center of her forehead and, in a voice sounding much higher than she intended, said, "As your host, I must ask: what do you prefer to . . . eat?"

The vampire's face twitched with enjoyment at her obvious apprehension. "I think you know," they said, smooth as glass.

Sara nearly dropped the trunks on their heads.

They grunted what Sara could only imagine was a gruff attempt at a laugh. "I brought some supplies. That one," they said, pointing to the trunk with buckled leather bands, "needs to be refrigerated. And since I swore an oath not to kill within your forest, I will need to hunt outside the wall."

The blood drained from her face, and Sara shook her head to clear a sudden lightheadedness. She cautiously asked, "How much hunting of the outside population are you suggesting?"

"Ten percent."

"Wha—No! Five percent at most, and only a mercy killing of the old and sick animals."

"I'll accept five percent, but it won't be the animals you're thinking of."

Sara halted. *Normals.*

Ian told her the vampires in Ware Woods only killed an occasional animal. But Lethal . . . fed exclusively on normals. And at over a thousand years old, Lethal must have killed scores of populations.

"To not complicate matters for you, I won't drain them completely. They'll survive, albeit with a nasty hangover. But . . . if they've been naughty"—Lethal's eyes glazed over—"I'll take every last drop. You're welcome." They angled their head toward Sara, hair falling forward in a golden curtain. "By the way, I would have settled with three percent." They completely ignored her death stare.

She was beginning to hate that pretty face.

"If you summoned me for knowledge, here's your first lesson: never trust a vampire." They shot her a cunning closed-lip smile and stalked ahead—right into the cemetery.

Great. Being High Witch was going along smashingly. Her spell for help in dealing with Samson and the Shadow Mother had led her to invite a viper into her garden.

Instead of hosting the vampire for even a night, perhaps they could have one epic meeting today, glean all the information Lethal knew about dark witches, and then send them back to whatever hellish coffin-filled site they came from.

Sara studied the entrancing vampire as they hesitated among the colorfully decorated graves. Had she not already witnessed Lethal's arrogance, she would have considered their demeanor to be appreciative of the offerings and photographs. With a grumble, she whished the heftier trunk to the main deck of the treehouse and whished the leather-banded trunk behind her as she charged into the cottage.

When Sara dropped the trunk before the fridge, it hit the stone floor with an ominous whomp and faint sloshing. She nervously glanced through the cottage windows and sighed at spotting Lethal wandering the cemetery.

Sara returned her attention back to the trunk. *Let's see what you're hiding in here.* With a flick of her wrist, she tore off the bands and threw back the lid.

What looked to be two dozen bottles of high-end wine lay nestled in cool foam inserts. She whished a crimson bottle into a stream of sunshine filtering through the overhead skylight. Its contents swirled with thick decadence, darkening the bottle's sides. Sara gagged.

Steeling her stomach, she quickly whished all the bottles into the fridge, which had been bare save for a few leftovers from the sleepover. With a grimace, she made a mental note to obtain a new, untainted fridge as soon as this visit came to an end.

After squeezing the empty trunk behind the couch, Sara rushed from the cottage and intercepted Lethal as they approached the cemetery gate. The vampire's attention was pinned on the lake and the

Atwell island like an apex predator locking in on prey. Her heart skipped a beat. Despite her anxiety over what Lethal might do to the Ware Woods vampires and her rattling desire to grill Lethal about the Shadow Mother, she calmly redirected them to the treehouse.

Sara lingered behind Lethal, watching them spiral up the wraparound stairs. Here was test number three. If the oak didn't approve of the vampire, Sara would dump their skinny arse and their crimson bottles outside the wall.

The oak groaned, low and mournful, as Lethal ran a delicate pale hand along its trunk. They paused and slid Sara a seductive expression. "Do all your trees like to be stroked?"

Traitorous tree and cocky vampire. She frowned at them both. "No, and this one shouldn't be so easily pleased," she admonished as they strode into the main room. The tree shook itself, gently clattering Lethal's remaining trunk on the deck floorboards.

When a thin branch snaked down from the ceiling, Lethal stiffened. It caressed their long flaxen hair, then pointed up the original staircase. "May I?" they asked politely, gesturing toward the narrow stairwell.

Sara hesitated. Two rooms lay in that direction, and neither of them had a conference table. "Uh, of course," she said, closely following them. *I'm just as curious as you are.* Perhaps the tree created a new room—with vampire restraints.

They glided up the stairs and into the stately room with scrolled bedposts and quilt the same cool-gray color as Lethal's deadly stare. "This will do," they said, eyes closing and chest expanding with a deep inhale. "It smells like . . . lilies." Their gaze snapped open and flicked toward the open, private deck and the island beyond.

Shit.

"Does it? Because all I can smell is you." Sara almost sighed out loud when Lethal took the bait and turned their intense focus to her.

"And what do I smell like? A god?"

Pfft! Hardly. The scent had teased her on their entire walk to the treehouse until she had figured it out. It was the musty, rich fragrance of frankincense—the signature scent of a church . . . and funerals.

"Death," she said.

They shrugged. "True. Though I'm surprised you can smell anything besides your mate. Where is he, by the way? I've never known a bonded pair to be separated."

Sara froze. Maybe she'd left out one of Thomas's shirts. But how could Lethal possibly know they were bonded?

Definite amusement shone on their flawless face. "Lesson two: vampires have exceptionally keen senses. So. Where. Is. He?"

"He's at school."

"And why is he there and not here with you?" An innocent question, as if Lethal was just as curious to learn about her.

Sara cleared her throat. Since Thomas was safe at university, she saw no harm in sharing this information. "He's studying to be an attorney. His family protects the forest from normal-derived environmental threats."

A crease appeared between the vampire's icy eyes. "You don't *make* normals do this for you? Vampires and shifters use compulsion, and witches normally use spells or whatever other witchy things you do, like summoning me here. Why wouldn't you use your magic?"

Really? So this was why Lethal's confidant seemed robotic. She was being compelled. Mother below. Did all other magicals force their will on normals?

Her horror must have shown on her face, or Lethal simply smelled it, for they said in a low, dangerous voice, "Magicals are above normals. Do not ever show them grace or pity, for they do not deserve it." They brushed past her, the brief contact like slamming into a granite column, and flowed down the stairwell. "The hour is up, and your *family* is here," they gritted out.

CHAPTER 22

IN TRUE TREEHOUSE fashion, the conference room was much larger than logically possible. Its grandiose round table and honey-oak chairs easily accommodated all eight of them. Contrary to the inviting space and pleasant breeze drifting in through expansive window openings, a stifling, quarrelsome pressure filled the room. Indeed, they hadn't even all sat down before Gran ripped into Sara.

"Let's start this discussion with my granddaughter explaining why she summoned a vampire to our *once* safe and protected forest."

Sara winced. "First of all, the summoning spell came from a *very* trusted source. And second, I've exhausted all of my forest resources and we need someone with knowledge on how to defeat Samson and the Shadow Mother."

Lethal grunted. "I've never heard of a Samson, but you can't be serious about the Shadow Mother. How do you even know of her existence?" They leaned forward, cutting a sharp stare at Sara. The furrow between their brows was not encouraging.

Shame heated her cheeks as she scraped an imaginary speck of dirt from her jeans. "Samson said I upset the balance between light and dark magic when I came into power and killed a dark witch. According to him, the Shadow Mother is pissed and plans to come on Winter Solstice and wipe out all the magicals and normals in this region." Sara left out the cryptic information provided by the Book. If Lethal was truly knowledgeable, they would already know the extreme danger associated with the Shadow Mother.

The vampire sat back and steepled their bone-white fingers. "Only significant swings in the balance attract the Shadow Mother's attention. If she is coming—and I *highly* doubt this—there must be another reason. Whoever this Samson is, they may be manipulating you."

"Samson is a sick bastard, and I'm sure he's playing us, but he has my brother and another witch hostage. So," Sara added with an exasperated sigh, "I made a blood bargain to help him if he cured Ian and released him and Dorcas once we faced the Shadow Mother."

Lethal blinked. Slowly. "You made a *blood* bargain with a witch you hate?"

Gran snorted, and Sara shot her a glare. "I'll do anything to help my brother and keep Ware Woods safe."

"Obviously," said Lethal. "I take it Ian is your brother. What's wrong with him?" Their calm demeanor reminded Sara of a condescending school counselor.

In a frustrated rush, Sara said, "Samson tried to kill him once, and there's a splinter of ice in his heart. But *supposedly* Samson can't cure him, and Ian has chosen to stay with him. For now. And did I mention, the bastard also ate my finger!" She held up her hand, heaving to catch her breath.

Lethal's stony façade never cracked. "And here I thought you had a broomstick mishap."

"This isn't funny," Sara fumed. "One of our witches was recently murdered outside the wall. I thought it was Samson, but it could have been the Shadow Mother. This is why I was desperate enough to summon help—because I don't know what to do." There. She said it. Admitted to being a clueless High Witch.

No one said a word.

The tree gently rustled its brittle fall leaves, and in the distance, a blue jay squawked.

"I see," said Lethal, breaking the silence. "I would like to inspect the scene of the murder, and I very much want to meet Samson. He seems to be a delightful devil."

Thank the Mother and the Father. The vampire *wanted* to help her. She'd worry why later.

Sara glanced at the darkening forest, the candles in the center of the table already flickering with her magic. "Naomi was murdered on the far shore. I'll take you tomorrow morning. As for Samson, I have no idea where he is. He comes when he wants."

"Fair enough," agreed Lethal. "We'll wait for him."

Sara slumped in her chair, relieved at having their assistance and troubled at having to host a vampire until Samson deigned to show up.

Charlie cleared his throat. "What do you know of the Global Council? We've been trying to reach them but have yet to make contact."

At this, the vampire conceded a tight-lipped smile. "We know. I'm from the Council."

Though Charlie huffed a laugh, his aura flashed a concerned shade of purple with green splotches.

"I was already on my way here when your witchery"—Lethal sent an accusing glance at Sara—"pulled at me and hastened my trip. We were aware of some unusual ripples in the magical balance and the possibility of a dragon in the area. Plus, until recently, your sacred site hasn't had a Magus leave the boundary for a very long time. Naturally, we were curious."

Seriously. They were already on their way here. *And* they had been watching Ware Woods and somehow knew about the dragon she saw at the beach. As much as she wanted to yell at Lethal for giving *her* a hard time for the summoning, she clenched her jaw.

"We've had no dragon," said Gran, shaking her head as if even the idea of one was absurd.

Sara shrank in her seat.

"Perhaps not," said Lethal. "However, there's no denying Ware Woods has remained unheeded for centuries. We have known this site to be *different . . .*" Their lip curled, revealing sharp white fangs. "As the only site with a mix of magical factions, you've been left alone like an injured animal. But you have deceived us. Instead of an abomination, this site is a vortex of powerful energy, as though the Mother herself sleeps below our feet." The vampire's eyes glittered in the candlelight.

Sara wobbled; the rest of them didn't move a hair. While she knew Ware Woods was special, she had nothing to compare it to. Unlike Lethal, who was ancient and from the Global Council and must know many sites.

Lethal shifted their gaze to Sara. "My advice is to remain hidden and keep this a secret. Too much power exists here. It will make other magicals nervous, envious, and reckless with want. It's how wars are started."

Sara gripped the edges of her chair. Considering their ancient age, Lethal had no doubt seen and participated in many wars. Her heart raced with a whole new level of anxiety. As if being High Witch wasn't enough pressure, she was High Witch of an extremely powerful site that the whole magical world might covet. There was the distinct possibility she might faint. She should have eaten something today.

"I will help you with whatever petty regional squabble you have with Samson and the rogue magical who killed your witch. Then I will slip away, effectively concluding the Council's inquiry and taking your secret with me."

"Just like that?" Uncle Larry's voice boomed from across the table.

The vampire shrugged. "More or less."

"Deal," said Gran. And before anyone could object, she rose from the table and declared, "I agree with Sara. This meeting is adjourned."

Sara jolted in her seat.

As Gran shoved Bill and Uncle Larry toward the stairs, she projected into Sara's mind, *"You're not the only one famished at this table. And if what they say is true, the sooner we can be rid of them, the better."*

Sara nodded at her grandmother as Kane rushed to her side.

"I can stay or send Violet to be with you tonight," he offered, fatherly concern in his blue eyes. Mother, how she missed Thomas's brilliant blues.

She dropped her gaze and waved him off. "I'll be fine. Thanks all the same."

Kane hesitated before shooting a warning glare at Lethal and flying out the window opening.

"Firecracker," projected her father. *"Contact me if you need anything."* He gave Sara a quick hug before Gran grabbed his arm and ushered him down the stairs.

"Make sure you eat the rest of the leftovers. And don't let that hungry vampire out of your sight," Gran ordered, their footsteps receding.

"Yeah, yeah," said Sara. *I wasn't planning on it.*

When the treehouse was silent once more, Lethal grunted. "How endearing. They *care* about you."

Sara stilled. Of all the wild things they had just discussed, this is what they commented on? And because a thousand years was a long time and because she couldn't stop herself, she asked, "Didn't anyone ever care about you?"

The flicker of pain in their rigid countenance said volumes.

"No. They only cared about what I could do for them. Like you. You only want my knowledge."

Sara reared back as if struck. While she did want their knowledge, she wasn't a cold-hearted monster intent on sucking them dry. She scowled at the irony. "I don't even know you. Besides, what I want right now—in this moment—is dinner. Come on, I'm sure you could use a glass of *wine*." She stormed down the stairs, flew to the cottage, and yanked open the fridge. After plunking a perverse bottle on one end of the kitchen island, she stood at the other end and annihilated her cold leftovers.

Sara's ears perked at the far-off yip-howl of coyotes filtering in through the open cottage door. No footsteps. And the vampire's distinct frankincense scent remained in the treehouse. She glanced at the far side of the kitchen island and choked on her last bite.

The bottle was gone.

Can vampires whish? She hastily rinsed her dishes, extinguished the lights in the cottage, and flew to the treehouse.

There they were, sitting in a chair on their private deck, drinking directly from the bottle. Sara hovered in the crisp night air, not daring to invade Lethal's space by setting foot on the deck.

"How did you do that?" she asked, pointing at the bottle. "Can you whish?" Father above, she hoped not.

They pulled their eyes from the island and met her gaze. "A tell for a tell?" they suggested, and took a swig from the bottle.

Sara put her hands on her hips. "Gaa. Fine."

"I can move very quickly and silently, and I can mask my scent."

Wonderful. But I'll still be up all night listening, anyway.

Lethal gestured at the open door and the warm, glowing treehouse behind them. "How do you do this?"

Sara softened her expression at their genuine curiosity and beheld the oak with affection. After a moment of consideration, she explained, "The tree is its own sentient being, but my magic heats the interior and lights the candles."

"You," said the vampire, shaking the bottle at her, "are most unique."

That sounded like a compliment. "Are you drunk?"

"Hardly." They returned their intense gaze to the lake. "I know you're hiding vampires on your island, and I am going there tomorrow. Before any murder scene investigation."

Sara folded her arms. *Crap.* Yet the reality that Lethal hadn't already crept off and visited the island, coupled with the oath they'd sworn, had her chewing her lip. If the vampire was intent on going, she'd rather it be under her watch and with very strict rules.

She relented. "Fine. I'll see you in the morning. Pleasant dreams or whatever it is you do." Hopefully not slink off and wipe out five percent of the outer forest in one night.

She flew to her adjacent room, angling herself through her window opening when she heard Lethal's voice drift through the tree: "I rarely sleep."

That makes two of us.

CHAPTER 23

Despite her best effort to maintain a vampire vigil all night, Sara ripped awake at the sound of splashing and the light of dawn filling the treehouse. Throwing back the covers and stumbling to the window opening, she spotted the very pale backside of Lethal, golden hair flowing to the middle of their back as they stalked into the lake.

Shit.

Sara threw on some clothes, not bothering to lace her boots, and flew to the water's edge. "You don't have to *swim* to the island. Mother below! The water must be freezing! Get out. We'll take the boat."

"Cold doesn't bother vampires. I wanted to feel the lake. It has . . . a sad energy. And I intentionally splashed to wake you up. You've been asleep for hours, and I was growing impatient." Lethal stopped, waist deep in the water, and turned toward her.

Sara gasped, her gaze fixed on the vampire's chest. Slashed across the front of their upper torso was a vicious, jagged scar surrounded by numerous smaller marks. Someone—or something—had once stabbed them multiple times and cut open their chest as if intent on taking their very soul.

Lethal glanced down at themself in a curious manner before slowly raising their gaze to Sara's. "This is why I despise normals.

They did this to my mortal body. Abused me for years, using me for their sadistic pleasures, and then blamed their perversions on me and attempted to brand the devil from me." Lethal's tone was detached, either from time or pain—or perhaps both. They twisted their shoulders and swiped their hair to the side, revealing scores of black crosses branded onto their back.

A hot mix of shock and anger gripped Sara. How could anyone do such atrocities? She clenched her fists, palms burning, and forcefully stilled the energy thrashing inside her.

Lethal released their hair and squared their shoulders at Sara. "They mutilated me until I died. I keep the scars to remember all that I was, all that was done to me, and all that I now am." They flashed their fangs.

Sara's scalp prickled a warning. If Lethal was trying to intimidate her—to test her mettle as High Witch—she couldn't show any fear. Fighting the instinct to run, she held her ground and stared at the vampire's perfect face, their pale, powerful arms corded with muscle, their narrow shoulders, and their lacerated chest. Lake water dripped down their defined abs and trim waist.

Lethal took a step toward her, and she immediately averted her gaze. Eyeing the vampire's discarded shirt, leather pants, and boots on a nearby Adirondack chair, Sara felt her cheeks redden. With a hasty flick of her hand, she summoned a towel from the cottage and practically threw it at them.

She stuttered, "So, uh, you were a normal once? How did you become an immortal vampire?" While witches and shifters lived for hundreds of years, they didn't live for a thousand. Hells, if vampires lived forever, no wonder no one cared for them. They'd be hardened by time, crotchety and arrogant like this one, and think themselves gods above normals as well as witches and shifters. And if Lethal couldn't be killed, her best bet would be to chain them to the bottom of the lake if they broke their oath and unwisely decided to stir trouble in Ware Woods.

Lethal splashed out of the water, undoubtedly making noise for her to track their movement. From the corner of her eye, she saw the towel drop and leather pants being pulled over smooth, toned legs.

"Death granted me vengeance and brought me back to life," said Lethal, voice quiet with a clipped edge.

Sara glanced up as they grabbed their shirt and slipped it on.

"I'm not immortal, and I'm not your typical vampire. I was made by Death, not turned. Most vampires are created when an Elder bites them and then offers their blood. If they accept the offer, they are turned into a vampire who is blood-bound to their Elder sire. If their Elder dies, they die too."

Not immortal—thank the Mother. And not an Elder as summoned by the spell, but something just as powerful—if not more. The result of performing the spell on Samhain when Death was listening. Sara swallowed hard at the thought of Lethal creating a legion of super vampires. She shifted, partially sinking into the sandy lakeshore, and watched them as they eased onto the Adirondack chair and donned their boots. "Have you turned anyone?"

"No," said Lethal, immediately. "Being turned is excruciating and comes at a high price. The mere existence afterward is a fresh hell I don't wish on anyone."

Aha. Their statement suggested a sliver of benevolence existed somewhere deep inside their stony presence. Sara also hoped it meant there were no other vampires like Lethal. This was a lot to unpack, and yet she needed to know so much more, especially if they were to visit the island. "Do vampires kill other vampires?" Feigning nonchalance, she bent down and tied her boots.

"Yes."

Another quick answer, this one ratcheting Sara's heart rate as she stood and stepped in front of them, blocking their view of the recessed island.

Lethal continued, "Vampires are territorial. We are driven by ego and an instinct to protect our food supply. Elders are the original few vampires created by the Mother. Like High Witches and Alpha Shifters, Elder Vampires protect sacred sites, but unlike the other factions, there are only a dozen Elders, each with a small colony of subordinates. Any rogue vampire seen outside of their sacred site is immediately killed by an Elder . . . or by me." The barest hint of a smile graced their angelic face as they dragged their icy eyes to meet Sara's burning glare.

She let energy flicker in her palms. Lethal didn't falter in the slightest. "You swore an oath not to kill anyone in Ware Woods," she said, voice low, slowly enunciating her reminder.

"True." The shadowy smile remained as they stood, barely taller than Sara and somehow infinitely grander.

She narrowed her eyes at them. Though Lethal was likely guilty of killing countless normals during their lifetime, they were somehow pure of heart—otherwise the sap would have killed them. "You *are* a light magical . . . aren't you?"

"I'm neither light nor dark. I just am."

Wonderful. Pompous ass is what you are. "We will *briefly* stop at the island on our way to Naomi's murder scene on the far shore." With a flick of her finger, she whished the discarded towel from the sandy shore and draped it across the back of the chair, then strode for the weathered rowboat with the vampire at her heels.

While Lethal sat in wide-eyed astonishment at the self-moving boat, Sara projected their imminent arrival to Lily, *"We're coming. They promised not to hurt anyone, but be ready."* She added, *"And please have breakfast available for me. If they cause trouble and I have to chain them to the bottom of the lake, I'll definitely be starving."*

Lily's response came as a thumbs-up-shaped cloud over the island.

When they neared the dock at the top of the island's retaining wall, Lethal stretched their upper lip in a half-smile, revealing the tip of a fang.

The bloodstone at Sara's chest thumped a warning. She lunged, but the vampire's cool, hard skin slipped from her fingertips as they disappeared down into the island.

All Hells, they could move extremely fast! Sara rocketed into the chalky morning sky and rushed for the Atwell house—for the Death Vampire now pacing before a dome of ice protecting the Atwells in their front courtyard.

Sara hoped the spell she'd cast on Samhain would still deliver experience and power, because she was about to obliterate the knowledge she needed to handle Samson and stand against the Shadow Mother. With a roar, she launched a comet of white-hot energy at Lethal's golden head. But before it struck true, Lily burst through the ice dome and rammed into the vampire, sending them both tumbling to the pebbled courtyard. Sara's energy screamed past them, searing Lethal's hair and detonating a nearby weeping willow.

Sara slammed into the ground beside them. Her violent impact rocked the courtyard and shattered the ice dome. "Lily!" She hauled up her friend, but Lethal was faster, clamping on to Lily's arm and rising with her.

Tugged between them, Lily shouted, "Stop!" She released a blast of wind that blew back Sara's hair and what was left of Lethal's.

Sara immediately let go, and to her utter shock, so did Lethal.

Lily straightened her jacket and raised her chin. "No fighting," she ordered them, staring down Lethal's hungry gaze.

Kingsley, the oldest of the Atwells, and—with Dorcas gone— the oldest in all of Ware Woods, laughed, his mirth echoing across the courtyard. "You tell them, Lily," he said, and promptly walked off into the Atwells' ranch-style home.

Lethal grunted and raked their piercing focus across the present Atwell family, nostrils flaring at Elizabeth Atwell—Lily's mother— and Lily's siblings: James, Johnny, and Ophelia. When the children smiled widely and waved, Lethal took a step back. Sara would have paid money for a photo of the angel of Death's perplexed expression. They grunted again and turned their attention to Elizabeth's mother, Claire, and her uncle, Ben, standing stiffly at the edge of the group. "You two have some explaining to do."

Sara gaped. Claire and Ben were the vampires?

Claire stepped forward, dipping her head toward Lethal as though they were royalty. "Apologies for the . . . situation." Her voice was deep and raspy with a touch of a flowery accent. It was the first time Sara had ever heard her speak. "When I was pregnant, our Elder had left for a Council meeting. While she was away, the colony tried to kill me and my child." She stole a glance at Elizabeth. "My mate died so I could escape." Claire bowed with grief and supplication to Lethal, who indeed held an unwavering, regal posture.

Sara's wide eyes darted from Claire to Ben to Elizabeth. *Not two, but* three *vampires.*

Elizabeth smiled, her usual kind but closed-lipped smile, while Orsen clasped her hand.

Ben, wearing all black, his raven hair in a low ponytail, came to Claire's side and said, "I was rogue from another colony—having been kicked out for preferring animal blood to humans—when we met. She was heavy with child and to avoid discovery by . . . you, we took a chance on seeking refuge in the one place known for deviance." Ben shifted his mahogany eyes to Sara. "Your ancestor, Ann, graciously accepted us and helped deliver Elizabeth. She suggested we pose as brother and sister and keep a low profile."

Sara held a hand to her chest, over the bloodstone hidden beneath her jacket and autumnal layers. Her great-grandmother had delivered a vampire child? She faced Lethal. "You said vampires were turned by Elders. How is this possible?"

Lethal adjusted their cuffs, doubtlessly making Sara wait in return for her demanding tone. "I said *most* vampires are created by Elders. On rare occasions, vampire mates will birth a living vampire. I have only known this to happen a few times. Subordinates usually kill the child because a born vampire is not blood-bound and outranks them, second only to Elders.

"But what I have never seen is this." Lethal gestured to Lily and her younger siblings. "Half-vampire, half-witch. I felt your power when you knocked me back, and yet you have no fangs—no need to harvest death with witch magic in your veins." The hungry look returned to their eyes as they blatantly studied Lily.

Sara felt her head might detach and float away in the clouds. Lily was part vampire, as were her siblings? No wonder Lily's strength exceeded her demure appearance.

Lily held her ground, calm and collected as usual, totally unimpressed with Lethal's obvious curiosity, which only seemed to further fuel the vampire's interest. "My family and I will answer your questions while Sara eats breakfast. Then"—Lily paused with her finger in the air—"you, Sara, and I will go to the far shore, and you will tell us what killed Naomi, agreed?"

Lethal jerked back. For a heartbeat, Sara wasn't sure if she should intervene or wisely step away. She opted for the latter.

The vampire grinned something cruel and beautiful—all four deadly fangs on display. "Agreed."

For hours, Lethal pressed the Atwells with questions and asked for magical demonstrations while Sara and Kingsley ate breakfast *and* lunch. By the time Sara settled into the boat with Lethal and Lily, her belly was full and her mood optimistic. Perhaps Samson had fooled her bullshit detector and Lethal could somehow determine that Samson—rather than Sara—was the one responsible for upsetting the magical balance and causing Naomi's death. And that the Shadow Mother had no interest in Ware Woods.

Her wish was not to be. After taking one long sniff of the quiet meadow on the far shore, Lethal assured Sara it was no dark witch that had attacked Naomi, but something *other*. Indeed, she had been targeted for quite some time. While Lethal wasn't convinced it was the Shadow Mother, they didn't exactly dismiss the idea. The vampire remained quiet for the entire trip back to the treehouse, only grunting once when Lily jumped from the boat and walked atop the water's surface to return to the island.

For the rest of the day, Lethal sat on their private deck, drinking from another bottle, and staring at the lake. Sara took the quiet moment to grab a quick shower, begrudgingly picking up another of Lethal's discarded towels, and then scarfed down a nearly forgotten, stale piece of cake and a late dinner of mac-n-cheese.

She and Thomas could be pasta professionals. Stars above, she missed him but didn't dare leave Lethal alone long enough to fly to her father's house and text him.

As she floated up to her room, she paused before Lethal. Two drained bottles sat on the table beside them. They held still as a marble statue, eerily lifeless, until their gray eyes slowly shifted to her with a touch of annoyance for interrupting their view—or thoughts, perhaps. They appeared perfect as usual, except for one thing.

"Sorry about the hair," said Sara. Not really.

"Don't be."

Okaaay.

She didn't care to stop herself from asking, "Would you have killed a pregnant woman?"

Lethal averted their eyes. "Not a woman, but a vampire."

Though it wasn't exactly an answer, the conflict in their voice was more than Sara had expected. She hovered for a quiet moment.

"So now what? Do we just wait like cattle for Samson and the Shadow Mother to maybe show up on Solstice?" she asked, her voice high with irritation and fatigue. She still had no idea who exactly the Shadow Mother was, but she figured Lethal could probably run circles around her; plus, Sara was still hoping the spell would deliver on providing an Alpha Shifter and High Witch to help her too. Whoever the Shadow Mother was, she wouldn't stand a chance against the four of them.

Yet there came a nagging thought from the back of her mind. If Ware Woods was as special as Lethal said—and the Death Vampire would know—did she want two additional Magi discovering their secret?

"First of all," drawled Lethal, possibly slurring their words, "no one in this site is *cattle*. And second, I intend to extract all the information we need from whoever this Samson is long before Solstice."

Given the vampire's glittering eyes and polished nails cutting into the arms of the chair, Sara felt a tiny flicker of sympathy for Samson, but then it was gone. She said, "Good, because I too look forward to *extracting everything* from him." Mother help me, she pleaded. Hopefully, Samson 'fessed up to tricking something *other* into murdering Naomi and lying about the Shadow Mother. After all, deceit was his specialty. Sara would gleefully let Lethal kill Samson, the witch's death taking his dark magic with him so Ian would be healed, and the Shadow Mother would leave them alone. Any Magi showing up at the wall would be sent on their merry way, thus securing their secret. The hopeful delusion wrecked her with exhaustion.

Sara flew to her room and crashed into bed. Her intentions for staying up for another night of vampire vigil immediately melted under the warm covers.

CHAPTER 24

A RHYTHMIC THUMPING reverberated around Sara, rattling her ribs and knocking the bloodstone against her sternum. Velvet darkness brushed against her legs and arms, tugging back her hair, whispering in her ears. The sensation reminded her of looping through the forest's soul trees but somehow falling deeper, farther.

Sara threw out her arms, forcing herself to stop, and landed on her bare feet in a shallow puddle. With a rapid inhale of humid air, she stood and surveyed her cave-like surroundings. The walls and high ceiling were smooth stone, as was the warm floor beneath her feet. On her left yawned a circular opening to a roaring waterfall, backlit enough to pleasantly flood the cave in a soft glow. Along with the rush of water, a gentle low-toned hum, similar to a singing bowl, filled the cave.

To her right knelt a man on a straw mat, his feet tucked beneath him, his hands resting on his knees. Trim yet slightly pointed black nails tipped each finger. His glossy obsidian hair was tied in a loose bun, his eyes obscured by small, round, darkly tinted glasses. He wore a wrap-around white tunic which gaped open at the top, revealing a smooth, powerful chest with golden-beige skin. His clothing reminded Sara of the karate gi she once wore for self-defense classes. She adjusted her stance, unsure if this was a dream or real. At least she was wearing sweatpants along with Thomas's shirt.

"What are you doing here?" he asked, his voice rich and slippery and somehow arcane. It was the way his lips moved that grabbed her attention, like they were hiding lots of teeth. And the fact that he had asked, "*What are you doing here*" and not "*Who are you?*" As though he already knew her.

Okay. She'd play along—long enough to determine if this was real and if he was a threat. "I don't know. Where exactly is 'here'?" The truth.

"If I told you, I'd have to kill you. And I don't think I want to do that." He tilted his head undecidedly. Nightmarishly. Whoever he was, he was palpably dangerous, for his sudden shift in mood radiated off the walls and threatened to crush her.

The hum intensified. Not a singing bowl, she determined, but his energy. Sara was definitely out of her league. Diving through the waterfall to whatever lay beyond seemed the best exit strategy. That or waking up.

She pinched herself. *Damn it.* Maybe she could reason with him . . . or maybe . . .

"I—I asked the Mother for help. Are you to help me?" Her voice sounded much too weak.

"You think the Mother listens to you? An ordinary witch?" His fingers splayed and gripped his knees.

Though she should be terrified, the way he said *ordinary* pissed her off. White flames flared at her palms.

"Careful. You are in *my* house. And it is *you* who will help *me*." His lips tightened into what was either a grin or a grimace, which was disturbing enough—never mind the promise of many pointed teeth behind his closed mouth.

Sara's flames guttered out. "Help you? Hells, I don't even know your name."

His hands relaxed. "I have many names."

"Magicals are so cryptic," she muttered. "Just pick one."

"Jin," he said, and swift as a river snake, lunged and struck her, sending her into the roaring waterfall.

Sara fell back, not through water but through the thumping, whisper-soft darkness, and slammed into her bed. The treehouse groaned along with her as she bounced up, morning light illuminating her room, and came face to face with Lethal.

The vampire's alabaster skin had paled an even deathlier shade of white. "Where in nine Hells did you go?" they uttered.

Nine Hells? I thought there were only seven. Sara swatted away Lethal's nectar-sweet breath. "I have no idea. Was I really gone?"

"Yes," they hissed, "for a while. You screamed on your way out *and* on your way back. Is this a regular witchy thing? Because it was disturbing . . . my meditation." Lethal leaned back and folded their arms over an ash-gray shirt, their gilded hair cascading down the front.

Their hair! Without thinking, Sara reached up and tugged a lock. "How did this grow so fast?"

Lethal grabbed her wrist, their grip as cold and firm as marble. "Don't touch," they ground out, eyes hard.

"Yeesh, sorry," Sara apologized, retracting her hand and rubbing her wrist.

They stepped away from the bed, shutting their eyes with a tortured face. "No. I'm sorry. It's just—I don't let anyone get close." They sighed and opened their eyes.

Before Sara could launch a sarcastic comment about a certain Goldilocks vampire not letting anyone get physically *or* emotionally close, Lethal held up a hand and scented the air.

"Lily is here," they said, face brightening. "And"—they sniffed again and frowned—"someone else."

Moira's husky voice sounded from the main room, "Sara! Get your ass out of bed." In a quieter tone, she commented, "Mother below, the blond anti-Christ *stinks*."

"They do not," chastised Lily, her delicate voice ringing with laughter.

Lethal raised a brow at Sara. "You let a shifter talk to you with such disrespect?"

"We're friends, ash-hole. Now get out of my room so I can change."

Stunned silence filled the room. And because the vampire clearly had difficulty processing her double-edged statement, she shoved them from the room—grousing with the effort of forcing their stony body—and ordered, "Go hang out with them downstairs. I'll join you shortly." And to Sara's delight, the treehouse sprouted a door and slammed it in Lethal's befuddled face.

By the time she changed, made a trip to the bathroom, and approached the tree's wrap-around staircase, Lily's sunshine laughter echoed through the treehouse. Sara crested the stairs and paused at the sight of Moira rapidly phasing between a repertoire of animals while Lethal stared, slack jawed.

"What's going on?" Sara asked, entering the room.

Lethal swung their head toward Sara. "Can *all* your shifters do this?"

Sara stifled a chuckle. She had seen more expressions on the vampire in the past half hour than she ever thought possible. "Well, Moira is the fastest and has mastered more forms than the rest of her family, but they all have an impressive range of species."

Moira stopped in her human form and grinned ear-to-ear.

"Most shifters can only phase into *one* animal, never mind dozens," said Lethal, slumping back on the couch with such force the furniture creaked in offense. "I've never seen them, but supposedly there are a few like Moira on the other continents."

Moira plopped into a chair, draping her legs over the side. "Those are probably my siblings," she said, inspecting her perfectly manicured nails.

Lethal grunted. "I hope they don't tell anyone where they come from."

"Nope," said Moira. "Otherwise, the packs don't accept them." She shrugged. "Are we going to the Main House for breakfast or what? All that shifting has made me *hungry*." Her last word was more of a growl.

Noting Lethal's relaxed and content demeanor, and considering their obvious adulation for Lily and Moira's magic, Sara seized the opportunity to pawn off vampire sitting. She projected to her witch and shifter friends, *"Are you cool with keeping an eye on Lethal while I meet with Gran and Alice?"* She desperately needed to consult her grandmother and great-aunt—and the Book.

Moira snorted a laugh and Lily beamed.

"I'll take that as a yes. Thanks!"

Lethal tilted their head and slowly looked at the three of them. "Are you—"

"Great idea," interrupted Sara. "You all go ahead to the Main House, show Lethal around the forest, and I'll meet up with you later today." And before the vampire could comment, Sara flew out the open archway.

CHAPTER 25

SARA TORE THROUGH the sky, upsetting a red-tailed hawk who screeched at her as she rushed to the blue house and threw open the door. She crashed into the living room, whishing a table lamp back into place and slamming the front door shut before barging into the kitchen.

Gran and Alice dropped their candle making, molten wax splattering the wood counter. From the second level, Albert yipped awake, most likely from his favorite sunny spot, and thundered down the stairs.

"What happened? And where is that narcissistic vampire? You weren't to let them out of your sight," scolded Gran.

Sara panted. "It's fine. Lily and Moira have them wrapped around their little fingers." She held up her four-fingered hand and spat a laugh before turning to her grandmother and great-aunt. "Do you know of a Jin?" she asked, hoping he was perhaps a famous High Witch or Alpha Shifter and somehow part of the spell she cast.

"No, honey. What is it?" said Gran with a glance at Alice.

"Is it a genie?" offered Alice. With a wave of her hand, she kinetically scraped wax from the counter and sprinkled it into the bubbling pot on the stove. "I don't know if those really exist.

But, then again, it's good practice to believe anything is possible with magic."

"Not a genie and not a what, but a who. At least . . . I think so." Sara stilled, recalling hidden eyes and preternatural speed. "I had a *transportive* dream and met someone who said they went by many names, including Jin. Where's the Book?" she asked, taking in an array of new herbs hanging overhead before scanning the cluttered farmhouse table. Candles of all colors, as well as bolts of fabric and lumpy gourds, covered the surface. Albert, her great-uncle trapped in wolf form, released a whiny groan and sprawled out in the archway to the living room.

Alice gave her wolf mate a tender smile before facing Sara and asking, "Transportive? Did you astral project somewhere?"

"No, I *physically* went to some cave," said Sara. She lifted a jumping mound of midnight blue silk and discovered the Book, trembling with indignation. "Show me who Jin is," she requested, pushing aside a cornucopia of warty gourds while the Book unfurled.

Its pages ruffled furiously, then slowed, then picked up again, as if unsure where to stop. Finally, it halted on a page with an ouroboros lazily spinning in a circle.

After waiting a few excruciating spins of the tail-eating serpent, Sara glanced at her grandmother. "What's this? What's the Book doing?"

Gran twitched her nose. "It's thinking."

"Thinking?" exclaimed Sara. "Gaa! This thing is slower than Charlie's dinosaur of a computer."

Alice peeked over Sara's shoulder. "There are too many variables—too many past, present, and future unknowns—for the Book to decide what to reveal."

Sara rolled her eyes. "I *saw* him. He's real. Maybe the Book knows him by a different name."

"What exactly does he look like?" asked Gran, raising a brow.

"I couldn't see his eyes, but he has perfect skin and dark

hair. He's smooth and sharp at the same time, and he's incredibly aggravating."

Gran snorted. "You sure you weren't dreaming of Thomas?"

"Positive," she gritted out, then sighed. "Maybe it was nothing. Maybe I just need to stop eating spice cake before bed. In fact, it's been giving me heartburn." She rubbed her chest, just below the bloodstone.

A deep frown marred Gran's face. "You're a High Witch. You don't get heartburn. I think you and Thomas have been apart for too long."

Sara's heart twinged in response. "You're probably right. I'm gonna go call him. First, though"—she turned back to the Book—"can you tell me when the next two Magi are coming?"

The page flipped and one word appeared:

Trust.

"*Two* Magi?" shrieked Gran.

The Book startled and slammed shut.

"Don't worry about it," said Sara, giving her and Alice a peck on their cheeks and a ruffle to Albert's head on her way out the front door. "I've got this all under control," she called over her shoulder, taking off for the brown house next door. *Not in the slightest . . .*

Sara slipped in through the back patio, relieved to have the first level all to herself. Ted and her father usually worked in the basement office, where all the computers and Ian's gaming servers and equipment and whatever else he used were carefully networked.

Conveniently sitting atop the diner-style table were three phones. She tugged hers free from the white charging cable and hit Thomas's avatar—a photo of him on the beach with sunglasses and swim trunks. On the third ring, he answered.

"Hello, monster," he whispered, the timbre of his voice kindling her insides.

"When you come home, I'm going to pin you down and torture you with my wicked tongue," she said.

He chuckled. "You can do whatever you'd like to me *after* I take my sweet time stealing the breath from that smart mouth of yours."

Her grip threatened to crush the phone.

"As much as I want to continue this conversation," he said in a low voice, "I'm in the middle of a riveting lecture on soils case studies."

"Sounds dirty," she whispered as if she were in class with him.

Thomas huffed a laugh. "Everything okay?"

"Yes," she lied, hating herself for it but knowing he needed to stay focused on his classes and not worry about the myriad of magical problems weighing on her. "I miss you. My heart physically aches for you, Thomas."

"My head pounds with thoughts of you. All. The. Time. I miss us—together." He sighed. "Just six more weeks—five if Matt and I can talk our professors into letting us take finals early."

She grinned. Of course they could charm their professors, especially if they removed the brown contacts they wore to hide the magic in their eyes. "Five weeks it is. I'm counting—"

The two phones on the table and the one in her hand all buzzed at the same time. Ian's avatar popped up on the screens along with a message:

Samson is coming. Now.

Her breath hitched. Thomas must have heard it, for he asked, "What's wrong?"

She smiled, forcing her conjured calm through the phone. "I forgot about a meeting. Sorry to cut it short, but you need to get back to class anyway—seductive soils and all. Talk later. Love you." Her words came out in a rush as she stood and peered out the adjacent window. Dark clouds gathered overhead, obliterating the sun.

"Right," he said, dragging out his response. "We'll pick up this conversation later. I love you too."

Her heart and the bloodstone hammered in response to both the intensity of his words and the darkness awaiting her.

Sara ended the call and gently placed the phone down. Shutting her eyes, she inhaled to the count of three, held it for three more, then whooshed out her breath. *I can do this.*

As High Witch, she banged out the back patio door, flew to the stone wall near the Sullivans' house, and faced the open fields on the opposite side. It was the exact location of their last meeting and also where Samson had nearly killed her when she first arrived at Ware Woods.

Since she couldn't penetrate Lethal's mind—she had shamelessly tried before and the vampire simply gave her a disgusted look—she projected to Lily and Moira, *"Tell Lethal that Samson is coming."* The vampire's extraordinary senses would no doubt tell them exactly where she waited.

Moira's wolf howl sounded through the forest, and before her soulful note faded, Lethal appeared at Sara's side.

The vampire glanced at the sky before giving Sara a smug one-fang smile. Strapped to their back was a short sword, its guarded grip and scepter-like pommel peeking above their relaxed shoulders. "This will be torturously fun," they drawled, reaching back and wrapping their stony white fingers, one by one, around the hilt.

CHAPTER 26

THE CLOUDS ABOVE the outer field darkened and swirled, spinning faster and faster as they funneled toward the center of the cropped expanse. Upon impact with the hard soil, a burst of black smoke and red sparks erupted into an atomic shroom. Sara squinted against the blast, her hair stirring. A subsequent chilly breeze cleared the dramatic entrance, revealing Samson—no top hat this time—sitting at a cocky angle before a table piled with food, his arms outstretched and beckoning her.

Lethal grunted and released the grip on their sword, hands falling slack at their sides.

Sara cast a glance at the stunned Death Vampire and scowled. *Coward.*

She didn't need them, anyway; she had been practicing her magic, and if she struck first, surprising Samson, she gambled she could best him.

Leaving the vampire in their stupor, Sara flew over the stone wall and rushed toward Samson with glee in her thundering heart. What a fool he was to show up alone—not a stained henchman in sight.

First, she'd drive him into the ground with enough force to not-so-accidentally break his fingers before questioning him about Ian, the Shadow Mother, and his involvement in Naomi's death.

Samson maintained his relaxed position and calmly held up a hand, his power pushing her back though not stopping her entirely.

She gritted her teeth and willed herself close enough to see the amused glint in his onyx eyes. Not an ounce of surprise shone from him.

"No need to rush. There's plenty of food," he jested. As if she would ever dine with the sick bastard who ate her finger.

Sara's bloodstone pulsed, her temper raging and crackling around her like lightning. Staring at the dark witch who killed her mother, a violent need crept over Sara—a need to *hurt* him as he once hurt her.

Utilizing the trick she learned from Abby, Sara formed a multitude of white-hot energy spheres around Samson and, with a roar, pounded him. The explosion knocked her back, skidding through the field. With a groan, she picked herself up and faced her devastation.

The table of food had detonated. Scraps of wood and meat and smashed fruits littered the hard-packed ground.

Standing in the middle of the detritus stood Samson, eyes flashing red. He appeared completely unharmed save for his burnt jacket floating away in ashy wisps.

Sara stumbled. Nothing should have survived her angry attack. And yet, there he glared at her, bare chested. The energy flickering on her skin snuffed out when she took in his ghastly, emaciated torso and the dozen bloodstones hanging from silver chains around his neck. Only one stone was red; all the others were as black as a rotten soul.

Samson snapped his fingers, and a new jacket instantly clothed him. Smoke billowed from his sleeves and slithered in thick tendrils toward Sara. She summoned a wall of wind to disperse them, but they morphed into black vines, wrapping around her legs, yanking her to him. Her bloodstone pulsed, and she released a surge of energy, burning free from the vines and shooting into the sky. Someone hollered her name; the cry choked off as a storm engulfed her, blinding her with darkness and squeezing her with icy cold.

Disoriented, Sara instinctively curled into herself and focused on gathering her energy. She managed a weak light just in time to glimpse a monstrous hand of black fire burn through the clouds and smash into her.

Sara threw all her magic into maintaining her protective shield, only to have it contract against her as Samson's force pummeled her through inky darkness. She hit the ground with a bone-snapping crack, the impact reverberating through her limp body and flooding her with pain.

She couldn't breathe, couldn't think, couldn't heal herself.

The smoke dissipated, and she blinked at a light-gray sky and Samson looming over her—his magic still pinning her down. "I didn't come to fight," he said, frustration edging each word.

She wanted to spit at him but could barely choke down a gasp of air while slowly mending her shattered spine and ribs.

"If I let you up, you must behave and *listen* to me. Otherwise, I will have to beat you again in front of your family, and I don't think you want that. Deal?" he asked, extending a stained hand as if to help her.

Face tingling with shame and healing energy, she managed a scowl before tucking her chin and conceding a curt nod. Her bloodstone thumped, filling her with warmth and accelerating her physical recoveries. She took another gulp of air and, ignoring his hand, pushed herself to her knees.

Her gaze flicked toward the forest, at Lethal and Lily and Moira and a small crowd, including Gran and her father, standing behind the wall. The vampire appeared to say something to Lily before gracefully leaping the stone barrier. In a blink, they crossed half the field, approaching Samson, and said, "You crafty bastard, it's been too long, O—"

Samson whipped around with his hand out, palm up, magically silencing the vampire. Fury bloomed on Lethal's face as they shimmered with near-invisible movement and four daggers penetrated Samson—one in each limb.

"Hello, Lethal," seethed Samson. "It's been so long, I'm sure you forgot my name is Samson." A dark wetness leached from his wounds as he kept his steady focus on the vampire.

Sara stiffened, eyes flitting between Samson and Lethal. *Father of Night! They* know *each other.*

Lethal grunted and advanced. "I see you're still playing games and amassing new powers." They waved a finger at the smoke clinging to Samson's legs. "But if you ever hush me again, Kindness will take your head, dear friend." They nodded toward the sword on their back.

"You still have that thing? You never did like to get your hands dirty," said Samson with a grin. "Ouch, by the way," he added, whishing the daggers back at Lethal and magically healing himself—his dark clothes pristine once more.

Lethal plucked the weapons from the air and sheathed them too quickly for Sara to track where the vampire hid them. A faint smile graced their otherwise placid face.

Samson considered the smug vampire before turning his focus to the wall, his fierce stare stopping on Lily. "I'm surprised she still lives. Have you gone soft in your old age?" he asked, flicking his gaze back at Lethal.

The vampire's face hardened. "She is different, and you know it. The question is, why do you care?"

Sara remained frozen in her crouched position, her attention darting between them as if watching a ping-pong match with a live grenade.

Samson gave them a lazy smile. "I'm curious if there are exceptions to the rules."

"There are *always* exceptions, as we both know," snarled Lethal.

Samson shrugged, his smile deepening. "Does this mean you've staked your claim on her?"

"You know better than to suggest such a thing," said Lethal, their voice rough as grinding stones. Twin daggers appeared in their hands.

"Pity. Because I truly wish you happiness someday, Lethal."

And before Sara could demand to know what the Hells was going on, Samson turned on her. "Do you know how *lucky* you are? Foolish girl. I *cannot* believe you invited this bloodsucker into your little garden."

Anger heated Sara's core, healing the last of her injuries as she sprang up to face him. She may be inexperienced, but she wasn't stupid. "They drank the sap," she gritted out.

Samson snorted a laugh, which promptly turned into a choke.

She jumped back when he pounded his chest and spat a dark slug of phlegm at her feet. *Disgusting.*

Samson wiped his mouth with a silken black scarf he pulled from his pocket and twirled a finger at Lethal. "They could drink acid and never flinch."

Nooo.

Sara slowly turned to the complacent vampire, who was casually tucking the twin daggers into their boots. No wonder they threw down a full thermos and never batted an icy eye.

"Fabulous," said Samson with an exaggerated sigh. "You'll trust a fanged monster over a fellow witch." He waved his arms, tendrils of smoke curling around him as the ruined dinner was magically replaced with a new table and chairs. Samson sank into an ornate wingback chair at the head of the table draped in a pristine white cloth and signaled for them to sit. "No offense, Lethal."

"None taken," said the vampire, sitting in an equally ornate chair. Their eyes lit up when a goblet of thick red liquid appeared before them. The distinct metallic tang of blood in the air further wrenched Sara's queasy stomach. She pushed back her shoulders, steeling her barely there bravado.

With an inky thumb pointed at Lethal, Samson shot her a look she could have sworn was a touch soft with concern and asked, "Why are they here?"

Thoroughly confused by his expression and cavalier attitude

with the Death Vampire, Sara merely blinked, unable to utter a word about the spell she cast.

Lethal broke the silence and said, "Global Council inquiry."

Samson choked on another laugh. "I'm shocked they even care about this little region. I take it you got lonely and decided to try something new."

Lethal gave the tiniest of shrugs and picked up the goblet.

Sara glanced at Ware Woods—at her family, watching their every move from across the field and behind the safety of the wall. Her father looked extremely pale, and Gran seemed liable to ignite with frustration.

Samson flicked a finger, and a wall of dark clouds erected along the old road, blocking her view of her family. *Everything's fine,* she mentally projected to them, but her words echoed flatly in her mind.

A sudden clatter drew her attention back to the table, where a metal plate piled with bread and a tin cup of water settled in front of the seat before her. Samson gestured again, and Sara reluctantly sat on the edge of the folding chair. In the harshest voice she could muster, she said, "Ian better be fine and nowhere near that psycho Brad."

"Brad?" Samson's face pinched for a heartbeat before smoothing into a leer. "Tut, tut. *You* were the one who bit that ox. No wonder he came to me looking for dark magic and so eagerly volunteered to divert you at the beach while I took—as you put it—my bargaining chip." He waved away her furious glare. "Don't worry, only Mr. Motley is allowed near my . . . guests."

Sara frowned, unsure if this was good or bad information. "Tell me where Ian is and everything you know about the Shadow Mother," she demanded. Since her plan to torture him had failed, perhaps he'd voluntarily run his mouth so she could trap him with his lies about the Shadow Mother.

Lethal arched a brow and leaned back in their chair, swirling the contents of the goblet. It stuck to the sides, painting the entire glass a murderous red.

"Unlike you, your brother has impeccable manners," said Samson with a grimace. "At least try to be nice and—"

"You destroyed my family and ate my freaking finger!" She held up her hand, white energy flickering on her remaining fingertips.

"Partially true, and I'll explain. But first . . . I noticed you didn't ask about sweet Dorcas," said Samson. A knowing smile graced his pallid lips. "You could at least thank me for picking your rotten apple."

Sara blanched. While she suspected Dorcas was a niggling threat to Ware Woods, Sara preferred having the shifty witch contained within the wall instead of beside a dark witch like Samson. Mother help them all if those two questionable witches teamed up.

Sara swallowed the burn at the rear of her throat and lifted her chin. "I trust you're keeping Dorcas on a short leash as promised. Because you sure as Hells haven't kept your end of the bargain by healing Ian."

"I've tried healing your brother." Samson sighed heavily and coughed up another inky phlegm slug. He ignored Lethal's displeased glance. "But Ian's condition is caused by the Shadow Mother, and I don't know the cure."

Sara scrutinized his apologetic demeanor. He seemed to be telling the truth, yet she didn't want to believe him—because why would the Shadow Mother target Ian? And if Samson wasn't at fault . . .

Sara's mind frantically spun as she fought to remain calm.

What if she truly was responsible for upsetting the balance and certain death was coming for them all?

Dread raked ghostly fingers down her back.

CHAPTER 27

SARA BLANKLY STARED at the barren field, grateful for Samson's smoky wall so her family couldn't see the fear and shame she knew darkened her face.

Lethal set down their drained goblet and, in a calm voice, asked Samson, "Why do you think the Shadow Mother is at fault?"

Samson shot a sly smile at the vampire. "You know I'm no saint and there are reasons for my actions, but I also got lonely and once foolishly thought I deserved to be loved—by a Hills witch, no less."

"Bit off more than you could chew, eh?" said Lethal with a hint of friendly ribbing. "The Hills were powerful witches. It was a shock to the Global Council when a dragon exterminated them. Nothing remains of their forest. I saw it myself."

Sara snapped from her daze and bristled, fighting the angry urge to throw more futile energy at Samson. *Pfft!* "No. Samson killed them all, except for Naomi, whose mysterious murder scene you recently visited."

"Naomi was a Hills witch?" asked Lethal.

The fact that they didn't question Samson's involvement incensed Sara. She cast them a dirty look, but they were already deep in thought, their brow furrowed.

Samson placed his stained fingers to his temples. "As I was saying"—he glared at Sara and Lethal—"I was foolish and drank the Hills sap, trying to prove to Winona as much as to myself that I was pure of heart." He chuckled, setting off another round of wet coughing. "It didn't go well. The Hills kicked me out, and when I lay dying, I was a coward and used the last of my power to summon whatever darkness could save me. The Shadow Mother came. In my weakened state, I didn't fully recognize her and stupidly agreed to a wealth of shadowy power in exchange for a few 'favors.'

"A couple of years later, she used me to kill Winona and Ian— only we didn't know Ian lived. I died all over again that day," said Samson, his raspy voice trailing off as his eyes glazed over with the memory.

With a shake of his head, swaying his long, corded hair, he continued, "I thought I paid my price and she was done with me. For nearly twenty years I never heard a whisper from her, but then she showed up, stronger than she had been before, and used me again to attack the Hills site. She nearly killed everyone by the time I forced her out of my body. As punishment for my defiance, she inflicted me with this extremely annoying and painful poison. Then promised to be back on Winter Solstice to end me and all magicals in this area." He coughed again, chest rattling, and dabbed his mouth with the foul scarf.

Sara pushed away the plate of bread, sickened by both his explanation and his hacking. Judging by Lethal's green-tinged countenance, she gathered the stoic vampire felt the same. But what, exactly, did Samson's confession have to do with her? She stilled, mind racing.

Bastard.

"You lying snake!" Sara spat. "You accused me of upsetting the magical balance and summoning the Shadow Mother when this is all *your* fault. Not mine. Yours! And it's *you* who need *my* help." She jumped up from the table and paced behind her chair.

Gaa! How could I be so stupid? She threw him her nastiest death stare, magic tingling in her palms.

"If you're so innocent, why did you kill my mother and repeatedly attack me?" she roared, unconsciously summoning wind, which tugged at the tablecloth and blew back Samson's hair as well as Lethal's golden locks.

Samson snarled at her. "Snake I may be and an expert at half-truths and omissions, but never a liar. Now let me finish." He wheezed, fighting to get air into his lungs. "You kids drive me crazy," he muttered into his scarf before tucking it away with a flourish.

Sara yanked out the chair and plopped down with a slight grin at knowing Ian—wherever he was—must have been giving Samson a hard time as well. She raised a haughty brow for him to continue. *This better be good.*

"Of course, I was furious at being used and a tad worried about her increasing strength. So, I did what I do best," said Samson with another inside smile at Lethal. "I played the villain to win back her confidence, determine her motive, and find a way to eliminate her— or at least send her back to whatever hell she crawled out of. That's when she instructed me to 'Finish the job' by killing Ian and Naomi. And, for rotten measure, she added wiping out the entire Lochton family. Which is no easy task given your little impenetrable bubble." He waved a hand toward the wall of smoke and the forest behind it, then settled his pitch-black eyes on Sara. "I did not intend for the truck to barrel into you and for your mother to die. That was truly an unfortunate accident, and I'm sorry for your loss."

Damn him. He was telling the truth; she could feel his regret radiating from his dark-gray aura. "Pfft!"

"I was trying to get close enough to you and figure you out. For someone so young, you have an incredible amount of power, but it twists and turns as neither entirely light nor dark magic."

Lethal nodded in agreement.

What the Hells is he insinuating? "I'm *not* a dark witch," Sara growled.

"He's not insulting you," said Lethal, their angelic face perfectly impassive. "Being a light witch does not make you inherently better. Both light and dark are equally important to the balance. You cannot have one without the other. Did you not kill the dark witch, Makwa?"

Sara froze. Lethal struck with deadly accuracy at the hidden part of herself—the questionable part that would do *anything* to right a wrong and to protect her forest family, even if it meant getting her hands dirty. Maybe she should invest in a sword.

"Perhaps the three of us are more alike than you care to admit," said Lethal, their words a knife twist to her punctured soul.

Father above, she hoped not. Before she could stammer a weak denial, Samson plowed ahead.

"I admit working with Makwa was not one of my best ideas, but I had no other way of getting into Ware Woods. And then *you* came at me all fired up," he said with a wet chuckle. Sara fought the urge to retch. "As you may recall, you were not in a listening mood, and time was running out. To confirm your power and your intentions—and since I was still playing the villain to ensure the Shadow Mother's trust—I impulsively ate your finger."

Samson paused with a grimace. Sara gripped the table, singeing the white cloth with her rage. He said, "Tasted *terrible,* but then I knew without a doubt that you have the power to face the Shadow Mother. Which is good because she is coming for us on Solstice. She seeks to exterminate potential threats, like your family, and to absorb all other magical powers. And once she is strong enough, she will use discord and violence to strike the heart of every normal."

He doubled over with another coughing fit, and Sara contemplated ending him right then and there—putting them all out of his misery.

Lethal leaned back and grunted. The vampire sat in silence while Samson finished a particularly nauseating hack, and as he wiped his mouth, Lethal coolly asked him, "Why does this concern you? You made a bargain with the Shadow Mother and defied her—now you must pay with your death. Do you think stopping her will somehow release you of your bargain and cure you? Or do you have a particular interest in preserving Ware Woods?" They smiled, revealing two upper fangs.

Samson froze, a fox cornered by a wolf.

Sara straightened in her seat, the wood table groaning under her tight grip as she stared at the witch and the vampire.

Shit. Lethal took cunning to a whole new level.

Clearing his throat, Samson dramatically placed a hand to his chest and proclaimed, "I am doing a favor to Ware Woods by warning you of this threat and joining forces against the Shadow Mother—as a means to make up for my past transgressions."

Lethal held their clever smile.

Samson scowled at them and promptly began gagging as if struggling not to puke all over the table.

Sara's stomach turned. Placing one hand on her belly, she raised her other hand and flicked a kernel of magic at him—just enough to get him to stop coughing. Her speck of white light hit him square in the chest and sent him tumbling back, chair and all.

Lethal shot out of their seat, eyes wide at Samson sprawled on the ground. "*Futuo*," they whispered.

With a gasp, Samson sprang up, immaculate stain-free hands patting his chest. Appearing somehow taller and stronger, he turned to the vampire. In a clear, rich tone, he said, "I don't care if you believe me or not. Clearly, she is powerful. But she is woefully inexperienced and apparently needs to get her head out of her ass and truly master her magic."

He faced Sara, his fierce countenance failing to hide a rattled mix of concern and relief. "Remember the bargain you made with me. Be ready by Solstice. Because she is coming for *all* of us." A cloud of black smoke erupted around Samson and swallowed him whole before contracting upon itself and winking out, taking the wall of smoke and the table and chairs with him.

Sara fell to the hard ground, her backside colliding with a fieldstone. "Mother below, what just happened?" She groaned, picking herself up and meeting Lethal's flummoxed appearance. If she hadn't been pissed off at Samson's admonishment, she would have burst out laughing at Lethal's perfectly rounded mouth.

"You *rutting* healed him!" they exclaimed, pivoting and striding for the forest wall and everyone behind it.

Sara scrambled after the vampire. "That's ridiculous. All my power barely smoked his jacket. There's no way a flippant spark cured him."

Lethal slowed their pace, letting her catch up. "There must have been a loophole in the curse—'only to be cured by his enemy' or some such nonsense. By healing him, you took away his death payment to the Shadow Mother. *Now* you have created a significant ripple in the balance, and she will surely be coming for you and everyone you care about."

She halted, mouth dry. Impossible. *Right?*

CHAPTER 28

SARA FLEW AHEAD of Lethal, rushing to the crowd anxiously waiting beside the stone wall. Despite not fully trusting Samson, and despite the possibility that the Shadow Mother had irreparably damaged Ian's heart and perhaps targeted her, Sara forced a thin smile and assured her family that Ian was fine and that, yes—aside from her pride—she was fine too.

With unconvinced expressions, Lily and Moira excused themselves, mumbling something about meeting up with Caleb, and promised they would see her later. Her father, Gran, and the rest returned begrudgingly to their late afternoon activities, while Sara marched for the treehouse with Lethal in tow.

Summoning a stronger wind than was necessary, she shoved leaves and pinecones from the path and chewed her lip until the coppery sting of blood worried her tongue.

There's no way I healed Samson. No way I am ever *going to lose to him again. And no way I am anything like him . . . or Lethal, for that matter.* She stole a glimpse at the vampire walking beside her, their brow creased with their own thoughts, and frowned. The idea of Lethal and Samson being *friends* was equal parts terrifying and intriguing.

She opened her mouth to ask the question burning her tail, but Lethal shot her down.

"No," said the vampire. "We are not requesting Global Council aid to fight the Shadow Mother. Because then everyone would know about the power in Ware Woods, and we'd have a much bigger problem on our hands. We need to handle this mess ourselves."

Sara jerked back at their fervency, guilt flushing the tips of her ears at expecting two more Magi to visit the forest before Solstice. Yet she couldn't bloody well undo the spell—she had no idea how to do such a thing and doubted it was even possible. Besides, the Book said to trust, and she had no other option but to do so.

"Right," she agreed with a firm nod, as if this had been her question. More leaves fluttered from the path. She waited a strained moment before asking, "Enlighten me. How is it that you and Samson know each other?"

Lethal strode a few paces before answering. "I suppose you could say we were comrades once. Years ago, in my region, we wreaked havoc together and delighted in one another's company. While I killed normals whose bloodlust matched my own, 'Samson' infiltrated dozens of dark magical groups and usurped their rogue Magi." They arched a brow at Sara. "Don't pretend to be horrified. We maintained the balance by eradicating darkness before it could grow out of hand." They tore off an errant low-hanging branch from the maple to their right, letting the limb crash to the ground. "Similar to pruning."

Sara flinched for the tree.

While she wanted to be horrified, deep down she understood the desire to stop madness before it spread like a cancer. And damn it, Lethal knew her inclination.

But just because Sara understood Lethal's and Samson's motivations didn't mean she was like them. The world's mayhem was not her responsibility, and she had no intention of getting involved in whatever didn't concern her. The only thing she was responsible for was Ware Woods—her family. And to protect them, she would set aside her pride and perhaps even a few of her morals to learn all she needed from Lethal and whoever else the spell brought her.

They followed the path around two dogwood trees and ended up at the edge of the clearing between the lake and cemetery treehouse. Lethal paused.

Sara slowed and beheld the open clearing—the treehouse and stone cottage near the far side.

I refuse to be "woefully inexperienced." And my head may not be on straight, but it is not up my ass. She fisted her hands and, before she could stop herself, rushed into the center of the meadow, and called to the vampire, "Spar with me. And don't hold ba—"

Fire ripped through her leg as a dagger sank into her thigh. Mother below, Lethal hadn't even looked in her direction. The strike had been so quick and jarring, Sara fought to remember how to heal herself. She had taken the occasional knife while sparring with Kane and Violet, but this blade burned with fire and ice. She grabbed the handle and yanked out the weapon while summoning healing energy.

Another blade pierced her other leg, severing tendons, and she collapsed.

In a heartbeat, Lethal stood over her. Sara stared in horror at the hilt of the sword peeking above their shoulders. Without warning, the vampire yanked the daggers from her leg and hand. "I'll go easy on you, but at least *try* to stop me."

The bloodstone pulsed, healing her and pushing a wave of energy at the vampire. They disappeared, their movement too fast for Sara to track. She leapt to her feet and spun around, only to go down again with daggers buried into both of her calves. Pain sliced through her, and despite herself, she cried out. A swift breeze smelling of frankincense rushed behind her as both blades were mercifully removed.

Lethal stood ten paces before her, flicking blood—her blood—from their daggers. "My weapons are kissed by Death. A mere cut kills normals and, I'm told, is excruciating to magicals." They didn't smile or taunt her while she hissed through her teeth and healed herself.

Shit. The fact Samson had taken four and remained standing astonished her with respect for the witch.

These weapons would be the end of her. Since she was nowhere near as fast as the vampire, she had to somehow slow Lethal's movements and disarm them.

Sara smacked her palms on the ground, fingers digging into the soil and connecting with her earth magic.

Vines burst at the vampire's feet and twined up their body. They jerked back with seeming amusement as the green vines turned to stone and constricted. But before Lethal's hands could be bound against their body, they flicked a dagger straight into Sara's shoulder.

She screamed.

Son of a— Her cry turned into a roar as she whished the dagger free and hurled it at Lethal's angelic face.

The blade grazed their cheek, sparking and emitting a harsh scrape but no injury before thudding to the ground. Sara stared in disbelief, the vines crumbling along with her shattered concentration. Her gash healed as she levitated, feet a whisper above the marred ground.

"What's happening?" resounded her father's voice in her head at the same time Lily, Moira, and Caleb came running into the clearing, arms laden with baskets of food from the Cahills' farm. Their wide eyes relaxed upon seeing Sara unscathed and hovering before the smug-faced vampire.

Caleb nodded in admiration at the broken vines and said, "Cool. You'll have to teach me that trick."

Moira scrunched her nose. "Torn jeans are definitely not in style."

Lily frowned at Lethal; to Sara's shock, they took a step back.

"She asked me to spar with her," they explained, sheathing the dagger.

"*Sara?*" shouted her father.

She sighed and, at the same time, both mentally projected and said, "Everything's peachy. Lethal's showing me the finer *points* of their sparring methods."

Her father huffed a laugh. *"I'll tell your grandmother to put the stakes away."*

Lily shifted her basket, green carrot and beet tops spilling over the sides, and in her sweet, delicate voice ordered, "Fewer sharp edges and more helpful instructions while we make dinner." She strolled to the cottage with a sniggering Caleb beside her.

Moira loosed a soft howl and murmured, "Served," before heading after them into the little stone building, its inner light casting a glow across the chilly meadow.

The vampire straightened their cream tunic and stepped out of the vine rubble. "Change your thinking. Instead of waiting for your opponent to make a move, anticipate their action. Use it to your advantage. Strike them when they least expect it." They widened their stance. "Again."

Without a moment's hesitation, Sara launched into the sky only to have Lethal grab her by the boot and throw her to the ground. When they shimmered with movement, Sara rocketed up again—this time at an angle and with a swirling cloud of dirt and dry grass to mask her direction. She slipped past them.

Lethal whirled, looking up at her. "Better. Now see if you can hit me."

She blasted them with enough wind to knock over a house and yet they still stood, completely unfazed. Sara summoned water from the lake, froze it into spears above the meadow, and then assaulted them from above. In a blur, Lethal pushed back their sleeves and blocked each strike with their forearms, ice splintering upon impact as if the vampire were solid stone.

Seriously? Let's see how you like kinetic power. Sara hurled two spheres of flaming white energy, the brightness illuminating the evening sky.

Lethal dodged out of the way—squinting against the light.

Sara smirked. It was a small crack in the vampire's armor, but it was all she needed to hit them when they least expected it.

She summoned more water from the lake, creating a barrier of ice behind and to the right of Lethal. The vampire inched forward a step, and Sara drove a blinding ball of white-hot power directly at them. As the light glinted off the icy wall and Lethal pivoted to dodge left, Sara barreled into their side, smashing them both through the frozen barrier. The ball of energy exploded above them, the ice crashing down, pummeling the shield she hastily threw up to protect them both.

When the last of the energy fizzled out, Sara rolled off the vampire, gasping, and healed her hand—every bone having been broken from colliding with Lethal's unyielding body.

What are they made of? Granite?

Lily threw open the cottage door, window box flowers trembling with her force. Her tense posture visibly melted at spotting them lying unharmed on the ground. "Clean up. It's time for dinner." With a shake of her head, she tossed a kitchen towel over her shoulder and disappeared back into the cottage.

Sara picked herself up. "Yeah, yeah, we're fine, thanks for asking." She twirled a hand, restoring the clearing to its original pristine appearance.

Lethal sprang to their feet, smoothing their shirt and swiping back errant golden strands. "Though incredibly messy, you did manage to knock me over," they said, genuine approval in their honeyed voice.

"Yeah, well, thanks for not showing me any *kindness.*" Sara nodded at the sword and strode past them, stomach growling in response to the savory scents drifting from the cottage kitchen.

CHAPTER 29

L ETHAL REFUSED TO eat or drink while the rest of them dined. Instead, they sat beside Lily, keenly observing the entire meal and every scrap of the group's banter. Caleb nervously cracked his knuckles a few times, and Sara pretended not to study the vampire studying them with blatant curiosity.

"You can truly eat anything?" they asked Lily, watching her pop another roll into her heart-shaped mouth.

"Yes, though dairy doesn't always agree with me," she confessed.

"Me, either," said Sara. "But it doesn't stop me from eating ice cream."

Caleb swallowed a mouthful of braised chicken. "Nothing could stop me from ice cream." He helped himself to more roasted beets and jerked his chin at Moira. "Have you talked with Matt lately? I bet he's having a great time partying at university. Sure was bouncing around and ready to go like a stud horse about to be released." He snickered, his green and gold-flecked eyes twinkling.

Moira pointed at him with a half-eaten chicken leg in her hand. "That's because Gran told him she had a premonition about him meeting someone *special*." She sighed. "Maybe I should go to university—"

"Gran should keep her thoughts to herself," interrupted Sara.

I definitely need to have a chat with my sweet, ornery grandmother. "Her premonitions are ridiculously vague."

"Not true," said Caleb. "She said I'd have a good time at the beach, and I did. Well, until the call, of course."

Moira leaned across the table, giving him her sly ear-to-ear grin. "I knew it. What's her name?"

"Doesn't matter now," said Caleb, dropping the tone of his voice and waving her off. "She *told* me her number, so there's no chance I'll see her again."

Everyone fell silent until Sara couldn't take the awkwardness anymore. "Why would that be a problem?" she asked, sharing a questioning look with Lethal across the table.

He hunched his broad shoulders and shot her a grin that didn't match the dull look in his eyes. "I'm dyslexic." Without skipping a beat, he added, "So, what was the big crash earlier? Lily thought a dragon smashed into the meadow." He arched a brow at Sara before knocking back the rest of his birch beer.

"Oh," Sara breathed, nearly getting whiplash from the rapid change in subject. As her mind stumbled to process Caleb's disclosure and his obvious avoidance of the matter, Lethal suddenly perked up.

"Have you seen a dragon?" they asked, icy eyes scanning the group.

Sara avoided the vampire's gaze by helping herself to a baked apple and carefully cutting it into *very* small pieces.

"No," said Moira. "Wouldn't we be dead if we saw one?"

"Not necessarily," responded Lethal. "They don't always kill everyone—depends on the dragon's disposition. Some are mindless killers, while others are more discriminating."

Their pensive tone pulled at Sara, and she dared a glance, catching the vampire's eye. The knitted brow was on prominent display.

Lethal continued, "Since it wasn't a dragon that wiped out the Hills site, I don't believe a dragon has been seen in this region for years." The vampire sat back, folding their arms. "It's not terribly unusual for dragons to be absent if magicals are behaving, but O—Samson," they corrected themselves, "said the Shadow Mother destroyed the Hills site. Such a brazen attack would have called a dragon, and yet none came."

Sara stopped chewing her apple and swallowed hard. "So, not seeing a dragon in a long time is bad?" An absurd question given the concerned look on their usually serene face. But she wasn't about to confess to *misbehaving*—as a High Witch, no less—and having a fight with Takers on the beach and coming face-to-face with a very large, very blood-red dragon that could have swallowed her whole.

Lethal said, "It's not good."

"Wait a minute," said Moira, pushing her plate away. "You're saying the Shadow Mother, whoever she is, and *not* Samson, killed the Hills witches? You believe the smoky, dark witch?"

"Yes. I believe this is true. And I believe she was involved with Naomi's murder. I also believe Samson intends to help protect Ware Woods."

"Then I believe it too," said Lily, rising from the table and gathering empty plates.

Lethal gave her a radiant, deadly tipped smile.

Beautiful, arrogant vampire. While they may have swayed Lily, Sara was not convinced of Samson's claims. He was a master of deceit—practically admitted it himself. And even if Sara had somehow cured him, how would the Shadow Mother know it had been her?

No. Sara shook her head. To fully believe the Shadow Mother—a force Samson *and* Lethal seemed to fear—was indeed coming for them, Sara would need proof. Because readily accepting this fate would be accepting their imminent deaths, and she refused to do this.

Lily approached her chair, interrupting Sara from her brooding, and asked, "Is it okay if we spend the night again? It's late and just started raining."

"It is?" Sara turned her frown to the cottage's skylight, listening. On cue, fat raindrops splattered the night-dark glass. Lily didn't need to make it rain for an excuse to stay. "Of course, silly. You're always welcome. Caleb, you gonna stay this time?" she asked while they all stood and began clearing the table.

Her cousin warily watched the vampire slip out the cottage door. "As tempting as that is, I don't want to get stabbed with a dagger because of my snoring."

Sara huffed a laugh. "Suit yourself. I got this," she added, taking the stack of plates from Lily. "You all made dinner. The least I can do is clean up."

As Lily and Moira headed to the bathroom for the toiletries they'd *conveniently* left behind from the last sleepover, Caleb took the dishes from her hands and set them down.

In a low voice, he asked, "Is this a good idea? You know, *they* didn't exactly eat dinner yet."

She paused. He was right to be concerned. Lethal had no qualms about killing, or even inflicting pain during sparring. And yet, given their respect for Lily and genuine concern when Sara had transported from her bedroom, she trusted the vampire would be true to their word and never hurt anyone in Ware Woods. She hoped that wasn't a grave mistake given Lethal's first lesson: never trust a vampire.

Avoiding Caleb's gaze, she said, "Yes. They sit in a chair and stare at the stars all night. Besides, the oak would stake Lethal if they even looked at our necks."

"You know that's a fairy tale, right? Uncle Larry says the only way to kill a vampire is with dragon or witch fire."

Sara blinked at him. Well, *that* was an interesting tidbit the Book had failed to share with her. And it explained why Lethal shied away from her flickering kinetic energy. Perhaps next time she and Lethal sparred, she would surprise them with witch fire. She troubled her lip, weighing the possibility of Lethal wielding Kindness in return.

With a chuckle, Caleb pulled her into a hug, his chestnut and mossy-green scent enveloping her. "Your innocence is very reassuring in these trying times, cousin."

She playfully pinched him, and he laughed again before releasing her and heading for the door.

"But seriously, do your mind-meld communication if you need anything. I promised Thomas I'd keep an eye on you, and I'm a male of my word." He zipped up his jacket and stepped out into the rain.

"Thanks, Caleb," she mentally called after him. Of course, Thomas would have sought out her cousin before he left. And how very Caleb to describe her lack of experience as innocence. *Pfft.*

Hopefully the second and third Magi would arrive soon—a powerful Alpha Shifter and an experienced High Witch—to round out Lethal's knowledge and give her an edge over the supposed Shadow Mother. And if the Shadow Mother was not a threat, Sara would have all the knowledge, power, and experience to finally be rid of Samson. Then Ian would be healed and finally home, and Dorcas would be back in her protective custody. With luck, the Magi could also keep a secret. Sara sighed, hoping it would be that easy.

Sleeves rolled up, she tackled the dishes and put the kitchen back in order, Lily and Moira chirping good night and retiring to the treehouse long before Sara finished. Once the kitchen was clean, Sara savored a long shower, each drop of water trying and failing to ease her anxiety.

By the time she entered the treehouse, it was quite late and silent save for the soft whispers of the flickering candles and the light patter of rain. Leaving her boots in the main room, Sara tiptoed to Moira's bedroom.

She was asleep, a trio of squirrels curled up beside her on the leaf-patterned quilt. On the back of a nearby chair rested Trouble, beak tucked beneath his wing.

Sara checked the remaining rooms for Lily and eventually tracked her flowery scent to the room she previously used—the room Lethal now occupied. When she padded to the top of the original narrow staircase, she spotted Lily through the open bedroom doorway.

The half-vampire, half-witch lay tucked into the gray covers, her eyes closed, pale blonde hair cascading like water over her petite form. Sara panned the room to Lethal, who was sitting with their back to her in their usual chair, staring at the night sky. No bottle of red tonight.

The vampire remained still as death, a cold, classical statue.

Hoping they wouldn't move until dawn, Sara retired to her own room, crawled into bed, and instantly fell into a dreamless sleep.

CHAPTER 30

THE MURMUR OF quiet conversation, accompanied by the soft birdsong of a new day, roused Sara from her cozy four-poster bed.

"There is no laundry service," said Lily, her airy voice carrying from the adjacent room. "Clean it yourself. Or better yet, stop hunting the nearby towns. Go to the brown house and call whoever you need to order more shirts and bottles."

Sara's eyes flew open, her body coiled and ready to spring from the covers if Lily so much as gasped at Lethal's response to her directive.

They only grunted.

The next day, two new trunks were delivered to the wall.

Sara had just whished them to the treehouse and resumed practicing with Moira and Lethal, passably deflecting daggers and claws with a combination of her powers, when the forest shushed. Not a leaf dropped, nor an animal stirred. Even the oak tree ceased its gentle creaking.

The prevalent furrow appeared between Lethal's brows as they tilted their head, listening to the disquieting silence. Moira, in the form of a mountain lion, crouched, muscles tense, furred ears swiveling. She hissed, the harsh warning causing every hair on Sara's skin to stand on end, and then tore off toward the Walkers' house.

The ground shivered, nearly knocking Sara off her feet. In the aftereffect, waves slapped the lakeshore, trees swayed, and flocks of birds took flight. She glanced at the cornflower blue sky dotted with fluffy clouds. Not a trace of darkness overhead. Whoever— or whatever—drew near was not Samson or the Shadow Mother. Besides, Winter Solstice was almost two months away.

From the west side of the forest, near the Walker home and where the private road met the forest wall, a series of throaty barks filled the air. The back of Sara's neck prickled at recognizing Bill Walker's wolf sounding an alarm. His wife, Shannon, barked in unison along with Moira, who must have changed form to join them.

Assuming Lethal would keep up in their own way, Sara launched into the sky and flew for the Walkers. Either Matthew and Thomas had returned early, which was concerning since they needed to finish their semester to complete their degrees, or the second Magus had come, which was also concerning given how annoyed Lethal had been by Sara's spell when they first arrived.

As she flew, her insides twisted at the thought of meeting another grumpy, powerful Magus—one who may not be inclined to keep the forest's unusual power a secret.

Nearing the edge of the forest, Sara spotted a gray muscle car with heavily tinted windows parked in the road alongside the Walkers' sprawling, green-paneled home. In the front yard, just behind the wall, loomed Bill, thick arms folded and chest puffed out, Shannon and Moira by his side. Joining them were Alice and Albert, along with Gran, Charlie, and Caleb.

Sara landed with a weighty thud beside Bill.

With his gaze steadfast on the car, he said, "It's a pack of shifters. This here is the scout, and they better have a damn good reason to be showing up at our door." He ended his words with a threatening growl. Beside him, Albert bared his teeth and snarled, white fur standing on end.

A whole pack? Sara leaned against the wall and peered down the road as three more muscle cars—one red, one orange with black stripes, and one solid black—rolled into view. Deep bass music seeped from the orange car, thumping in time with the throaty purr of the engines.

Father above, she only needed the help of an Alpha Shifter, not an entire pack.

The gray car's engine cut, and the driver's door opened. Bill widened his stance and grimaced as a young male wearing wrap-around sunglasses gracefully emerged and faced them. He was tall and lean, dark hair pulled into a short ponytail with spiky, bleached-tip ends. Even with his hands in his pockets, he moved with a preternatural ease, similar to Moira's and Matthew's fluid elegance. But unlike the twins, this shifter possessed a wild power that flickered in a golden aura around him.

Sara narrowed her eyes. Bill said he was a scout, yet this male's energy was Magus level. And whoever he was, he had magic outside of a sacred site.

Despite the cool autumn day, the visitor wore a white T-shirt, accentuating his golden umber skin. A tattooed line of black dia-monds adorned both of his outer forearms.

Bill growled. "Remove your sunglasses and tell us why you're here before I decide I don't care and rip out your throat."

Though Sara knew Bill's magic couldn't cross the wall, his threat rang true. He would tear into this shifter with normal hands if given the slightest affront. And if he needed any help, Albert would jump the wall and assist.

The shifter's expression remained respectfully tranquil—no arrogant teasing smile, which surely would have ignited Bill. After a heavy pause, he slipped his hands from his pockets, revealing matte-black fingernails with slightly curved points, and slowly removed his glasses.

Sara froze, her mind distantly ringing. If the nails weren't enough of a warning, his eyes shone like liquid gold, and his pupils were black vertical slits. Elysian eyes.

Her jaw dropped.

Caleb nudged her and whispered, "If this is the scout, I don't want to know what's in the rest of the parade." He angled his head at the remaining cars, whose engines idled with a deep rumble.

"You have dragon eyes," whispered Alice, drawing back a step.

The bloodstone at Sara's chest pulsed. His stare was wondrous—not cruel per Gran's fearsome Samhain tale, but dazzling with power.

The shifter swept his extraordinary gaze from Bill and Shannon to Albert and then Alice. "I'm half-dragon. And I'm confused. Which of you is the pack leader?" Though his words were blunt, his voice was smooth and polite. He turned his attention toward Moira and tilted his head with a slight frown, as if finding lack.

Bill growled again and edged in front of Moira. "Why are you here—all of you?" He jerked his chin at the line of cars.

The shifter inclined his head further. "Apologies. We thought we were expected. Our site was recently destroyed, and we were . . . pulled here."

A whimper escaped Moira, and Bill snarled.

"Sara Lochton!" yelled Gran, steel blue energy snapping around her.

Sara cringed.

Her father arched a brow at her. "Why did you summon an *entire* pack to our forest?"

Caleb wisely took a step back as Sara responded, "I didn't mean to *pull* the entire pack, just a powerful Magus to help with our *current situation*."

"An Alpha Shifter's power *is* their pack. And nothing comes without a price. They may help now, but they will take in return. Factions are only loyal to their own," said Gran, completely ignoring the half-dragon shifter, who didn't refute her statement.

Great. This was another nugget of information that would have been nice to know before she cast the spell. Everything she did seemed to be a crash course on how *not* to be a High Witch.

Sara eyed the shifter, who remained intensely studying the Walkers. A faint grin tugged at the corners of her mouth. "Then we're in luck. Because the Walkers are shifters." Without hesitating in the slightest, she leapt over the wall and faced the visitor. In what she hoped was a confident High Witch tone, she proclaimed, "I'm the one who summoned your Alpha. Can I speak to them?"

Bill stepped closer to the wall. Albert jumped atop it, claws digging into stone.

The shifter tensed, nostrils twitching, golden aura flaring as he scanned Sara with his strange gaze. "Perhaps it is you who can help us right now. I'll take you to him," he said and strode toward the other cars without looking back to ensure she was following.

Sara hurried after him. As they passed the red muscle car, the windows lowered. Inside, three identical females removed their glasses and set three identical amber gazes on her. Sara steeled herself, feigning what she hoped was a steady High Witch appearance.

The shifter continued past the orange car with black stripes, its male driver tapping the steering wheel and nodding to his music, which had been noticeably turned down. Though dark sunglasses veiled his eyes, his head slowly swiveled as he tracked Sara's movement.

Upon reaching the black muscle car—the only four-door in the group—the driver's window rolled down and a scrawny teen boy, his pale face speckled with pimples, stuck his head out. "Yo, Tobio, he's not doing so well." He adjusted his backward baseball cap, his gaze nervously darting from Sara to the back seat of the car.

"That's about to change," stated the shifter—Tobio—as he put his hand on the rear door handle and turned to Sara. "You'll need to heal him before he can shift and speak with you." Confidence blazed in his gold eyes.

She retreated a step, shocked he knew she had healing magic while also deftly negotiating with her so they could both get what they wanted. Maybe his eyes saw far more than the typical magical—far more than even her ability to see auras. She threw up her mental shield, tucking away the questionable bits of herself, and narrowed her gaze at him. Savvy half-dragon.

He opened the door. Inside lay a massive black wolf, sprawled across the entire back seat, his left flank horribly burned.

Potent magic and a robust stench smacked into her, flaring her hair and burning her eyes. "What happened?" exclaimed Sara. She scrunched her face, shoving down the urge to empty her stomach, and crept closer to the wolf. His head hung limply over the seat on the far side, eyes shut, jaw open, pink tongue lolling with each labored pant.

Sara leaned into the car and placed her hands above his red and black-charred flesh. The wound's heat seared her palms. Gritting her teeth, she summoned a cooling energy to soothe and heal the injury. Frosty white light leapt from her hands and onto the wound, sizzling as flesh restored itself and fur regrew until the injury completely vanished.

The wolf rotated an ear toward her and groaned, his guttural resonance vibrating the windows.

Tobio, holding the door, replied, "A dragon attacked us."

CHAPTER 31

SARA STOOD, SMACKING her head into the car's door frame. "Dragon?" Images of the red-and-gold dragon from the beach swam in her mind, her skin burning at the memory of its fire licking her protective shield.

Tobio remained silent as the scent of frankincense descended upon them, mixing with the choking odor of burnt fur and flesh.

Sara pulled away from the car and rounded on Lethal, who casually stood in the road beside them. "Where have you been?" she demanded.

"Holy shit," squeaked the teen, rolling up his window as Tobio released a deep-throated, pulsating hiss. Goose bumps erupted on every inch of Sara's skin.

She dug in her heels and glared at the half-dragon shifter. "No fighting," she grumbled. Burning Hells, this spell had more unexpected dangers than sparring with Violet and her vestment of hidden knives.

"Lethal!" boomed a voice so deep it rattled Sara's teeth. She jerked her gaze back at the car. Perhaps the largest person she had ever seen—aside from Bill Walker—emerged from the back seat. He wore dark jeans and a gray thermal shirt, which hugged every bulging muscle in his enormous shoulders and arms. Sara gawped. Father above, his neck was as thick as his head.

Tobio slid one foot back, his fiery glare fixed on the vampire as the titanic Alpha Shifter approached and rumbled, "You're a long way from home."

Lethal raised an unamused brow at him. "Dean. Your testosterone is suffocating, as usual."

The Alpha bit back, "As is your pleasant demeanor."

Lethal's death stare put Sara's to shame; she hoped never to be on the receiving end of that glare. When the Alpha didn't flinch, Lethal said, in a scythe-sharp tone, "Choose your words *very* carefully." Dean's gaze narrowed a fraction, and Lethal continued, "I'm equal parts curious to know *why* you and your wolf pack are disobeying a direct order from Council and *why* a dragon attacked your Blue Ridge site."

Dean grunted or cleared his throat—the sound so low and quick, Sara wasn't sure which. "We were *pulled* here. Have been for a while and couldn't resist anymore," he said, and Sara felt his low-toned aching voice in her bones. He flicked his amber gaze to the wall before squaring his shoulders to Sara. Towering over her, a faint smile on his chiseled ebony face, he took her hand in his and gave a firm shake. His clasp was warm and dry, astonishingly gentle given his burly hand completely dwarfed hers. "I'm Dean. Thanks for healing me. We're at your service now." He released her hand and gestured to Tobio and the others waiting in the cars, engines off.

Lethal impatiently folded their arms, perfect nose crinkling. "Clearly, shifter instinct and witchy spells override Global Council. Now, explain the dragon."

Tobio hissed again, a distinct warning.

Lethal didn't even blink.

With a quick shake of his head at Tobio, silencing him, Dean turned his attention back to the vampire. "Ah, yes. Dragon. We hadn't seen one in years until a few nights ago when a vicious flat-eye attacked—*for no reason*. It burned our house and soul tree to the ground and went straight for Tobio. He drove it off, but the damage was done. So we fled, tails tucked between our legs." He gave a resigned shrug, yet Sara saw the crushing blue-black grief in his aura.

One soul tree? She held in the question, which surely would have tipped him off to Ware Woods' many trees and unique magic.

"Did you notice anything odd about the dragon?" inquired Lethal, heartlessly ignoring the loss of Dean's house and soul tree.

"It wasn't a family member, if that's what you're asking," said Dean, frowning at the vampire. "The scales were a dull orange, not fiery like we've seen before. And shadows clung to it."

The crease puckered Lethal's brow. "I'm amazed your brother is still alive," they said, glancing at Tobio. "You'll like it here, half-breed," they crooned to the elysian-eyed shifter before disappearing in a blur of movement back into the forest.

Brother? Sara bounced her gaze between Dean and Tobio.

Dean stared after Lethal. "You'd think that vampire would have learned some manners by now. Why are they here anyway?" he asked, shoving his giant hands into his back pockets.

Sara faltered. This Alpha Shifter was much bigger and much younger than she expected. And though power projected from him, and he fearlessly stood up to Lethal, there was a gentle softness to him. She guessed Dean was a few years older than her, perhaps Caleb's age, and he was staring right at her . . .

"Oh," she stuttered. "I pulled Lethal too. There's a dark witch harassing us, and a *teensy* possibility the Shadow Mother is coming on Solstice, so I cast a spell for aid. Are you cool with helping us?" Her words tumbled out, and she resisted the impulse to slap a hand over her mouth.

To her shock, Dean grinned, revealing dimpled cheeks. "I don't know anything about a Shadow Mother, but we'd love to." He cut a sharp whistle, and the rest of his pack emerged from their cars. "This is Wes." He nodded at the teen boy with the ball cap.

"That's Luke." He jerked his chin at a sun-tanned surfer-style blond jauntily leaning against the orange car. "And those are my cousins, Moesha, Alesha, and Iesha." The trio of identically gorgeous bronze-skinned females waved down low at Sara.

She immediately responded by returning the magical greeting, then swept her gaze across the entire pack, counting.

Seven shifters. Sara plastered on a smile. *"Dad?"*

Charlie softly chuckled in her mind. *"Yes, firecracker?"*

"Can you please bring a gallon of sap to the wall?"

"Ted's got it. Alice and I are escorting your grandmother home before she spouts off some rather personal premonitions." He paused. *"Well done, kiddo."*

Before Sara could reply, Dean said, "Ah . . . we had to leave in a hurry and would really appreciate anything you can spare." His tone was apologetic and hopeful, not the demanding fierce Alpha Shifter she had been expecting but a gentle leader who cared for his pack—a pack that likely had only the clothes on their backs and were thoroughly exhausted.

He ran a hand over his cropped hair and clarified, "Short term, of course. We have plenty of means. Mo just needs time to access our funds and order what we need."

Moesha—the triplet with double-plaited braids—wagged her phone at Sara with a confident smile.

Sara returned the grin. "Of course. I know I speak for the entire forest in saying we are sorry for the loss of your home and soul tree. We have plenty to share. You all can stay at our Main House, and I'm sure we can find some temporary clothes." Sara scanned the pack again. Tobio and Luke could easily fit into Matthew's and Ian's spare clothes, and she and Moira could share with the triplets, while Wes could borrow some Cahill kids' clothes. Dean, however . . . Sara glanced at Bill.

Though his arms were folded, his scowl seemed halfhearted as he gave her an approving nod. Beside him, Shannon was nearly jumping up and down with excitement. "They're just pups, Bill! They're not even a proper pack yet."

"It's the *yet* that worries me," muttered Bill. His amber gaze slid to Moira, who was flirtatiously tossing back her red hair. Luke stared, a bit of drool on his lower lip, until Dean growled at him, and he quickly looked away with his head down.

Mother below, bringing a wolf pack into Ware Woods would be tricky. Sara tapped a finger to the center of her forehead, thinking. *How should a High Witch handle this?*

She inhaled deeply, gathering her confidence, and faced the new shifters. "Welcome to Ware Woods. Besides the crotchety vampire of Death, the rest of the forest is delighted to have you."

Shannon squealed, and Ted gave a hearty, "Hear, hear."

Encouraged by their enthusiastic support, Sara continued with the first of her two hastily considered requirements. "I know Dean is your Alpha, but inside Ware Woods, all shifters will answer to Bill Walker." When she pointed at Bill, he rocked back on his heels and gave a toothy smile, dominance exuding from his massive frame.

Though Dean and the pack grumbled, they lowered their heads in agreement.

Sara sighed. If the pack was willing to defer to Bill, they shouldn't have any qualms about her second request. She eyed Ted, who held a jug of sap in one hand and in his other, the ornate metal cup typically used when teens came of age and officially pledged themselves to protect Ware Woods.

Perhaps the sap had zero effect on shifters, as with Lethal, but it still gave Sara peace of mind and seemed the right thing to do. She looked up at Dean and explained, "It's customary for newcomers to drink our sap and pledge themselves to protect this forest as if it were their own." She left out the part about being pure of heart. While the pack seemed trustworthy, here was the true test and one Sara hoped would also ensure they kept the secret of Ware Woods' powerful magic.

"We will protect Ware Woods," said Dean, solemnly, speaking for his entire pack. He lifted his chin toward Tobio, a silent command.

Tobio held his brother's stare for the briefest of moments before accepting the cup from Ted and taking a tentative sip. Sara remained transfixed on the half-dragon, waiting. When nothing happened, Tobio took a longer pull from the cup, handed it back to Ted, and fluidly hurdled the stone wall.

Upon crossing the threshold, Tobio froze, his aura and golden eyes blazing as he first scanned the forest edge and then everyone gathered beside him. With predatory ease, he pivoted back to the road—to Dean and the pack—and lifted his chin approvingly.

As if not to be outdone, Luke grabbed the cup from Ted and quickly did the same. The three sisters immediately followed, drinking the sap and crossing the wall as one. Their beaming smiles and content purrs caused Caleb to nervously crack his thumbs and avert his attention to the next wolf shifter stepping up to the wall.

With a muttered, "Thanks," Wes politely accepted the refilled cup from Ted and knocked it back, draining the contents as if he hadn't drunk in days. The teen barely set the cup on the wall before he stumbled and fell to the ground, convulsing.

Shit.

Sara and Dean rushed to his side, but as soon as Sara extended a healing touch, Wes jumped up and laughed.

"Kidding! Dang, you should see your faces." Wes reared back with a howl until Caleb leaned over the stone wall and smacked him upside the head.

Sara would have throttled the young teen herself if she hadn't been a puddle of relief.

"Smartass," chided Caleb. "The role of resident goofball is already filled."

Wes straightened his cap and squinted at Caleb. "We'll see about that," he quipped with a competitive grin and hopped over the wall. As his athletic shoes hit the grassy yard, his eyes nearly popped from his skull. "Holy shit."

"Watch the mouth, ash-hole," warned Caleb with a hint of teasing. He proudly beckoned him and said, "Come on, sidekick, I'll show you to the Main House. We've got plenty of room and food for you all." Caleb turned and strode for a path at the rear of the Walkers' yard.

With a yip at the word "*food*," Wes phased into a small gray wolf and chased after him, playfully nipping at his heels. Luke phased into a gray wolf as well, followed by the girls turning into three identical black wolves. Tobio merely quickened his pace to join Caleb's side.

Clearly eager to catch up with them, Dean swallowed the last of the sap, then faced the Walkers and flashed a dimpled smile. "Thank you for having us," he said, wincing slightly as he dipped his head to Bill. It obviously pained him to defer to another, but he quickly recovered his grin and leapt the wall, phasing into a hulking black wolf and bounding after his pack.

In a furry blur, Moira turned into a russet wolf and chased after him, tail high.

Sara sighed through her nose. This second part of the spell—seven shifters—was even more surprising than the arrogant vampire. Yet, if the sap could be trusted to work on shifters, the pack was pure of heart and in genuine awe of the forest's magic. They pledged to protect Ware Woods and seemed willing to help, which was more than she could say for Lethal, who hadn't been completely forthright with all they knew about the Global Council.

Although she supposed it worked in their favor to have other magicals forbidden to visit Ware Woods, why would the Global Council order this if they didn't know of the forest's unique power? She needed to speak with Lethal, but first . . .

Sara levitated and slowly spun in the air, studying the four muscle cars parked in the road.

"Don't worry," said Bill. "I'll have them pull the cars into our drive tomorrow, and we'll keep an eye on the seven of them. Just like old times when all the kids were home." He put an arm around a glowing Shannon, pulling her close while steering them back toward their house.

Ted chuckled. "Must have been some spell you cast on Samhain." He grinned up at her with approval.

"Pfft. I guess we'll see on Solstice," she uttered, hoping to the Mother and Father that her amateur efforts would somehow protect them all from whatever dark magic might come their way.

"Everything will work out as it should. And right now, everyone is happy. Even Ian—wherever he is—called earlier and was truly content. You're a great High Witch, and I know you have plenty to do with getting the pack settled into the Main House, so skedaddle." Ted waved her off as he walked in the direction of the Lochton homes.

Sara nearly fell from the sky. *If only I were a great High Witch.*

"You are," Ted projected into her mind.

And despite not believing her uncle, she mentally whispered, *"Thanks,"* before soaring above the trees and racing toward the Main House.

CHAPTER 32

Through thinning autumn treetops, Sara easily spotted Caleb and Tobio walking along a pine needle–strewn path. The rest of the pack sniffed and searched the immediate forest, with one of the triplets scouting the lead and Dean bringing up the rear. Caleb gestured to different parts of Ware Woods, and Sara caught portions of his conversation as he explained the five families' roles and magical gifts. Despite being surrounded by a pack of shifters, including a half-dragon at his side, Caleb was completely in his element. Either he readily trusted the newcomers, or he knew Moira slunk behind them all, cautiously surveying their every move.

Sara raced ahead, pondering the best way to tell the Cahills that a pack of hungry shifters was about to move into the Main House. When she landed on the deck and entered the main room, Helen Cahill—resident matriarch and head of the Main House—called out to her from the kitchen along the back wall.

"Ted mentally told us about our new guests. I've got a couple pots of chili started and fresh bread in the oven. All the rooms have been made and ready ever since we rebuilt after Makwa's fire."

Sara paused midway through the sea of wooden lodge-style furniture. "You've been expecting them since Makwa died?" That was months ago—long before Sara even considered casting a spell.

From across the kitchen island, Helen's husband, Eddie, and Caleb's mother, Rebecca, waved at Sara as though it were just another typical day.

Helen looked up from chopping tomatoes, her face rosy, gray hair arranged in her signature braided wreath around her head. "Gran instructed us to make the Main House bigger, so we did. You know how your grandmother's premonitions are. She didn't know who would be moving in, just told us to be ready."

Sara panned the voluminous room with its overhanging second-story balcony. Gran's foresight was glitchy at best. And while the arrival of the shifters explained the Main House additions and possibly the multiple bins of beef jerky Gran had insisted Helen stock up on, it did not explain the multitude of child-sized mittens she had been obsessively knitting nor the random fire extinguisher she'd brought to the treehouse. As if a High Witch with water powers would ever need such a thing.

"They're here!" Uncle Larry's voice thundered from the deck patio.

Helen grabbed a towel, wiping her hands as she and Rebecca rounded the island and joined Sara in filing out onto the deck.

"Oh, my," whispered Helen, her gaze falling on Tobio and his unusual liquid gold and slit-pupiled eyes.

Tobio stopped before the deck, scrutinizing the present Cahills before turning back to Dean. The Alpha immediately phased, followed by the rest of the pack. Behind them, Moira phased as well, hands on her hips, studying Dean with a distinct foxy luster in her amber eyes.

Caleb made introductions, humbly apologizing when he mixed up the triplet sisters' names. A tense silence followed a chorus of polite "Hellos" until Dean cleared his throat. "Excuse us if we seem aloof. Most of the witches we've seen were rogue and tried to kill us."

"You've seen a lot of rogue witches?" asked Moira, her presence startling Dean as he jerked and rounded to face her.

He eyed her warily while she sauntered up beside him. "Ah . . . yes. Our site doesn't have a wall like yours. We had to regularly defend ourselves from dark magic trying to take our energy and soul tree."

Moira blinked at him, and Dean went wholly still.

"Welcome," called Uncle Larry from atop the deck stairs. "We rarely see dark witches, or dragons, for that matter. The only danger here is Helen trying to overfeed you. Which"—he paused, stroking his snow-white beard and regarding Dean with a grin—"may not be possible for shifters." His focus drifted to Caleb. "Come on, Caleb, you can help me, Eddie, and your ma tend to the chili while Helen shows them the house." He untucked his thumbs from his overall straps and retreated toward the kitchen with Rebecca.

Wes nervously adjusted his ball cap, flipping the bill to the front. "You're gonna cook for us?" he asked hesitantly.

"Don't let it go to your head, Jokey. We cook for everyone," said Caleb, mounting the stairs and following his mother and Uncle Larry.

Whether or not Wes caught the hint of humor, he timidly approached the deck, sniffing the savory aromas already drifting from the kitchen. Tobio pushed past him, boldly striding up the stairs and into the Main House. He halted, gaze skipping around the grandiose room as the rest of the pack followed and froze beside him.

Similar to the original Main House, the new construction included multiple live trees—their trunks functioning as pillars, their canopies forming a vaulted ceiling. The Cahills' earth magic kept the trees in a perpetual state of vibrant growth, giving the sprawling house a treehouse village ambiance.

Around the room sat clusters of deeply cushioned couches and chairs, arranged in intimate settings, each with its own area rug and coffee table scarred by booted feet. Behind the upholstered furniture were groups of dining tables and chairs with enough seating for dozens of people. Along the back wall and tucked beneath the overhanging second-story balcony stretched an enormous granite-countered island with a commercial-sized kitchen beyond it. A grand staircase flowed down the right side of the main room, while on the left, a floor-to-ceiling stone fireplace towered, its hearth alight with an inviting warmth.

Helen brushed past the gawking pack and stood in the center of the room. "We recently made upgrades including a loft space with a central room and multiple bunk beds, which you are welcome to have," she said, pointing to the second level. Her hazel eyes crinkled, subtle wrinkles fanning from the outside corners as she bobbed her hand in the air and silently counted the shifters. "But we also have a new wing with seven private suites—each with its own bath."

One of the triplets whooped. Or it could have been all three in unison.

Helen beamed at the excited sisters. "Follow me," she said, escorting the entire pack past the fireplace and down a new hallway with multiple open doors. "The rooms are all fully furnished and stocked with linens and bathing essentials. But please let me know if you need anything else. Oh, and there's a door to the rear yard at the end of the hall so you can come and go as you please." She elbowed Moira and added, "I know how shifters get antsy, especially during a full moon."

Moira only shrugged.

Though the golden wood–paneled hallway was plenty wide enough, Dean swept beside Moira, his arm grazing hers, sending a blush to her cheeks as he approached Helen.

Sara coughed to hide her chuckle.

In his deep, rumbly voice, Dean said, "It's perfect, thank you."

Yelping with delight, the triplets began checking out the rooms.

"We're glad to have you," said Helen before turning back toward the kitchen. "Now, if you'll pardon me, I need to check on your dinner."

As she bustled away, Wes approached the open door closest to Sara. He peered inside at the spacious room with a full bed, sitting area, small desk, and archway to a private bath. With a wistful look at the hunter-green quilted bed, he said, "It's nice, but . . . It's Iesha's night off."

"Off?" inquired Sara to the triplet with two puffed ponytails.

"It's my night to take a break," said Iesha, her voice feather soft. When Sara raised a brow, Iesha explained, "We agreed to protect Ware Woods as if it were our own. So, this means we will defend the forest at all times. Our pack takes turns with one of us resting."

"While the *remainder* of you are on patrol?" questioned Sara. She exchanged a wide-eyed glance with Moira.

"Yes," said Alesha—the triplet with short locs—jumping in for her sister. Her voice was deeper, husky, and had the commanding bite of a seasoned fighter. She casually leaned against a door frame, seeming at ease, yet tension and perhaps grief bracketed the sides of her mouth. A faint scar traced her cheekbone. "That's how most packs operate. Caleb said the Walkers"—she nodded at Moira—"and Sullivans guard Ware Woods. Do you not take turns as well?"

Moira said, "We rotate, but only one or two of us patrols at night. No one approaches our wall in the daytime. You'd think the idiots would realize it's still impenetrable at night."

"Even to dragons?" asked Tobio, the gold in his eyes swirling, vertical pupils razor-thin in the late sunlight casting down the hallway.

"I should hope so," said Sara, biting back a gasp at both his gaze and the idea of dragons tearing into Ware Woods. She sent a silent plea to the Mother that the wall was indeed impenetrable. There was a beat of awkward silence. "I'm sorry for the loss of your soul tree and home."

Tobio dropped his gaze. "The tree is a great loss, and we hope it will grow back. The house was no big deal. Wasn't the first time we've lost our structure."

"Mm-hmm," chimed in Moesha, not bothering to look up from tapping her phone. "We've rebuilt a few times. The last house was my least favorite—it was much too big and drafty." She frowned, likely at their plight and the lack of phone service.

"The dragon did us a favor by burning that house to the ground," said Alesha, bending a knee and casually resting her foot on the doorframe behind her.

A dragon with shadows clinging to it. Sara twisted her lips in thought and glanced at Tobio, assessing his wary surveillance and slightly sluggish movements. The many questions she had for him regarding dragons would have to wait until he was in a well-rested and more trusting mood.

"Dean?" probed Iesha in her light voice, drawing his attentive gaze away from Moira as well as interrupting Sara's contemplations. The three sisters stood within the thresholds of three individual rooms, their warm-sunset eyes pleading with Dean.

Sara swung her head to him.

"They'd like to shower before eating," he explained, then inclined his head at his cousins, giving approval.

Their faces shone with gratitude as they promptly closed their doors.

Before the clicks finished echoing, Alesha's door flung open. "This is *my* room," she growled, kicking Luke into the hallway.

He banged into the opposite wall with the force of her toss, laughing until Tobio put him in a headlock and dragged him back to the main room.

Dean leaned toward Moira. "Only one to two sentinels, huh? Maybe I could join you when it's your turn. That is, if you'd let me." He grinned, his dimples flashing.

Moira's blush quickly melted into a coquettish gleam. When a deep purr vibrated in Dean's chest, she raised a manicured brow and turned on her heel, tossing her red mane behind her. "I'm checking on the chili," she called over her shoulder, an obvious saunter in her step.

Dean trailed after her with Wes in tow while Sara lingered in the hall, considering the pack's disclosures. It troubled her to know they had needed to rebuild often and spent most of their time on high alert for dark magic. Yet what bothered her more was the dawning awareness that magicals were constantly fighting. And that a dragon could swoop in and destroy a site.

Sara buried this worry for another day. She already had too many worries, including one in particular she wanted to address tonight. Rushing into the main room, she whished a tray of drinks from the kitchen island to a coffee table surrounded by comfy couches and chairs, then beckoned the male shifters standing idly by the fireplace to join her.

Caleb's laughter rang out from the kitchen, followed by Moira's.

"We can help too," offered Dean, a slight longing in his tone. He wavered before Sara, his shoulders facing her while his hips faced the kitchen.

Despite his brother's hesitation to relax, Tobio collapsed into a chair, grabbed a glass of water, and instantly drained it before reaching for another.

Sara held Dean's gaze while she sank into an oversized chair beside Tobio. "Thanks, but you all must be exhausted." She motioned to the empty seat on her other side.

"True," mumbled Luke, pulling on headphones from the front pocket of his sweatshirt and stretching out onto a couch. Wes flopped onto an adjacent sofa and lowered his cap over his closed eyes.

"Shoes," growled Dean, settling into a chair, the wood groaning under his massive frame.

Both Luke and Wes kicked off their shoes, letting them clomp to the floor. No sooner had the echo faded when Shannon burst into the room. In her hands were multiple backpacks, stuffed full.

"Between Moira and her other siblings, we have plenty of clothes for you with more on the way," panted Shannon in a manner suggesting she had run from her house.

"Thank you," said Dean and Tobio at the same time, clutching the arms of their chairs as if unsure an offer to help would be appreciated or insulting to the forest's alpha female.

Shannon plopped the bags on a nearby table, said, "Our pleasure," with a bright smile, and headed into the kitchen.

"Even other shifter packs aren't this welcoming. Is everyone here this nice?" asked Dean, his features slightly drawn as he stretched forward and picked up a water. The glass looked ridiculously miniscule in his dinner plate–sized hands.

"Pfft!" Sara glanced at Moira, catching her staring in their direction. "Mostly. Although you are definitely getting a much kinder welcome than I received." As she recalled, Kane nearly drowned her and Moira threatened to kill her, never mind the bear witch, Makwa, who had literally cursed her.

Tobio crunched a piece of ice, curious doubt in his elysian eyes. "You're new here?"

Sara waved a hand as if shooing a fly. "It's a long story." Divulging her inexperience as a High Witch was not what she wanted to discuss. Not in the least.

From the kitchen, Shannon could be heard telling Moira, "You are *forbidden* from spending the night here."

"Fine," came Moira's whispered hiss. "I'll stay at the treehouse."

"So," said Sara, a bit too loudly, distracting Dean and Tobio from the mother-daughter conversation while readying to ask the question she could no longer hold back. "What did Lethal mean when they said you were disobeying an order from the Global Council?"

Tobio crunched another piece of ice, his face once again impassive.

"Ah . . ." stumbled Dean, tearing his eyes away from the

kitchen. He cleared his throat and shifted in his seat. "Global Council has a direct order that no one approach Ware Woods. I'm sure Lethal knows why."

Not exactly an answer. Sara tried to assume Tobio's poker face. Either they were too hungry and tired for a full-on explanation, or they didn't know. It didn't matter. She'd go straight to the source to get an answer.

"Then I need to speak with Lethal," she said, rising from her chair. Helen and Uncle Larry looked up from spooning chili into bowls the size of buckets and met her gaze. Mentally projecting to them, Sara said, *They're exhausted and should crash after they eat. I'll be at the treehouse if you need anything.* They gave her knowing smiles and nodded reassuringly.

Sara turned to Dean, whose honey-yellow eyes shimmered with a touch of fatigue. Tomorrow she would test his power and learn all he had to teach her. But for now . . . "Eat and rest. None of you need to run patrol. You're safe here." She huffed. "Well, at least until Winter Solstice."

Dean's responding grin was pure wolf, as though nothing scared him. "Danger, we're used to. The opportunity to rest is new and greatly appreciated." He tipped his glass to her as she flew from the room and directly to the vampire—Hells-bent on extracting information and sharing a sense of foreboding doom.

CHAPTER 33

SARA TRACKED THE scent of frankincense to a certain private deck of the treehouse, finding the vampire exactly as she expected.

Lethal sat in their usual chair, bottle in hand, watching the setting sun. Not even bothering with a hello, Sara dropped into the chair beside them. "How is it that you know everyone?" she fired at them. A warmup jab of a question.

Without shifting their gaze, they drawled, "Global Council. Plus, I've been around a *very* long time."

Sara grinned at the perfect setup for her blazing left hook. "Speaking of Council, why did they order other magicals to stay away from Ware Woods?" She pinned them with her stare, intent on getting an answer.

The vampire took a swig from the bottle before responding. "Because you're different, and a mixing of factions is despised."

This was the paltry reason? Sara scowled. "That is incredibly backward and something I'd love to take up with the Global Council myself someday. Assuming we all survive the Shadow Mother and the dragons she apparently now has on her side." There. She landed her last punch, hoping it didn't seal their fate to be adding dragons to the Solstice party lineup.

Lethal didn't move.

Sara coaxed a breezy warmth from the adjacent open bedroom, letting it wrap around her and the vampire—even though cold didn't bother them. Her stomach growled. She would have grabbed some chili to go, except it would have inflamed her persistent heartburn. With a few impatient flicks of her hand, she whished herself a birch beer and sandwich from the cottage kitchen. Might as well get comfortable.

Lethal grunted. "Figured it out, did you? Then you know your Samson is telling the truth and you must trust him implicitly if you are to join forces and fight off the Shadow Mother."

Damn it.

Sara knew this to be true, but to hear it spoken out loud was like one of Lethal's Death daggers to her soul. Trust a dark witch with multiple black bloodstones, Takers, and a sadistic sense of humor. A witch who had eaten her finger, made a bargain with the Shadow Mother, and perhaps brought this all on them. She sighed. Loudly.

Samson also admitted to wanting to be loved and apparently had spent most of his life eliminating the dark magic he pretended to be. And though he had taken her brother, Ian was somehow happy. Ian, who she loved and trusted with all her heart, had told her to trust Samson.

Burning Hells.

She downed half the birch beer in one go. The irony did not escape her at having to trust the witch she hated most in order to save what she loved most. So she would suck it up and do what needed to be done. *Trust.*

She drank the rest of her beer, choked down the sandwich, and sat in grim silence with Lethal as the sky blackened and stars began to twinkle through the oak's mainly bare branches.

Hearing Lily and Moira enter the cemetery—recently tidied of the Samhain offerings—and ascend the treehouse stairs, Sara bid goodnight to Lethal and rushed to the cottage for a long, hot bath.

By the time the condensation on the bathroom mirror and shower glass had vanished, Sara's nine fingers and ten toes were thoroughly wrinkled. Preoccupied with worry, she had let the water grow cold. She carefully loosened her grip on the wildest of magic buried deep inside her. A tiny flame of witch fire slipped out and into the bath. It bubbled up, reheating the water, and popped from the surface in steamy bursts. She held her breath and sank under, relishing her weightlessness in the giant marbled wooden tub.

Maybe trusting Samson wouldn't be terrible. And maybe, with Lethal and Dean and a mystery High Witch by her side, defeating the Shadow Mother and curing her brother would be terrifically easy.

She lay still beneath the water and envisioned the perfect outcome—a smiling forest family, Ian healed, and her and Thomas holding hands in a peaceful, snowy forest. When her lungs burned for air and she couldn't stay under any longer, Sara released the image and rose from the tub.

After toweling off and donning sweats and another of Thomas's T-shirts, Sara padded up the treehouse stairs and peeked into Moira's room. Her friend lay fast asleep with a flushed grin upon her freckled face, the squirrel trio tucked in beside her and Trouble perched on a branch dangling from the ceiling.

Seems I'm not the only one pleased with the new shifters. Sara shook her head, sniggering, and wandered toward her room. At the top of the narrow staircase, a puff of air blew back her hair. She looked up—and froze.

Lily sat in the gray bed with a book and flickering candle, a finger to her lips. Beside her lay Lethal, arms folded across their slender chest, eyes closed, golden hair flowing over the pillow. They looked exactly like a sculpture atop a sarcophagus. No wonder they rarely slept; someone might truly bury them.

Lily, her voice quiet as snow, whispered, "They fell asleep while I was reading to them."

Sara squinted at the book in Lily's lap. It was the spicy novel she had brought to the beach. How anyone—besides herself—could fall asleep to that tantalizing literature was beyond Sara. She stifled her laughter and, with a wave goodnight, promptly fell asleep in her own cushy bed, hugging the spare pillow and dreaming of Thomas.

The following day, Sara woke feeling lighter, as if she had thrown off a heavy cloak she hadn't noticed was weighing her down. Either choosing to trust Samson had relieved her stress, or she was truly excited to learn as much as she could from Dean.

According to the spell, the Alpha Shifter symbolized power. And it was power she would need to drive off the Shadow Mother and any dragons she brought with her.

While Dean's tremendous size exuded strength, Sara needed to know what he was capable of and how she could emulate his powerful magic to defend Ware Woods. And with Winter Solstice less than two months away, she would need to be a fast learner.

Eager to meet up with the Alpha, she jumped from the bed, startling a line of sparrows off the windowsill, threw on some clothes, and raced through the treehouse, checking up on her companions. Everyone was asleep, save for Lethal who sat in their chair, reading. They didn't even look up from their page as they waved what was either a two-finger good morning salute or an I'm-busy-don't-bother-me gesture.

Sara rolled her eyes and flew to the Main House, pulling her black jacket close against the morning chill. Her excitement over meeting Dean for a long, informative breakfast was instantly dashed when she burst into the quiet main room and found only a handful of Cahills at the kitchen island.

"Where's the pack?" she asked, a touch winded as panic washed over her. Had they changed their minds, wisely deciding the Shadow Mother wasn't their problem, and left Ware Woods in the middle of the night?

Uncle Larry slid a mug of coffee at her. "They're all sleeping in."

Sara relaxed her shoulders and grabbed the mug and a cider doughnut from the platter of pastries on the counter.

"If these shifters are like the Walkers," said Helen, setting a basket of fresh eggs beside the restaurant-sized flat stove top, "they'll sleep until almost noon, and breakfast will be brunch."

Sara let her shoulders sag further, coffee burning her tongue as she gulped it down. She hated waiting, especially with the countdown to Solstice looming over her amateur head.

Uncle Larry chuckled and stroked his beard, an impish grin on his ruddy face. "There's a thatch of brimstone briars by the marshy section that could use some tending to."

"I'll do it," replied Sara, slamming down her half-drained mug and gratefully taking the opportunity to be of use. She scarfed down the donut and, with a quick, "Thanks," for the breakfast and not-so-subtle distraction, rushed to the marshy area of the forest, where briars had indeed multiplied over the past month. The serrated thorny vines covered most of the marsh and half of Dorcas's home.

Sara shuddered at the dilapidated and foul-scented hut, which she refused to enter despite the fact that vines had wormed their way under the door and down the chimney. Though tempted to burn it all down, Sara left the dwelling for Dorcas to contend with upon her return and instead focused on the visible briars.

After an hour of eradicating vines and a crop of toxic parsnip, Sara patrolled the forest. She inspected every soul tree and every stone in the wall until the sun was high, and even then, she waited until Moira finally woke and dragged Lily and Lethal with her to the Cahills.

By the time Sara returned, the Main House was abuzz with the midday meal and many curious family members. Moira and

Violet sat with the shifters, passing around food and laughing with the triplets, while Lily and Lethal occupied a small table off to the side. Sara eyed the empty seat beside Dean, but before she could join him, Tobio slipped in and sat with a yawn.

Gaa! Fine, it's not like I can privately talk with him while they're the center of attention.

Sara settled onto a barstool at the kitchen island, accepting a plate of food from Rebecca and absently eating while she racked her brain for a way to observe Dean's power. Asking him to shift and display his magic as if he were a dog doing tricks would be horribly impolite. She rubbed her temple until a simple yet hopefully effective plan took root.

With a smug smile, she swiveled in her seat and scanned the room, taking in the jovial gathering and feeling quite pleased with herself until meeting Lethal's sharp stare. Given the vampire's damned enigmatic expression, she couldn't tell if they were annoyed or amused by the pack's lively presence.

Sara deepened her grin and considered trying her telepathic magic on them again when Dean rose from his table and brought his empty plate to the kitchen, the rest of the pack following his lead.

"We'd like to help clean up if that's okay with you," Dean said to Helen, Eddie, and Uncle Larry.

Helen beamed at him, clearly enthralled by his good manners. "Set your dishes in the sink, and I'll take you up on your offer another time. Because—based on Sara's devious grin—I do believe you're in for a Lochton treat."

Sara jolted. "I wouldn't call it a *treat*." Too many sets of amber eyes and one of molten gold stared at her. She hopped off her stool. "It's more of an *activity*."

Sara assembled the pack in the Cahill common along with Moira, Lily, Caleb, and Violet, who welcomed a break from her studies. Lethal followed, feigning disinterest in the gathering until Violet begged to see their daggers—oohing and aahing over the exquisite blades.

"Are we playing target practice today?" asked Caleb, eyeing the daggers and playfully grabbing Wes as a shield. "Or is this an official Lethal fan club meeting?" He winked at the vampire and then quickly shoved Wes aside as a dagger shot for his head. The blade froze a foot away from Caleb's ashen face. His swallow was audible as everyone whipped their gaze at Lethal.

The vampire's stone-cold countenance held the faintest of smiles.

Sara whished the dagger back at Lethal, who snatched and sheathed it in a blur of movement. She frowned at them, as did Lily, and said, "You're sitting out for obvious reasons while the rest of us play a game."

"Woohoo!" cried Wes, bumping shoulders with Dean's cousins—the 'Eshas, as he called the trio of sisters. "What're we playing?"

"The seven of you against the five of us." Sara gestured to herself, Moira, Lily, Caleb, and Violet. "Your team tries to reach the largest birch in the grove near the northeast portion of the forest, and we try to stop you."

Dean rubbed the back of his neck, uncertainty on his wide face. "Do you want Tobio on your team to even the numbers?"

Sara glanced at the half-dragon shifter, his elysian eyes as beautiful as they were unnerving. She had yet to see him shift into anything—wolf or dragon. Maybe he couldn't and was a liability to the pack. But that didn't make sense given the golden aura emanating from him.

Sara shook her head. "No. The five of us have home advantage. Besides, four of us are witches, and you haven't seen what Moira can do yet," she teased.

"Ooooo," howled Luke, the triplets joining him. "You're going down." He snapped his gleaming white teeth at her and grinned.

Dean arched a brow at Moira, who smiled sweetly and flicked her hair. A deep rumble, like the purr of a tiger, sounded in Dean's chest.

Trouble cawed a stuttering laugh from where he circled overhead. Evidently, Sara wasn't the only one closely watching the Blue Ridge pack. She cleared her throat. "Everyone plays fair. You can immobilize opponents, but no injuries." Sara narrowed her eyes at Tobio. Though he was definitely a mystery, she needed to stick to her plan and stay focused on Dean and his powerful aura of black-and-gray flames.

"Anything else?" drawled Luke.

Before Sara could respond, Tobio bolted for the closest forest edge, while the rest of the pack shifted and tore down the center of the common, straight for the birch grove.

Lily flicked her hands, and a sheet of ice appeared in the wolves' path. They instantly split apart, running in separate directions and avoiding the ice.

With a screech, Moira phased into a falcon and flew after them.

Lily took off in a blur, white-blonde hair vanishing into the forest.

Sara gaped after her. "I didn't know she could move like that."

"I taught her," said Lethal, casually reclining atop a picnic table.

"Why didn't you teach me this trick instead of using me as a pincushion?"

"Vampires only."

"Gaa!"

Caleb sprinted for the forest edge. "I'll get Tobio," he said, understory bowing out of his way as he charged into the woods.

Sara rose into the air, tugging Violet with her. "You rush ahead and stop anyone from reaching the tree while I take down Dean." Violet nodded and flew off while Sara rushed after the large black wolf who had already cleared the Cahills' farm and was tearing for the old birch as if he knew exactly where it was located. A stiff wind lashed Sara's face while she sped after him. Reaching out with her power, she summoned a wall of boulders and fallen trees in his path.

Dean leapt, much higher than a normal wolf could have, and easily cleared the wall.

Well, shit.

Sara grew an even taller wall of brimstone briars, which he smashed through like it was paper. By now, he was at the edge of the grove. When she threw a sphere of energy in front of this path, he deftly pivoted, and her magic exploded a group of young saplings. With a silent apology to the trees, Sara surged ahead and nearly crashed into him when he skidded to a halt.

Before them dominated a massive bear, one clawed paw raking the air while its other paw pinned a gray wolf to the leafy forest floor. Sara's heart skipped a beat at recalling the bear witch, Makwa. Unlike Makwa, this bear had no interest in Sara. Instead, it shook its mighty head and roared at Dean. The bear's fierce warning blew back the Alpha's thick, dark fur and echoed through the forest.

Sara smirked. Moira wasn't holding back.

Behind Moira, hovering mere feet from the old birch, was Violet with her arms outstretched, kinetically restraining Moesha, Alesha, and Iesha. Though their lupine bodies were frozen, the sisters managed to slide their gazes to Dean and Sara.

Lily stood in front of the tree, spears of ice jutting out of the ground at her feet.

To their right, Caleb panted with his hand pressed to his side.

"Where's Tobio?" asked Sara, searching the immediate forest.

"Got him right here," said Caleb, patting a mound of boulders.

"Hardly," said a voice from within the pile of rock. The ground shook, and the pile erupted, huge boulders scattering like pebbles as a magnificent black-and-gold dragon rose from the center.

Caleb fell back, Violet's kinetic power flickered, releasing the 'Eshas, Moira phased into her human form, and Lily's spears melted. Everyone's jaw dropped while the dragon wound its serpentine body among the birch trees.

Similar to the red dragon Sara had seen on the beach, Tobio swam through the air without wings, shiny black scales gleaming with a golden luminescence in the afternoon sun. Spikes tipped in gold lined his back and his compact arms and legs. He was half the size of the red dragon and positively exquisite. After circling the grove and showing off with a puff of fire, he phased back into his human form and soundlessly landed beside the three sisters. "We won," he said as the 'Eshas also phased back with proud smiles.

Beside a still-stunned Moira, Luke phased and barked a laugh.

Caleb sat hard on a boulder, and Violet rushed to Sara's side, a touch of fear in the wide-eyed gaze she kept on Tobio.

"I'll be damned." Caleb stared at the central birch tree and the small gray wolf peeking around its trunk. "Jokey made it to the tree."

CHAPTER 34

WITH A VICTORIOUS growl, Dean phased into his human form and folded his muscular arms over his chest. He faced Sara with a dimpled grin. "The pack's strength is in our numbers and teamwork. You fell for our diversions, *and* you thought I was the greatest risk."

She huffed a laugh at him. *True.* "How did you all know the tree's exact location?"

Luke answered, "We scouted your entire forest last night. Turns out, your cell service is strongest to the east, you all have enough cut wood to last multiple winters, and you have *many* special trees." He tucked his blond hair behind his ears and slid her a dazzling smile.

Caleb erupted with laughter. "I'd be careful with that smile, dude. Her mate will skin you alive if you even think of sniffing her."

Luke's throat bobbed. "What mate?"

"My brother," said Violet, casually playing with a sizzling ball of energy in her palm.

Sara threw a scowl at Caleb. "Thomas will *not* skin anyone alive. He and Moira's twin are at school, but they'll be back before Solstice. I have a brother too, and he should also be home soon." She intentionally failed to mention Ian's unknown whereabouts, preferring to avoid a messy explanation of how she bartered her own brother.

235

Tobio straightened, his aura flickering an iridescent purple. "You have a twin?" he asked Moira.

"Yeah. You're wearing his hoodie," she said, twirling her finger at him.

He jerked back, one hand clutching the front of his sweatshirt as he tucked his chin, brow furrowed.

Dean cleared his throat and in a low voice asked Moira, "Do *you* have a mate?"

Her cheeks flushed as red as her hair. "No."

A dimpled smile. "And you can phase into a wolf *and* a bear?"

Moira placed her hands on her curvy hips and gave him a wicked grin, eyes blazing like embers in the late afternoon sun. "Oh, I can phase into most *anything*."

Dean leaned toward her, massive chest resonating with ardent approval.

"Okay," interrupted Caleb. Sara could have kissed him. "Who's ready to help make dinner? We're eating early tonight, so we can start prepping for a special celebration tomorrow."

With another yip, Wes, still in wolf form, pranced around Caleb and head butted him toward the Main House. The rest of the pack, Moira included, shifted and chased after one another in the same direction.

A moment of silence filled the grove before Violet kicked a pile of lemon-yellow leaves and said, "Sorry I missed the little guy."

Sara shook her head and chuckled. "No apology needed. You stopped all *three* of the 'Eshas. And now I know how their pack operates." Strength in numbers, teamwork, and everyone seamlessly knowing their role. She chewed her lip, contemplating the pack's power and how Ware Woods could function like a pack—instinctively working together as one insurmountable power to defend the forest.

"All the same, I won't let it happen again," said Violet with the typical Sullivan determination and stubbornness that Sara knew all too well. "I gotta get back to studying. See you at tomorrow's party," she said and flew off.

"What party?" Sara whirled to the last person in the grove. Ware Woods seemed to have more parties and celebrations than Sundays. But, Sara supposed, it helped break up the possible monotony of their magically long lives by focusing on celebrating life's little pleasures.

"We decided to throw a welcome celebration for the pack and Lethal," said Lily, strolling toward the Main House. "Speaking of Lethal, I promised to spend the rest of the day with them. You should take a dagger-free moment for yourself." She gave Sara a serene grin over her shoulder, then disappeared in a shimmer of motion.

The birch grove fell silent again. Sara hovered above the ground, staring after everyone. Part of her wanted to rush back to the Main House and know more about this celebration and to pepper Tobio with questions. Since he was part dragon, perhaps he knew how to defeat one. But . . . a vampire-free moment meant she could call Thomas.

She launched into the sky and rocketed for the brown house. Within a few minutes, she barged through the back patio door, nearly tripping over a pile of boots on her way into the empty kitchen. Panting from her full-throttle flight, she mentally called out, *"Hello? Where is everyone?"*

Charlie immediately answered. *"We're at the Main House. Bailey too. Do you need anything?"*

Perfect. No one to hear her in case she and Thomas got into a pleasantly heated conversation. Her cheeks tingled. *"Nah, I'm good."* She picked up her phone from the collection charging on top of the dining table and saw two new texts from Ian:

Hey, I'm counting down the days until Solstice. If all goes well, I have something incredible to show you. BTW, we're thankful you healed Samson. He may not tell you, but he is grateful.

*I heard a shifter pack moved in. *surprised emoji* Sounds like you have lots to tell me too. Let Lily know I'm happy for her—she'll understand.*

Pfft. *We?* How many people did Samson have in his secret hideout? And what exactly would Lily understand? *Never mind. Not my business.*

Sara texted back:

I'm counting down the days too. Everything will go well. I'll tell her. Love you.

Then she texted Thomas:

*Hello, spice packet. Ready to chat? I have the whole house to myself! *winking emoji**

Thomas instantly replied:

I'm in a study group. Talk later?

Her heart fell.

Sure. Love you.

A heartbeat later, he responded:

Love you more.

Sara loosed a long sigh. As if that were possible. Father above, her heart physically ached for him. After this semester, she hoped they would never be apart again. She left her phone with the others and softly closed the patio door on her way to the treehouse.

By the time she removed her jacket and boots and sat on her bed, wrapped in her blue blanket, rain pattered the forest. It drummed against the oak and pinged the glassy surface of the lake, growing in a rhythmic crescendo.

Scents of decaying leaves, crisp air, and earthy musk filled the treehouse. Soon the temperature would drop, and winter would cover the forest. She usually looked forward to Solstice—playing in the snow with her parents and decorating their home with evergreens and candles. Now, she dreaded it.

Instead of drowning in sorrow and fear, Sara redirected her thoughts to the shifter pack and their formidable strength as a unit.

This was the power portion of the spell—to show her strength in numbers and teamwork. She clutched the satin edges of the blanket and scrunched her face in thought. What if, instead of the forest families acting as separate magical forces, they could harmonize their powers? With their numbers, they could easily form a cohesive defense *and* attack at the same time—catching the Shadow Mother off guard and sending her back to wherever she belonged.

Sara closed her eyes, letting her thoughts drift with the soothing rain. Dean was indeed large and powerful, yet humble—a giant teddy bear beneath his muscled exterior. Much like Moira, who feigned a fierce demeanor to protect her affectionate heart.

Sara chuckled. Perhaps the Mother herself, and not just Sara's spell, pulled Dean to the forest—to Moira.

She sighed again, thinking of Thomas this time. Five more weeks seemed an infinity when she had already waited so long. The bloodstone and her heart beat together, warming her as if Thomas's arms and soul embraced her. She yearned to feel him—to see him.

A strange sensation prickled her skin, and her insides dipped, reminding her of riding a roller coaster. Sara swayed and opened her eyes. Instead of her bedroom, she was surrounded by darkness. The distinct double-thump of a heart replaced the patter of rain.

She snatched for the blanket only to feel velvety strands slip through her fingers. A weightless feeling, similar to looping through the soul trees, lifted her, softly brushing back her hair. Her stomach twisted and shrank, the sensation like being pulled by the inside of her belly button, and in a flash of light she was standing in an apartment-style room—efficiency kitchen and small dining set to her right, couch and coffee table to her left. Books and papers littered the table, and on the couch sprawled Matthew, red hair now shoulder length, eating from a bowl of chips precariously balanced on his athletic chest. His gaze, muted by brown contacts, flicked to her and he stopped, mid-bite.

"Shit!" he exclaimed and sprang from the couch, the bowl and its contents crashing to the floor.

Sara ignored his lunge in her direction, for her attention was riveted on Thomas and a woman standing near a door on the other side of the room. The woman wore a tight sweater, and her long blonde hair had been thoughtfully curled. Though her back was to Sara, the flirtatious tilt of her hips and head suggested she was very much interested in Thomas, who stood before her. His brown gaze looked over her shoulder and locked on to Sara. A muscle twitched along his jaw as he grabbed the woman and pulled her into a firm hug.

Sara's heart cracked, and before Matthew could reach her, she fell back into the velvety darkness, falling through the thumping beats and losing all sense of time and direction until slamming into her bed.

CHAPTER 35

SAPPHIRE TWILIGHT FILLED the quiet bedroom. Not a drop of rain or squirrel chatter to offset the sound of her choked gasps. Sara jumped from the bed and paced the room, shaking her hands and sending sparks of white energy skipping across the floor. "What the Hells just happened?" she demanded. The treehouse quivered in response. "One moment I'm thinking of Thomas and the next . . . I'm there. At least, I think I was." She paused. Maybe she had imagined it. She *must* have because Thomas would never have done that to her.

Right?

Only one way to find out. She yanked on her boots, grabbed her jacket, and flew back to the brown house.

In a cold gust, Sara burst through the patio door. Whishing on the lights, she rushed to the kitchen table. All three phones—hers, Charlie's, and Ted's—vibrated and jumped with texts and calls from Thomas and Matthew.

Crap. It did happen.

She slumped into a chrome-and-blue-pleather diner chair and reluctantly accepted Thomas's call.

"Sara! Where are you? What just happened?" Thomas's voice was near hysterical.

Sara sat in silence. No words could possibly describe the bizarre looping—the sudden tilt to her world as if she were trapped in a fun-house nightmare—the vast hole in her heart.

"Sara?" asked Matthew through the speaker, his cautious tone resembling a negotiations officer talking someone off a ledge. "Were you just here?"

Fixing her unseeing gaze on the kitchen's gauzy curtains, Sara breathed, "Yeah."

Thomas cursed in the background while Matthew continued his careful exchange. "*How* were you just here?"

"I don't know," Sara whispered, and paused. "Who is she?"

A rustling and a faint click sounded as the phone was taken off speaker. "Sara," said Thomas. "I—I couldn't let her see you. She was on her way out from our study group. And when you suddenly appeared, I grabbed her so she wouldn't turn around and see you. Hells—you were *glowing* like the Mother. She's a classmate and nothing more. It—it isn't what you're thinking."

Sara focused on her rapid heartbeat, on the sugar bowl left out on the table, on the steady hum of the fridge behind her. Of course it wasn't what she was thinking. Their bond was too strong for anyone to ever come between them. Right?

His shaky breaths hushed through the phone, his panic matching hers.

"Baby," said Thomas, his voice catching.

Sara could count on her four-fingered hand how many times he had called her "*baby*." On the surface, it was an endearing term; underneath, it revealed a raw vulnerability—one they equally shared in expressing and accepting their deep love. No one but Thomas could ever call her this. Every time he said it, their bond grew stronger.

Through the following silence, she *felt* their connection squeeze her heart and kiss her soul. A tear trickled down her cheek, and she whispered, "I miss you so much it's hard to breathe."

A shuddered sigh blew through the phone. "I know," murmured Thomas. "I feel the same."

Silence again. No words necessary. Sara cradled the phone to her face, rose from the table, and trudged up the nearby stairs.

To remind them both of the reason behind their trying separation, she said, her voice hoarse, "Tell me what you learned today."

He huffed softly, and she knew he understood why she asked— why she needed to hear his voice as she curled up on Ian's bed and drifted off to sleep with him pressed against her ear.

When she woke in the morning, the phone was still clutched in her hand. Thomas had texted her:

Five more weeks. I love you.

She sighed, resisting the urge to text back and distract him during his morning class. After setting her phone on Ian's nightstand, she pushed back the quilt, swung her feet over the side of the bed, and nearly stepped on Bailey, lying on the floor beside her.

The yellow Lab bounded to her feet and shook herself silly, pressing her wet nose into Sara's lap.

"Hey, girl," Sara crooned, tugging the sides of Bailey's face. "Did you keep me company all night?"

Bailey barked and pranced in a tight circle as Sara slid to the floor and put on her boots. They had been sitting too perfectly under the nightstand for her to have kicked them off in her sleep. She glanced at Ian's alternative music posters and the many high fantasy books on a shelf above his tidy desk. The distinct aroma of baked cinnamon filled the air. Though Ian's room usually smelled of pine and cinnamon, this was much stronger and . . . mixed with coffee.

Her father's cheerful whistle drifted up the stairs, and for a moment Sara imagined herself back at the house on Green Brier Lane—her mother still alive and enjoying a cup of morning tea, which she preferred to coffee.

Bailey circled again before barreling down the stairs. With a groan, Sara picked herself up, shoved the phone into her pocket, and thumped down after her, one hand squeaking along the lacquered golden-paneled wall. She stumbled into the kitchen, squinting at the sun shining through the window above the sink, and blinked at her father.

Without saying a word, he handed her a mug of coffee with extra cream, exactly as she liked it. Beyond the archway into the living room, Bailey hopped into a chair and stared out the window.

"Where's Ted?" Sara asked, noting a stained coffee mug in the sink.

"He and Uncle Larry are meeting the latest delivery truck at the end of the road. It seems part of the shipment includes items Moesha arranged for the pack, and the rest are things your grandmother took upon herself to order for them."

Of course Gran did.

"Rough night?" her father gently prodded.

"Mm-hmm," Sara murmured before taking a sip of coffee. Yep, exactly as she liked it. She took a few gulps, deciding to skip the inexplicable looping and simply share the true reason why she had slept in Ian's room. "Thomas and I had a *misunderstanding*. Everything is fine now, but . . . my heart still feels empty." She plunked her phone onto the table, then sank into one of the dining chairs and looked up at her father. "I miss him, and I miss Ian, and I miss Mom. There's this gaping hole inside me."

Charlie smiled a tender, sad smile.

Unable to speak, she projected, *"How do you do it? How do you live with the ache?"* Her father and mother had shared a bond, and Sara could not fathom how difficult it must be for him.

Sighing, he leaned heavily against the counter. "I miss them too," he said, and Sara knew he was referring to Winona as well as her mother and Ian. "Sometimes I feel their spirits, and sometimes I need a quiet moment, but mostly I focus on being here with you, Ted, and Gran and everyone else—and Ian when he gets back, of course. This"—he motioned between them—"is what I live for."

The oven beeped, and he grabbed one of Gran's handmade potholders and pulled out a tray of cinnamon rolls.

Sara's mouth watered at the comforting, sugary scent. "Are those Mom's?"

"Same recipe, yet somehow they taste different." With a shrug, he plated one and handed it to her. He held on to the white-and-blue CorningWare until she met his gaze. "We can talk about Mom or your bond with Thomas, or we can talk about what's really causing you to bite your lip."

Sara released her lip.

Grinning, he let go of the plate, then turned back to the stove and cracked eggs into a skillet.

She studied him and huffed. *Alrighty, since you asked and probably already know with your fancy intuition.* "Based on the pack's account of the dragon that attacked them, Lethal and I believe the Shadow Mother is a definite threat and may have dragons somehow working for her."

Charlie merely nodded and whistled a short, upbeat tune while he finished scrambling the eggs.

Staring at his unfazed demeanor, Sara questioned, "How can you be so calm?" She poked her cinnamon roll to the edge of her plate as he dished out half the eggs to her and put the remaining eggs on a plate for himself.

He settled into the seat beside her, sunlight streaming across his chest. "Because now is the moment that matters. Not what was, not what will be, just now."

Sara leaned back, the pleather seat sighing, and studied him. "How very metaphysical of you."

He chuckled. "I'm not making light of the situation. I'm just choosing not to let it control me. The dangers are real, but so are our magic and passion. Our forest is special—*you're* special."

She rolled her eyes, and he fell silent.

Oh, crap. He's being serious.

He beheld her with an intense fatherly expression. "I believe *anything* can happen. Don't you?"

Sara's mind reeled with their past discussions regarding philosophy and energy—discussions she recently realized had everything to do with *real* magic. And with this simple statement, Sara knew he meant if she set her intentions and worked for it, she could triumph over anything.

The bloodstone at her chest pulsed, and she thought of the spell she cast—of Lethal and Dean and their assistance. She swallowed. "I think things are already happening."

Her father's eyes twinkled. "Indeed, they are, firecracker. And today is a day of gratitude for our good fortune." He picked up a fork and dug into his breakfast.

CHAPTER 36

BLAZING SCARLET AND gold leaves adorned the Main House's fireplace mantel and grew among the branch balustrades of the interior second-story balcony. A living garland, the fiery foliage extended along the balcony, down the grandiose stair rail, then up into the tree at the base of the stairs, where it blended into a vaulted ceiling of vibrant autumn colors.

Pumpkins and gourds of all sizes, mixed nuts, and dried ears of calico corn—their rainbow-hued kernels glistening like beads of glass—decorated every surface inside and outside the Main House. Delectable aromas of roasted meats, root vegetables, breads, and spicy-sweet desserts filled the air.

Sara relaxed into a chair on the deck and crossed her ankles, surveying the festive scene.

Before her, in the center of the Cahill clearing, children played tag around the chestnut soul tree, shrieking with laughter as Wes, in wolf form, chased them. Dean and Tobio sat at a picnic table with Bill and Kane, deep in conversation, while Luke tossed horseshoes with Caleb. Beside them, Violet, Moira, and Lily played croquet with Moesha, Alesha, and Iesha. The group laughingly teased and taunted each other, equally sparing no mercy on whacking the colored balls. Nearby, along the clearing's edge, Lethal hung in the shadows of a line of pine trees with Lily's younger siblings.

Sara squinted at the grinning faces and blurred movements of the half-vampire, half-witch children and chuckled.

Throughout the afternoon, the forest families took turns welcoming Lethal and the new shifters. For them both, a table was soon overflowing with gifts of books, handmade soaps, and various pointed weapons. Whispers circulated that the Cahills had magically constructed the pack a den-like gathering space, tucked into one of the forest's quiet rock ledges.

Sara glanced at Gran, Ted, and her father beside her on the deck, multiple outdoor fireplaces comfortably heating the exterior space. The day would have been perfect had Thomas, Matthew, and Ian been there—and had the Shadow Mother not been a looming threat.

Gran stirred in her seat, her gaze on Dean and Tobio. "I had another premonition last night," she said, a quiet sadness in her tone.

"Ma." Ted shot her a warning look and shook his head, lips pursed.

"Not about the shifters," she replied with a slight glimmer in her eyes. "This was different, and I think it applies to Sara."

Hmph. "Do I need another fire extinguisher?"

"I don't know, maybe. All I grasped was death and dragons."

Sara startled at recalling the fiery red dragon coming nose to nose with her on the beach. But since sharing her near-death experience would only upset her family, Sara put a different spin on Gran's message. "Well, we already had a death—Naomi's—and now we have a dragon." She waved her hand toward Tobio.

Gran's face wrinkled in thought. "I suppose . . ." She trailed off and, to Sara's relief, dropped the subject when Helen announced it was time to eat.

Like a game of musical chairs, the entire forest ran to snag a plate and a seat at one of the many indoor and outdoor dining tables joyfully decorated with mini pumpkins and clusters of capped acorns.

With an understanding nod from her father, Sara grabbed some food and joined Dean and the pack at a table near the center of the deck. Settling into a chair beside the Alpha Shifter, Sara skimmed her gaze across the other tables, exchanging a grin with Connor at the Sullivan table and a wave with Lily among the Atwells.

"Ian texted and wants you to know he's happy for you," she projected to her, feeling awkward at being the messenger of something that seemed private. Lily only smiled and turned to Lethal, sitting quiet as a mausoleum in the chair beside her. The table space before the vampire was bare.

For a nervous moment, Sara considered making a speech and thanking Lethal and the pack for providing assistance. But what could she say? *Thanks for supporting a misfit, sacred forest protect itself from an epically dangerous darkness with dragons on her side. Oh, and I sincerely hope you don't die.*

She shook her head, catching her father watching her with a curious look. Perhaps she should take a page from his book and simply focus on enjoying the present, grateful moment.

At the pack's table, everyone except Dean sat stock still, eyes on their overflowing yet untouched plates. The Alpha Shifter flicked his amber gaze to each pack member, then politely set his napkin on his mighty thigh, picked up a roll, and ate it in one bite. The rest of the pack immediately feasted, wolfing down food with an appreciative gusto that rivaled Caleb's.

Following Dean's lead, Sara remained silent for the meal, stealthily waiting until Luke and the 'Eshas left to get third helpings before turning to Dean and Tobio. With any luck, they would be pleasantly sated and in a talkative mood. She plucked a tiny speck of lint from her sleeve and asked, "So, how does one become half-dragon? Were you bitten by one?" Father above, she sounded ridiculous. She should have asked the Book instead.

Ears burning, she took a swig of her birch beer and choked

on it when Tobio gave her a sly smile and said, "I was made the old-fashioned way. Isn't that how witches are made?"

Dean's deep-chested laugh shook the entire table. At the opposite end, Wes paused from gnawing on a turkey leg and gave Sara a questioning look as if asking, "Is it?"

Tobio tightened his spiky ponytail with a swift yank, and for a split second, his poised demeanor and broad cheekbones seemed familiar. "Elysian-eyed dragons can shift into human form and mate with other magicals. My mother is an elysian-eye. She gave me to our wolf shifter father when I was born—before another dragon could kill me. Herself included, I suppose."

Sara struggled to swallow her mouthful. How could a mother kill their own child?

"Dragons are fierce predators and will kill lesser dragons for dominance and sport," said Tobio, resting his forearms on the table and clicking his black nails against his water glass. "A half-breed is the lowliest of creatures in all magical factions—especially to dragons. Fortunately for me, most wolf shifters will accept any pup, so my father and his pack took me in hoping I would be more wolf than dragon."

"But," ventured Sara, "you're more dragon than wolf. So what happened? Did you two just leave the pack and start your own?" She glanced at Dean.

Dean rubbed the top of his head, palm scraping his closely cropped hair. "Our Alpha father died in an accident, and most of the pack left, leaving me as the Alpha."

"*I* was the accident," admitted Tobio, slicing a sharp gaze at Dean. "Dragons are volatile, and I'm no exception. When I was young, I didn't know how to control myself, and I accidentally killed our father."

Sara set her beer down with a hard thunk. While she knew it wasn't her fault, she still felt responsible for her mother's death. She ached for Tobio and his situation. "I'm sorry," she said, feeling numb with uselessness, wishing she could magically ease his emotional pain.

With a slight shrug, Tobio lowered his gaze to his empty plate.

The following uncomfortable silence ended when a nearby table of Cahill children rang out with laughter. They bolted from their chairs and ran into the common, chasing each other and tossing around a small pumpkin.

Sara internally cursed herself for causing Tobio distress—during a celebratory dinner, no less—and for desperately needing to ask her next question. But as a High Witch expecting the Shadow Mother and dragons to descend upon them all too soon, she quietly asked, "How can a dragon be defeated?"

Tobio's head snapped up, his eyes boring into her. "Care to share how a witch can be defeated?"

Sara didn't hesitate. "We're mortal and most of us are powerless outside the forest's boundary." Her vision wavered at thoughts of her mother and Naomi.

Tobio's face softened. "Except for you."

"I'm High Witch and have healing magic. I also have a wicked temper and strong will to live." She grinned at him, attempting to lighten the conversation and steer them back to the cheerful celebration.

He hissed a laugh, golden eyes flashing. "Well, then, we have a lot in common."

Sara stilled as he downed his water and sat back, crunching on ice and considering her with a mixed expression of amusement and respect.

With that sly grin of his, he said, "Dragons are nearly impossible to defeat. Brute force can drive them off, but the only way to kill one is to pierce its soft spot, which is usually at the base of the skull, heavily protected by spikes and bone frills. To even get close to a soft spot is incredibly risky."

Risky, yet not impossible. Sara dropped her stare to a knot in the wooden table, pondering, as Luke and the 'Esha sisters returned. They plopped down with their extra helpings and dug in once more.

Tobio's attention swiveled to the food; ignoring Luke's growl, he snatched a meat-stuffed roll.

Since his mouth was full and Sara had learned what she needed from the half-dragon, she shifted her shoulders to Dean and asked her next burning question. "How did you attend Global Council meetings? We can't figure out where to find them, and Lethal has been tight lipped about it." She flicked her gaze to where Lethal had been sitting at the Atwell table. The seat was empty.

Dean followed her line of sight to Lethal's vacant chair and sighed.

Sara whished another birch beer to him.

He chuckled, leaned toward her and, in a low voice, said, "Most sacred sites have one soul tree that can transport its magicals to other sacred sites. The Magus can also transport through the tree to anywhere they wish, including Global Council. The dragon burned our tree last week, which is why we came here by car."

Sara slumped back in her seat. "Anywhere?" she murmured, mind reeling. But Lethal also arrived by car—and plane, she assumed, since they came from overseas. Perhaps that was how the vampire preferred to travel. And Ware Woods didn't have one soul tree, it had many—which only looped to each other. They didn't have a tree that transported to other sites. Or maybe . . . they didn't know they had one.

The bloodstone quivered under her flannel shirt. Twice now she had magically transported while in the oak tree. The first time, she had asked the Mother for help; the second time, she had ached to see Thomas.

Father above.

The entire treehouse was a portal to anywhere in the world. And if she was right, she wouldn't have to wait for the third part of the spell—she could find the High Witch to help them, and she could also find Ian.

She pushed back her chair and gave Dean a clumsy hug. "Thank you," she gushed just as Moira came by with a tray of desserts.

"Ah . . . you're welcome," said Dean, sounding more like he was asking a question than making a statement. He scrubbed his jaw and turned to Moira with a nervous smile. "I'll have one of everything." His warm eyes lingered on her instead of on the sweets.

From the other side of the table, Luke purred, earning an elbow jab from Tobio. The 'Eshas snickered while Wes continued eating, eyes wide as he stared at Dean.

Sara jumped up and practically shoved Moira into her chair. "Here, take my seat. I gotta go."

"But you didn't even have pie yet," objected Moira. She set her dessert tray in the center of the table, and Luke immediately helped himself. "And we're all gonna stay up late and watch movies. Caleb set up one of Ian's projectors in the new loft, and even Violet is staying." She stuck out her lower lip, pouting. Sara swore she heard someone whine.

The pies did smell delicious, and Sara hadn't seen a movie in forever. But she had a High Witch to find, a game plan worthy of vanquishing the Shadow Mother to devise, and a brother to save. "I'll take a rain check on the movies, and I'll have leftover pie for breakfast," she said, her tone dusted with a sugared apology.

"Between me and Dean, there won't be any leftovers," said Luke, his whiskey-colored gaze roaming the family tables and pausing on Violet. Dean growled a warning as Tobio punched Luke in the shoulder and then stole his apple tart.

Luke barked in protest and grabbed another from the tray.

"We'll save you some pie," promised Dean.

But it wasn't until Moira waved off Sara with a genuine smile that Sara took to the sky and flew directly for the treehouse.

She skidded into the main room, rumpling the pale-green

area rug, and sprinted up the narrow stairs—two at a time. Relief washed over her at spotting Lethal in their chair on the private deck. They held a full goblet of crimson drink in one hand, and in their lap was an open novel.

Sara paused, catching her breath. "Why did you leave? The dinner was for you, too."

Lethal clapped the book shut, placed it on a side table, and drained half the goblet before answering. "I prefer to dine alone since my dietary *restrictions* make people uncomfortable. It's organically sourced, by the way," they added with a ghost of a smile and tilted the thick drink at her.

"Oh," was all Sara could manage. Now was not the time to ask *exactly* where their bottled food source came from. Besides, Sara wasn't sure she truly wanted to know. She shook off the thought, refocusing herself on why she left the party and why she sought out the vampire. "I need your help," she said.

Lethal grunted. "I know. That's why I'm here." They finished the rest of their liquid snack and gently set the goblet beside the book.

Their unwavering arrogance was both grating and comforting. "I'm done waiting for the third portion of the spell to arrive. In fact, what if they *can't* come on their own because of the Global Council's edict for no one to visit us?" She threw them a scowl. "I'm going to find the High Witch on my own, and I need you to watch Ware Woods while I'm gone." Her heart clenched at openly admitting she needed to leave the forest—something she swore she would never do again. But to be ready by Solstice, she needed to obtain the last and perhaps the most important part of the spell— an experienced High Witch.

Lethal slowly shifted in their chair, icy gray eyes staring into Sara's soul. "You trust me?" they asked, surprise in their entrancing voice.

"Yes." Father above, if Lily heartily trusted the ancient vampire of Death, then so did she. "This tree is a portal, but I don't know exactly how it works or exactly how long I'll be gone," Sara explained while striding into her adjacent bedroom.

Lethal trailed after her, hands in their pockets. "Does this involve you screaming and disappearing into thin air?"

Sara sat cross-legged on her bed, keeping on her boots and thick, flannel shirt—unsure if she would need them wherever she was going—and released a nervous breath. "Most likely," she admitted.

The vampire gave her a rare four-fang smile, angelic face glowing with acknowledgment of what she was about to do—of what she had asked of them. "Good luck, witch."

CHAPTER 37

WITH ONE HAND clutching the bloodstone through her layered shirts, Sara shut her eyes and mentally recited the last part of the spell:

"Expertise I ask from one of my kind,
A witch with mastery for me to find."

Nothing.

She strained to hear even the faintest thump of the tree's heartbeat but only heard Lethal easing into the chair beside her bed.

Come on. Think. What did I do differently last time?

She dropped her hand into her lap, mind fluttering with insecurities about this truly working. The anxiety had to go. With a whooshing exhale, Sara stilled her thoughts and grounded herself by focusing on the gentle sway of the oak tree and the soft tapping of the last of its brown leaves in an autumnal wind. Wherever the High Witch was located, Sara trusted the tree to safely loop her to the proper location. Perhaps the High Witch was waiting for her. Perhaps everything she needed to protect Ware Woods was a velvety kiss away.

The bloodstone pulsed and a deep, resonate hum filled her ears. It grew louder, vibrating her entire body as a warm breeze caressed her face. Sara relaxed and fell back, expecting to sink into pillows. Instead, she drifted into a dreamy void that lifted and tugged her in different directions. Unlike transporting in the forest, the looping became agitated. It jerked her back and forth while simultaneously bouncing her against a wall of elastic darkness.

Mother below, if this wild ride kept up, she would retch into the Aether. Sara pleaded for the unusual transporting to cease—and promptly dropped onto a very hard stone floor. Her knees throbbed in pain, her palms burning from slapping the smooth, damp surface. With a groan, she released a flicker of power, healing her slight injuries, and sat back on her heels.

Behind her flowed the steady rush of a familiar waterfall. Before her, in the cave-like, spacious room, stood Jin. With his back to her, he moved in a fluid, concise dance, equal parts meditation and shadow fighting. He wore only loose-fitting white pants, his exposed upper body muscles rippling with his controlled movements. His long, unbound, obsidian hair swished across his bare back with enough vigor to reveal a heavily inked line of diamonds running along his spine. The same tattoo pattern marked both outer forearms. He finished his maneuvers and turned to her, whishing his tinted sunglasses into place before she could glimpse his eyes.

Sara scrambled to her feet, her black ass-kicking boots ridiculously clunky in the humid cave. Jin was definitely not a High Witch—he was something altogether more powerful and completely terrifying. She eyed the waterfall, weighing her options. Though a watery escape was tempting, the tree looped her here for a reason.

Hoping he was in a better mood than the last time she dropped in unexpectedly, Sara pushed back her shoulders and forced a confident smile. "I'm looking for a specific High Witch. Do you know where I can find them?"

He grinned ever so slowly. Each heart-pounding moment revealing more and more pointed teeth. If he removed his glasses, Sara had the distinct feeling she may faint. She averted her eyes from his face and shifted her foot toward the waterfall. Perhaps this was a test and Jin was the fierce guard of the High Witch waiting for her on the opposite side of the water. Maybe all she had to do was leap through the waterfall.

She inched closer to the round opening.

A vehement hiss filled the room, and her traitorous muscles seized, her gaze flicking back to him. "Here I thought you willingly came to join me. Yet, again, you dare ask me for assistance," said Jin, bare feet planted wide, hands loose at his sides.

Burning Hells, he was more arrogant than Lethal. For a stupid second, she forgot her fear and fired back, "I can't help where my tree looped me."

He took a step toward her and paused with a curious tilt of his head.

Sara held her ground, hands trembling with the effort to summon the faintest flicker of power.

The nostrils of Jin's obstinately straight nose flared. "You're being pulled by a spell. But you can't get there by looping. Only an essence doorway or smoke and ash can reach this High Witch."

"Fabulous," muttered Sara. Her first time intentionally looping through the oak tree, and she royally screwed it up.

Jin's keen grin widened. Sara's heart thundered as he circled her, shadowy ash trailing behind him like a serpentine tail. "I'll send you, but she is growing stronger, and the next time we meet, you will stay and help me." Before Sara could blink, much less lunge for the waterfall, Jin's ring of ash swelled and swallowed her whole.

Though his ashy method of looping squeezed her insides and was far less pleasant than traveling by soul tree, it was certainly quick. She landed on splintered charcoal, sinuses stinging at a heavy burnt odor. With a choking cough, she waved away the last of Jin's ash and fully opened her eyes.

Surrounding her was a scorched and barren landscape. Fallen trees, their sooty remains like used matchsticks, littered a ground marred with rock outcroppings. An occasional vertical blackened trunk speared the hazy sky.

A plume of smoke erupted beside her, and out stepped Samson's right-hand Taker, Mr. Motley.

His bloodshot eyes widened. "What in nine Hells are *you* doing here?" he exclaimed, nervously surveying the immediate area.

Wonderful. Even Jin hadn't looped her to the proper location. A public bus would have delivered her to the High Witch sooner than all this magical travel.

Sara scrunched her nose against the sharp odor of spent forest fire. "I have no idea. Apparently, magic is glitchy today. I'm looking for a High Witch." She narrowed her eyes at him. "What are *you* doing here?"

He frowned. "Either you have terrible or impeccable timing," he said, scanning the sky. "Besides you, the only High Witch here is this one." He stepped aside as a cloud of black smoke unfurled between them and Samson materialized.

Sara stumbled back. The dark witch was no longer skeletal but healthy and glowing, eyes glittering with excitement, hair flowing in soft waves instead of irregular thick cords. He seemed taller, bigger, and somehow . . . happy. Words escaped her as Sara stared dumbfounded at both his appearance and the creeping realization that Samson was the third part of the spell.

He flicked his wrist, and the smoke contracted upon itself and disappeared. "It's about time. I have three things to tell you," he said, voice clear and strong and, much to Sara's chagrin, sounding like a parent scolding their child. In the far distance, a roar echoed. "Make that four," he added. Mr. Motley fidgeted, hand clutching the stone pendant around his neck as if preparing to vanish at any moment.

Samson twirled an unstained finger at her. "First, you stink like ash. I hope you didn't sell your soul for a one-way ride here. All you had to do was conjure a simple doorway from all the phlegm I graciously left you. Still the rookie. Tut, tut." He shook his head, grinning all the while, clearly enjoying his reproval.

Sara lunged for him. "I'm going to strangle you with my—" Her sentence was cut short as her entire body froze.

"Second," he said, and she managed a scowl against his magical hold on her. "I'm glad you finally realized I'm the High Witch your clever spell devised. Since you wouldn't listen to me, we all needed to wait for you to figure it out on your own and come to me when you were ready. Ian did say you were stubborn." He released his hold, and Sara nearly fell face first into the charred ground.

Seriously?

How had she been so blind? She had wasted weeks stewing over Samson's motives—not trusting him—and counting down the days until Solstice, when she should have been harassing him with questions and learning how to be a High Witch from the most experienced witch she knew.

Sara glared at his smug smile. She still wanted to strangle him. Mother help them both if his mentoring skills included constant barbs. But she was here because she trusted him and, apparently, the Book did too.

Another roar echoed across the barren landscape. Closer this time. Sara looked from Mr. Motley's tense shoulders to a nearby cluster of boulders. They were completely alone. "Where are Ian and Dorcas?" she asked, slowly turning and surveying every blackened tree behind them.

"Ian is safe, but we have a tiny problem with Dorcas," confessed Samson, putting his palms together and wiggling his fingers. "The third thing I have to tell you is—for *fun*—I let Dorcas tie me up last night, and that witch took her opportunity while I was incapacitated. She slipped off with the help of your number one fan, Brad, but not before managing to kill all my Takers except for Motley. Which leads me to my fourth bit of good-news-bad-news, which is Dorcas and Brad are back—but with dragons."

The sky darkened as something massive flew just above the low-hanging gray clouds.

Sara cursed. Loudly.

CHAPTER 38

SMOKE BILLOWED AROUND Samson's legs. "I'll take care of Dorcas and Brad while you two handle the dragons." He jerked his chin at Motley before vanishing in a puff of smoke.

"Gaa!" She was definitely going to strangle him, provided she lived through the next few moments. The sky dimmed again as two massive bodies circled overhead.

Black flames sizzled in Motley's palms. "If they're flat-eyes, we stand a chance. Just don't get hit by their fire," he explained, grinding his combat boots into the burnt forest floor as an enormous, soot-smudged, orange dragon descended through the clouds.

It reminded Sara of a bloated worm with rows of spikes along its back and a massive head armored with a flare of horns. Finding its soft spot would be nearly impossible and probably deadly.

Power flared around her, tingling in her hands as she summoned her magic. The monster was easily twice the size of Tobio's dragon and much heftier than the red dragon she saw at the beach. Fortunately, its size slowed it down.

By the time it swooped toward them, Sara and Motley had dodged aside, avoiding its open mouth of ghastly arm-length teeth while blasting it with enough energy to level a freight train. Their blow only loosened a chunk of molting skin from its flank.

The monster bellowed, shaking the ground with its prehistoric roar, and whipped its tail at them as it sailed past. Motley yanked Sara to the ground with him, the wet tip of the dragon's spiked tail cutting within inches of Sara's face.

"Don't get hit by the tail, either. Their poison is fatal," he warned, jumping to his feet.

Great. This keeps getting better and better.

Sara sprang up just in time to catch a fiery blaze coming at them from their right. Her protective shield barely formed around her and Motley before flames engulfed them. The intense dragon fire turned her shield molten red, threatening to cook them alive until a cold blast cut the heat. She gulped the cool air and looked up at Samson, who was hovering overhead and extinguishing the ember-strewn forest floor with a coat of ice.

He gestured at a dirty yellow dragon doubling back toward them. "You let that one sneak up on you. And you're too reactive with your magic. This isn't time for singular parlor tricks. You need to combine your powers and use your head." His tone was matter of fact, without a hint of mockery. "I'm still playing with Dorcas and Brad in the valley. Surely the two of you can handle a couple of flat-eyes." He vanished in a cloud of smoke.

"Right," grumbled Sara. "They're like puppies with bad breath."

Motley whirled, blasting the orange behemoth overhead.

Magic crackled in Sara's palms, and before she could add her magic to his, the bloodstone pulsed a warning. On instinct, she shifted, placing her back against Motley's, and faced the yellow dragon barreling directly at them. Its jaw dropped, readying to spew flames or swallow them whole—or both.

Sara launched a stream of ice water into the dragon's mouth while erecting another protective shield around herself and Motley.

The dragon choked, puffing steam and ash, and slammed into her invisible barrier. As its spiny head scraped along the shield with a bone-splintering whine, Sara glimpsed its solid matte-black eyes—as flat as the killing gaze of a shark and completely void of any soul.

"Incoming!" warned Motley.

Before Sara could whip around, the orange dragon rammed into them, shattering her barrier. The impact propelled Sara into an alpha-sized boulder and sent Motley sailing in the opposite direction.

A sickening crack followed by a blood-curdling scream pierced the forest wasteland.

Sara scrambled to her feet, healing herself, and rocketed toward Motley, who lay broken beside a charred pine stump. The bloodstone throbbed again as she furiously shook her hands, gathering energy bombs to launch at the two dragons diving for his injured body. But before she could take aim, hot ice grabbed her ankles from behind and her power misfired, detonating a nearby stack of rock. Stones hailed upon her while she fought to turn and blast the assailant who had bound her lower legs with crushing black smoke.

Enough!

She summoned all her energy into throwing a protective shield around Motley and burning off her shackles.

When she twisted around, Brad stood before her, jagged, inky shadows whipping around him like black chains.

Sara staggered and gasped at the acrid air, willing her magic to recharge itself from what little energy the devastated forest could offer her.

He grinned, slow and sadistic. "I'm going to make you cry and beg," he said in a low voice, a lover's promise.

Though her panicked heart skipped a beat, Sara snorted a laugh at him. "We've been through this before, and I left you a vomiting mess in a locked cell." Of course, he hadn't been a freaking dark witch with crushing chains of death at the time. She rallied her swagger and eyed the darkness pulsing around him—from him. Black stains coated his fingers. "What happened to you? Get a taste for the bad stuff and decide to team up with Dorcas because being a lackey Taker wasn't enough?" Sara stole a glance at Motley, lying by the far tree stumps, momentarily protected by her shield while the dragons circled above.

Brad swirled a hand, gathering black flames in his palm and stirring his shadows. "I was never Samson's lackey. I just pretended because the Shadow Mother wants what he has."

All Hells.

"You're *with* the Shadow Mother?" Fear twisted in the pit of her stomach. Sara inched away from him and closer to Motley's too-still body, the dragons hovering dangerously close.

Dragons. At the beach, Brad had said, "*Soon they won't be a problem.*" He had known of the Shadow Mother's plan to control dragons. Her scalp prickled.

The bastard ran his tongue across his upper lip, his red-tinged gaze eating her up. "Her Dark Glory sought me out after you escaped. She gave me everything I've always wanted—power, respect, and a means to force others to my will. Maybe I'll let you live long enough as my pet to see her and our thunder of dragons destroy your precious Ware Woods and everyone in it," he leered—and attacked.

His chains wrapped around Sara's legs and waist, pulling her against him, his thick hands encircling her throat. The pressure drew stars to her vision and lit a fire within her. White energy exploded and bit back at his chains and hands, but still he held on. Desperate, she tried to absorb his magic—to take away the poisonous darkness that infected him—yet he only grew stronger.

Lungs burning for air, Sara clawed at his vise grip and then, remembering Kane's brutal instructions to always go for an opponent's weak spot, she drove her white-hot thumbs into his eyes.

Brad roared, the dragons joining him. Their bellows shook the entire decimated forest as Sara pushed away and hovered out of his reach, gratefully sucking in the foul air.

Eyes leaking black blood, Brad spat at her, "I'll see you on Solstice, bitch." His shadows snatched him, and he vanished. At his departure, the dragons screeched and flew off into the bruised clouds.

In an explosion of smoke, Samson appeared, deep scratches gouged into his cheeks.

"What happened to you?" she and Samson asked at the same time.

Samson gingerly touched his face. "Dorcas is feisty, and it seems she and Brad are taking orders from the Shadow Mother."

Sara groaned. "I know—"

"Where's Motley?"

Shit.

Sara pivoted and rushed to the pine stump, but he was gone. In his place was a smoldering briquette.

Samson swore and pulled at his hair. "I loved that guy. You have no idea how hard it is to find good help these days," he lamented. "And as much as I'd like to hold a three-day funeral dirge, the rest of us need to leave—*now.*"

Sara put a hand to her chest, grasping for the solid presence of the bloodstone, and swallowed the bile at the back of her throat. Even while hovering, she swayed with lightheadedness.

Samson seized her by the shoulders, concern etching his bloody face. "You drained yourself. *Damn it, rookie.* Never use all your power at once, and never absorb dark magic. Witches like us can gather darkness and send it back, but don't ever absorb it."

Sara blankly stared at him. *Who* was *this?* Not the Samson she had hated and was Hells-bent on destroying.

She touched a glowing finger to his cheek, confirming he was real, and inadvertently healed his wounds. Despite her fatigue, she giggled at the utter shock in his expression.

He said, "You're delirious, which is the perfect time for me to convince you to let us all into the safety of your perfect little Ware

Woods bubble. I need you to agree to this before I can bring you to Ian and everyone else."

Well, that was sobering.

She pulled back, remembering Brad's words ". . . *the Shadow Mother wants what he has.*"

Father above. Lethal was right: Samson was hiding something. And whatever—or whoever—it was, he wanted them all to have refuge in Ware Woods. Including him.

Sara blinked. What would the forest families think if she willingly let him into their sanctuary? What would Gran say? And to shelter Samson and his secret would surely bring the Shadow Mother banging on their door. Then again, Brad had already promised a Solstice party with a thunder of dragons. And, as Sara had learned from Dean and the shifter pack, there was safety and power in numbers.

Sara inhaled for three counts and exhaled for three more while Samson tensely waited. "Okay," she drawled. "But everyone drinks sap upon arrival."

He blanched. "They can, but I can't. Will you accept my true name instead?"

Her eyes widened at his inconceivable counter. He was either truly desperate or truly trusting to offer his greatest weakness. Sara studied him. Perhaps his name wasn't his greatest weakness; perhaps it was whatever he was hiding. She held his gaze, noting the hope and trust in his dark eyes, and nodded.

"Excellent," he said with a wide grin. "My true name is Oded. But, please, call me Samson." As he yielded his secret, a cloud of smoke billowed around them, and Sara felt the recognizable tug of being looped to a new location.

CHAPTER 39

S AMSON'S INKY CLOUDS blotted her vision, softly brushed her cheeks, and swirled her hair. His method of looping was pleasant, and she secretly hoped he would teach her how to conjure such clever magic. When her feet gently landed on firm ground, the smoke contracted and vanished in a puff.

Sara tilted back her head, raptly taking in the enclosed cavernous space around her. Overhead, an image of a sunny sky with fluffy clouds was magically projected onto a vaulted ceiling dripping with stalactites. Though they seemed to be underground, trees flourished, and a grassy lawn carpeted the forest-like expanse. Small, round tents of various primary colors dotted the landscape, giving it the appearance of an encampment jamboree.

In the center of the retreat, a dozen children, their skin tones a blend of whites and browns, sat crisscross applesauce on the ground, facing toward Sara. Before them sat a young couple, their backs to her, as if conducting a lesson. When the children grinned, the couple looked over their shoulders and met her gaze.

Sara's heart skipped at recognizing Ian and a vaguely familiar female.

Samson waved a hand at the scene. "We're under the Hills forest. These are the children I saved from the Shadow Mother, and this"—he gave an affectionate smile to the young female—"is Kira. My daughter."

Sara stumbled forward a step, remembering the masked magical from the beach encounter with Brad. But Kira wore no mask here, and when she smiled at Sara, vampire fangs pressed against her bottom lip. A rare half-vampire, half-witch, like Lily and her siblings. And similar to Lily's aura, liquid silver shimmered around Kira.

Sara huffed. Clearly, Samson had been busy since Winona turned him down. And this explained why he had been interested in Lily and questioned Lethal on exceptions to the rules governing magical factions.

Kira, who Sara guessed was close to her age, stood and followed Ian as he bounded to her and Samson.

"Sara!" Ian exclaimed, throwing himself at her and wrapping her in a tight hug. Mother below, it felt good to embrace him and smell his comforting pine-and-cinnamon scent. "Glad to see you finally trust Samson. I've got so much to tell you. Sorry I couldn't say anything before—we couldn't risk anyone knowing about the kids. They're all from the Hills—my mom's family. Oh, where are my manners?" he babbled, pulling away and putting his hand on the small of Kira's back.

Sara swore Samson stiffened.

"Kira, this is my sister, Sara."

Kira beamed at her. "It's nice to finally meet the witch my father raves about. *And* Ian tells me we have the same taste in books," she said with a conspiratorial wink. The many braids hanging down her back clacked their beaded ends when she cocked her head and took the tiniest of steps closer to Ian.

Sara hovered, afraid her knees would give out from shock. Kira radiated kindness as well as a poised power that was no doubt capable of shredding any opponent; she reminded Sara of a friendly panther. *And* she had good taste in books.

Sara swept her attention to Ian. He was positively glowing with excitement, not sickly and tortured as she had once feared he would be in Samson's captivity, and he was also arching a brow at her . . .

Oh! She flicked her gaze back at Kira and stammered, "I—it's nice to meet you too. I had no idea your father was so . . . *protective.*" It would have made everything much easier if Samson had shared all this information at the very start. Except Sara had been blinded by her hate for him. The devil had played his part well—too well. She turned to him with genuine surprise. "You raved about me?"

He shot Kira a playful scowl. "She means raving mad."

Giggles erupted from the children. One small boy pointed at Samson and said, "He's funny when he's angry. Smoke comes out of his ears."

"Enough chitchat," said Samson, clapping his hands to quiet the children. "You have one minute to grab your emergency bag. This is not a drill—we are leaving for Ware Woods, *now.*" The children immediately scampered to the tents.

"What happened?" asked Kira, her voice rising an octave.

Ian dropped his grin, eyes darting around. "Where's Mr. Motley?"

"There's been a complication," admitted Samson. Though he casually inspected his stain-free nails, Sara noticed the dusky grief flickering in his aura. "Dorcas and Brad are in cahoots with the Shadow Mother, who apparently is amassing a cadre of flat-eyed dragons, *and* they all know I'm hiding something valuable down here."

"Shit," breathed Ian, which is *exactly* what Sara would have said if she hadn't been rendered speechless by the entire revelation that Samson had been hiding a magical refugee camp.

In a shimmer of movement, Kira rushed off to the tents, returning with two bags and a small red cooler clinking with medicine bottles. With a soft, "Thanks," Ian shouldered the bags and grabbed the cooler while the children gathered around with their own meager possessions.

Samson turned to Sara, smoky tendrils extending from him. "I'll loop us all there, but first you need to invite us into Ware Woods," he stated.

The blood drained from Sara's face at the thought of looping again so soon. Her stomach hadn't fully recovered from witnessing Motley's remains, and her magic was still drained from her encounter with Brad. In a shaky voice, she said, "As High Witch of Ware Woods, I, Sara Lochton, invite you, Samson, Kira, and the Hills children into our sacred forest."

"You okay?" asked Ian, his worried face the last thing she saw before velvet-kissed smoke enveloped them.

Sara stirred awake at the vexed conversation of multiple voices.

"Are you sure she'll wake up today?"

"Ask me again and I'll throw you in the lake."

"Yeah, but *he* said the last time this happened, she was only out for three weeks. And we don't have much time left."

"We all know."

"Father above. Don't you have a grimoire that should have told her never to absorb dark magic and burn all her energy at once?"

Certain that last question would cost someone a prized body part, Sara snorted and opened her eyes. She lay in her four-poster bed, surrounded by the anxious stares of Gran, Charlie, Samson, and Lethal.

"Finally," muttered Samson, rolling his eyes.

"Mmph." Sara frowned at her thick, wooly tongue and swiped away a spot of drool from the corner of her mouth. Her father whished her an open thermos, and she gratefully plucked it from the air and gulped down crisp sap. "How long have I been asleep?"

she asked, glancing at her unchanged silvery-gray hair and guessing a few hours—a day tops.

"Weeks," said Gran.

"No!" Sara howled.

She shoved back the covers, relieved to be fully clothed, and swung her feet over the edge of the bed. Weeks closer to Solstice. Weeks she should have been training and preparing and catching up with Ian and getting the Hills children settled and—

"Calm down," said her father with a wince, his fingers pressed against his temples. "Ian, Kira, and the kids are doing well. And Samson has filled us in on . . . well, everything." Charlie exchanged a sad smile with Samson as if the two of them had reached an understanding in their shared grief for Winona and all the unfortunate events that brought them to their current situation.

Sara chewed her lip. Weeks also meant— "Thomas and Matt are coming home soon," she blurted, excited and terrified at the same time. They would be leaving the safety of a public university and risking an opportunity for dark magic to attack them on their way home to Ware Woods.

"Today, actually," said her father.

Samson paused his pacing and quirked a brow.

"Thomas is her mate," explained Lethal. "Her *bonded* mate."

"Are you kidding me?" asked Samson with an incredulous chuckle. When no one answered, he paled. "That's impossible. The angry, chiseled witch who tried to attack me with mere knives is *not* your equal."

A snarl escaped Sara. "He *is* my equal."

"I beg to differ." Samson held her stare, his lips a razor-thin line. Energy sizzled around Sara until Samson conceded an exasperated sigh, throwing up his hands. "Fine. You're *bonded and apart from your mate* while the Shadow Mother plots against you? Bonded pairs are stronger together. No wonder you depleted your magic so quickly. Father of Night! What's so important that he left in the first place and hasn't returned yet?" He glanced around the group, onyx eyes wide.

Charlie cleared his throat and, in his best authoritative professor voice, said, "Thomas and Matthew left for one semester to finish their degrees. Education is very important to us."

"Yes, but not if you're dead or have a mate in stasis," scolded Samson.

Sara flinched, as did Charlie and Gran. Lethal held an I-told-you-so expression while the treehouse shuddered, swaying the room. Sara bit her lip again, mind whirling for possible solutions, and glanced out the window opening at the oak's bare waving branches.

Of course!

Though her last attempt hadn't been flawless, she grinned and said, "I'll just loop through the tree and bring them home."

"It doesn't work that way," Samson said with a dismissive wave of his hand. "Only Magi can loop to and from non-sacred sites. And it's not a good idea for you to go by yourself. Not with the Shadow Mother likely watching our every move." He glanced at Charlie, who nodded in agreement. Samson continued, "And since she already wants my head on a pike, if I loop or smoke to a non-sacred site, I'll attract her attention and put everyone with me in grave danger. So I can't go."

"I'll go," offered Lethal. "But I'm not looping—makes me sick." The vampire crinkled their perfect face in disgust.

"You're such a prima donna," muttered Samson.

Lethal went dead quiet, icy eyes shooting daggers at the witch.

"Great, so we'll drive," announced Sara, jumping from the bed and standing on shaky legs between the two fuming Magi. "I'll ask Tobio to join us too. There's no way anyone would be stupid enough to face a witch, a vampire, and a half-dragon. Plus, Tobio has a kick-ass car."

CHAPTER 40

S ARA'S TENSION SIMMERED with each passing mile and each example of utter normalcy from truck stop gas stations to tour buses filled with sightseeing foreigners enjoying the quaint roadside towns and hoping to catch the first snowflake of winter.

Although the picturesque villages whizzing by her window were merrily decorated for the coming holiday, Sara rarely looked away from the phone clutched in her lap. Thomas and Matthew had packed up and left university moments before she had called them and informed them of her plan. For the past two hours, Sara and Matthew had been continually texting their status and location.

Sara twisted and glared at Lethal in the back seat, their arms folded and stubbornly refusing to wear a seat belt. If it came to it, she'd pin the vampire with her magic to stop them from going through the windshield. With a sigh, she redirected her gaze to Tobio. The half-dragon wore his signature spiky ponytail, wrap-around sunglasses, and another of Matthew's sweatshirts. He drove like a demon, weaving between cars and semitrucks and shifting gears with such precision he seemed to be one with the gray muscle car. Though he remained focused on the road, Sara smiled sweetly in his direction and asked, "When Solstice is over, can I drive your car? I know how to drive a stick shift."

"No."

Not even a "maybe" or "I'll think about it." A *hard* no.

Lethal grunted. "Dragons are very possessive."

"Clearly." Sara flopped against the black leather passenger seat. "Fine. It smells like wet dog and reptile in here, anyway." She grinned as Tobio took a tentative sniff.

The corner of his mouth drew up. "Is this your twisted way of thanking me for my superb driving skills?" He coolly downshifted in response to the slowing traffic.

Before she could quip back at him, her phone pinged with another message from Matthew:

Running into traffic . . .

Sara quickly punched back:

So are we.

They crawled for another mile before coming to a complete halt. Sara checked the locator app for possibly the hundredth time—they were both stopped at the same accident. Not great news, but not bad either. They were close enough to walk to each other if the traffic didn't budge soon.

Ping. This time from Thomas:

The road is a parking lot. Ppl have turned off their engines. We're going to case it out.

Seriously? She texted back:

No—YOU stay put. We're at the same accident. My death squad and I will check it out.

Ping.

Already on the move. Meet us in the middle. I'm dying to see you.

Sara shoved the phone into her jacket pocket. "They're here too. We're gonna check out the accident and meet up on foot." She looked at Tobio, who nodded, and then glanced at the surly vampire and their sword in the back seat.

Tobio cut the purr of the engine and dangled a spare pair of sunglasses at Lethal. The resulting icy magic in their eyes could have frozen the Ware Woods' lake. Solid.

"I am not wearing those," said Lethal, "nor am I leaving Kindness in the car. Dragons don't bother me unless I taunt the normals." Lethal pushed Sara's seat forward, ignoring her indignant yelp, then slipped out the door and began stalking down the road shoulder. Sara and Tobio rushed after them, falling into formation beside the vampire in an attempt to block normal views of their sword-strapped figure.

After passing dozens of cars and a school bus full of kids, Sara skidded to a stop. A few more cars ahead of them lay a colossal tree blocking the road. She grabbed Lethal and Tobio, holding them beside her as she studied the enormous pine and its exposed roots. Roots too thick to have simply let go and topple the giant. This was no accident.

Beneath her layers of clothes, the bloodstone quirked a double beat. Sara scanned the dense forest on both sides of the road, the many people exiting their cars, the gloomy sky, and—Her heart skipped a beat. Thomas and Matthew were just ahead, ducking under the massive trunk and striding toward her.

She wanted to rush into Thomas's arms and smash her lips to his, but the bloodstone pulsed again in warning.

Tobio jolted. "To be clear, the ginger is *not* yours," he said, voice a low, possessive growl, and launched forward.

With lightning speed, Lethal grabbed the hood of Tobio's sweatshirt and wrenched him back with one hand while unsheathing their sword with their other. In a blur of movement, the vampire swiped the sword around them, rapidly deflecting multiple objects with a series of metallic clangs. "Ambush," they spat.

Sara tossed her sunglasses aside and beheld a half dozen arrows laying in splinters on the road. Sucking in a breath, she lifted her face to where Thomas and Matthew had hesitated beside the tree trunk.

A keen whistle arched through the air, followed by a dull thunk as an arrow sank into Thomas's upper chest.

Time slowed, cementing Sara's feet to the gritty pavement.

Thomas looked in disbelief at the arrow in his chest. The shaft was so embedded, the arrowhead stuck out his back. Had it struck a few inches lower, it would have skewered his heart. He raised his shocked gaze to her, and she stopped breathing, her soul silently screaming into the Aether. Blood welled down the front of his jean jacket as he sank to his knees. Another whistle and Matthew collapsed, an arrow piercing his thigh.

People shrieked, high-pitched cries of terror. Some scrambled for cover, while others simply tottered in confusion.

Tobio snarled, the sound an ancient promise of death that prickled Sara's skin. Black spikes tipped in gold began to erupt through the arms and back of his sweatshirt.

"No," snapped Lethal, getting into Tobio's face and breaking the shifter's concentration. "That's exactly what they want, so a dragon much bigger than you will come and kill us all."

Sara's shock melted under white-hot anger. Energy crackled around her, stirring her hair as she hovered on her tiptoes. Lethal hissed something, their words distant as Sara directed her focus to the forest on their right—at the myriad of whistles headed their way. Day briefly turned to night as a flock of arrows vaulted above the trees, aiming to rain upon *everyone* in the road.

Sara flicked her gaze to Thomas and Matthew, bleeding beside the tree, shouting at her to go—to leave them behind—and then she took in the scores of panicked and trembling normals.

Consequences be damned.

Surging into the air, she met the arrows with a blinding burst of energy, incinerating them into ash. The bloodstone thrummed as she rose higher, clearing the trees and spotting Dorcas and Brad on a knoll to her right—shadows twisting at their feet, a fury of arrows hovering behind them. Sara summoned more power, bracing to splatter them into all nine Hells, when the cloudy sky opened up, and two dragons plunged for her. Orange Worm and Dirty Yellow.

Shit.

The dragon pair spewed flames. Sara instantly erected a protective shield, fortified with ice, as fire engulfed her. She gritted her teeth, the ice sputtering into steam, and counted the agonizing heartbeats until the onslaught stopped. A fetid roar blasted her from behind, and she spun to face the open maw of Orange Worm. With no time to hit it with magic, Sara rolled aside as a smudge of glimmering blackness rammed into its plated belly, sending it off course. Rotten, jagged teeth sailed by so closely, Sara glimpsed the raw remnants of Worm's last meal.

The dark smudge swished in a tight figure eight, slowing just enough for Sara to recognize Tobio's gilded black dragon before he attacked Dirty Yellow in a ripple of swift movement. Though Tobio was half the size of the other dragons, he was significantly faster and more agile. The moment he collided with the flat-eye, a storm of arrows sailed up from the ground and bombarded his flank, three finding purchase while the rest bounced off his shimmering scales. Tobio pulled away from the yellow dragon with a furious screech.

Sara whipped her attention back to Dorcas and Brad, determined to end them and their damned arrows. Hands blazing with spheres of energy, Sara reared back to unleash herself when a thunderous crack split the sky open again. A shrill roar shook air and land alike as the fiery red dragon from the beach descended upon them all.

Sara's energy faltered, too many sets of spiked teeth and poisonous tails surrounding her. The red dragon flew in a wide loop, massive horned head swiveling while its elysian eyes surveyed the entire scene. It gave another piercing roar and spit jets of fire at Orange Worm and Dirty Yellow.

The two flat-eyes bellowed back and launched themselves at the red dragon. With a swift coiled twist, Red clobbered both dragons with its armored head, then ripped open their scaly hides with the speared tip of its tail. Dark blood spilled forth. Shrieks filled the air as both monsters retreated into the murky clouds.

Their cries fading, Sara dove for Dorcas and Brad, who were

now preoccupied with fighting off Lethal and Kindness. Before she could sweep Lethal aside with a blast of wind and fire her energy at the dark witches, their shadows swallowed them whole—Brad's smoky rude gesture a parting gift.

With a guttural holler, Lethal savagely swiped at the waning shadows.

Sara's own fury at letting Dorcas and Brad get away was cut short by a roar from the red dragon. Instead of a high-pitched warning, this vocalization was deeper toned.

She rushed back to protect Tobio as he hovered, bleeding and bowing his head before the red dragon. *"What are you doing? This dragon will kill you!"* she projected at Tobio, straining and failing to kinetically move him out of harm's way.

With a flick of its serpentine body, Red slammed Tobio, sending him snapping through the branches of a giant pine before crashing beside Thomas and Matthew. His impact shuddered the road, rocking the nearby cars.

A fresh wave of shrieks and sobs erupted from the normals.

Hauling himself by his forearms, Matthew crawled toward Tobio's spiny head, blood pooling around them both.

Sara turned her gaze to Thomas, who held on to the arrow shaft lodged into his chest. His attention remained fixed on the sky behind her, his eyes wild with fury and fear. "No!" he yelled, and the desperation in his voice pierced her soul.

Sara heard the distinct rasp of the red dragon's scaled body and the hiss of air passing through many teeth as it came to collect her—the price for using her magic before normals, even if it was to save them.

Summoning her remaining magic, she fired a burst of white healing energy at Thomas, Matthew, and Tobio. And when a forked tongue caressed her face and darkness crept over her, Sara reached for Thomas, her fingertips glowing with love and a heartbreaking apology. The anguish in his eyes bored into her, searing her soul, before the dragon wholly claimed her.

CHAPTER 41

THE GENTLE WHISPER of rushing water drifted into Sara's consciousness. With a slow inhale, she cautiously gathered the rest of her senses: the scent of rain tickling her nose, the soft surface she was lying on, the muted light seeping through her closed eyelids. Definitely not the fiery digestive system or burning Hells she had expected.

She cracked open an eye and took in the white-paneled walls of a small room. Sensing nothing and no one else in her enclosure—for lack of a better term—Sara pushed herself up on the cot she lay upon and scanned the room. No visible doors.

Fear ripped through her at being trapped in a mental ward—a horrible reality she had barely survived after losing her mother in a car accident.

Her heart raced. Perhaps this was her own personal hell for failing to protect Ware Woods—for failing to be a worthy High Witch—for failing Thomas. And yet no sadistic orderly loomed over her. They didn't have to; being taken from her family, her friends, her forest, her mate was brutal torture enough.

She blew out a long breath, thinking of them. With any luck, her death had corrected the natural balance between light and dark magic, appeasing the Shadow Mother into leaving Ware Woods alone. In her absence, Samson would be the experienced High

279

Witch her family needed, and Thomas would move on to find a new mate who could bear children.

Pain squeezed her chest as if a giant hand were wringing every drop of blood from her heart. She gasped, eyes wide, mouth open in screamless agony. Her body threatened to explode until her vision darkened with a new promise of death, and then the torment stopped.

Sara gulped down air. Either the pain was a physical manifestation of her mental and emotional anguish, or it was an unwelcome bonus to an eternal, all Hells membership. Both possibilities sucked.

She bit her cheek, waiting for tears that did not come. Crying was pointless if you were dead. Besides, she regretted nothing and would do it all over again if it meant saving Thomas, Matthew, Tobio, and all those unwitting normals.

Actually, she did have one regret—not killing Dorcas and Brad. Then again, she wouldn't want to spend eternity with them. Assuming their deaths, although not by dragon, would have dumped them into this singular paper-white, doorless room.

Sara frowned. *Death and dragons.* Gran's premonition rang in her head, and she wondered if her grandmother had known she would die.

Her frown deepened. Maybe the Book had known too, and the spell she cast was a covert way to bring replacement Magi in the event of her death. At least Sara had trust in Lethal, Dean, and Samson to protect Ware Woods.

She huffed a laugh. Smart Book.

The bloodstone pulsed, startling Sara and sending a wave of warm energy through her. She slapped a hand to her chest and gripped the stone through her favorite black jacket with an asymmetrical zipper. Tucking her chin, she glanced down at her four-fingered hand, her jeans—torn by Lethal's daggers—and her socked feet.

This version of hell lets me keep my bloodstone but has a no-shoes policy?

Sara peeked over the edge of the cot and spied her take-no-prisoners lace-up boots directly beneath her. She immediately put on her shoes, all the better to run at—or away from—whatever horrors dwelled outside her enclosure. Yet, despite her hyper-awareness, all she sensed was the gentle flow of water.

Sara slid off the bed and inspected the walls. They were all constructed of thick, white paper with a dark-brown lattice frame. Along the bottom and top of one of the walls was a slender track. She lightly touched the wall, half expecting to be zapped with energy for prodding her cell. To her shock, a portion of the wall slid open, exposing a room of smooth stone, softly lit by a familiar circular opening on her far left.

Sara darted her gaze around for any trace of the tattooed and sharp-toothed Jin. But the room was empty save for the sound of water streaming down the outside of the round opening.

When she crept toward the water and cleared the threshold of the paper room, the door closed behind her and vanished, leaving a wall of solid stone in its place.

Well, crap. Glad I grabbed my shoes.

With nothing in the desolate cave, and no other means of escape, Sara slunk to the waterfall. It parted, revealing a thin river with black stepping-stones. Beyond the stones welcomed a garden paradise of sculpted trees, ornamental shrubs, perfectly pruned grasses, and aged boulders. Ribbons of gently flowing water, smooth-pebbled pathways, and brushed-white sand wound through the landscape. Definitely the opposite of what she'd expected.

Sara hopped across the stepping-stones and approached the snowy pink blossoms of a cherry tree on the grassy bank. Her mother had loved creating cherry blossom floral arrangements, and on more than one occasion explained to her that the fragile springtime blooms represented renewal and the delicate balance between life and death. Perhaps someday, Naomi's tree would be as grand as this one.

She plucked a five-petaled flower and twisted it between her fingers. Savoring the delicate green fragrance and starry pattern in the center of the blossom, she looked up and froze.

On a nearby boulder perched Jin, staring at her—without his tinted glasses.

The flower fell from her hand, fluttering to the pristine cropped grass as Sara beheld his exquisite silvery eyes and slitted pupils. Eyes of the red dragon.

"Am I dead or is this real?" she whispered, unable to look away from him for even a moment to wave at the exquisite garden. The energy radiating from him shimmered in the soft sun, prickling the back of her neck. He had enough power to crush her bones and obliterate entire cities without breaking a sweat.

"Real," he answered, voice sleek and dangerous.

Despite the deadly threat before her, Sara's shoulders relaxed a fraction.

Not dead . . . yet . . . . According to the magical rules enforced by dragons, she should be dead for exhibiting magic in front of normals—for what she had done at the beach and along the road.

She squinted at him. He wore loose black pants and a wrap-around sleeveless white top. The diamond-pattern tattoos on his forearms were similar to Tobio's marks. Marks she now realized indicated the location of spikes in his dragon form.

Unable to rein in either her curiosity or her smart mouth, and to confirm he was indeed the red dragon, she blurted, "Twice now you haven't killed me. I'm not complaining, but why?"

He only blinked at her, and her heart skipped. Dragons supposedly killed *all* magicals involved in an exposure incident.

Her panicked gaze swept the quiet garden. "What happened to the others?" she squeaked.

In one fluid motion, Jin leapt from the boulder and began walking along a pathway of intricately arranged pebbles toward a raised rectangular pavilion—its paneled walls fully retracted into four wooden columns. She lurched after him, desperate to hear anything he would tell her.

"You healed them, and I corrected the situation by wiping magic from normal minds. To the other magicals, you are gone. To me, you are very much alive and finally by my side." He stepped onto the grass mat inside the pavilion and, with an almost imperceptible flick of his hand, a tea setting for two appeared on the floor.

Sara jerked back. Thank the Father, Thomas and the others were alive, but . . . "*finally by my side*"?

She looked from the steaming pot of tea back to Jin. Smooth as flowing water, he lowered to the floor and knelt, bare feet tucked behind him. "Is this punishment for my failures? To *serve* you?" she asked, incredulously.

Jin remained quiet, his face unreadable while he poured two cups of tea and delicately placed one before her. The distant hollow thunk of a bamboo water feature filled the tense silence.

He squared his shoulders at her, his silver eyes like liquid metal. Gesturing to the garden and indicating himself with a slight curl of his fingers, he said, "You see this as punishment?"

Sara glanced at the garden and the tea, her chest tight. This was wrong.

Pain stabbed her heart, and she winced, pressing her palm to her chest until it subsided.

Jin angled his head. "Is something the matter?" His tone was the slightest bit softer.

With a shake of her head, she stammered, "I—I don't belong here." She had broken a magical rule, failed to stop Dorcas and Brad, and utterly failed Ware Woods as High Witch—letting down everyone she loved. Having tea in a too-perfect garden was not where she belonged. Instead, she should be stoking the fires of all Hells or suffering an eternity as a catatonic mental-ward wretch with Brad looming over her.

Jin flashed a knowing smile full of bright white pointed teeth.

"You belong here. The Mother said you would help me. Now, please sit." He nodded at the mat.

Sara's mangled heart skipped another beat. "You know the Mother?" She sank to the floor, hoping her compliance would tease a proper explanation instead of a cryptic response.

Jin frowned at her boots before dragging his arresting gaze back at her face. "All elysian-eyed dragons know the Mother. We are her servants in overseeing the magical factions and maintaining the balance between light and dark."

All? Sara immediately thought of a small black-and-gold dragon with elysian-eyes. And either she whispered his name or Jin read her thought, for he said, in a harsh voice, "Not Tobio. He is a half-breed mistake who shouldn't be alive."

A lie. Sara sat back on her clunky shoes, copying Jin's position, and twisted her mouth in thought. He could have easily killed a wounded Tobio during the ambush. But instead, Jin had appeared to scold and dismiss him. And Tobio allowed it, as if they knew each other. Regardless of their relationship, Jin had clearly taken pity on him.

Sara narrowed her eyes. "What exactly did the Mother say about me?" *That I'm a mistake too—incapable of being a High Witch and the perfect mate Thomas deserves?*

She held her breath, ignoring another stab of pain. Perhaps Jin had taken pity on her as well.

He held his cup with both hands and took an infuriatingly long sip before saying, "The Mother said you and I will help each other. She also said love will correct the balance." Jin set down his cup and leaned back, staring at her with that damned unreadable face.

"Help *you*—an elysian-eyed dragon?" She snorted a laugh. But then her curiosity tugged at her and she added, "With what?"

His fingers fluidly tapped his knees, black pointed nails clicking at a faster tempo than the slow thunk of the meditative water feature. He seemed to be thinking awfully hard as to how a defective witch could indeed help him. "I assume to save dragons from the Shadow Mother."

Sara arched a brow, partly in disbelief and partly in hoping for more information.

Much to her surprise, Jin explained, "For centuries, the Shadow Mother has bided her time—stealing moments of imbalance and quietly growing stronger. While this is natural to a certain degree, a sudden shift in the balance was not expected, and she has grown powerful enough to infect flat-eyes with her shadows. The lesser dragons now serve her and no longer obey me. And I am currently unable to summon another elysian-eye for help."

A sudden shift?

Sara rubbed her chin, her thoughts racing. Samson had said she was responsible for an imbalance by coming into her powers and destroying Makwa. But surely the utter destruction of the Hills sacred site, at the hands of the Shadow Mother no less, also affected the balance.

Ignoring or oblivious to her ruminations, Jin continued, "If she grows strong enough to infect and control elysian-eyed dragons, she will have enough power to destroy all magical factions." The concern in his silvery eyes was unmistakable, yet the idea of anyone holding sway over him or destroying all magicals seemed impossible.

"That's absurd. Why would she do such a thing if there would be none of us left to terrorize?" The resulting frown on Jin's face made Sara feel terribly small.

He stopped drumming his fingers. "The Shadow Mother is sentient like the Mother and Father. However, there is no reasoning with her. She is a wild darkness that thrives on discord and violence. Like a tempest of death, she will absorb and obliterate all magic and then destroy the normal world as well. Her entire existence is to consume."

Oh, well, if that's *all.*

Sara swallowed around the knot in her throat and eyed the cup of tea. Despite her thirst, no way would she drink or eat anything in this garden. The likelihood of the tea being infinitely more magical—and deadly—than sap was a distinct possibility. Though she knew Jin needed her and wouldn't kill her just yet, she pushed away the cup with her knuckles and folded her arms.

Think. How can I negotiate my way out of this garden?

Sara studied Jin, contemplating how he had said, "*love will correct the balance*." Mustering her swagger, she inquired, "And you think *love* will magically stop the Shadow Mother?"

Keep dreaming, because my tiny, ragged heart belongs to Thomas— even if he thinks I'm dead.

Jin shrugged, the gesture so humanly normal that Sara's frown melted into a wicked grin. The dragon's lack of assuredness in how to proceed was all she needed to gain leverage over her predicament.

She leaned toward him. "How about we pay the Mother a visit so she can explain *exactly* what kind of love she is implying."

CHAPTER 42

Surprise rippled from Jin, and he shrank back as if Sara were the serpent. "We can't. She has gone quiet—perhaps sleeping, as she and other dragons often do."

Pfft! Like dandelion fuzz in the wind, there went her plan to implore the Mother to protect Ware Woods and get a direct explanation on what type of love and help she expected from a failed witch. She scowled at him.

Jin tilted his head. "Is there more than one kind of love? I only know of mating." His silver eyes gleamed, a sensuous grin pulling at the corners of his mouth and exposing many pointed teeth.

Sara choked and debated throwing her hot tea in his lap, but the genuine sincerity in his voice stayed her hand. Father above, he was serious. Gran's cautionary tale of dragons being void of love flashed in her mind.

She fidgeted, boots cutting into her backside, mind scrambling for a witty comment to dig herself out of this hole. Since her smart mouth had gotten her into this situation, her best tactic would be the truth.

She blew back a stray lock of hair, stealing another moment, as he patiently waited.

"Well, yeah, there's physical love when you *desire* another . . ."

Her cheeks burned at recalling Thomas's fervent kisses and roaming hands.

Jin's sharp smile broadened, his nostrils flaring, likely scenting the tingle along her skin and through her center.

Cursing herself for forgetting the acute senses of shifters—present dragon included—Sara clamped her knees together and cleared her throat. In a louder voice, she said, "But there's also caring love for friends and family. The kind of love that wraps your heart in a hug and reassures you that you're never alone. The kind where you'd do anything for their safety and happiness—and they'd do the same for you. The kind where you wholly accept and love what makes them unique."

Like Moira's feistiness, Gran's bluntness, and Thomas's fighting instinct. Even Caleb's snoring and Ian's nervous tapping. Sara chuckled softly, her vision clouding with remembrances.

Jin stilled.

"And then"—she gave a wistful sigh—"when desire and caring combine, there is a third type of love so absolute your hearts and souls entwine as one."

A gentle breeze stirred her hair, and she closed her eyes, savoring the memory of Thomas's embrace, his musk-and-ash scent, and his unconditional support and genuine acceptance of all her quirks. Her love for him would never waver, no matter how long they were apart—even for an eternity in a dragon's garden.

She straightened, a sudden realization warming her like a cheerful fire on a cold day. As bonded mates, their feelings were reciprocal. Which meant, of course Thomas felt the same about her. Despite her quirks and flaws, and regardless of what the future held, she *was* his perfect mate. And he would always love her, just as she would always love him. Now and forever.

The bloodstone pulsed and energy crackled around her.

And, Mother below, the love she had for her forest family was fierce and irreplaceable, and of course they felt the same way toward her. It had never been knowledge, power, and experience she needed to be a worthy High Witch. She had only needed to trust their mutual love.

Another wave of energy surged from the bloodstone and sparked around her, bringing with it a second revelation that could very well change everything.

The tension she hadn't realized she'd been holding melted into fiery determination.

She needed to get back to Ware Woods—to where she belonged.

Sara snapped her eyes open and fixed her gaze on Jin. The dragon had ever-so-slightly scooted back and was studying her intently, hands still gripping his knees. "How long have I been here?" she asked, her tone a rushed clip.

He tensed, black nails digging into equally dark pants. "A day."

Relief flooded her. "Perfect! We can help each other by facing the Shadow Mother together. Winter Solstice is a week away— plenty of time for you to bring me back to Ware Woods and for all of us to be ready when she attacks us on the darkest day. Between you and the three Magi I summoned, we'll defeat her and find a cure for the dragons. And life will be peachy for everyone," she rattled off, finishing with a smug smile.

Jin slowly shook his head, the movement similar to a snake swaying before striking. "You belong here at my side until the Mother awakens and tells us what to do. Besides, the Shadow Mother has no reason to attack a reclusive sacred site."

White flames flaring around her, Sara jumped to her feet. She had already waited for far too much and was done *waiting* for others to dictate her fate.

Looking down on him, she warned in a frosty voice, "I am no one's possession. And I do not wait for *anyone* to tell me what to do. I am *helping* you by telling you where the Shadow Mother will be on Solstice."

Jin rose, muscles quivering in his bare arms, and snarled—the sound like boulders being ground into dust. The garden trembled, rocking the perfect flowering trees and pavilion. Between them, their teacups wobbled and spilled, staining the grass mat. But before Sara could summon a sphere of energy and start a brawl she would surely lose, Jin stopped growling and redirected his furious gaze at something behind her.

She whipped around and beheld a dark plume of smoke erupting in the garden just outside the pavilion. Her jaw dropped.

Impossible.

How would Samson even know where to find her? *She* didn't even know where she was.

With a whispered clap, the smoke contracted and disappeared. In its place stood Samson, Tobio . . . and Thomas, his vest of knives loaded with weapons, eyes blazing with rage.

Sara froze at his healthy appearance—no arrow protruding from his chest. Though Jin said she had healed him, she had never thrown out her healing power and had no idea how well it had worked. She flicked her gaze to Tobio. While his demeanor was anxious, he was otherwise perfectly fine as well.

Jin's hissing growl, promising a slow, painful death, shook the garden. Slate tiles from the pavilion roof broke loose and smashed to the ground as pink and white blossoms filled the air like sleepy snowflakes.

In an ancient, guttural voice, Jin threatened, "You have two seconds to tell me what you are doing here before I incinerate all of you."

"Sara!" Thomas lunged for her, only to be flung aside by Jin's magic and slammed into one of the pavilion's columns. He slid to the tile-strewn ground, blue flames in his eyes as he fought against Jin's power pinning him down.

Jin bared his pointed teeth, and Thomas responded by somehow managing to hurl a lance of cobalt energy and a fistful of knives. In midair, the magic and blades instantly disintegrated into wisps of ash.

"Stop," pleaded Sara, rushing to Thomas's side, hoping Jin would hold his fire and spare them both. She crouched beside Thomas, holding the sides of his face and pressing her brow to his as he pulled her into his arms. Light-blue energy erupted from their touch and flickered around their embrace. The pain in her chest—her heart—melted, and she gasped, tears welling in her eyes.

Thomas tightened his grip. "I knew you weren't gone," he whispered, voice trembling. "I felt your pain—*our* pain from being *forced* apart. With or without magic, I will always find you."

Against all odds, he had come for her. Sara's healed heart pounded at holding him for the first time in months. She wanted to stare into his eyes and feel the rise and fall of his chest for the rest of their lives, but Jin growled again, sending the pavilion to the verge of collapse.

A popping hiss menaced behind her, and she glanced back at a furious Jin. Fiery red spikes protruded from his forearms.

"Ryujin," warned Tobio, and in a softer tone added, "brother." He stepped toward Jin, his words halting the dragon's transformation.

Sara twisted in Thomas's arms to face both dragon shifters. "You're *brothers*?"

Tobio slid her a sly grin. "I'm the much younger, better-looking brother."

"Half-brother," snarled Jin. "Mother should have killed you. She'll be appalled to learn you still live with wolves."

Tobio shot back, "I'll gladly take the pack over this lonely existence." He gestured at the garden before slipping his hands into his pockets.

Sara gaped at Tobio's bold confidence given his dragon was half the size of Jin's.

"One second to explain yourselves," demanded Jin, spikes tearing through the back of his sleeveless tunic.

"Well," declared Samson with a smoky flourish, clearly relieved to finally get a word in. "I was enjoying the family reunion. But, since you asked so kindly, the Shadow Mother and a thunder of dragons are circling Ware Woods." His shrewd gaze studied the two dragon shifters as if calculating a complex formula.

"You're wrong," said Jin. "I would have felt such a disturbance in the magic."

"Oh, it's true," crooned Samson, twirling his hands in the air, sending tendrils of smoke around himself and Tobio. "Terribly inconsiderate of them to arrive early, especially while Sara was out having tea." He quirked a brow at the ruined tea set and then winked at Sara with pure cunning in his eyes.

Sara bit her lip to hide her grin. *The crafty devil is plotting to outsmart a dragon.* She mentally projected to Thomas, *"Get ready."*

He responded by grabbing her hand, their fingers interlacing with a tingle of energy as they readied their crouched stances—like this had been their plan all along.

Samson tipped his head in a slight bow to a fuming Jin and said, "Apologies, dragon, but we're late for our own party."

Sara pulled Thomas with her as she surged toward Samson's billowing smoke, and in a velvety dark flash, they winked from the garden and transported to the center of the Cahill common—Jin's unhinged roar reverberating in the marrow of her bones.

CHAPTER 43

THE GROUND PITCHED, and Sara stumbled to maintain her footing from the rapid looping, a united cheer filling her ears. Thomas released her hand and put a secure arm around her waist as they faced the crowd surrounding them, relief in everyone's expression.

Her father rushed forward and hugged her, crushing the air from her lungs. "Thank the Mother and Father you're okay," he said.

The forest families sighed and clapped Tobio and Samson on their backs.

From over her father's shoulder, Sara spotted Dean and Matthew beaming at Tobio while Kira launched herself into Samson's arms. Sara flicked her eyes to the tense faces of Ian and Lethal, the latter wearing Kindness strapped to their back. Then she took in the churning dark sky pressing upon the forest. The shadowy outline of something dreadfully huge skirted above the clouds. Before her, the Hills' children whimpered and joined hands, drawing closer around Ian.

Sara pulled away from her father, sweeping her gaze across her people—her entire forest family. "I—I don't understand. It's not Solstice." How could this be happening? She wasn't ready. She would never be ready. An eternity of time couldn't prepare her for this sickening moment.

Dean cracked his neck, his hands on his hips in a formidable stance. "Either the Shadow Mother wanted to throw us off our game, or she knew you were gone and thought us weak. Doesn't matter—we're ready."

His Alpha confidence bolstered Sara's spirit. The bloodstone pulsed along with another tingling wave of realization as she panned the crowd.

It was never just her facing the Shadow Mother, but all of them together: a pack of witches, shifters, and vampires, and even a half-dragon. A combined unit with strength in numbers *and* diverse abilities.

She swallowed. Aside from facing Makwa, she had no experience in organizing a battle strategy. She turned her gaze to the person who had successfully protected Ware Woods for decades— her toughest instructor and the forest's de facto general—Kane.

Thomas's father didn't even blink before saying, "Ware Woods has never fought dragons before, but you Magi have." He lifted his chin to Sara, Samson, Lethal, and the pack. "We defer to you."

Samson smoothed his jacket, this one midnight blue instead of black. "Flat-eyed dragons are mindless mongrels. No big deal." He flashed an easy smile.

Lethal countered with a head shake. "Not true. While they can easily be outsmarted, they have the fire power to burn you to ash, and their tails are tipped with poison."

"I've been licked by their fire a few times, and it was no picnic." Dean thumped his wide chest, his wince dissolving into a hint of a dimple as Moira joined his side.

Sara caught Tobio's eye and raised her brow at him, a silent request for permission to share the information he had revealed to her. When he nodded his approval, she spoke up, voice cracking at the gruesome memory of Mr. Motley's remains. "Dragons have a weak spot at the base of their skull, but it's heavily armored. Our best tactic is to use blunt force to beat them back. They are being used by the Shadow Mother and shouldn't be killed unless necessary."

Lethal grunted. "Fine. I don't intend to get close to one anyway."

"None of us do," said Caleb, folding his stocky arms at the vampire.

The families whispered anxiously until Samson cleared his throat. "While dragons are bothersome, it's the Shadow Mother we need to be wary of. She can worm into your mind and turn your darkest thoughts against you. If she corners you alone, she will control you like a puppet and make you do things you don't want to do." A muscle twitched along his clenched jaw as he looked at the Hills' kids, shame and regret shining in his onyx eyes.

A moment of heavy silence was immediately shattered by a chorus of dragon roars. From the barn at the far side of the common, livestock fretfully lowed in response.

Energy flared around Sara. Like Hells she would let dragons or the Shadow Mother into Ware Woods.

She hovered a few feet above the ground and spun in a slow circle, assessing their strengths as a whole and reading the trust and love in everyone's presence. *"We can do this,"* she said mentally. And as another shadow swept overhead, she unfolded a plan she hoped would save them all.

"Atwells are to stay focused on the dragons—blast them with ice and water to stop their fire," she said, making eye contact with all the water and air witches. To the few vampires among them, she added, "You all watch their backs. Make sure nothing sneaks up on them." They nodded gravely before Sara shifted her attention to the Sullivans. "Sullivans are to attack anything that tries to get through the barrier from above, and"—she turned her gaze to the Cahills—"Cahills will protect the barrier at the ground level."

Sara swung her focus to her father, Gran, Ted, and Ian. The Lochtons had a diversity of magics, but the most useful in this moment would be their telepathy. "Your role will be to provide mental communications among the families and, with Kira's help, to safeguard all the children here in the central common. If all Hells break loose, everyone falls back to the common to protect each other." Sara glanced in the direction of the treehouse. Though looping through the oak tree to a safer location was a possibility, she knew none of them would willingly leave Ware Woods. Like herself, they would defend it to their dying breath.

A murmur of agreement drifted among everyone present while parents hugged their children and gathered them toward the Lochtons. Ian ruffled Connor's hair as he joined Lily's younger siblings and the many Cahill kids now holding hands with the Hills children.

Sara swiveled to the shifters, who had naturally clustered together: the Walkers, Dean and the pack, and even Alice and Albert. "Shifters are to roam and protect the other families as needed with Bill and Dean co-leading this defense. Tobio, this includes you too. I want you staying inside the forest barrier and being our fail-safe against any dragons that make it past the families."

Tobio sliced a smile and clenched his fists, golden-tipped spikes protruding from his forearms. Beside him, Matt gave a nod, his copper hair pulled back into a short ponytail, amber eyes aglow.

Sara lifted her chin in return and then flicked her gaze to Wes, already in his juvenile lupine form and looking deceptively innocuous beside Albert's massive white wolf. She grinned. And because the best defense was a sneaky offense, she launched into the second part of her plan.

"Samson, Lethal, and I will make an offensive strike against the Shadow Mother. If she truly thinks I'm not here, she won't be expecting our attack outside the wall. Together we may be able to drive her off and avoid any damage to Ware Woods." Not just injured animals and fallen soul trees, as had happened in her battle with Makwa, but unspeakable casualties.

She considered her family, all the children, every magical, and each creature in the forest. Her bloodstone pounded with energy, emitting a reddish glow through her shirt and unzipped jacket.

Her father caught her eye, opening his mouth as if to say something, when two shadowy dragons slammed into the barrier directly above them. The entire forest quaked. With hands over her ears to block the deafening reverberation, Sara looked up and stilled. Fire sprayed against the invisible dome and cast them all in a deathly orange glow.

A short, shrill whistle pierced the air, bringing everyone's attention back to their gathering. Gran yelled, "You know your roles. Work together and retreat here if needed. Ware Woods does not tolerate shadows and overgrown reptiles. Present company excluded, of course." She inclined her head at a composed Tobio before shooing them all away.

The families immediately scattered with the shifters close at their heels.

As his family rose into the sky, Thomas lingered. Hovering before Sara, he cupped her face with his hands and pulled her to him. "I wish I could go out there with you. Be safe, my monster, and make sure you come back to me—to all of us." His voice was rough, his thumbs swiping her cheeks.

Sara clutched his arms, light-blue energy sparking around them. "Of course I will."

"I love you." He pressed a kiss to her forehead before releasing her and flying off.

"Now and forever," she projected into his mind, swallowing against the lump in her throat as he flew after Violet toward the lake. When they disappeared over the trees, Sara turned to spot Samson hugging Kira.

He reluctantly let her go and, in a stern, fatherly voice, said, "Stay with Ian and the kids. No hero business."

"Look who's talking." Kira rolled her eyes at him, giving him another hug before trotting off after Ian.

A smile teased Sara's mouth. If they made it through this, she looked forward to getting to know Kira, swapping books and tormenting Samson with identical eye rolls.

"*Sara,*" projected her father, and she twisted in the air until spotting him with Gran and Ted, gently steering the children closer to the chestnut soul tree. "*Be careful.*" His eyes shone as he held her gaze.

Sara didn't need magic to read his distraught look. He had witnessed too much tragedy, and she'd do everything in her power before causing him anymore.

"*Careful is my middle name. Besides, anything is possible.*"

Her father snorted a laugh. "*Only one of those is true.*"

"*It's enough.*"

He smiled stiffly and blew her a kiss, which she returned.

"Are we done?" drawled Lethal.

Sara whipped around to the vampire, ready to comment on the embrace Lily had given them, when the sky turned orange again with dragon fire.

"Yes," stated Samson, sprinting toward a new path at the edge of the common. Sara flew after him while Lethal strode with vampire ease. "Your forest is very clever with shortcuts," said Samson with a mixture of awe and appreciation. "Lethal hates looping, and I need a moment to give you a crash course in facing the Shadow Mother. Protect your energy and do *not* absorb her shadows—do *not* listen to her silken lies."

"So, our plan is to cover our ears and blast her while Lethal hacks away?" asked Sara, eyeing the hilt of the vampire's sword.

Samson shook his head, jaw clenched. "It's not so easy. She speaks inside your mind. The only way to block her out is to fully accept your own darkness and not let her see what you truly love."

Sara frowned. This might be much harder than she was willing to admit. She glanced at the vampire again. Maybe they should stay behind since a sword was useless against a shadow, anyway.

Samson twirled a hand, smoke drifting from his fingers. "Lethal will be fine. They have little heart and no conscience, not to mention nothing to lose." Though Lethal growled, Samson continued, "You, on the other hand, have a lot to lose. As do I." He regarded Sara with concern in his dark eyes as the path abruptly stopped at the stone wall.

Sara froze, his warning twisting in her soul. Going after the Shadow Mother was clearly insane, but so was waiting for her like rooted rabbits.

She tore her gaze from Samson and looked past the wall. Where the fallow fields should have been was nothing but a curtain of dark, undulating shadows.

Shit.

Samson smirked, yet his eyes remained haunted. "I'm sure this will be delightful. All the same, let's stick together as we send this bitch back to her circle of Hell." He vaulted over the wall and was swallowed by darkness.

"Always so dramatic," complained Lethal as Sara grabbed their stony wrist and heaved them over the wall with her.

CHAPTER 44

SARA GROUND HER heels into the soil between Samson and Lethal, pulse hammering while her eyes adjusted to the sooty dimness. The air was as heavy as a lead coffin and bitingly colder than inside the forest. Overhead, dragons roared. Their thunderous echoes rattled Sara's spine and prickled the nape of her neck. But her concern about the flying beasts was quickly eclipsed by the rapid thudding of feet as multiple panting creatures surrounded them.

So much for a sneaky offense.

Lethal pulled away from her and unsheathed their sword, the bright sing of the blade instantly gobbled up by the thick air. By the time the shadows shifted and Sara caught her first terrifying glimpse of the dozen bruised-eyed Takers surging toward them, Lethal was already a choreographed blur of movement. Within two heartbeats, the Takers were all dead, their black blood leaching into the stubbled field.

Sara fought the urge to vomit and grabbed on to Samson's arm, stopping herself from pitching into the filth creeping their way.

"Why so surprised?" asked Samson. "You chose Lethal to accompany us for this exact reason, right?" He lifted a brow at her.

Nope. I didn't even think about the possibility of Takers. Just seemed like a good idea to have the vampire of Death by my side.

Sara grumbled an unconvincing, "Yeah, yeah," and stepped back from Samson, chin up. Her gaze flicked from him to the fresh horde of Takers encircling them. But instead of advancing, the Takers parted and remained standing at attention as a voluptuous, shadowed figure slithered from the gloom.

Sara held her breath—afraid to absorb even one speck of the ghastly entity.

The Shadow Mother drifted forward, her faceless form steadily convulsing in and out like a beating heart. Her nebulous edges faded into the dim light, while her dense core swirled with all the sinister pull of an ethereal black void.

To Sara's horror, Samson crumpled to the ground, hands gripping his head, his face contorting with pain. Lethal soon followed, all four fangs bared, trembling with the effort to hold on to Kindness. Sara debated grabbing them both and lurching back into the safety of the forest when her own voice sounded in her head: *"Hello, monster."*

Sara froze, every inch of her skin quivering under an icy touch. The voice was hers and for a dizzy moment, she questioned if she'd said the words herself. "Get out of my head," she snarled.

Laughter echoed inside her. *"I am your head, your heart, your soul—I am you. The* real *you, full of anger and violence."*

"This is not me," she screamed at the Shadow Mother—at herself. The bloodstone pounded in time with her rapid heart rate, but not a flicker of magic could be summoned from her veins or from the spoiled field. It was as though the Shadow Mother had sucked away her magic.

"Imagine how liberating it will be for you to embrace your darkness. Your power. You can righteously kill thousands and own the fire burning inside you."

Sara shook her head, denying the Shadow Mother and trying to dislodge the claws scraping the inside of her mind and soul.

From the Shadow Mother's void, dusky whips unfurled and

lashed out with a snap. Their jagged edges tore into Sara's legs, forcing her to her knees as their icy cold crept through her body. She threw her head back and mentally beseeched the Mother and Father for the strength to end the dark abomination before her.

Instead of a divine response, dragons writhed in the sky.

Laughter filled her ravaged mind, and the Shadow Mother slunk closer.

"You do not need the Mother. She has forsaken her darkness. But not you. We both know your heart is full of vengeance. You have already willingly hurt and killed a few to save many. It feels good, does it not?"

Sara cried out as the shadow whips tightened, threatening to shatter her bones. A memory of slaying Makwa with a spear of red energy flickered in her mind, followed by an image of Brad choking under her magical hold and a vision of killing an old friend's abusive uncle. The reflections and whispers of the Shadow Mother struck true. Sara had done monstrous things to protect herself and others.

"When you join me, I will gift you the smoke magic you covet and so much more. Then you can wipe out all the dark energy you so fiercely despise."

Sara slid her eyes toward Samson, whose hands still gripped his head as if he could dig out whatever horrors she was planting inside his mind. Was this the lie she fed him so long ago?

The darkness beckoned with vaporous fingers. *"Come. If you truly care for this forest—for your family—for Thomas—you will do them a loving favor by leaving them and taking your darkness with you. Come with me, where you truly belong, and I will make you the perfect High Witch—one to rule all others."*

Never. Sara had no intention of ruling over others, and she already knew the darkness inside her. She had made peace with knowing she would instinctually do anything for those she loved. And though it wasn't until she was in Jin's garden, Sara had also accepted her faults and imperfections. The forest, her family,

Thomas—they all loved her imperfect self. The only loving favor she wanted to grant them was to banish the Shadow Mother and her insidious deceptions.

"Lies," Sara rasped. She inched one hand toward Samson's sleeve and her other toward Lethal's golden hair. Perhaps together they could summon a scrap of magic to throw at her. And if not, at least they would go out together.

Laughter filled Sara's head again, the earlier pleasant tone now harsh and laced with poison. *"You are a failure of a High Witch. Your incompetence is so great you must bespell others to do the many things you cannot do yourself. Without me, you will always be weak and unworthy."*

Hanging her head, Sara admitted, "You're right. There is much I have yet to learn." The whips loosened, and a self-satisfied hum oozed from the Shadow Mother. "But," added Sara, pausing to give a reckless huff before lifting her gaze to the black void, "it's not weakness to ask for help. And if you think I'm not good enough, you can kiss my imperfect ass."

The Shadow Mother hissed, spitting black ash that sizzled and melted like liquid tar upon the ground. Her jagged hold constricted, and despite herself, Sara screamed. *"Then you are of no use to me. I shall enjoy forcing you to die by your own hand and taking your magic, just as I did with the Hills witch."*

"So it *was* you," panted Sara, stalling for precious time. The memory of Naomi's smile and laughter, and the promise to destroy her killer filled Sara. Distantly, a tear spilled down her cheek. She reached out, her fingertips grazing Samson and Lethal. *"Come on, you two. Wake up and let's get out of here!"* she mentally shouted at them.

The bloodstone at her chest pulsed, and again she attempted to summon energy. Instead of her magic flaring in her palms, the Shadow Mother's invisible power forced Sara's four-fingered hand away from Lethal and to her throat—and squeezed.

"I'll make it quick. A reward for bringing me two fine gifts. One I will enjoy taking apart for his deceit; the other, I will savor for a very long time." The Shadow Mother's greasy-tongued eagerness snaked inside Sara's mind, her clutch threatening to burst her lungs.

A strangled gasp gurgled from Sara, yet she refused to yield. Like Hells she would let this bitch touch Samson or Lethal. She didn't need magic when she had pure defiance and rage keeping her alive. Eyes mere slits, she fixed a death stare on the Shadow Mother. She would *not* fail her friends and family—her forest. No. She would destroy this vile monster with sheer will alone.

Deep within Sara's soul, an ember sparked, its warmth shooting through her. Witch fire. A magical power so fierce and volatile, it often did as it pleased. She could have sworn the entity flinched.

Before Sara could pry her hand from her throat, a skull-splitting screech erupted from the sky with such fury the entire field trembled, dirt and rocks rising from the surface. Another and another shriek followed. The force controlling her hand stopped, and Sara sucked in a harsh breath. She faced the roiling clouds—and the distinct rasp of a slick-scaled serpent ripping toward them like lightning.

In a thunderous crack, the red dragon broke through the clouds and dove for the Shadow Mother. Her dark figure guttered, shadowy whips reeling back into her core as she fully released her magical hold on Sara.

Energy flooded Sara's veins and crackled around her, the bloodstone once again pulsating with a steady beat.

Expelling a venomous hiss, the Shadow Mother contracted upon herself and retreated into the gloom, dragging the Takers with her.

Sara struggled to her unsteady feet as Jin roared. The sound jarred her entire body, nearly knocking her back to the ground before he closed his tremendous, sharp-toothed maw and pinned his attention on her.

She wanted to scream at Samson and Lethal to get behind the forest wall or blast them back with her magic. Yet she stood transfixed by the ruby-red dragon, who was either going to take her back to his garden or actually swallow her whole. And despite the ferocious risk, the boneheaded vampire and fellow witch rose and stood beside her.

To Sara's surprise, Jin hovered before them, his quicksilver gaze taking them in. Huffing smoke through his wide nostrils, he shook his massive head toward the sky full of panicked flat-eyes. With another roar, he shot after them.

Lethal stumbled back, using Kindness to hold themself upright. "*Futuo*," they spat, then vomited blood onto a dead Taker.

Of the three of them, Lethal was the most rattled, which seemed at odds for a vampire spawned by Death herself. When they heaved again, Sara's own stomach clenched in understanding: Lethal did indeed have a conscience, coupled with over a thousand years of dark thoughts for the Shadow Mother to twist like a dagger in their alabaster soul.

Sara swallowed the burn at the back of her throat and turned to Samson, who also looked about to retch.

"We owe Jin a new pavilion," he rasped, staring at where the Shadow Mother had disappeared. "Father of Night, that bitch has gotten stronger than the last time I faced her."

Sara scanned the darkened fields and willed her energy to continue recharging and chasing away the Shadow Mother's icy touch. The fields were barren—no sign of her or the Takers—which should have been a relief but instead struck Sara with terror.

Her scalp tingled in warning. "She's using the dragons to distract Jin while she and the Takers try to break into the forest. We have to stop them."

Lethal wiped their mouth, smearing crimson across their perfect cheek. "Agreed," they said, cleaning Kindness on the nearest body before sheathing the beautiful blade.

With a hand over her bloodstone, Sara contemplated a battle strategy of simply outlasting the Shadow Mother. Perhaps they could patrol the wall until every Taker was dead and she left from boredom, taking the dragons with her. Sara's thoughts were cut short when a delicate laugh sounded from just inside the forest wall. She pivoted to where Dorcas stood, preening among the understory.

"Hello, darlings," she trilled with a wave and toss of her long, blonde hair. "So nice of you, Sara, not to revoke my residency." She caressed the stone wall, blew a kiss to Samson, then dropped her perfect façade by cackling something wicked.

Samson snarled and threw out a smoky tendril. Before it could crush her, Dorcas vanished into the forest. "I have unfinished business with that witch," he seethed, rushing over the wall and chasing after her.

"Get in line," shouted Sara, close on his heels with Lethal at her side. "You take the north half, Lethal take the south, and I'll search the middle," she ordered, and then flew into the heart of Ware Woods.

CHAPTER 45

Wind and straggly branches tore at Sara, the trees unable to bow out of her way fast enough as she zipped through the canopy, scanning for any sign of Dorcas. *Where are you, you traitorous witch?*

Overhead, the sky flashed orange and red, followed by a dragon ramming into the barrier. Sara glanced up at a mottled brown-and-yellow serpentine body scrabbling against the invisible wall, a bloody gash in its side. She slowed and searched the clouds for a glimpse of Jin's fiery red dragon, hoping he wasn't injured, when a bellow of sheer frustrated anger erupted from the forest floor to her left.

Sara yanked herself back, silvery-gray hair flaring around her. The only time she had ever heard such a holler from Caleb was when the original chestnut tree burned and crashed to the ground.

She raced toward his yell, smashing through the tree canopy until she spotted her cousin and Dorcas strangling each other with vines beside a rotted stump. Sara rushed closer, losing a precious moment to swerve around a massive spruce tree.

Dorcas's belladonna-sweet voice rang out, "So strong, but not strong enough." A flash of dark-purple energy shot from her.

Sara pushed away from the spruce and threw out her power, punching Dorcas aside with a gust of wind while simultaneously trying to pull back the dark witch's magic. Like a slippery eel, the purple energy slithered through Sara's grasp, striking Caleb square in the chest.

The vines immediately turned to ash. Caleb slumped to the forest floor, his eyes glazed and unseeing, as Dorcas's dark magic flickered and dissipated from his rigid body.

Sara slammed into the leaf- and ash-strewn ground beside him. Placing one hand on his too-still chest, she hurled a wall of white power in Dorcas's direction. But the witch had vanished again. Sara's power struck a young stand of pine, razing it entirely to the ground.

"No!" Sara frantically pulled Caleb to her, engulfing him in healing energy. Again and again, she tried to revive him, but all she felt was his heart failing, each slowing beat like the winding down of a clock.

No. No. No.

She'd plead with Death herself to save him. The thought sparked her bloodstone, casting her and Caleb in a red glow.

Death. If her magic couldn't heal Caleb, perhaps another type of magic could bring him back. Sara clutched his unyielding body and summoned the one person who knew death all too well.

"Lethal!" she projected mentally and audibly into the forest with such force, the trees swayed. With unsteady hands, she clasped the sides of Caleb's face, repeatedly begging, "Hold on," until the understory rustled, and the scent of frankincense drifted to her sniffling nose.

Lethal crouched beside them, Kindness sheathed at their back, black blood staining their hands and once-white shirt. The gore appeared too fresh to have been from the dozen they had slain outside the wall. Sara gritted her teeth; more Takers were not her immediate worry.

She held the vampire's gaze, her lower lip trembling. "I can't heal him, but you can."

Lethal's face contorted with anguish as they slowly shook their head. "Turning is not healing. It is a form of death itself."

"Please." She wept, her vision blurring with tears. "I refuse to lose him to the stars if I know he can live like you."

Lethal ran filthy hands through their hair and swore. "I've never turned anyone. The price is too high. You don't know what you're asking of me—of him." They turned away, spewing a litany of curses in multiple languages.

Sara choked back a sob, grip tightening on Caleb. "Please."

Lethal fell silent. They slowly spun around and looked at Caleb, their expression tortured and apologetic. Then they pierced Sara with an intense gaze. "I'll do it, but only because we can't have you fall apart right now. When he comes back, he will have lost the one thing he loves most. And once he realizes this, he may not want to live—especially as a bloody vampire. This is all on you, Sara. You must take full responsibility for whatever happens—whatever he becomes."

She bit her lip and nodded.

I will not fall apart.

Their grave silence was shattered by a screech like metal on metal as portions of the barrier overhead were ripped open by flames of dark-purple magic. Dragons pushed and clawed their way through the frays, roaring in triumph and spraying the forest with fire.

The bloodstone glowed brighter through Sara's layers, her magic—the forest's magic—screaming in response to the breach.

"Leave us," ordered Lethal. "You don't need to see this. It may take a while, and I must stay with him throughout his change, which means I can't rejoin the fight."

Giving another tight nod, Sara gently laid Caleb on the forest floor, his heart barely fluttering, and kissed his cheek, already chilled with imminent death. Not a goodbye, as Thomas would say, but a "see you later." She embraced Lethal and, despite the vampire's rigid posture, placed a kiss on their cold cheek as well.

I will not fall apart.

Without looking back, she rocketed into the sky, toward a rip in the barrier above the Cahill common—where the Shadow Mother poured into the forest like smothering black sand.

Phantom talons shredded Sara's soul. Insidious thoughts of tiny hands against tiny throats, pierced hearts, and violent murders flashed in her frantic mind. She surged faster, the forest below a smudge of browns and greens, a mad-hatter plan to drag the Shadow Mother out of Ware Woods taking root. It would take all her magic and likely her life, but Sara was out of options. She only hoped she could haul the Shadow Mother far enough away and remain in control of her magic long enough to unleash an inferno of witch fire so violent it would consume them both.

Sara sped over the tree-lined edge of the Cahill clearing, arms outstretched, summoning wind to gather the nebulous Shadow Mother, when golden light exploded up from the common. Sara wrenched to a halt, instinctively throwing up her hands to protect her eyes against the exultant brightness.

The Shadow Mother shrieked, her unholy cry reverberating throughout Ware Woods with such fury the entire magical region no doubt felt her outrage.

Sara squinted through her fingers to see the dark entity retreat from the brilliant energy pushing her back to whence she came. Collapsing into a jagged clawed creature, the Shadow Mother clung to a gash in the forest's protective barrier. Eyes glowing with Hells' embers met Sara's stare. With a spitting hiss, the Shadow Mother scuttled out the rip and disappeared into the roiling clouds overhead.

A cheer rang out from the common as the shield of light was joined by steel blue power and amber witch fire, the three magics working together and sealing the fray before moving on to repair another rip in the barrier.

Mouth agape, Sara peered down at the common and nearly fell from the sky. Though Alice's witch fire was no surprise and Gran's energy was a slight shock, it was the golden light emanating from Ian and the Hills children that captivated Sara.

Here was the valuable secret that Samson had been protecting—magic capable of standing against the Shadow Mother. No wonder she had forcibly used Samson to eliminate most of the Hills' witches—witches with special gifts for spell breaking, protective charms, and force fields.

Sara pursed her lips. Later, she would throttle Samson and Ian for not telling her about the children's special gift. But first, with her family and the Hills children repairing the barrier, she needed to eliminate all the dragons and dark magic that had snuck in—starting with Dorcas.

Sara launched high above the common and surveyed the forest. Around the outer portion, wolven shifters darted among the trees as they hunted and attacked Takers. In their wake lay ribboned bodies and pools of black blood glistening like inky stains. Throughout the forest flashed pockets of green energy as the Cahills restored trees and vegetation damaged by dragons. At the western edge of the forest, Tobio looped in the sky, easily outmaneuvering and attacking a brown dragon with a stubby tail. Along the northern half, near the marshy section of the forest, Samson's smoky clouds and bursts of red magic dominated a pair of massive, sallow dragons. And by the lake, barely above the tree canopy, blazed a distinct blue energy, fighting to hold off a dragon swarm.

Thomas.

Sara flew for him, her heart lodging in her throat when a streak of dark-purple fire sniped up from the forest floor and arched toward his blue lights. He dodged just as a jet of sleet mixed with sparkling, violet-hued energy punched up from the ground and eradicated the dark fire.

Without slowing, Thomas zipped and swerved above the trees, luring a muddy-orange dragon directly into another blast of ice and violet power from where Lily and Violet lay in wait. Sara pulled up, gulping down tangy, magic-filled air, and added a shot of white energy to their coordinated attack. The dragon roared and fell into the lake with a large slap, sending out a wave of water that rocked the shoreline.

Before Sara could slump with relief, a sickly yellow-green beast spewing fire descended upon Thomas. He veered and rushed higher, barely escaping the licking flames.

Sara swished her hands, pulling water from the air to join Lily's rain cloud and extinguish the blaze, while Thomas hurled a sphere of blue magic at the dragon. Yet the dragon, gaunt with dark shadows clinging to its flaky skin, paid no mind as it swiveled its head and set its flat-eyes on Lily and Violet. It reared back, taking aim.

Sara summoned a flurry of wind to sweep them aside, but Lily had already disappeared in a blur at the same time Violet shot up behind the dragon. With pinpoint accuracy, she drove a spear of energy into its momentarily unguarded weak spot. The beast screamed and fell from the sky, snapping and breaking a swath of trees before violently slamming against the forest floor.

"We'll handle the dragons. You deal with Dorcas," shouted Thomas, ducking a ray of bruised purple energy. He hovered and flashed Sara a reassuring grin.

Her heart skipped a beat as it always did when he smiled at her, and then she nearly fainted when he narrowly avoided the sudden lash of a muddy-orange tail. Thomas rushed off in a zigzag pattern, dodging dragon fire and another blow of dark-purple magic.

Dorcas.

Anger surged through Sara and crackled in white-hot flames

around her. Dorcas would pay for harming Caleb and assaulting Thomas—for betraying all of Ware Woods.

Sara whipped her attention to a glint of blonde hair in the thick understory. And with energy snapping in her palms, Sara launched herself at the traitorous witch.

CHAPTER 46

DORCAS FIRED A crack of energy at Sara, her aim sloppy as she turned and ran, using her power to push trees and shrubs out of her way.

A cruel grin spread across Sara's face. Not only was Dorcas running from her, but she was also leaving a wide-open path to track her every move. With a four-fingered flick, Sara conjured brimstone briars to erupt from the forest floor and ensnare Dorcas. While hitting the witch with energy and instantly killing her would be satisfying, it would also be too merciful. Entrapment and suffering would be a befitting end for the dark witch who had betrayed Ware Woods.

The razor-edged vines clamped on to Dorcas, yet she merely laughed, her typical melodic peal now grinding like a broken music box. With a surge of dark-purple magic, the briars disintegrated. Dorcas spun and launched another burst of energy at Sara, the purple and black flames as quick and sinister as the power she had forced on Caleb.

The magic struck Sara, only to spark and fizzle out against her glowing protective shield. Her attack hadn't even nudged Sara from the sky. Clearly, Dorcas had drained her powers, which explained why she had been running away.

As if knowing she was caught by a bigger spider, Dorcas

merely stood her ground. In her sickly-sweet voice, she asked, "How's Caleb?"

Angry fire swelled inside Sara. She pounded into Dorcas like a furious comet. Bright energy detonated, momentarily blinding Sara and razing the surrounding trees with a cannonade of brittle snaps. Splinters, rock, and dirt rained upon them as Sara reinforced her protective shield and hovered above Dorcas, pinning her face down on the forest floor.

The witch coughed and spat a slug of black phlegm before managing to flop over with a vile grin.

Sara drew back, her anger fading into utter shock. Gone was the beautiful woman, and in her place was the revolting hag Sara had first known Dorcas to be. Her few remaining rotten teeth were coated in black blood, her once-flawless skin now dull and pocked with festering sores. Her eyes, which had been clear blue, had returned to cloudy voids.

Bitter cold crept over Sara. It had all been a glamour—Dorcas's entire appearance and goody-two-shoes act after Makwa's death had been a lie. "Why?" Sara demanded.

Dorcas writhed in the shallow crater of Sara's blast, seemingly trying to free herself. Sara pushed more power at the witch. *No way will I let you escape this time.* Sara clenched her jaw and fought to block out the clash of dragons and magic behind her, refusing to look away for even a second from the hideous witch.

"Because," guttered Dorcas, her true voice as grating as broken glass, "I hate normals and witches who sympathize with them. Normals hung my mother and imprisoned me as a child—made me do and say things against my will. And it was *your* family that tricked and imprisoned me in Ware Woods.

"For centuries, I had to bite my tongue, living among *lesser* witches and shifters and even foul vampires and half-breeds." She spat again, darkness running down her scarred chin. "When Samson came to the forest wall, I sensed the Shadow Mother on him. But Makwa didn't believe me and was too small minded with her own agenda, so I used her and manipulated you, biding my time for the Shadow Mother's reckoning. And then"—Dorcas choked on a thick laugh—"you *let* me go. Foolish girl. Now I'm doing my part to help Her Dark Glory eliminate all normals."

"You're insane," said Sara. "The Shadow Mother is using *you*— she will destroy normals along with every single *magical* until no one is left."

Dorcas grinned a foul taunt. "It doesn't matter. I still get what I've always wanted—making people suffer as much as I have. Your face when I killed Caleb was divine. It's a shame I didn't kill Thomas too."

Sara roared, the entire forest shaking with her wrath. White-hot anger flared from her and struck Dorcas with such force the witch's back broke and twisted at a ghastly angle. Sara hovered closer, rage narrowing her vision. "No one else will suffer at your hands, Dorcas."

At hearing her name, the witch visibly relaxed, her dark-purple aura fading.

"Did you really think it would be this easy to kill me?" Dorcas rasped. "I choose this. My death is my salvation. I freely give the Shadow Mother exactly what she wants—more imbalance and discord. Now, no one can stop her."

The witch ripped back the top of her dress, revealing Makwa's black bloodstone around her neck. And in less than a stuttering heartbeat, Dorcas plunged a six-fingered hand into her own chest and pulled out a greasy black stone.

Sara recoiled, numb with horror, when Brad suddenly appeared beside Dorcas. He grabbed the two bloodstones, slashed a vicious grin at Sara, and then looped away, leaving behind a cloud of shadows.

Sara jolted back to her senses. With a scream torn loose from her soul, she pummeled Dorcas's lifeless body with stones and broken trees, burying her under a mountain of debris. When she had nothing left to throw at her, Sara's cry became a high-pitched wail of anguish, the entire forest trembling.

Her energy surged into witch fire, burning everything around her, choking her with flames. Too much. She panicked, and the fire blazed hotter and brighter. Her lungs seized as she burned from within, the wild magic threatening to consume her and the forest.

A hard body slammed into her and, despite the searing flames, flew them both into the clearing between the lake and treehouse. Thomas.

"Stop," he commanded, grabbing her shoulders and forcing her to see him through the inferno. His blue energy pushed back at her white fire, emitting a shower of sparks as he held her gaze. "Sara, stop the fire."

She gulped. His power was cool and soothing, his tone calm even while his skin blistered along beside hers. Clinging to his strength, she willed her magic back into her core and down into the ground, drawing the witch fire with it. The forest sighed, trees regenerating, charred earth restoring into sleepy early winter soil.

With a crowd gathering around them, Thomas clasped the sides of her face and pressed his forehead against hers. "It's over."

I wish that were true.

As if reading her thought, Thomas added, "For now, it's over."

Sara nodded with him and wrapped her arms around his waist, frowning as her hands met a slick, hot wetness. He winced as she pulled back and stared at the red blood—his blood—on her hands.

Impossible.

Their bond automatically healed him whenever they embraced; the fiery blisters already gone. Maybe she had expended too much magic, sent too much back into the forest, and just needed to recharge. Sara's heart quickened as she summoned a soft glow of energy into her palm and held it to his blood-soaked side.

Thomas winced again and shrank from her touch, falling flat onto his back. "It burns," he gritted out.

Kane, Dean, and Tobio darted from the crowd and joined Sara as she fell to her knees beside Thomas.

Kane grabbed Thomas's hands and nodded to Dean, who then ripped apart the bloody vest of knives, exposing Thomas's torso.

Thomas groaned, eyes rolling back. The gash along his ribs emitted a hiss of steam into the chilly air. From the oozing wound, a red-hot rash of flames covered his chest and crept up his neck.

Burning pain stabbed Sara, hot and quick, through the bond. Every nerve broiled in agony for a shared moment. *Mother below, how had he even been standing?* She hovered her hands over the angry wound, summoning more healing energy.

"Don't!" called out Tobio. "You'll make it worse."

Sara pulled back at the warning and grim look in Tobio's elysian eyes, her heart sinking like a boulder to the bottom of the lake. *Poison.* Thomas had been hit by a dragon's deadly tail. Her magic was useless against such a fatal strike, and she had no idea if a cure existed. Her mind raced. The Book might know, but it refused to leave the blue house, and judging by the rapidly spreading rash, she didn't have enough time to physically consult it.

This can't be happening! She loved him too much, their bond too strong for him to suffer—to die. Her heartbeat thundered in her ears.

"Does anyone know a cure?" she hollered, loud enough to rattle every tree in the forest. Loud enough to send waves slapping against the nearby lakeshore. Loud enough for the Mother and Father to hear.

Someone whined.

Sara tore her eyes from Thomas, frantically scanning the crowd for Samson. Surely he had experience with dragon poison and his smoky tendrils could leach it away. But the witch wasn't in the clearing. Neither was Lethal. Maybe they were still changing Caleb and couldn't, or wouldn't, save Thomas too. Her mind skipped, desperate. Perhaps another vampire . . .

Her panicked gaze sought out the Atwells clustered near the rear of the gathering and fell upon ancient Kingsley, Lily beside him. The bloodstone thumped.

Kingsley placed a hand to his chest, eyes glistening with an emotion Sara couldn't place, and said, "Dragon tears will heal him."

Beside Sara, Tobio confirmed, "He's right. I'm only half-dragon and my tears don't work, but Ryujin's will." He threw back his head and searched the sky.

Sara did the same, tracking his line of sight, until she spotted the vibrant red dragon flying a figure eight through the dispersing clouds.

Tobio turned to her. "The barrier is repaired. You'll have to invite him into the forest."

Sara hesitated. What if Jin —Ryujin—refused to help Thomas? What if he took her back to the garden?

She ground her teeth. If Jin cured Thomas, she would do whatever he asked of her. She glanced at Kane—Abby and Violet behind him. When they nodded in unison, Sara closed her eyes and mentally projected, *Jin? I—I need your help. As High Witch of Ware Woods, I invite you into the forest.*

Tobio and Dean rose and backed away from Thomas as the red dragon swam through the sky, streaking directly for them. The surrounding forest family members tensed at the massive elysian-eyed dragon, his presence and power acutely superior to the flat-eyes they had just fought. In a puff of rain-scented ash, Jin landed in his human form—wearing black flowing pants and a red wraparound tunic—and approached, liquid silver eyes scanning the crowd before settling on Sara.

"Apologies for not believing you earlier and . . . for not realizing you are bonded," said Jin, tucking his chin slightly. "Had I listened, perhaps this could have been avoided." He gestured to the forest and to Thomas, whose breaths had become distinctly labored.

Sara shook her head. Regret was a dangerous illusion that only caused pain. She knew all too well because she continually struggled with it. She met his gaze. "You're here now, which is what matters. Thank you for helping us, but I must ask another favor. Can you heal dragon poison?"

Muscles feathered along his broad cheekbones. "Dragons only heal other dragons. If I shed a pure tear for your witch mate, I do not know what will happen or how it will affect your bonded future. He could be healed and unchanged, or he could turn into a dragon. Either way, his life will be bound to mine. If I die, he dies. And if I call him to serve me, he must obey."

Sara's heart quavered as she looked at Thomas. Despite the risk, if he hadn't been conscious and able to make this decision for himself, she would have chosen this for him. She bit her cheek over the agonizing choice she had made for Caleb and hoped her cousin could someday forgive her.

Afraid her healing magic would cause Thomas more pain, she held her palm just shy of touching the side of his sweat-slicked face, poisonous heat radiating from him.

His nostrils flared with each panted inhalation, but his blazing blue eyes were clear as he held her questioning gaze. "I made promises to you that I intend to keep." His voice was rough, strained, and Sara felt another burning stab of pain through the bond. He tightened his grip on his father's hands and hurriedly nodded his agreement at Jin to proceed.

Jin crouched beside him, and Sara said, "If Thomas will be bound to you, then I will be too."

"I know," responded Jin, his tone soft. "The Mother said we would help each other, and so we will." He closed his eyes and leaned over Thomas's wound. Within a few anxious quakes of the nearby oak tree, a single tear of swirling silver formed at the edge of Jin's eye. Sara's heart fractured at the intense sadness Jin must harbor to shed a tear so easily. With a plink like a coin being cast into a wishing well, the silvery tear dropped onto Thomas.

He hissed through clenched teeth and passed out, his body slack as the wound closed and the flaming rash disappeared. A peacefulness descended upon him, and he appeared to be comfortably sleeping with a steady rise and fall of his chest.

"Thank you," whispered Sara. She pulled Jin into an awkward embrace, catching a hand in his long hair. Though he stiffened, she held on to him, inhaling his scent of fresh rain and tea, until he lightly put an arm around her. His touch was timid, as if he had never hugged someone before, and in an instant, he slipped away from her, rising and retreating a polite step.

Averting his gaze from Sara, Jin motioned to Thomas. "I'll remain until he wakes. Young dragons can be . . . unpredictable." He shot a glance at Tobio, who merely clenched his jaw. "In the meantime, I'll correct any magic that may have been seen by normals." Jin vanished in a puff of ash.

Placing one hand on Thomas's chest and feeling the stable pulse of his heart, Sara looked past the 'Esha sisters, coated in black blood, and locked eyes with Lily. Mentally projecting to her, Sara asked, *"Can you please check on Caleb and Lethal? I left them alone . . . on the far east side of the forest."*

Lily's eyes knowingly widened, fear and concern shining in her pale face before she vanished in a blur.

Sara swept her gaze among the present shifters, Atwells, and Sullivans. "Are there any more injuries?" she asked, hoping for nothing significant that would warrant yet another excruciating choice.

"There are a few minor injuries in the common," answered Dean, his deep voice composed and steady—the voice of an Alpha Shifter.

Sara nodded her thanks for the information and the gentle

nudge in his tone—whether intentional or not—reminding her of her role as High Witch. With one more scan of Thomas's peaceful face, she rose and hovered above the meadow. Beyond their gathering, the oak beckoned with waving branches.

Sara turned to the Sullivans. "You're welcome to take Thomas to the treehouse and make yourselves at home while I check on the rest of the forest."

As Abby responded with a weary yet appreciative smile, Sara flew off over the trees, directly toward the common.

CHAPTER 47

RACING THROUGH THE setting sun's rose-tinged rays, Sara shook out her hands and inhaled deeply. *Relax.*

Though Dean had said "*minor injuries,*" her mind tormented her with images of devastation and gore—Makwa's fiery damage to the original soul tree and Main House still fresh in her memory.

Cresting the edge of the grassy clearing, she whooshed a breath and slowed her flight. The chestnut tree mass in the center of the common stood tall and healthy, a few stubborn fall leaves and spiny burred nuts still clinging to its branches. Around the tree ran Bailey and a few of the Hills and Cahill children. And at the Main House wooden deck, her family and the Cahills lingered. Sara dove for them, pulling up at the last second to land not-so-gracefully on the deck's wide stairs.

"I give that landing a five out of ten," joked Ian with a stiff grin. He sat at a nearby table with Ted beside him, Gran and their father on the opposite side.

Relief flooded Sara at his barb, and she dished it right back at him. "I'm about to land my fist in your face for not telling me about the golden shield you and the kids used to repel the Shadow Mother."

Gran snickered.

Sara placed her hands on her hips and threw a mock scowl at him, but her teasing abruptly stopped when she noticed an empty medicine bottle among the water glasses on the table. He always took his daily medication in the mornings. "Did you take an extra dose?"

"Yeah. Facing the Shadow Mother put a cold squeeze on the old ticker," he admitted, rubbing his chest, then quickly added, "I'm fine now." He slipped the bottle into his pocket and firmly patted Ted's arm.

No one looked convinced.

Though Ian's other hand anxiously tapped the side of his chair, color bloomed in his cheeks and a brightness shone in his eyes. Sara studied him, contemplating holding the Book over an open flame until it explained what type of love would finally heal Ian.

"Stop staring at me and tend to the Cahills." He jerked his chin toward the deck behind her.

Sara huffed at him as she whirled and spotted Helen sitting with her feet up on a spare chair. One foot was wrapped in ice and, Sara determined with a sniff, a salve containing garlic and willow. But when she rushed over to help, Helen waved her off and said, "See to Uncle Larry first."

Sara levitated and looked around, noting Alice and Albert on the far side of the deck appearing fine, before she spotted Uncle Larry. He lay on a couch just inside the open archway, nursing a possible broken leg. Her grandfather shook his head of white hair at her and pointed a thick finger at Helen. "Nah, don't worry about me. You fix that old bird first."

"Pfft!" responded Helen. "All I have is a minor sprain which will heal on its own soon enough. I wouldn't have even gotten this if the barn animals hadn't been in a ruckus over those damn dragons." She adjusted the bag of ice on her ankle and in a quieter voice added, "Tend to Becca. I think she is hurt worse than she is letting on."

Sara strode toward Rebecca, casually sitting in a rocking chair near the deck's edge and watching the children play in the common. A white patchy burn covered her entire left arm and hand, her barn jacket and underlying shirt singed back to the collar. Sara gasped. Either Caleb's mother was in shock, or she had an incredible tolerance for pain.

Sara knelt before her and looked up into her moss-green eyes—eyes like Caleb's, except his had flecks of gold. At least, Sara hoped Caleb's eyes were still golden green and not icy gray. She swallowed and tenderly placed a healing touch on Rebecca's mottled and cracked skin.

Rebecca sighed in relief as her arm glowed with white light and the injury disappeared. "Thanks, love," she said, placing a hand on Sara's cheek. "Have you seen Caleb?"

Sara stilled. Telling Rebecca everything at this time wouldn't be helpful since Sara didn't know exactly what had happened after she had left Caleb and Lethal. She put a hand over Rebecca's, holding it to her cheek. "Caleb was injured, too. But he's safe with Lethal and Lily right now."

Though Rebecca paled, she forced a smile and said, "Thank you. I'm sure he's fine and will be home soon."

I hope so.

"Well," said Rebecca, rising from her chair, "I best grab a new jacket and check on the littles." She nodded her goodbyes before descending the stairs and strolling toward the chestnut tree.

Ignoring the concerned looks from her father and grandmother, Sara tended to Helen's sprain, then healed Uncle Larry's leg—and apparently the arthritis in his ruddy hands. After nearly sustaining a cracked rib from his jubilant embrace, she stood before Ian and folded her arms, one black boot tapping.

"Explain."

Ian bounced a leg and smiled guiltily. "I never said anything about the shield because I didn't know if it would work. And I didn't want to pressure the kids. But when Dorcas ripped the barrier, they insisted on helping."

"And," interjected Gran, "Alice and I knew to add our own power because the cranky Book had opened up a few days ago and suggested we practice concentrating our magic."

How convenient. If the Book had revealed any of these special powers to Sara months ago, maybe Caleb and Thomas would still be fine.

She studied Gran and Ian. While her crafty grandmother was difficult to read as usual, her brother's aura shifted curiously. He was still holding something back.

Or someone.

Sara glanced around the Main House, the back of her neck prickling. "Where are Samson and Kira?"

"Samson is disposing of all the bodies in some pocket of Hell, and I'm hoping Kira is with him," said Ian, his voice thin with worry.

Sara inclined her head, waiting for more.

"I can't find her," he confessed, the tips of his ears reddening.

Aha, here it is at last. The corners of her mouth drew up.

He ignored her smirk and continued, "Usually I can feel her presence, but when I was focused on sealing the barrier, she disappeared. I figured she went off to hunt down whatever had been trapped inside, but . . . she's still not back."

Sara's mind jarred with the image of Brad winking in and taking the black bloodstones from Dorcas—as if it had been planned all along. What if the bastard had taken Kira? What if he had *planned* to take her as well? She shuddered. *Samson will go ballistic. And so will I.* She almost felt sorry for Brad. Almost.

Sara regarded Ian, Gran, Ted, and Charlie as they wordlessly expressed their concern with one shared glance. Father above, being part of a psychic family was both a blessing and a curse—today most definitely being a blessing. But just to be clear, she stated,

"If Kira doesn't come back with Samson, we tell him and start a search party."

They nodded in unison.

She slumped her shoulders, relieved no one argued on this directive. With a heavy sigh, she pressed her fingers to her temples and considered having an emergency Council meeting right then and there.

"Firecracker," said her father, his tone matching the concern in his face, "you're exhausted. Everyone here is fine. We'll contact you when Samson *and Kira* return. In the meantime, I believe you are needed at the treehouse. You should rest with him." He gave her a slight, knowing smile.

Either word had already spread through the forest, or her father had read her emotions—or aura, or whatever it was he did—and simply knew about Thomas's condition. Sara didn't care. It was one less thing to explain when she was already tired and dealing with too much.

She sighed again and raised her face to the evening sky. With Solstice days away, nighttime came early, and with it a penetrating cold. Turning in and checking up on Thomas was definitely desirable. But since she knew he was resting peacefully, there was someone else she needed to confirm was alive and well.

"You're right," she admitted, and hurried to give them a group hug. "Tell me straightaway when Samson and Kira get back. And please inform everyone that we will have an emergency Council meeting tomorrow." Their collective agreement was a distant whisper as she launched into the air and, instead of heading to the treehouse, flew straight for the last place she had seen Caleb alive.

The dense evergreen canopies on the east side of the woods forced Sara to land and run toward the rotten pine stump, the scents of blood and magic heavy in the somber evening.

Like a white-blonde ghost, Lily emerged from the bushes. She rushed at Sara, hooking arms with her and dragging her back the way she came. Farther away from Caleb.

"Now's not a good time," Lily explained, tugging her along. "Caleb isn't ready to see anyone yet."

Sara dug her boots into the leafy forest floor, halting Lily's firm escort. "*Anyone* or just me?" Sara asked, afraid of the answer. From overhead, an owl hooted, its call seemingly echoing her question. Sara gritted her teeth, bracing herself. She had taken Caleb's free will and made a choice for him that she hoped to the Mother and Father had been the right one to make.

"Both," confessed Lily, wringing her petite hands.

Fair enough.

Sara could live with him being furious at her. She deserved it. "But is he *okay*? I saw him dying, Lily. I just need to know if he's okay."

Lily sighed. Her watery gray eyes shone with understanding, and Sara knew her friend didn't fault her for the choice she made. Yet Lily didn't offer a solid assurance of Caleb's well-being. She only said, "He will be . . . eventually. Right now, he needs time to process."

Biting back a storm of emotions ranging from grief and frustration to guilt and relief at knowing he was still alive, Sara said, voice quivering, "Tell him I love him, no matter how he may have physically changed, no matter if he hates me forever. He's family and I love him."

"I will." Lily gave a comforting squeeze to Sara's arm before vanishing back into the woods.

With a heavy heart, Sara stared after her until her nose stung and her hands and feet hurt with the chilly bite of coming winter. Instead of using magic to warm herself, Sara welcomed the punishing cold as she turned and fled toward the treehouse— toward Thomas.

CHAPTER 48

S ILVER MOONLIGHT SHONE upon the forest, glinting in the calm surface of the lake and accentuating the dark shadows of the trees. A mix of bare branches and evergreen boughs waved as Sara flew overhead. Below the tree canopies, a pair of foxes scurried about their normal activities as if the devastating day had never happened. The forest's resiliency was astonishing, as was its blessed innocence of what was yet to come.

Unease twisted in Sara's belly like a bucket of earthworms on a one-way fishing trip. Because if Dorcas's sacrifice for the Shadow Mother had been true and if Brad had taken Kira, their entire magical world would irrevocably change.

With a shiver, Sara approached the treehouse and hovered outside her bedroom window opening. Thomas lay sleeping in the four-poster bed, his parents and Violet by his side. She figured Connor was spending the night at the Cahills with the other children. Reassured by their vigil, Sara flew to the cottage, devoured a protein bar someone had left on the kitchen counter, and then took a brutally hot shower. The water did little to soothe her anxiety.

Exhausted to the bone and about to collapse, Sara summoned the last of her energy and flew into her room, where the Sullivans waited. Holding it together for a round of greetings and a brief exchange regarding Samson, Kira, and the forest's miraculous recovery—no doubt thanks to Jin and the Cahills' earth magic—Sara welcomed them to stay in whichever bedrooms they wanted and to whatever they could find in the kitchen, save for Lethal's decadent bottles of blood, of course.

As Thomas's family exited the room, the treehouse slowly closed the bedroom door and sighed along with Sara. Huffing a laugh at the oak, she ran an appreciative touch along one of the bedposts and slipped under the covers, where she shimmied up beside Thomas.

His body was pleasantly warm, not burning hot with poison, and his face remained contentedly relaxed. It had been so long since she had lain beside him that she simply stared at him, cherishing the sculpted contours of his face and every shared breath until she finally convinced herself this was real and not a dream.

The bloodstone pulsed as her fingertips gently smoothed the silken hair at his temple. Leaning over him, she kissed the corners of his mouth, her touch soft as a butterfly's wings. She could have sworn he whispered her name. With half a thought, she extinguished the candles flickering atop her bookshelves and windowsills. Then she wrapped her arms and legs around him—melding their bodies together—and placed her head on his bare, broad chest. Either he had been working out at university or they had clearly been apart for too long. Perhaps both. She closed her eyes and smiled. The steady beat of his heart, the familiar warmth and feel of him, the scent of musk and ash, and the pleasant fact he wasn't covered in an angry rash or dragon spines—yet—quickly swept her asleep.

A warm roughness scraped Sara's cheek and the bed softly jostled, pulling her out of a deep sleep. She grasped at her dream—of snow and flowers, her mother's laugh and the steady thrum of the bloodstone echoing through her waking consciousness. Her bed was extra cozy, cuddling her in a way she hadn't felt in a long time. She wiggled under the covers and then froze as arms wrapped around her waist and a very solid body pressed against her.

"Sara," croaked Thomas, his voice as scratchy as a shagbark hickory. The events of the day before slammed into her, and she was afraid to open her eyes and discover he now had the head of a dragon. "I feel . . . different." He cleared his throat and coughed.

A bright light accompanied by the distinct roar of fire engulfed Sara. Her protective shield instinctively responded, encasing her in energy while her magic sparked awake and smothered the flames filling the room. Her eyes flew open.

Thomas jerked back and slapped a hand over his mouth, faint curls of smoke emanating from him and shrouding his face.

Sara scrambled up in bed, taking in the singed quilt, clumps of ash floating in the air, and soot covering her bookshelf and art supplies on the far side of the room. Heart hammering, she turned to Thomas and threw a hand over her own mouth.

Crap.

The treehouse shook, clacking its barren branches. Sara summoned a puff of wind to clear the smoke and ash from the room and get a better look at Thomas. He seemed himself except for one striking difference. His eyes were molten blue with slitted pupils.

He blinked.

From beneath his hand, a stubble beard peeked. He said, "Are my eyes different? Because I'm seeing some weird shit."

She nodded, and carefully asked, "What are you seeing exactly?"

He blinked again and glanced around the room, wide eyed. "Everything is . . . clear. Like I was only seeing two dimensionally before, but now, I'm seeing . . . everything." He slowly lowered his hand.

Sara tracked his graceful movement, noting his clear, trimmed nails. At least those were normal. With a quick inhale, she steeled herself and said, "Smile."

He did, and her heart skipped a beat at his perfectly straight white teeth. She pulled down the covers and turned Thomas back and forth, her rapid hands-on inspection eliciting a tickled snicker from him. She traced the diamonds tattooed along his spine and along the backs of his sculpted calves and corded forearms. Tattoos similar to Tobio's and Jin's. She glanced at his shorts and quirked a brow. "Is everything else . . . normal?" Father above, she hoped so.

"Yeah. I checked there first," he readily admitted.

Pfft! Males.

He tilted his head, eyes tightening. "Did you just say, '*Males*'?"

"*All Hells, you can read minds now.*"

Thomas's answering grin was pure wickedness.

Bam. Bam. Bam. "Everything okay in there?" Kane's voice boomed through the bedroom door. "We saw fire and smoke."

"*No, everything is not okay,*" Thomas said mentally. "*I'm coughing fireballs.*"

Sara put a finger to his lips and held his gaze as she called out, "Yes. We're fine."

Violet's voice responded, "Are you guys decent?"

And damn the treehouse as it opened the door and let in Violet, Kane, and Charlie.

Sara quickly adjusted the scorched covers around her. "*I can't believe our fathers are in our bedroom. I'm only wearing your T-shirt.*"

Thomas chuckled and pulled her closer to him. "*Our bedroom. I like the sound of that.*"

"Finally, you two are up," complained Violet, striding into the room like she owned it. "Today's Solstice and—" She halted, Kane and Charlie running into her while they all stared at Thomas.

He rubbed the back of his head and stated the obvious, "I, ah—seem to be part dragon." Puffs of smoke hung before him, and he clamped his mouth shut again.

Kane folded his arms, surveying Thomas and the blackened room with concern. "Evidently."

Sara shook her head, counting on her fingers. "We—we've been asleep for almost a *week*?"

Charlie whished a thermos at them.

Sara grabbed it and took a grateful sip of cool sap while Violet continued, "Yeah. Most everyone is at the Main House celebrating right now. I was on my way there when Charlie asked me to bring some of Thomas's clothes, his razor, and—something else." She tossed a bag at Thomas, who deftly caught it in one hand while accepting the thermos from Sara in the other.

He gulped down the contents, his stomach loudly sizzling as if the sap were dousing an internal fire.

Sara lifted her brows at her father—of course, he would have known when they'd wake.

Charlie shrugged. "Take a minute to get cleaned up. Then meet us downstairs. Ryujin needs to speak with you before we go to the Main House."

"Wait," exclaimed Sara. "What about Kira and Samson?" She searched her father's face for any hint that all was well. She didn't dare ask about Caleb. Whatever had happened to him, she needed to see for herself and apologize if need be. Maybe he was fine and clinking wineglasses with Lethal.

Charlie shook his head, and her heart sank. "I found Samson in the birch grove after he collapsed from using all of his magic. He woke this morning, and when we told him Kira was missing, he took off to find her."

"We need to help him," said Sara.

Thomas's hold strengthened, stopping her from jumping out of bed.

"We are," confirmed Charlie. "Just get dressed and come down-stairs." He eyed the burnt walls, letting out a low whistle, before following Violet and Kane out of the bedroom.

As soon as the door snicked shut behind them, Thomas turned Sara into him, his molten eyes causing her heart to race. He tucked a lock of hair behind her ear, fingers lingering before winding into her silvery-gray tresses and cradling the nape of her neck. "I take it Kira's absence isn't a good thing, and the Shadow Mother is still out there, and we're expected downstairs for a meeting, and I'm fighting the urge to cough another fireball, *but* I need a selfish minute with you." He pressed his brow to hers.

Energy sparked between them. The bond tugged at Sara, stronger than ever before, filling her with warmth and physically drawing her closer to Thomas.

The weight of being apart from him for months, of helplessly watching an arrow pierce his chest, and of nearly losing him to dragon poison slammed into her. He was her bonded mate, ordained by the Mother and Father for whatever fateful reason, the one who accepted and supported her and fearlessly tracked her to Jin's garden, and she needed more than a minute to breathe him in.

"Hmm," she considered, melting into his embrace. "Let's take five minutes——"

In a blink of ashy smoke, they were both naked in the cottage's glass-enclosed shower, warm water raining on them.

"Gaa! Thomas!" She playfully punched him in the chest. Hard.

He snorted a fiery laugh, instantly steaming up the room. "Oh, I'm definitely liking this dragon magic," he said, voice low and thick as he pressed against her and ran his wet hands down her slick back. A shiver tickled her spine, and she arched into him as he put his mouth to her ear and said, "Maybe now I'll be your equal both inside *and* outside the forest."

Sara pulled back and regarded him. Beneath the hint of amusement lay a raw truth to his words. Her heart turned liquid, the bloodstone flaring red between them. "We have always been equals." She placed her lips to his.

Energy burst and sizzled, further steaming the shower as she gently kissed him, her lips barely parting in a coy hello-there-haven't-seen-you-in-forever curl.

The bond blazed through her like wildfire, fusing her soul and magic with his. She gasped into him, his fingers digging into her hips, their power flaring together. Without intending, she slipped into his mind just as she felt his presence slip into hers—filling her thoughts and caressing her from the inside for the first time. Sara trembled, his love flooding her, their magic equally entwined.

Thomas moaned and intensified their kiss, his tongue sweeping hers with spicy fire. Constraint be damned. After being apart for months, five minutes was either going to be perfect timing or frustratingly not enough. She slid her arms around him and—

Pain stabbed her hands.

Sara reared back, crying out and startling Thomas, who had unknowingly started to shift. Blue spikes tipped with silver protruded from his forearms and, Sara glimpsed, jutted out his back. With a hiss and a pop, his dragon spikes retracted into his tattoos. He released her, terror and guilt shining in his elysian eyes. Though Sara immediately healed herself before he could see the damage, she couldn't hide the bloody water swirling down the drain between them.

"I'm sorry," he practically shouted, backing against the misted shower glass and staring at his arms.

She flung herself at him, grabbing his shoulders and pinning him with her body before he thought to disappear. "It's okay. You— we just need to learn how to control it." She held him, staring into his molten eyes, until his jaw unclenched and his energy relaxed. "In the meantime, we'll take cold showers." With a twist of her lips, she whished on the cold water and nearly jumped out of her skin.

He winced, his groan audible over the drumming of the shower, and scrubbed a hand over his face. She pulled his hand away and gave him a chaste kiss, relishing in the surprise that flickered in his eyes. Hells-bent on completely wiping away his guilt, she deepened her grin. But instead of riling his passion and the likelihood of more dragon spikes, she struck at his competitive nature and challenged him, "Let's see who can get ready the fastest."

Big mistake.

In a blurry wisp of movement, he showered, shaved, and changed—having whished over his bag and a set of clothes for her too. Her mouth was still slack as he grabbed a bite to eat from the kitchen and then waited, patiently holding open the cottage door while she hurried to magically tie her boots and dry her hair with a blast of hot air.

Thomas smirked at her flustered state, no doubt pleased with himself and considering how she could later reward him for winning the challenge. She knew that devilish grin.

"What's taking you so long?" her father projected, mild curiosity in his echoed tone.

Sara jolted at the interruption. *"Coming!"* She clasped hands with Thomas and flew out the door, her stomach in knots over how to find Kira and Samson. And although Jin hadn't seemed inclined to order Thomas into servitude, the possibility wound tightly around her heart.

CHAPTER 49

As Sara and Thomas mounted the oak's wraparound stairs, Jin's voice floated from the main room: ". . . no one has seen him for centuries." He stopped his conversation and swiveled his head, keenly studying Thomas when they entered the room.

Jin sat on one of the couches, black hair unbound, hands on his knees per usual. Gran perched beside him while Charlie and Kane reclined in two of the adjacent oversized chairs grown by Caleb.

Sara's gaze lingered on the chairs. Mother willing, Caleb still had his witch powers.

Thomas slowed their steps and nodded at Jin. "Thank you," he said, voice solemn.

Jin inclined his head, ever so slightly. "You appear to be doing exceptionally well. I suppose I shouldn't be surprised given how special this forest is. All the same"—he shifted his quicksilver eyes to Sara—"do not let him out of your sight until he can control his dragon."

"Wasn't planning on it," she said sweetly, relieved he trusted her and didn't appear the least bit interested in ordering Thomas to his side. And to prove her point to him and Thomas, she yanked Thomas with her to the opposite couch.

"So aggressive," he drawled in her mind as they plopped onto the cushions together.

She squeezed his hand. *"Oh, you have no idea—"* Her thought screeched to a stop when Charlie fidgeted uncomfortably and Jin smirked.

Sara straightened, noting everyone's attention on her, and remembered her role as High Witch. A flood of responsibilities and anxieties crashed into her with such force, she choked as though Brad's hands were around her throat. She attempted to pass off her strangled garble as a cough, and judging from the troubled expressions, failed miserably.

I can do this. Sara held up a hand, staving off questions while she took a moment to focus her thoughts.

With today being Winter Solstice, she couldn't spoil the forest's festivities by holding an emergency Council meeting, but she could discuss important information with the present group. She had to. What had happened with Caleb and Dorcas burned at her soul and needed to be shared. Though she assumed Jin had called this meeting with information of his own to reveal, she couldn't help blurting, "Dorcas killed Caleb. My magic wouldn't bring him back, so I—I begged Lethal to save him."

Thomas jerked. "As in turn him?" he asked, voice rising.

Sara dropped her gaze and nodded as Gran answered, "Yes. We know. Lethal and Lily have told us everything. You had to make a tough decision—one with consequences that need to be dealt with. That said, the entire forest is grateful for Lethal's *gift*." Her last word had a touch of a mocking bite. Gran never sugarcoated anything.

Sara winced at her grandmother's confirmation that Caleb's turning into a vampire did indeed bear consequences, ones she hoped mostly applied to her and not Caleb. But Sara was also relieved the families knew and were grateful to still have him— better a vampire than gone forever.

Steeling her nerves, Sara gripped Thomas's hand and plowed

ahead. "After Dorcas attacked Caleb, she tried to kill Thomas and—I lost it. I played right into her sick game by killing her and increasing the imbalance for the Shadow Mother to grow stronger. And if that wasn't enough, Brad swooped in and took Dorcas's and Makwa's bloodstones. They must have planned it, and I bet he took Kira too." Sara released a shaky exhale and added, "I'm sorry."

A bone-chilling growl escaped Thomas, one she had never heard before. It sounded like talons being scraped across stone—utterly unnerving and pure dragon. "You have nothing to be sorry for," he said, voice low and deadly. "I would have gladly ended her myself."

"As would I," agreed Gran, eyes glittering. From the adjacent chairs, Charlie and Kane grumbled in concurrence.

Jin, his voice as calm and smooth as the still lake water, said, "We will find Kira and Samson. And the cause of Dorcas's death is irrelevant. What matters now is how we act. We know the Shadow Mother is already strong enough to control flat-eyed dragons and attack multiple magicals at once. Although we stopped her from destroying Ware Woods and eliminating the last of the Hills witches, her power may continue to grow and eventually affect elysian-eyed dragons."

Sara's heart constricted as he shared a grim look with Thomas.

Jin spread his fingers, jet nails biting into his stark white pants. "This situation has escalated past a regional threat and is now a global concern."

The room fell quiet until Thomas coughed a burst of fire. Jin and Sara raised their hands at the same time, squelching the flames in midair, while Kane, Charlie, and Gran pushed back in their seats, eyes wider than a full moon.

Jin scrutinized Thomas. "Tobio will teach you how to control your dragon impulses. I suggest you meet with him soon."

Sara flinched at the warning in his command and at recalling the unfortunate fate of Tobio's father.

"Why not you?" asked Thomas.

"Because Lethal and I are leaving to petition the Global Council for assistance in finding Kira and stopping the Shadow Mother. It'll be the first time a dragon has ever asked for help from other magicals, but with all the other elysian-eyes still sleeping, I have no other choice. We need to come together and stop the Shadow Mother before she has the chance to control all dragons and slaughter everyone—magical and normal."

"I'm coming with you," said Sara.

Thomas growled again and snaked an arm around her waist, holding her to him. Charlie, bless him, tried to stifle his chuckle.

"No," said Lethal, popping up the stairs and stalking into the main room.

Sara scowled at both the vampire's rebuff and the sight of Kindness strapped to their back. *Why would they need a sword to visit the Global Council?*

The vampire shot a wary glance at Thomas and explained, "Ware Woods needs to remain a secret until we secure the support of the Global factions. If other magicals aren't ready to work together, then they aren't ready to accept how *unique* this site is. It'll start a war that the Shadow Mother will delight in, a war we can't afford. We need to bring all magicals—light and dark—together to defeat her."

Sara bit her lip and considered the weight of Lethal's statement. It seemed their fate was tied to the acceptance of all magicals. And if so, she intended to be involved. She eyed the slim vampire, their angelic demeanor belying centuries of death, war, and—apparently—political posturing. With their experience and connections, Lethal was Ware Woods' best hope in securing aid, but the instinct to protect her forest would not keep Sara on the sidelines for long.

She said, "And you think you can convince the Global Council?" *Without me?*

Lethal's seductively slow four-fang smile was pure arrogance and promise. Sara's scalp instinctively prickled, and she thanked the Father for keeping her mouth shut on the last part of her question.

Lethal slid their stony white hands into their pockets. "Let's just say I have *considerable* sway over the Council."

Despite the deadly power radiating from the slight vampire, Sara arched a brow—unable to resist poking their pride.

They simply fixed her with an icy stare. "Do not visit your cousin until he is ready to see you. And do not touch the trunk I left in my room."

Her brow climbed higher. *Fine, but "their" room?* Though Lethal's audacity irked her, she was secretly pleased to know they intended to return.

The vampire added, "Since my confidant will be here soon, I'll need the other trunks delivered to the wall." They paused before gritting out, "Please."

Thomas choked and clamped a hand over his mouth, smoke curling from his ears, while Sara debated a myriad of snappy quips over hearing that pretty word from Lethal. But before she could say anything, Jin rose and adjusted his wraparound tunic.

"That won't be necessary," Jin said, eyes shimmering with molten silver. A sleek smile graced his lips. In a blink, he and Lethal vanished, leaving behind a faint stir of ash and the echo of Lethal's roar.

Gran stood and clapped her hands. "They'll be back soon," she said with profound confidence. "And no, I don't have any premonitions about Kira or the Shadow Mother. All I see is snow." She gestured toward the arched doorway, and Sara twisted on the couch to see fluffy white flakes drifting down from a bright white sky.

Charlie and Kane rose as well, the latter asking, "Are you two coming to the Main House? Everyone is excited to see you both, especially Abby and Connor."

"Of course," replied Sara, before scanning Thomas up and down. "But we'll stay outside in case Dragon Boy has a hiccup.

I'm sure Moira will have a legit hissing fit if the decorations go up in smoke."

"Dragon Boy?"

"It's better than the Impaler."

Thomas jolted before his surprise melted into a smoldering gaze. The tips of her ears burned as light-blue energy crackled between them.

"Jackets are in the closet," Gran called over her shoulder as she and Charlie left in a hurry. Kane, face flushed red, launched off the deck and flew toward the Main House.

Ignoring Thomas's heated gaze, Sara studied the seamlessly wood paneled room and exclaimed, "We have a coat closet?" The treehouse responded by opening a hidden door near the rear archway and revealing a new addition that was more of a walk-in mudroom than a closet.

Sara whooped her appreciation, and the oak proudly shook itself. With a snorted laugh, she whished over their jackets and looked at Thomas. "Did you know you moved into the treehouse? Because the oak thinks so." The floorboards rippled as if in laughter.

"I'm honored," said Thomas, rising from the couch and buttoning his jean jacket—an identical replacement to the one that had been pierced by the arrow and soaked in his blood. "But we'll have to visit *our* studio regularly when the vampire roommate returns."

She flicked her hair back and narrowed her eyes at him. "Already thought that far ahead, did ya? Pretty bold of you, Sullivan."

"Oh, you have no idea," Thomas rumbled, tossing her words back at her. Sara's toes curled, and she considered summoning Tobio to immediately begin Thomas's dragon self-control lessons.

With a smug smile, he held out his hand. "Come on, let's walk and cool off before I ruin this jacket."

Sara jumped up from the couch, laced her fingers with his, and pulled him down the stairs and into a fresh blanket of snow. Thomas stared at the falling snowflakes, as if seeing them for the first time.

She reveled in his dreamy distraction for a few moments before her gaze instinctively drifted to her mother's headstone, merrily draped with evergreen garland and red holly berries. A cool breeze caressed Sara's cheeks, accompanied by a lilac-scented, invisible embrace. Though Sara's heart ached at this first Yule without her, she took comfort in knowing her mother's spirit pleasantly swirled around them. The still circle tattoo on her upper back tingled with warmth.

With a wistful sigh, she continued strolling through the cemetery with Thomas, Naomi's grave now before them. Despite winter, the cherry tree and rose bushes remained in full bloom. Sara tilted her face to the milky sky and hidden stars above, hoping Naomi was at peace and somehow knew the Hills children survived. Snow caught in her lashes, and she lowered her head.

Ian had said the kids wanted to stay at Ware Woods, and, of course, everyone was happy to have them. But perhaps someday she could help the children restore the Hills forest, and they could return if and when they were ready. Similarly, she'd help Dean and his pack too if they wished to rebuild their Blue Ridge site.

Thomas gave her hand a squeeze as they stepped over the low cemetery fence and onto a forest path carpeted in fluffy white. "You're too quiet given this," he said, gesturing to himself and coughing a ball of flames that immediately sputtered out in the falling snow. "And you were surprisingly agreeable in trusting Jin and Lethal to find Kira and Samson *and* petition the Global Council."

Sara searched his liquid blue eyes, his slitted pupils sending a thrill through her, and noted genuine concern behind the mask of levity. She smiled. "A very wise person once told me, '*We can't stop living today for what may or may not happen tomorrow.*'"

He huffed a smoky laugh, then leaned over and kissed the side of her brow. "A very wise person indeed," he agreed, blue and white energy sparking around them, the muffled crunch of snow beneath their boots.

"But seriously," he pressed. "What are you thinking? I know you, my little monster. And I know you're plotting something."

She smirked, feeling his mind politely nudge hers. Thankfully, he hadn't read her fear of the Shadow Mother possibly controlling him someday or of what it meant for him to be dragon-bound to Jin.

"I have every intention of enjoying today," said Sara, swinging his hand. "As for your dragon condition, I'm sure you'll be a fast learner from Tobio, given certain motivations." She leaned into him and kissed his neck. Thomas quickly returned her taunt with a nip to her jaw, his lips a fiery warmth against her cool skin.

She bit back her gasp. Perhaps being part dragon wasn't so bad after all.

Waving off another of his smoky chuckles, she said, "And I do trust Lethal and Jin. But too much hinges on the aid of the Global Council and all the factions."

She frowned at the possibility of other magicals coveting the power in Ware Woods, at the idea of Kira and Samson being manipulated by Brad, at the ramifications of Caleb being a vampire, at the sliver of ice still lodged in Ian's heart, and at the Shadow Mother's suffocating darkness threatening them all. How much time did they have to stop their entire world from unraveling?

"Trusting is one thing. Waiting is another," said Sara.

She glanced behind them, down the path and at the cemetery oak tree—her portal to anywhere.

"I am High Witch, and I wait for no one."

LEAVE A REVIEW

If you enjoyed *Death & Dragons* (well, maybe not the death part, but definitely the dragons), I would be extremely grateful if you could leave a review at your online retailer of choice. And heck yeah, you can leave the same review at multiple locations and then bask in the good karma. Thank you! ~ Sonja

Review links can be found at:
www.sonjafblanco.com/d2review

Reviews are important to this author and help spread the word so other readers may discover and enjoy this series. Sharing your review on social media or around the proverbial water cooler and shouting it from the rooftops is also encouraged.

Thank you! Or as Lethal would say, *"Grazie."*

DISCOVER MORE

Get your FREE copy of *Witch of Ware Woods – Flood & Fire*, the series prequel where magic, love, destruction, and sacrifice combine in the spellbinding creation of Ware Woods.

Free download at www.sonjafblanco.com/f2

Witch of Ware Woods – Book 3 . . . coming soon!

Get sneak peeks, giveaways, and insider info
by subscribing to Sonja's newsletter at:
www.sonjafblanco.com/subscribe

ACKNOWLEDGEMENTS

Let me start by saying this book was a blast to write. While I'm an overthinker and plot out story lines and character developments, I also let a story organically grow and breathe by leaning into scenes and giving characters free rein to shine. And Death & Dragons stepped up to the plate with characters ablaze. I love this part of writing, for this is when the magic happens—at least for me it does. I hope the magic shone through on these pages for YOU and became YOUR story just as much as it is mine and Sara's.

That said, writing the second book in a trilogy is daunting, and I could not have achieved this without the assistance, support, and love from so many people.

To my dear husband, David—Thanks for your continuing support, poop loads of patience, and my fancy seat and back cushions. Fork 'em Devils!

To my children, Mia and Jason—Thanks for running the blender less often while I wrote this story, for offering your opinion on character names and cover designs, for the eye rolls and laughs, and for reminding me what's truly important in life. (Ha ha! No sooner had I written this than one of you brought home a friend specifically to use the blender. It's a Ninja, in case any of you are wondering.)

To my parents, Don and Donna—Thanks for being my biggest cheerleaders and emotional support team and gifting me noise-cancelling headphones (for said blender and so much more). I am grateful for you and love you beyond measure.

To my brother, Chris—Thanks for all the witty sibling banter and "friendly" ribbing. Keep it coming, Pillow-son.

To my frister, Tami—I am thankful to the stars and back for our friendship. Thank you for gently pushing me to do better, for providing quick feedback when I call you in a panic (which is often), and for always being there for me.

To my family and friends—Thank you! Your enthusiasm for my writing means the world to me!

To the Rogers, Carey, and Kilhart families—This series is strongly inspired by your mutual love and caring (and forest paths!). Thanks for all the shenanigans and dedication to your land and family.

To my cousin, High Priestess Lady Jesamyn Angelica—I am in awe of all that you do. Thanks for being a bright shiny light, for confirming and correcting my magical elements, for your editing expertise, and for all your love and support. It is freaking amazing to share this story with you, seeing as how you knew the original Gran AND lived in the "blue house."

To my beta readers, Maya, Tamra, Jesa, Regan, and Danielle—I am profoundly grateful for your support and incredibly insightful comments—each and every one, from the gushing to the brutal. Thanks for being honest, constructive, and enlightening with your feedback.

To my sensitivity readers, Sara, Mandy, and Brigid—Thank the gods for your involvement in examining this story from multiple lenses and for all your gracious comments.

To Dr. Elizabeth Schmied—Thank you for answering my many questions (no matter how bizarre) and for providing your expertise on sensitive conditions.

To my editors, Hannah and Kelly—Many thanks for your keen eyes, patience, attention to detail, and passion for this series. Your hard work is greatly appreciated.

To my international design team, Stef, Maria, Marina,

Damonza, and David—Terima kasih, grazie, multumesc, and gracias. Your creativity and digital art prowess are astounding and swoon worthy. Thank you!

To my writer friends and social media peeps—THANK YOU! Writing can be lonely and frustrating at times, but I know I can always count on you for support (and vice versa). We have a wonderful community that I am honored to be a part of. Love you all!

Special thanks to Ashley Kay, Christine Hutton, Merrit Townsend, Ashley, Darin Nagamootoo, Katrina Tortorici, Jennifer Sargent, Ali Mills, Jess Dodge, Amanda Insco, Otto Schafer, Alexis Henricks, Stephanie Whitfield, Sara DeLaVergne, Sherry Shearhart, Mariya, Sara Fujimura, Dani Hoots, Rose Fairchild, Jennifer Milius, Laura Quinn, Alice Hanov, Rosalyn Briar, Bekah Berge, Penelope Daniels, Amanda Pavlov, Kacey Rayburn, T.J. Bateman, Marla Azinger, and Diana Georgelos. I am beyond grateful for your support and friendship.

Thanks to all the scented candles, Cheetos, chocolate, tea, and coffee that helped fuel this novel. And thanks to my cozy tortilla blanket. What can I say? I get cold easily.

To all you fellow wicked writers, musicians, and artists—Your creativity is NEEDED. Please continue to follow your heart's passion and enrich the world with your authentic talents.

To all you ah-mazing readers—Your support is everything everything (yep, meant that twice and to infinity). Every purchase, read, and praiseworthy review, word-of-mouth, social media post and/or comment is very much appreciated from the bottom of my tiny black heart.

And as always, thank you, Universe, for the magic.

ABOUT THE AUTHOR

Sonja grew up in New England, where she ran barefoot through the woods, chased lightning bugs, tapped maple trees for syrup, and built towering snow castles.

Having an ancestor who was hung as a witch, Sonja is naturally drawn to all things magical and fantastical—trees and cemeteries in particular.

At 5'2" she is often caught climbing tables, chairs, and small children to reach the upper shelves. She likes coffee and tea equally, both of which most certainly contributed to her diminutive stature.

Witty comics easily amuse her, as do heavily jowled Hell Hounds that talk in their sleep.

She writes fantasy as if it were real, because believing makes it so.

Get sneak peeks, giveaways, and insider info
by subscribing to Sonja's newsletter at:
www.sonjafblanco.com/subscribe
Follow and connect with Sonja at:
Goodreads: goodreads.com/sonjafblanco
Instagram: @sonjafblanco
Facebook: @sonjafblanco
TikTok: @sonjafblanco
Twitter: @sonja_blanco